For Love and Glory

A NOVEL

CINDY BONNER

Published by Deck Night Press

Yoakum, Texas

Design by Betty Martinez

Author Photograph by Ryan Rayburn

With thanks to Judy Alter for the careful editing.

This is a work of fiction. All names, characters, places, and incidents are either products of the author's imagination or are used fictitiously. No reference to any real person is intended or should be inferred.

Library of Congress Control Number: 2022904796

ISBN 979-8-9859225-0-9

First Edition, April 2022

Also by Cindy Bonner

Lily

Looking After Lily

The Passion of Dellie O'Barr

Right from Wrong

*For my Ol' Darlin' Wayne Myers who helped me find my way back
to writing.*

PART ONE

The Crash

JULY 1940

CHAPTER 1

"Becky"

The Curtiss banked in a steep-rising, almost perfect three-quarter loop. Lange thought of it like throwing a lasso, and he was the rope. Sky in his face. Wires singing with wind. The pull of "G" on his body. The roller-coaster down. Spotting the flagger. The horizon rosy with the sun already low in the west. He leveled out two feet above the field, right on the top edge of the cushion, opened the hoppers, and a white trail of dust clouded out behind him. He kept his eye on his speed, his altitude, the row of salt cedars at the far end of the field.

At the last second, he jerked the biplane sideways, and knifed the wings through the trees, cranking back on the stick. Dust flowered up from the floor of the cockpit. The cedars got dust, too, before he thought to cut off the hoppers. Arsenate of lead, for the midge eating up this field of grain.

The flagger waved him around, and he made his last two runs. There had been a crosswind all day that kept taking the chemical. Some of it always blew back on him. The chemical was the one part of the job he disliked. Flying was the part that galvanized him. Once the hoppers were empty, he circled back towards the flagger, waggled his wings, and headed for the airfield Red Hawk was using that week.

This was new territory for Red Hawk Aero-Dusters. Lange had a natural sense of direction, but even if he hadn't, all the barns and warehouses for miles around had arrows painted clearly on their rooftops, marking the way to the airfield. It was like following the yellow brick road across this country, flat and patch-worked with row crops, his shadow flying along ahead of him.

Once over the landing field, he circled the Curtiss into the wind and put it down on the grass in a soft three-point, taxied up to the hangar where the mechanic, Cooper, was waiting with his sack of spark plugs and wrenches.

"There's still a little flutter in the tail." Lange unsnapped his goggles and chin strap. He hiked himself out of the seat and dropped over the side to the ground.

"Reckon it's that new stabilizer," Cooper said, bending down for a look. "I'll see what I can do."

One of the hopper-loaders, a skinny kid of about fourteen or fifteen, came trotting up. "Can I pull her inside this time?" he said.

Cooper nodded. The kid's face lit. Lange remembered the feeling. He'd been there himself at fifteen, begging odd jobs around an airfield just to get a chance at one of the planes. He'd been willing to push a broom or lime an outhouse for a three-minute sit inside a cockpit.

He headed for the hangar just as the boss, Choke Hargrove, ambled out to meet him. Choke was a beer-bellied, red-faced man who walked with a swivel left over from a crackup in his younger, warbird days, back before he bought the four machines that made up his duster fleet. While the other pilots took the new Cubs and the Waco, Lange got the old, beat-up Curtiss Jenny, because he would fly anything, and everybody knew it.

"DeLony!" Choke said, around the cigar clamped in his teeth. He waved a yellow envelope at Lange. "Telegram come for you while ago."

Lange's heart skipped. He reached for the envelope, thinking *Papa*, or *calamity*, in that order. Another stroke. Maybe worse. People didn't send telegrams just to say *How are you?* He bit the leather glove off his right hand, spit out the taste of the arsenate. It was all over him. He tore off one end of the Western Union envelope and shook out the slip of paper inside. He turned his back to Choke.

The telegram came from his cousin, Julianne Williams. It was short, to the point, telegram-like. It was about Becky. *"There's been an accident. Your needed."* The *"your"* misspelled by the telegraph operator on one end or the other. Lange folded the telegram and stuck it back in the envelope. Choke was watching.

"It's my wife," Lange said. "She's had an accident." He thought about that old Ford Model T he'd left with her in San Antonio.

"Your wife?" Choke stared harder.

Lange grimaced, gave a nod. "I'm going to have to go see about this. I know we're busy as hell right now—"

"All these weeks you've been working for me," Choke's mouth clamped harder on the cigar, "and I don't know you've got a wife?"

Lange shrugged.

Choke's eyes narrowed. "All right," he said. "I'll hold your job, but you let me hear something pretty quick. I need to know when you're coming back."

Lange knew he was the most reliable pilot Choke had. Choke could act hard-line and make threats, but Lange knew the job would be here waiting.

"A goddamn wife," Choke muttered, as Lange strode towards the hangar.

Beside the rear door was a makeshift sink some thoughtful somebody along the way had rigged up by using a rain barrel and a gate valve. Wasn't much but it did the trick. A chip of a mirror was fastened to the wall. Lange's face looked ghostly white with the lead arsenate all over him. Only the skin around his eyes, in the shape of his goggles, looked human and normal. He stepped out of his jumpsuit, dropped it in a heap, and splashed soapy water on his face.

The telegram had rattled him. It didn't say exactly what sort of accident Becky had, but Julianne wouldn't have sent a telegram if it wasn't serious. She knew how things stood with him and Becky. It had to be that old Ford. Last time Becky wrote to him she hadn't mentioned anything about the car acting up. She had just asked him for more money, the same way she always did. She was still his wife, she said, and like it or not, the lease on the apartment was still in his name. So he had sent her all he could spare. But how long ago was that? Six months? Maybe longer. At least it wasn't Papa. At least that...

He dried his hands and face and watched as one of the other flyers brought in the Waco—a guy named Eddie or Mike, a new guy. He porpoised it all the way down the landing field before it finally bounced to a solid stop.

NOBODY on the bus to San Antonio seemed to want to sit beside Lange. He guessed the lead arsenate ran them off. No matter how hard he scrubbed he couldn't seem to get rid of the smell. They had been dusting for five weeks already so he was used to it and used to the coughing that came with it. Hazards of the job. But it was a flying job, and one he'd found for himself, so he wouldn't complain. Especially not when he thought of all those years on the ground, chopping cotton and pushing cattle around for Papa and Gabe.

Inside the bus it was sticky hot. He loosened his collar and tried to sleep but his window wouldn't raise. After a while the arsenate started mixing with his sweat and burning the skin around his wrists and neck. He tried to wipe it away, but he couldn't get his mind off the burning or off what was waiting for him in San Antonio.

At the Kenedy stop, a woman with two bawling babies got on the bus. The only empty seat left was next to him, so she had no choice. He didn't mind kids, but the bawling made him nervous.

He ended up with one of the babies asleep on his lap and shared his dwindling pack of cigarettes with the mother. She was on her way to live with her folks in San Angelo. She said her husband had just joined the Navy.

"He said he figures we's about to get into the war over in Europe. Wants to make sure he don't end up in some dirty stinking trench somewhere." She said it as if she wholeheartedly approved of his decision.

Lange couldn't imagine having a wife as agreeable as that. She gave him half a bologna sandwich, which he devoured in two bites. He hadn't even realized he was hungry.

When the bus pulled into the San Antonio station it was half past midnight. The woman said, "Sure hope your wife's all right," as he angled himself down the aisle. He raised his hand to wave thanks and goodbye and stepped off the bus and into the sultry San Antonio night.

Inside the terminal, he dug a nickel out of his pocket as he made his way to the bank of phone booths along the wall. He gave the operator the number, and when Julianne answered, said, "I'm here."

"Oh? Already?" She sounded sleepy. "You got the telegram then."

"Yeah. Can you come pick me up? Or do you want me to walk?"

"Of course not, Ding. Just give me a second to wake up. I'll be there directly."

He thought she must be really sleepy to call him by his old nickname. He'd done away with that years ago, or anyway, he thought he had. Who would hire a pilot with a nickname like Ding? His first name was Crawley, but he didn't care for that either. Back when he was a kid just starting school his sister had suggested he go by his middle name. Lange had been their mother's maiden name. It was short, easy to pronounce. He hadn't realized until later that he would have to constantly correct people—"Lange. Rhymes with hang."—to keep them from using the soft g or from sounding out the e at the end. He'd been called *Lang-ey* often enough to cause a couple of fist fights.

The bus station was empty except for an old bum asleep on a bench. And the snack bar was still open. He bought a plate of greasy French fries to quell the appetite the bologna sandwich had stirred, counted the cigarettes left in his pack, and bought another—Camels, the only brand behind the counter. His pocket change was fast dwindling, too.

Within fifteen minutes, Julianne drove up in a new Dodge coupe. It grated on him a little to see that new Dodge. Clearly, Sterling was bringing in good money now. She opened the door and got out to hug Lange, then backed off when she got a whiff of the lead arsenate.

"Whew!" She was dressed in a skirt, hair combed into a snood. Julianne was in her forties, but she'd kept her looks.

"Sorry," he said. "I didn't have a place to bathe."

She gave him the once-over. "You didn't bring a suitcase?"

"I didn't think I'd be staying that long." He smiled, but he figured it probably came out more like a grimace. He wasn't in a real smiling mood. "Good to see you, too," he said.

"Oh, it is good, honey. You know it always is." She grabbed his hand and gave it a jiggle. "Get in the car. You can borrow some of Sterling's clothes. Him and Troy Lee are up north anyway. Won't be home till the weekend."

Lange went around to get in on the passenger's side of the Dodge. He didn't comment on the car, but it smelled new. As if to add to his irritation, the engine purred like a hummingbird.

San Antonio was asleep this late at night. Julianne maneuvered the Dodge through the streets without meeting any oncoming traffic. When he lit up a Camel she reached for it.

"Forgot mine," she said. He lit another for himself, glanced at her. She had her face turned towards the road, smoking his cigarette. "Becky smashed her car into a tree," she said finally.

He let out his breath. He felt like he'd been holding it for hours. "I had a feeling it was that old Ford." He said it calmly, careful to hide his nerves. "When?"

"Last night. I didn't get specific in a telegram. I apologize. I guess I just didn't want to worry you."

He shook his head at her, but she wasn't looking. Any telegram was enough to put a person into a panic. She had to know that. He took a long pull on the cigarette and kept his eyes on the lonely swath the headlights cut in the dark street. "Is she OK?"

"I'm afraid it's not good, honey. She's in the hospital. In a coma. Her mother came in on the train this morning."

"In a coma? Which hospital?"

"It's way past visiting hours, Ding. We'll go first thing tomorrow."

"Which hospital is it? I'm going there now."

She looked at him. He heard her sigh just before she U-turned the Dodge.

HE FOLLOWED the nurse down a long corridor. The woman was all business, no small talk, crisply leading him through the ward doors. The place spooked him. Smelled too sterile, made him feel awkward and dirty. He wished Julianne could come with him, but the nurse had said visitors were welcome one at a time. Julianne was out in the waiting room with Laura, Becky's mom, who had apparently been there all day and wasn't leaving. He needed a smoke but reckoned it wasn't allowed, so he concentrated on following the starchy nurse.

The soles of her shoes squeaked as she walked ahead of him. Without speaking, she led him into the critical ward. It was bright and antiseptic. Curtained screens walled the patients from view. The nurse stopped at the third one on the left. She slapped back the curtain. He jumped at the sudden noise. She nodded at him to go, and he stepped sideways through the opening.

Becky lay flat on her back. A plasma bottle hung from a hook on the upper corner of the hospital bed. A tube ran from the bottle down into her arm, which was strapped onto a board. She lay still, her head turned slightly away. A bandage was wrapped around her forehead and over one ear. She looked small, ragged. He almost didn't recognize her. She'd cut her hair, or maybe the hospital had. A hard chair stood beside the bed. He braced it for balance and leaned forward for a closer look. Scratches and bruises decorated her face.

"Becky?" he whispered, coughed into his hand. He swallowed. "Becky?" He said it louder. "It's me. Lange."

"She might not hear you," the nurse said from behind him. Her voice startled him. He had forgotten she was there.

He backed away from the bed, self-conscious. He couldn't take his eyes off Becky, lying so perfectly still in the bed. She seemed lifeless, a wax doll. A picture of the last time he'd seen her snapped into his mind. How she'd run after him, tripping on the sheet she'd wrapped hurriedly around herself, hair bedraggled, face flushed with heat. *Lange, wait. Stop please....*

"Will she come out of it?" he asked the nurse. "The coma?"

"Sometimes they do. Eventually." The nurse fussed around with the plasma bottle. "She lost the baby, though. I'm sorry to say. Couldn't be helped...." The nurse reached for the back of the chair, scooted it towards him. "You can sit here for a bit. It won't hurt anything to talk to her. You never know."

"No, I think..." He cleared his throat. "I believe I'll let her get some rest."

He backed away and didn't think until later about how ridiculous that must've sounded. Rest, hell, she was in a coma. He ducked out of the curtained enclosure before the nurse could say anything else. He was suddenly anxious to put as many steps between him and Becky's pale, still body as he could.

Lost the baby. There'd been a baby? He focused on the floor tiles, the black toes of his boots. Whose baby? Was he still supposed to care? A baby...for crissake....

Julianne sat perched beside Laura in the waiting room. Both their faces rose towards him as he came in—watchful, troubled faces. They made him feel caged. The last thing he wanted right then was to have to talk to Laura. He wondered how much she knew about the situation between him and Becky. Should he tell her there'd been a baby? Maybe she already knew.

He stopped in front of them, gave them both a fidgety look. "She didn't know I was there," he said.

Laura jumped to her feet. "Oh, I'm sure she did. I know she did."

She grabbed hold of him, gave him a fierce hug. He tried to stop her. He tried to do it gently, so she wouldn't know how uncomfortable her clinging made him feel. "I'm pretty dirty." He gave Laura's shoulder a shallow pat.

"Laura's going to stay here tonight," Julianne said.

He studied Julianne. Did *she* know about the baby? "You're coming home with me," she said. "You look dead on your feet."

He didn't argue. She held out the car keys, and he took them, glad she was letting him drive. It would give him something to concentrate on. Something besides this whole damned messy business.

"I'll be back tomorrow," he said to Laura, as an afterthought. He didn't know if he'd just told her a lie or not.

JULIANNE AND STERLING had a new caliche driveway, and a carport for the Dodge. Their economic situation had clearly risen. A light burned in the kitchen. They entered through the back door.

"I could use some coffee, how about you?" Julianne said, as soon as they stepped inside. She put down her purse and started filling the coffee pot with water.

He lowered himself into one of the kitchen chairs, dragged the ashtray from the center of the table. He used a stick match from his pocket and the bottom of his boot to light a cigarette. He was already down to six. Inhaling deeply, he watched Julianne measure coffee into the tin pot. The aroma of it spread through the kitchen.

She glanced around. "Is coffee going to keep you up all night?"

He shook his head.

"You want to try a piece of this cake?" She motioned at a cloth-covered plate. "My neighbor brought it over this morning. Said it's made with Coca Cola. Sounds funny but it's pretty good." She smiled. So did he, but he shook his head at the cake.

She bent to light an eye on the stove and set the coffee pot over the flame. "It's not your fault this all happened, Ding. I mean, Lange. I just can't get used to it, sorry, honey."

He mashed the burnt match-head against an edge of the ashtray. A hard lump had settled at the top of his stomach. "I'm not blaming myself. I'm trying not to blame anybody." He let the match drop into the tray. He thought about Becky, lying silent and still in the hospital bed. "Did you know she was pregnant?"

Julianne sat down across from him. Her eyes had dark bags underneath. "Not till this morning. I haven't seen Becky since...I don't know when...last winter, maybe. I bumped into her at the dry cleaners one day."

Julianne slid a folded newspaper in front of him and tapped her finger on a spot near the bottom of the page—one paragraph about the crash. Lange read it silently. It said Master Sergeant Dwayne Sutherland, from Redfield, Arkansas had been thrown from the car. Died on impact. Broken neck. Sergeant Sutherland was twenty-eight, stationed at Fort Sam Houston.

The coffee pot on the stove started wobbling from the heat of the eye. The paper didn't say anything about Becky, just her name—Rebecca DeLony—and that she had been driving. It didn't say if she had been out drinking, dancing and drinking, or how she knew this Sergeant Sutherland, or if he was the father of her baby.

Lange swallowed. "I don't even know what I'm doing here," he said. "I mean, hell, Julianne, I haven't even seen her in near about a year."

She got up after something on top of the icebox. "The police came here after the accident. They had this as your address." She held out a big legal envelope, laid it on the table in front of him. "This was in Becky's car."

The envelope had his name on it, Julianne and Sterling's address. The return address on the envelope, stamped on the left corner, was an attorney's office on St. Mary's Street. The envelope was smudged with dirt and crumpled on one corner. He smoothed at the crumpled corner, then opened the envelope. He read the heading, skimmed down to the body of the document, read further.

"Desertion, she claims, of all the damned things..." His voice trailed off as he continued to read.

Julianne reached to pat his arm, but he moved it before she could and took a drag on his cigarette so she wouldn't think he was purposely avoiding her touch. He didn't want sympathy. What he was feeling didn't call for sympathy. He kept reading. The print was small and made his head hurt.

"It says she's expecting me to pay for everything," he said. " Wonder where in hell she thinks I'm going to get the money for that?" He set the cigarette in the ashtray and stuffed the papers back in the envelope. "If she wants a divorce then she can damn-well pay for it." A picture of her lying in that hospital bed flashed again in his mind.

On the stove, the coffee pot geysered brown liquid into the glass bubble on the lid. Julianne used a dishrag to grab up the pot and poured coffee into two cups. They were nice cups—pink Sunday china. Before she could set the cup in front of him, he scooted back his chair.

"Would you mind too much if I just went on to bed? I'd like a bath too, if it's not too much trouble."

Her shoulders straightened. She held the two steaming cups. "Of course not, honey. You know where everything is."

He smashed out the cigarette and stood. "I'll just sack out on the porch."

"Don't be ridiculous. You'll take Troy Lee's bedroom. I'll make sure the sheets are clean."

TROY LEE WAS Julianne's youngest, the only one left at home. Lange had slept many nights in Troy Lee's room, back when he worked for Julianne's husband, Sterling, nights when he'd come in from some job too late to go home.

The walls of Troy Lee's bedroom were covered with posters of different aircraft and of flyers like Lindbergh and Wiley Post. Models suspended with fishing line, hung from the ceiling at various levels. There was a recent model made from balsa wood of a German Messerschmitt 109. Lange gave the German plane a tap on the tail, and it swung into a flat spin.

Julianne fluffed a pillow and turned back the bed. She'd given him a pair of pajamas to wear. They hit him mid-calf. He didn't care. A deep tiredness had seeped into him. He felt heavy with it. Numb.

"You want the fan off or on?" Julianne raised the window beside the bed.

Lange spun the Me-109 in the other direction. "I guess Troy Lee got his private ticket finally?"

"Oh gosh, yes. A couple of months ago already. Morning of his sixteenth birthday. He was up at dawn for it."

"So he's working with the old man now?"

She nodded. "For the summer anyway. They've sure been busy."

She didn't realize Sterling's success hit a raw spot in Lange. That whole time of living in San Antonio was raw. But if he'd stayed here, stuck it out through those first hard months, maybe things would be different now. Maybe he would feel different, like a success, too, instead of living in one cheap hotel after another, flying a creaking, old crop dusting Jenny, covered up in lead arsenate all the damned time, chasing any job that kept him flying, maybe he would be making some real money now, too. Sterling had been trying to help, giving Lange a percentage and the use of his planes. It was Lange who had thrown in the towel, packed up and left town without a word to anybody. Because there hadn't been any words left inside him.

As soon as Julianne closed the door behind her, he stripped off the pajama shirt and flopped down on the bed. He reached to start the fan on the bedside table. It roared like the blades of a propeller. Cool air gushed across him. All the strung-up model airplanes danced in the breeze. The Messerschmitt kept twirling round and round in its flat spin.

Lange had known Becky was running around. Known it in his bones but just wouldn't admit it to himself. Clues were there, all over the place. She had an explanation for every slip-up she made. For the strange butts in the ashtrays—well, she worked in cosmetics at Joske's downtown, and sometimes she bummed cigs on her coffee breaks. For the river mud on the car fenders—well, one morning she and some of her girlfriends from the store took a wild hare to go catfishing. *Catfishing!* Hell, no idiot would believe that one, except he had. Sometimes those same friends came back to the apartment with her, put on a stack of records, and taught each other new dance steps—which was her explanation for how she suddenly knew the Lindy and the Shag that New Year's Eve he finally had money enough to take her out on the town.

Becky was lively, up on the latest of everything. She liked to go and do and be around people. Dances. Parties. Pictures shows. Coffee shops. Pretty clothes and nail polish and lots of colorful make-up, that was Becky. It was what attracted him to her in the first place. She laughed a lot, and drank beer, and would flirt and cut up. She liked men—yeah, OK, he'd know that from the beginning —and they liked her back.

He met her at Southwestern, that single year he spent in college, that one golden year. She was from a nearby small town. He was from a town even smaller where there were no girls like Becky Godshall. None with her sparkle. He fell in love instantly. She claimed to feel the same way. He married her mostly to keep anybody else from having her. She looked gorgeous on their wedding day, took his breath away. They went to Austin on their honeymoon, because he couldn't have made it any farther. There were a hundred tiny seed buttons down the back of her white satin gown. He made it through about half of them before he tore off the rest. And she didn't even get angry about it. She laughed at him, loud and boisterous, and never pretended to be the lily-white bride. That had been his fantasy not hers. His mistake.

You couldn't leave a girl like Becky by herself. Not as much or as often as he had to flying charters for Sterling. But it was the only dream he'd ever had, to fly and make a living at it. Even working for family—his cousin's husband—it took time to build confidence, to build a reputation, to get some experience under his belt. It took patience, more patience than Becky had to give. He hadn't been trying to catch her at anything, he really hadn't. Later, though, he wondered if maybe she had been trying to get caught.

On a night like this one: midsummer, sticky hot, might have come an afternoon shower, he couldn't remember. He didn't know what caused him to creep into the apartment so quietly. He was tired, had been gone for thirty-six hours on a charter to Odessa with two Houston wildcatters. And he thought she was asleep, except for that light on in the hall and some soft music playing on the radio— "All The Things You Are." Maybe she was just getting ready for bed. He thought he would surprise her, so he crept in. Well, he surprised her all right. Surprised hell out of her—*and* the Joe Blow from Men's Shoes.

Later on, he was glad he hadn't been able to see much, because the light in the hallway had been glaring in his eyes. About two steps from the door he recognized the sounds from inside the dark bedroom. He said something, he didn't remember what exactly. Her name probably. He knew he cussed. He almost reached around the corner for the bedroom light switch. Almost. Except all he wanted was to get out of there as fast as he could, wanted not to have chosen that moment on that night to come home, wanted to go back to being the dumb country bumpkin he'd been before, blind to all the signals, believing in marriage, trust and fidelity, in decent human honesty.

She came running after him, dark hair bed-messy, pink-cheeked, tripping on the sheet wound so modestly around her. Who the hell did she think she was kidding with that sheet? Especially with Joe Blow from Men's Shoes scrambling out into the hallway with his pants half on.

"Lange, wait! Stop please! Lange! Listen to me! I can explain...."

The slamming of the front door cut her off. It gave him a little satisfaction—about two seconds worth—slamming that door in her face. Explain what? Exactly what in hell had she been about to say? That it was an accident? That she hadn't meant to? That he hadn't just caught her cheating? Sometimes he wondered just what kind of an idiot she thought he was anyway.

THE TELEPHONE in the upstairs hallway woke him. Outside the window, bright daylight shone. Once he finally drifted off, he'd slept hard but with his neck in a cramped position. He sat up, rubbed at it. He could hear Julianne talking, her voice muffled through the closed door. He blinked at the Army Air Corps poster of a Bell P-39 Airacobra thumbtacked to the ceiling. All the model airplanes still swayed on their strings. He reached to switch off the fan.

A tap came at the door. "Lange? Honey? It's for you," Julianne said. "It's the hospital, honey. They want to speak to you."

The hospital? Of course, the hospital. Who else would call him here? He almost asked Julianne to take it for him—almost—but that would've been too cowardly.

He opened the door, just two inches. Julianne's face was there, morning-frazzled.

"It's the hospital, honey," she said again.

He walked across the hall to the black telephone. The receiver lay on its side. He stared at it for a moment, picked it up. He cleared the clog in his throat. "Hullo?"

"Mister DeLony?" It was a stranger's voice.

"Yes?"

"Mister DeLony, I'm very sorry to have to break this news to you, but your wife passed away this morning...."

The words went through him like something sharp—even expecting them, even knowing as soon as he picked up the phone that they were coming, they stabbed him anyway.

CHAPTER 2

"Nel-o"

When the bid got dropped on him, Dane glared across the table at Dellie, who was playing as his partner. She said, "Come on, Brother. I'll help you all I can."

He grunted. It had gotten so he hated playing anything but Moon. In Moon you didn't have a partner. You played for yourself. Dellie was too timid about bidding, which was why he was in the fix he found himself now, squinting at his dominoes, trying to make something out of this pitiful hand. A blank-six. One higher six. Otherwise zilch.

"Nel-o," he said.

"Huh?" Gabe couldn't hear worth a damn. He'd been in an artillery unit in 1918 and still had the thunder of war in his ears. He tended to shout everything he said.

"I bid Nel-o!" Dane shouted back, but he heard himself, and the words didn't sound like much.

"What did he say?" It was Ding who was asking Dellie this time.

Dane thought to himself—*well, if you'd come around more often*—but he didn't say it. The boy had enough piled on him after having just buried his wife. There was nothing easy about that task, let alone all that afterwards business, folks giving condolences, wandering in and out of the house all evening, laden with bowls of fried chicken or pans of cornbread, cakes and pies. He remembered how it was when Tessa died. The boy hadn't been but four, and thank God his sister Sunny was still at home to tend to him. Still, there was no way the three of them could have eaten all the food people brought. Just like now. There was enough food in Dellie's kitchen to feed the whole town. Even though this funeral had been held up at Georgetown where Becky's folks were from, news traveled around these parts pretty fast, too. Every neighbor within twenty miles had come to call.

"He wants to bid Nel-o," Dellie explained, as if Dane was a foreigner and she was his translator. But since his last stroke, she was the only one who understood a word he said.

"Nel-o?" Gabe reached across to feel playfully at Dane's forehead. Dane swatted his hand away. "He's betting he won't take a single trick. So it'll be our job to make him go set." Gabe arranged and rearranged his dominos.

"He just wants me out of the game for this hand." Dellie gave an accusing glance.

"Might as well be out of it," Dane replied, accidentally spitting on himself. He wiped at his chin.

Dellie slapped her dominoes face-down. "I'll go make us some more coffee." She pushed back from the table.

Dane tried to remark on Dellie leaving the table, but neither one of the boys could understand so he just tossed the ace/trey out there.

"Is that the best you can do?" Gabe said, eagerly scanning his domino hand. "You sure you don't need help, Uncle Dane?"

Dane made a face at him. It was frustrating to be talked down to and treated like an invalid. Bad enough he'd had to move into his sister's house and have her waiting on him hand and foot. He hated getting old, despised his feeble, liver-spotted hands. He wasn't one of those jolly old fellas, happy to finally have some age on him and the privilege that came with it. In his mind, he still ought to be out plowing fields and tending to his animals. But all his animals had been sold off, and his fields leased to other, younger farmers, and he was living under his sister's roof.

Dellie came back in time to see him lose the trick, which was the idea with Nel-o, so it meant he'd won that hand without her. He made it all the way through his hand, and even managed to slough off the high six. He slapped the table in glee and caught the dribble that leaked from the corner of his mouth.

"Go fix your papa a cup of coffee," Dellie told Ding. She could be bossy, but they were all used to it. Ding picked up the empty cup beside Dane's elbow and headed off for the kitchen. Gabe got up to follow him.

"You got to start bidding," Dane said when the boys had gone. He flexed his left arm. He'd just about got the use of it back, although it did still tingle some.

The Philco was set on a music program, the Hillbilly Boys playing live from downtown San Antonio. Dane glanced at the radio, then at the wall clock.

"Fifteen more minutes," Dellie said, reading Dane's mind. They never missed the news if they could help it. She stirred the dominoes on the table. They were already well-shuffled. "He looks awful," she said in an undertone. "His color's bad. And he's as skinny as a Scotch hen." She shoved the pile of dominoes away from her and into the center of the table. "He smokes too much."

"That ain't nothing new. He's been smoking since he was twelve."

Ding had been born hard-headed, a breech baby, thirteen years younger than Sunny and always kicking against the fence. Dane had tried whipping the rebellion out of the boy, tried restricting it out of him, tried scolding, but nothing ever worked. By the time Ding was fourteen, not only had he got hung up on cigarette smoking but he'd got the flying bug, too, and he never was good for a damn thing after that. Mixing up with that Godshall floozie—rest her soul—spoiling his chance at a college education. It had taken every dime he and Dellie and Gabe all three could scrounge up to send Ding off to college, right in the middle of hard times, too, and he'd just thrown it away, like you might toss out an old plowshare that had rusted through. Never had understood about sacrifice, that boy hadn't, or opportunity either.

"I've decided I'm going to give him the Oldsmobile," Dellie said, keeping her voice low.

"What?" Dane leveled his eyes on her. She was already picking her dominoes out of the pile, even though she knew good and damn well the one who shuffled was supposed to choose their hand last.

"I've been wanting a new car anyway." She lined up her dominoes the way she always did, four in front, three behind, rearranged them into some kind of mysterious order. "Maybe he can get some use out of that old car."

"Make him buy it from you."

"He doesn't have any money. You know that. And with all he's been through—" She glanced towards the kitchen. The boys were horsing around in there, making a racket.

"Hasn't ever one of us in this house had to go through it?" Dane said.

"Not at twenty-six. You were forty-nine when Tessa died, and I was fifty-three when I lost Daniel. Even Gabe was nearly forty. Ding's a baby compared to that. Things are harder at twenty-six. A person is not used to bad things happening yet, and people dying. Not at twenty-six."

"He'll weather it."

She pressed her lips and frowned. "Have you always been this cold in the heart, Dane? Or did it just come over you one day?" She shook her head and rearranged her dominoes again. "It certainly is not a becoming quality in you. I'll tell you that much for sure."

He was forming his reply when Gabe and Ding came out of the kitchen, cups brimming. One of the cups sloshed over onto Dellie's polished oak floor. She jumped to wipe up the spill with her handkerchief, fussing after Gabe to be more careful.

Once the boys were settled and started pulling in their domino hands, Dane gave Ding a more scrutinizing look, taking to account Dellie's words. Maybe she was right. Ding's color was bad. He'd gone plumb ganty, too, like he'd been off his feed a while. And he was sure-enough chain-smoking those ready-rolls of his. Worse even than Gabe, who always seemed to have a butt hanging from his lips.

Dane blew at his coffee, swilled in a sip. It was scalding hot, but he liked it that way. It tasted funny, though, and he realized it was laced with whiskey. He glanced up. Gabe gave him a wink. Ding grinned ear to ear but pretended to study his domino hand. So they'd been in there boozing, the two of them. No wonder they had sounded so jolly. Dane could smell it on them now, too.

Across the table, Dellie concentrated on her dominoes and bit at her lip trying to get up the gumption to bid, oblivious to the smell of liquor hovering in the air. Gabe thumped his fingers in time to the beat on the radio. Loud, fast fiddle music. A lot of damned noise, in Dane's opinion.

Before they could get that round played, the nine o'clock news came on and Dane halted the game. Dellie moved her chair and Dane's chair closer to the Philco. She helped him get situated, turned up the volume.

As usual, the war in Europe was the main subject of the newscast. It was bad over there and getting worse. The damned Nazis were attacking England now that France was out of it. Gabe got up and wandered off somewhere without saying a word to anybody. War news peeved him, made him feel like he and his fellow soldiers of 'Seventeen and 'Eighteen hadn't done their jobs properly the last time.

All Dane wanted was news of France, and Dellie listened for it just as hard. But there was still nothing, had been nothing for the last two weeks. Ever since the armistice was announced it was as though the whole country of France had evaporated.

The National Broadcasting Company gave a condensed version of FDR's speech to Congress from that afternoon, calling for preparedness and for Congress to discuss a draft lottery. Everybody thought the European war would be coming to America soon. Then dance band music started up, again, live from the Hollywood Dinner Club. Dane reached to turn the volume down.

"No word from Sunny's kids?" Ding had stayed at the table when Gabe left.

Dane wanted to answer the question but couldn't straighten out his words. Dellie watched him struggle, then said, "Situation's the same. At least as far as we know. I've written a mountain of letters...."

She pulled a stack of letters from the sideboard drawer and set them on the table in front of Ding. He picked up the one on top of the pile and started reading, but Dane couldn't tell if the boy's heart was really in it or not. Family matters had never been of much interest to Ding. He'd always done what he wanted and to hell with the rest of them.

The letters were all answers to Dellie's dogged inquiries about the situation with Sunny's kids. They were postmarked from Austin and from Washington D.C. One had even come all the way from the ambassador's office in Paris. But that was before Hitler had routed the French Army. Last news they'd had was that the American Embassy was on the retreat, headed for Bordeaux just like all the other refugees.

Trouble was the French government considered all three of Sunny's kids to be French citizens. The oldest, Nina, even though she had been born in the United States, had married a Frenchman—man named Emile Monnier—which they said made her a French citizen by marriage. The other two, Pete and Justine, had both been born in France, and so were considered naturalized French citizens. And Sunny had never bothered to straighten it all out that they were the children of two bona fide American citizens. Sunny always had a knack for making a big mess, and it was beginning to seem like it might be too late to fix this one.

Dellie came up behind Dane's chair to give the back of his neck a little knead. She was a toucher. He used to fight her off when she tried that, but lately he'd given in to it. "Don't work yourself up, Brother," she said softly, reading his mind.

Ding raised his face from the letters, like he thought she might be talking to him. Dane saw the one the boy was holding. It was the last letter they'd had from Nina back in April. She had asked them to stop worrying, that she and the other two wouldn't want to leave France anyway. She was expecting her first child and looking after Pete and Justine, who were seventeen and fifteen, now, after all, and nearly old enough to look after themselves. Her husband, Emile Monnier, had joined the army to fight off Hitler, and that made it her war, too, so she would stay. Dane wished he knew what had happened to her brave Emile since the fighting in France had stopped, if he'd been one of the ones to make it to England or if he was even alive. Either way, Dane wanted to know who was taking care of his grandchildren.

"It's a goddammed mess is what it is," Dane said, with too much force. He wiped spittle from his chin. Dellie gave his shoulder a lingering pat.

"I wonder what Sunny would've done," Ding said, "if she were still alive…"

"I've thought about that, too," Dellie answered, "and I don't think she'd have stayed in France with a war going on. I really don't."

"I'm not sure about that, Aunt Dellie. Evidently she loved it over there or she wouldn't have stayed for twenty years."

"Eighteen years," Dane corrected, but as usual, nobody listened to him.

Ding folded the letters back into a stack. He bounced his knee and shifted around, like the chair was uncomfortable or like he was about to take off on a sprint somewhere. Ding had always been full of fidgety energy. He was the only person Dane had ever seen who wasn't calmed by liquor.

"Gabe thinks we'll be at war before the year's out," Dellie said.

"Just as soon as Mister Roosevelt gets reelected." She went around the table to Ding, leaned over, and wiped his hair back from his forehead. He tipped backwards and smiled up at her. "Rough day," she said, and he gave her a nod.

Dane watched them and felt a twinge of the same old envy he'd always felt at their easy way with each other. Dellie was more like a mother to Ding than Dane had ever been a father. He guessed he should've been thankful for it. Somebody there to take up his slack. He never understood why it irked him the way it did. He grabbed his cane.

"I'm going to turn in," he announced and managed to lever himself out of the chair.

Dellie started over to help, but Ding jumped to his feet before she could. "I'll take him up." He mashed out his cigarette in the dish he and Gabe had filled with butts. "Come on with me, Papa."

Sometimes Dane had a hard time realizing his son was as old as he was, a grown man, really. Tall, wiry strong in his arms and shoulders. Those slim hands—he'd got those from Tessa, along with her handsome face. Dane's own hands were short and stout, farmer's hands. He hung on to Ding's neck, and the boy practically carried him up the stairwell. Many, many weeks had gone by since that staircase had been so easy to climb.

"Watch your step now, Papa," Ding said, just as if Dane was in control of his own two feet, which he wasn't. He couldn't have fallen if he'd wanted to.

DANE HAD FISHED for bream in Willow Creek for seventy years. As often as he could, which was more often now than ever before in his life, and if the weather was holding fair, he tried to make it out to the creek bank each morning. He had even brought out a chair to sit in, an old broke-down straight chair that nobody used anymore, and he had rigged a pole holder in the crook of a tree in case he wanted to doze a little. Many was the time he woke up to a bream flapping on the end of his line.

When he was a boy he used a porcupine quill to keep his bait from dragging bottom, but last Christmas Gabe had given him some fancy green-and-white bobbing corks, and so now he used those. But it didn't help the fishing. Willow Creek just didn't have the fish in it that it used to. Back in the old days you could smell the bream in there. It was nothing to have two milk buckets full of fish by daylight. A few weeks ago, he'd found this eddy that tended to hold a little deeper water, and he'd been getting a fair amount out of it, but still it took a couple of days or more to get enough for a fish-fry.

By ten o'clock the sun beating down on his back felt hotter than a stove pipe, and what wind there was felt like a furnace blast. He gradually lowered the brim of his straw hat till it was necessary for him to tip up his head to see any higher than the waterline, and still the sun seemed to burn at his nose. He had just about decided to pack it in for one day when he heard the horse at the top of the bank. If it was one of Gabe's horses grazing by, he decided he would try to catch it and ride it bareback to the house. Wouldn't that surprise his sister, seeing him come flaming up like a wild Indian on one of the ranch horses they let fatten around this place.

Instead it was Ding, riding Blue, a roan gelding that had long been a favorite of Ding's. The boy had helped Gabe gentle the roan when it was still just a foal.

Ding alighted and swung the reins around a limb. The horse was so tame it didn't even have to be tied tight. Spoiled was what Dane thought. All the horses on the O-Bar-J Ranch were spoiled to their bag of oats and coddled to the easy life around here. Gabe had put up a horse barn two years ago that was better built than Dellie's house.

Ding came sidewinding down the creek bank, ducking through button willows. "Catching anything?"

He smelled like cigarettes and alfalfa hay. He leaned over and peered into the milk bucket. A hand-and-a-half of water stood in the bottom, with four eating-size bream swishing around. Dane peered into the bucket, too.

"That'll feed the cats," Ding said, with a laugh.

Dane didn't appreciate the remark or that laugh. He knew that everybody thought he just wasted time down here, so he was glad when a fish out in the creek decided to tug his bait right at that second. He jerked it up one-handed and pulled the bream to the bank where it flipped around in the sand. But the fish really wasn't a keeper.

"Don't let him fin you," Ding said, in a teasing voice. "You might bleed to death before I could carry you back to the house."

Dane gave a little snort and pitched the bream back out into the creek. It disappeared in a swirl of water. He picked up his coffee tin and fingered out another worm, went to pinch it in half and his hands wouldn't work. The worm dropped squirming into the dirt. Ding knelt to retrieve it.

"Here. Let me do that, Papa," he said, catching hold of the hook on the end of Dane's line. Ding threaded half of the worm on the hook, dropped the other half back into the can.

Dane swung the bait into the creek. Ding squinted out at where the bobbing cork landed. Ding never would wear a hat to shade himself from the sun. A bit of vanity. Didn't want to cover up that fine head of black hair he had.

"Remember the perch we used to pull out of this creek?" Ding said. "Used to take all afternoon just to gut them."

"Creek's about fished out," Dane said, mouthing the words slow and careful so Ding could hear them.

"I'm fixing to head on, Papa." Ding plucked at a blade of bahia growing alongside the bank. "Just came down to tell you goodbye. I'll be back around in October. Gabe says he could sure use the help working calves about then, so I'll probably be here for that."

"Always is plenty of work around this place." Dane glanced out from under the brim of his hat at Ding. The boy was twirling the blade of grass between his thumb and finger, staring at the cork in the water. The current had moved it a couple of inches nearer the opposite bank.

"I know I ought to come see you more often. I'm just busy hustling work all the damn time. Dusting season will be over pretty soon, and then I might think about working for Sterling again. Maybe. His business is going good. He once told me there'd always be room for me. He's always talking, you know how he is."

"Sterling Williams is a jackass," Dane said.

Ding stopped staring at the creek and looked into Dane's face. "I think I caught that," he said, with a laugh. "You know, I'm starting to understand you pretty good."

Dane laughed then, too, and for a few seconds they were relaxed with each other. It felt nice, reminded him of times when they used to sit here fishing together or when they shot birds off the front porch at the old place, back when Ding would let somebody teach him a thing or two, before he got so's he thought he knew ever damned thing and wouldn't take advice anymore.

Just as suddenly as the easiness began though, it stopped. Ding's face sobered. His eyes wandered off again. He patted at the pack of cigarettes showing through the pocket of his thin cotton shirt. "Fact is..." He gouged the pack out of the pocket and tapped one of the cigarettes loose. "I need to borrow some money, Papa. I hate to ask you. God knows, I don't have any right to ask..."

"Thought you said you'd been busy working," Dane said. "Don't they pay you?"

The smell of sulfur came heavy off the match Ding struck against his boot sole. He lit the cigarette and waved out the flame. "I don't need a lot," he said. Smoke purled out with his words. "Just enough to settle Becky's hospital bill is all. I've got to get back over to San Antonio and get her things moved out. We weren't living together anymore. I reckon you didn't know that. Hadn't for nearly a year. She—well, you know Becky...she never did like me flying."

Dane hadn't known it for certain that the marriage had

soured, but he wasn't surprise by it either. The last couple of times Ding had come home, he'd come alone. But Ding wasn't one to confide his private affairs, and Dane never had tried to hide his poor opinion of Rebecca Godshall. She'd stolen the boy's education from him. From the first time Dane had seen her he hadn't thought she was worth the loss. Painted floozie was what she was.

Ding picked a speck of tobacco off his lip, took another drag. He knelt there, flicked ash off the end of his coffin nail and stared out at the bobbing cork again.

"I think I'm probably not meant to be with anybody," Ding said. "Probably too selfish for it. Probably too much like you." He laughed and gave Dane a glance. Dane just snorted and drew the cork away from the opposite bank.

"But we were still married, and the law says her debts are my debts, so...." Ding laughed without any persuasion, bumped the curve of his hand against the end of his nose, and started that aggravating damned twitching again. He played with the lip-end of the cigarette, flattening it and twisting the paper. Tobacco flakes dribbled onto the ground. "Anyhow—I need about fifty dollars, if you can spare it. I thought about asking Gabe for it, but—I don't know —I couldn't bring myself to do it. Didn't seem like a good idea, you know. I didn't want him thinking I expect money for helping around here or anything like that. I'll pay you back as soon as I can, Papa. Pay you with interest. However much you say. I'll even sign something if you want me—"

"Goddammit Ding..." Dane hooked the fishing pole under his weak left arm and reached into his pocket, pulled out a roll of cash money. "You don't have to sign nothing." He peeled off five ten-dollar bills. "I haven't got any use for it." He held out the bills. "Here."

The boy's eyes widened. He rose to his feet. "Papa? What in hell are you doing carrying around a wad like? You ought to have it in a bank not in your pocket."

"Well, it ain't in a bank. So take it." He shook the money. "Dammit, boy, I said take it."

Ding stepped forward. Reluctantly, he two-fingered the folded bills out of Dane's hand, as if the money were dirty, or poisonous. "I'll pay you back. Every cent."

"Hell with it."

"I'm going to pay you back," Ding repeated, digging in his heels about it.

"Thought you was in a hurry to get on the road." Dane pulled in his line. The worm was gone from the hook. He'd felt a nibble a minute ago. He reached into the coffee tin keenly aware of the boy's eyes on him.

"Thanks, Papa. I'll be back as soon as I can. October at the latest."

Dane pitched his cork into the water. Circles rippled out from where the cork hit. He felt Ding leave, and heard him, but didn't turn to speak again. He watched the green-and-white cork floating in the water. For a second, he imagined he heard the sound of an airplane engine, that rackety-rack whir coming up your spine. He looked in the sky, half-expecting to see Ding up there like that day he buzzed the old farmhouse, waving down from the flimsiest looking contraption, barely fourteen years old, flying the damn thing all by himself. Scared the chickens into a scatter. The milk cow broke out of the barn. Dog went bounding off through the corn field, barking up at the aeroplane.

The boy had always been full of promises, things he was going to do: build his own aeroplane. Start his own company. Get an engineering degree. Always had a head for doing sums, for pencil drawings, for figuring out the way a thing worked. He'd been a cheerful boy, bright, confident. Now, all that seemed to have gone out of him. Way he smoked and drank and twitched around like a weasel. There seemed to be something he wasn't saying, something bleak and disturbing.

Dane thought somewhere along the line, he must have failed

with his fathering. Hell, he'd been too old for it for one thing—forty-four when the boy was born. Too set in his ways to be raising babies. A man ought to be done with fathering duties by the time he reached the age of forty-four. A man ought to have some years in his life that were just for him, when he didn't have to worry about his offspring, when he could just sit and fish all day long if he wanted to or nap out in the sunshine.

Dane leaned his head all the way back and searched the sky. Nothing up there but a line of mare's tail clouds and the sun shining straight overhead.

CHAPTER 3
"Break Down"

As Lange drove Aunt Dellie's Oldsmobile out onto the road, he felt he could breathe again. He didn't know what was wrong with him—ungrateful bastard that he was—but he always felt that way leaving Papa and Papa's whole world. Shifting the gears on the Olds was like shifting into freedom.

Once he got through Bastrop and hit the black-top, he opened up the Oldsmobile full throttle and pushed it to its limit. He didn't think he could have stood another night cooped up in Aunt Dellie's house, having to watch Papa hobble around with a walking stick, spitting out incomprehensible sentences. Couldn't have stood another damned hour of dominoes either. But mostly, Lange was ready to get back in the air. Go clean out Becky's stuff, get rid of the memories, then head south again—and fly.

Except that just outside San Marcos, the car began to shimmy and clatter and cough up smoke, before it gave a shudder like an old dog shaking fleas and died. He managed to get it over to the pavement edge before the wheels stopped turning, but steam fumed around the seams of the hood. Smoke was even hissing out from the front wheel wells. He slapped at the steering wheel, swore. He got out of the car, lifted the hood and got a cloud of angry wet steam right in his face.

An hour later he was still at the same spot on the side of the road, only he'd given up trying to fix anything himself. No tools, but even so it wouldn't have done any good. Busted water pump. Another setback in time and money.

There was no traffic on the San Antonio road. The train had already gone by, in fact two trains had passed, two he should have taken instead of the car. But for the moment he was content to sit on the fender, gnawing on a chicken leg from the box of food Aunt Dellie had packed for him, and watching an Army Air Corps trainer zoom around overhead.

The sky was as clear as spring water, and the trainer was really getting up there, doing some altitude work. For a while all Lange could see was the vapor trail as the airplane hit cold air. Then it whooshed down to around 3,000 feet. There was the flash of silver, the clear outline of the plane, an AT-6 from Kelly Field, which was only about fifty air miles away.

Once upon a time—back when he was Troy Lee's age collecting posters and magazine articles and spending Saturday afternoons at the picture show watching *Wings* and *Dawn Patrol* and all those other warbird movies—he had thought he might go into the Army Air Corps. But you had to have your college time to get into the Air Corps, and you couldn't have a wife. So once he married Becky and dropped out of school his decisions were all made.

Watching that AT-6 soar around in the sky, he wished he had made different choices. He vowed to stop acting on impulse. From now on, he would take care and think things through, weigh everything he did. He was twenty-six, time to grow up. He didn't want to end up Papa's age, sitting around playing dominoes and longing for something he hadn't done with his life.

A Ford pickup came around the curve behind him and slowed to a stop. The driver leaned his elbow out the window. "You broke down? Or just enjoying the scenery?"

"Both." Lange tossed the chicken bone out into the ditch. "Could I trouble you for a lift into town?"

The driver, a farmer in coveralls, did better than just give Lange a lift. The man had a tow chain in the bed of his pickup. The morning had turned off July hot, so before they got the bumpers lashed together they were both dripping sweat. The man knew of a garage up ahead that stayed open on Saturdays. Lange got in behind the wheel of the Olds, shifted into neutral, and let the man drag him into San Marcos.

At the garage the mechanic didn't have a water pump on hand, so he got on the telephone and placed a call to somewhere in Austin. He took the cigarette Lange offered with a grin and a nod of thanks. "I can get you a pump, but it's gonna be a little while," the mechanic said. "If you can wait."

Lange didn't see any other choice. He grabbed another chicken leg out of the box in the back seat and set out to walk the two miles on into the town.

He found a movie theater on the courthouse square, Saturday afternoon matinee, a place to rest his feet. He bought a ticket, a nickel cone of popcorn, and let the usherette guide him to a seat with her flashlight. The newsreel was already on, a replay of Joe Lewis beating the sand out of Arturo Godoy. The people in the theater—mostly kids—groaned with each punch and applauded when the Chilean went down. There was a comedy that involved dogs on roller skates, and a Popeye the Sailor cartoon, before the newsreel came on, flickering pictures of Adolf Hitler as he stood before another massive crowd, gesturing like an orchestra conductor. A few chuckles rose from the theater seats. Someone in the audience booed. Another threw an empty candy box at the screen. Laughter rang out as goose-stepping Nazis trooped like a bunch of robots down a wide, tree-lined street.

As soon as Lange realized it was Paris he was looking at he stopped munching popcorn. A huge Nazi flag draped down the side of the Eiffel Tower, a shot of a well-dressed woman pinning a flower on a German officer's uniform. There were pictures of pilots running for their airplanes—British pilots, because they were leaping into British airplanes, Typhoons and Hurricanes—loaded down with parachutes, flying helmets, and oxygen masks, giving a thumbs-up to the camera. "The battle of France is over," the narrator said. "The battle for Britain has begun."

The picture show itself wasn't much—an Andy Hardy comedy —a bit of fluff. Lange couldn't concentrate on it. He felt overloaded suddenly, stretched thin enough to burst like the water pump on the Oldsmobile. He kept seeing the worried look on Papa's face last night during the radio news and that hopeless stack of letters Aunt Dellie kept in her sideboard. Lange remembered the last time he'd seen his sister, a few weeks before she left for France. He'd been all of eight-years-old. Sunny had been twenty-one, already had Nina, just a baby with straw colored hair and bright blue eyes. The other two kids hadn't been born yet. He'd never seen either one of them except in pictures. Nina was married now, and the younger two were both nearly grown.

A while back, right around the time Lange had married Becky, there was a lot of family discussion about Papa going over to visit Sunny and her kids in France, taking an ocean liner and staying for a couple of months, but nothing ever came of it. Money had been too short, for one thing, and then Papa's health began to fail. All that time, Sunny had been quietly battling TB, something she never mentioned in her letters. It came as a shock to Papa, that cablegram Nina sent, saying Sunny had died in her sleep. By the time the cable arrived, the funeral was already over. She was buried somewhere in Paris—the city where that swastika flag now flew.

Once Sunny died, a light went out in Papa. Three weeks later he had the first of two strokes. The second, more serious one, had come seven months ago, right after Christmas. Sunny had always been special to Papa in a way that seemed almost unreasonable with her three thousand miles away.

"That's exactly the reason why," Aunt Dellie had once told

Lange. "Haven't you ever heard? Absence makes the heart grow fonder. But make no mistake, Sunny was a trial to your papa when she was a girl. Just like everybody's always been a trial for Dane. His expectations are too high, so he's always disappointing himself when people don't live up." Aunt Dellie tried to smooth Papa's way with everyone, but the fact was Papa was a hard man to please. Lange knew *he* had never done it. Impossible to and Lange had all but given up on trying.

The instant "The End" appeared on the movie screen, he jumped up to beat the crowd out the door. He emerged light-dazzled like a gopher caught above ground. The sun was already sinking. He checked his wristwatch. Quarter after six. His feet still hurt. He thought about the long walk back to the garage, the even longer drive to San Antonio. He might get there before midnight. Maybe Julianne and Sterling would let him bunk on their couch.

He dreaded having to go back there. He didn't want to settle Becky's affairs, didn't want to know what all she'd been up to, or with who, these past months. He'd cured himself of any lovesick notions he'd had about her. That was the past. She was the past, and he wanted her to stay there.

Back at the garage the big overhead door on the work bay was shut tight. He rapped the back of his hand against it, a wasted effort. The mechanic had closed up and gone home, and tomorrow was Sunday. Lange heaved an angry sigh, hit the door one more time, as punishment to himself for going off to the picture show and to the door for being locked. A sign in the window said, sure enough, "Closed Sundays."

"Dammit to hell." Lange gave the door a solid kick, but all he did was hurt the aching big toe inside his left boot. He didn't want to have to spend two whole nights in this place.

The Oldsmobile was parked on the side lot, but the keys weren't in it. The door was unlocked, though, and as he got in he almost sat on a crumpled piece of brown paper sack. A note was scribbled to him:

Sorry but had a emergincy at home. Be bake to open up tomorow and will get this thing runing for you.

— BUD DOW

Lange leaned back against the car seat and let out one exasperated laugh and a sigh. "Well, thanks, *Bud*." He wadded up the paper, glanced at the seats, front and back, looking them over with an eye for comfort. Neither one promised much.

The box of food Aunt Dellie had packed was still in the backseat. He unwrapped a wedge of apple pie and bit into it. The crust crumbled all over his shirt. He swept it away with an irritated swat. What would really taste good was a beer. He counted his money. With Papa's fifty, he had a total of sixty-one dollars. Surely that was enough to pay for the water pump and a couple of beers. He remembered a little store he'd passed walking into town. His feet hurt but the beer began to work on his mind. He thought he'd noticed another route that might be a shortcut.

Less than a mile from the garage, he heard twangy guitar music coming on the wind, clear enough for him to recognize "The Cotton-Eyed Joe," and like a pied-piper the music drew him down a side road. Around the first corner he saw the lighted sign among the treetops—"The Western Palace." A beer-joint with a near-empty parking lot—too early, yet, for Saturday night honky-tonk dancing. Fiddle and guitar music flowed out through the open doors and windows. He decided to go inside.

The place was empty except for a man righting chairs to tables and sweeping the dancers' benches around the outside edge. A short, redheaded woman was behind the long counter, burying cans of beer into galvanized tubs of ice. She answered "Yeah" when Lange hollered were they open yet and punched two holes into a can of Pearl beer, which she slid down to him. He guessed he must've looked thirsty. Given a choice he might've picked a different brand, but the apple pie had lodged in his throat and the air was still July-hot, so he drank down that beer in four swallows. By the end of the second beer, he was humming along with the band, which was still warming up, playing a little bit, in fits and starts.

It wasn't until about an hour later that people started pouring in, coming in pairs, couples, then gangs of singles looking for a date. Shy boys, drumming up courage, hung out around the inside center post. Girls stayed to the outer benches, trying not to look too eager. They all seemed so young. Everybody appeared to know everybody else, lots more noise besides the rowdy music from the band. The dance floor filled up, the room got hotter, and Lange went to stand with his fifth beer by one of the screenless windows propped open with a broom handle.

By then, he was feeling better than he had in days. He watched the couples on the floor going in a wide circle around the room, almost like it was choreographed, except it wasn't. It was just a flow you got into when you were out there, to keep from running into each other as much as anything. He knew all about joints like this one. He'd been in plenty with Becky. She liked nothing better than a loud, sleazy, honky-tonk. Hell, he'd met her in one just like this place, full of the same kind of people.

He couldn't stop thinking about her, couldn't get that image out of his mind at the graveyard yesterday, the casket with her inside it going down into that deep, black hole in the ground—*ashes to ashes, dust to dust*.... Standing there he'd had to wall himself off from all of it: Papa next to him, and Aunt Dellie on the other side, patting his hand inside both of hers. Poor Papa, feeble in his black funeral suit, so old it had gone shiny in patches, Aunt Dellie's cameo brooch catching a glint of sunlight. She smelled of pressed powder and hair spray. At the end of the row of folding chairs, Laura almost collapsed. Becky's stepfather had been there to hold Laura upright....

"Are you trying to ignore me?" a loud voice behind him said. He realized then that the music had stopped. He looked around at the dark, smoky confusion of dancers coming off the floor. "That's right. I'm talking to you, sugar. I think you're ignoring me."

He looked again and saw the short red head from behind the bar. He narrowed his eyes—the beer had made them a little blurry. "Not intentionally," he answered.

"Don't you remember me?" she said, sounding disappointed. "Mona Faye. I got you that beer you're holding."

He smiled, held his beer up in a silent toast. He didn't recall her giving him her name.

She had just freshened her lipstick and had a bright red grin. "I finally got a minute to breathe, turned around, and you weren't there anymore. You haven't been here before, have you?"

"No ma'am," he said. "Just passing through. Broke down out on the highway."

"Don't you go ma'aming me. I'm not that old. And you can stop trying to play like some shy, backwoods hick, too. I see right through that." She put her hands on her hips and tilted her head. "Did you take your car to Bud Dow's place? Continental station up on the Austin highway?"

"How'd you know that?"

"It's a small town, sugar. Make sure Bud don't know you're just passing through. He'll overcharge you if he thinks he'll never see you again. Tell him you're my cousin or something. No, hell, tell him you're my ex-husband. That ought to shock him stupider than he already is." She stepped up closer and gave his shirt pocket a brazen tap. "I thought I saw a pack of Luckies in there."

She squeezed the pack of cigarettes out of his pocket and tapped a cigarette loose. He chuckled at her. She was brassy as hell.

"Allow me," he said—flirting, yeah, why not? The beer, and her smile, had made him agreeable. He cupped a match to light her cigarette. "Hey, you read me wrong. I *am* a shy backwoods hick."

She tipped her head to let out a gray plume of smoke. "And I'm Jean Harlow. The light's just bad in here."

He laughed, swigged at his beer. She kept smiling. Another number started up—"Treasure Untold," played a beat too fast.

"Are you going to ask me to dance?" she said. "I'm on my break."

"Well, I guess I am." He put his hand on the small of her back and steered her out onto the dance floor.

Once they were out there with the crowd, he pulled her up tight. Her body was solid, even chunky in places, but in a pleasing way. She followed him with a lightness in her step, but also rubbed against him at opportune moments. Desire crackled through him, strong and unexpected. His reaction didn't go unnoticed by her either. She seemed to enjoy it, laughed, arched back now and then to smoke her cigarette.

When the first song ended, she didn't let him go. "I'm still on break," she said, so they danced to the next one, too. And the next one after that, and the next, until he hollered uncle and broke for the bar. She followed him and took over the bar duties from the crotchety fellow back there shoveling cans out of the ice tubs.

Mona Faye started passing out beer to those waiting. She wise-cracked with everybody, and laughed at her own jokes, slipped a couple more beers to Lange, too, without charging him. "I'll collect from you later," she said, with a wink.

He leaned there and watched her, thinking about the invitation and the promise in that wink. He'd been around his share of Mona Fayes. In the past year he'd gone through a whole string just like her. Places down on the coast teemed with beer joints and easy women. Aileen and Nelda, Patsy, June, Ruby, a couple of Anns. He wasn't keeping score. It was just the ones he remembered. And besides, he'd usually been as drunk as a coot...paying Becky back.

Vaguely he wondered if that might have been his motivation all along, right from the first second he stepped foot inside The Western Palace, to get drunk, maybe get laid, to feel good for a little while. He had it coming, didn't he? After the last couple of days. Hell, after the past year.

He watched Mona Faye behind the bar, smooth little body bustling around back there, loading more beer into the ice tubs, laughing and joking with her customers. She seemed good-hearted, didn't have a wedding ring on her finger. She'd mentioned an ex-husband, but you never knew for sure, did you? Could be some poor chump waiting on her at home or out working his ass off so she could buy that red lipstick and those red leather cowboy boots. Lange thought he ought to leave some money on the bar where he was standing and walk out the wide-open doors when she wasn't looking. He even jangled the change in his pocket, trying to decide. Except she chose right then to raise her head in his direction and give him one of those half-timid, half-provocative smiles. His hand came up empty to rest palm-down on the bar.

HER BEDROOM WAS STIFLING HOT. Sultry air came through the windows. He couldn't stand the sheets against him. Couldn't sleep anyway with her sick-sweet perfume and all the beer rolling in his belly. When her breath began to come even and deep, he eased out of the bed. He managed to put on his pants silently so as not to wake her. He carried his boots in one hand, the rest of his clothes in the other, except for his socks. He couldn't find them in the dark. He tiptoed through the airless little shotgun house.

The screen door latch popped as he slipped it free of the eye bolt. It sounded like a firecracker going off in the dead quiet. He lifted his head and listened. Nothing moved inside the house. Relieved, he slid out the door, paused at the porch steps long enough to tug on his shirt, his belt, his boots. He had driven her car so he would remember the way back, and she'd been more than happy to let him. She'd pressed right up next to him, her head on his shoulder, and gabbed the whole way. He couldn't remember now what she had talked about, he didn't care. He figured he had about a four-mile hike back to the garage. He felt wobbly and a little sick from all the beer.

A few houses down from Mona Faye's, a loose dog joined him, soundlessly fell into step alongside him. He didn't mind; he'd always got on good with animals. The dog made him feel more like himself. And he needed to feel a little more human right then.

Sex with Mona Faye had been like riding a storm at 10,000 feet. It shook him to his core, and once it was done, shame overcame him almost immediately. What kind of a person was he anyway? Hadn't he just yesterday buried his wife? He pictured again the casket going down in that deep, dark hole.

His boots had already rubbed blisters on his sockless feet. The night was heavy and thick. No moon. No breeze. No cars came past him. No one stirred inside the houses. The steady gait of the dog kept him going.

What happened to that vow he'd made sitting on the fender of the broken-down Oldsmobile? Hadn't he promised himself to stop acting on impulse, to stop doing the first damn thing that struck his fancy? Did he have no willpower at all? No moral fiber? Papa was right. He was a sorry excuse for a man. Couldn't keep a steady job. Couldn't keep any money in his pocket. Couldn't keep a woman either—*damn you, Becky*.

The Oldsmobile sat in the side lot of the garage, a ghost in the dark night. He stumbled to the car. The dog hiked his leg on the front tire, sniffed around on the ground beyond. Lange crawled into the backseat, exhausted, nauseated. He wadded a bundle of dirty clothes underneath his head and didn't bother to push off his boots. The dog whined a little.

"Go on home, boy," Lange said, pulling at the collar of his shirt, giving his neck more room. He felt like he was strangling. Even his spit tasted dry and salty.

The dog raised on his hind legs and rested his big front paws on the door. He whined louder. Without looking, Lange fished a chicken leg out of the food box from Aunt Dellie and pitched it out the window. He didn't want to move too much, didn't want to think. The world was spinning, the car, the back seat. If he lay there perfectly still, he thought he might stave off the vomit.

"SURE SORRY TO HAVE TO LEAVE YOU stranded last night." Bud Dow was leaning both arms on the outside of the car window.

Lange opened his eyes, closed one, squinted. The sun was already well up, and the glare burst on him like it was trying to shine right through him. His head pounded.

Bud tugged down on the bill of his cap. "One of my kids sprang an ankle and the wife called me home. Had to run him up to the doctor's or I would of come back to see about you. You a coffee-drinker? I got a Thermos full of it in the garage there. Help yourself."

Lange shook himself awake. He sat up. The taste of soured beer lingered in his mouth. "Thanks," he mumbled and popped open the rear door. Bud moved out of the way long enough for Lange to emerge from the Oldsmobile.

"Got that pump you need inside," Bud said. "Me and the boy just shoved your car around here out of the way yesterday. But if we can get her rolled out to the front, I'll start work on her right now."

A sullen, pimple-faced teenager stood off to one side. He studied Lange up and down, didn't seem to think much of what he saw. Lange could smell himself.

"Yeah, OK." Lange got behind the wheel to take off the hand brake. Bud and the teenager positioned themselves on either side of the fender, and Lange steered as they shoved the car around the side of the garage to the front where all the tools waited.

"Coffee's in there." Bud pointed toward the cluttered desk just inside the work bay. "The wife sent you up a couple of cold biscuits. Ain't much. She worried you was going hungry."

"Well...tell her thanks." Lange wiped his cheek, smoothed at his hair. He wasn't ready to eat yet. He patted around his pockets for his pack of cigarettes. There were three crumpled ones left. He pinched the end of one closed so it wouldn't lose anymore tobacco, struck a match. He took a big, deep drag on the cigarette, and went over to the little desk where a tin syrup lid served as a well-used ashtray.

The silver Thermos of coffee stood there with an empty cup beside it. Two cold biscuits were wrapped in waxed paper. He poured himself some coffee and went outside to smoke. He left the biscuits untouched, took the front page of the Sunday paper with him.

It was the *Austin American*, and the headlines were still full of Roosevelt's radio address. "FDR In Favor Of Reinstating The Draft." Lange fought the breeze that kept trying to blow the paper out of his hand. "Nazi Warplanes Continue To Strafe Britain." They were still counting casualties from yesterday's tenement bombing in London. Parts of a Hitler speech were quoted—his promise to destroy the British Empire if she didn't surrender. The Italians were fighting the English in Africa. But there was nothing at all about the situation in France.

He thought about those government letters again that Aunt Dellie had shown him, and Papa sitting bent and withered, with his ear cocked on the radio broadcast. Lange hadn't really been paying much attention to the war over there. He figured it didn't have anything to do with him. Sad about all those people dying, but hadn't the Europeans been killing each other off for centuries? He knew Hitler was a bad man, everybody knew that, but there were bad men roaming all over the world just like they had been since the time of Christ.

A tiny paragraph on the back page of the newspaper caught his eye, a fill-in, there just to hole-up an inch of leftover space at the bottom of the page. The paragraph stated that Great Britain had begun to lobby the U.S. government to repeal the law prohibiting Americans from enlisting in foreign military units under threat of losing their American citizenship. The paragraph said Britain had the backing of several U.S. senators on the matter, including Morris

Sheppard of Wheatfield, Texas. And it also said that in recent weeks hundreds of men had flowed through Canada into the Royal Navy, the King's Army, and the Royal Air Force.

Lange read that last sentence again, crushed the cigarette under the heel of his boot, read it again. And one more time, just to make sure he got it.

He tore out the little article, stared out at the highway, at the few cars that passed. He'd heard about a couple of guys who had gone to Canada. One was the fellow, Buzz Kirby, who Lange had replaced at Red Hawk Aero-Dusters. There'd been talk around some of the airfields, back before France capitulated, of resurrecting the Lafayette Escadrille from the Great War, but it was just talk, had the ring of thrill-seeking to it, and bravado, like a hired gun back in the Old West. He folded the torn-out piece of paper in half and stuck it in his shirt pocket.

He knew Canada was up there, of course, to the North. But it was a mysterious foreign place to him. Not like Mexico, which was all around you when you lived in Texas. Hell, he'd even flown over part of Mexico a few times by accident. But he'd never seen a Canadian, let alone met one in person. He wouldn't know what they looked like or sounded like. He didn't know much of anything about them. Canada was just too damned far away from his world. Except—you *could* drive there if you set your mind to it. That much was possible, although it would take some doing to get there, and some time. Due north, he reckoned, up through Dallas and Oklahoma City and Missouri and all those other plains states stacked on top of each other until you got to the U.S. border. Could take as long as a week, provided you had a way to make the trip.

He gazed towards the garage, at the Oldsmobile sitting there with the open hood like a yawning mouth. Bud Dow had grease and oil all over his blue plaid shirt and down his right arm. He handed the old blown water pump to the teenager who stopped picking at his pimples long enough to heave it over into an empty oil barrel.

"I'll have you back on the road in half an hour," Bud Dow said with a grin. "This thing ought to go on slick as a gut."

Lange nodded. He felt a little woozy but exhilarated, like a preacher who has just heard the call. He glanced at the empty highway, gulped down the Thermos cup full of coffee.

"Here," Lange said. "Let me give you a hand with that." He dropped the newspaper back amid the tumble on the desk.

CHAPTER 4

Letters

Ottawa

Commonwealth of Canada

August 24, 1940

Dear Papa,

I have sat down to write to you at least a dozen times, but things were just too un-settled till now to tell you anything. You have probably been imagining me as still down around Rockport flying dusters when all this time I have been wandering all over the North American continent in Aunt Dellie's Oldsmobile, so I will start at the beginning.

I never did make it back to San Antonio. The car broke down before I got there, and it took all night to get it fixed, which left me with a lot of free time on my hands to do some serious thinking about things going on in the world and what this Hitler fellow is doing over there in Europe, and how we're all of us in this country just sitting by watching it happen, even though I'm pretty sure Mr. Roosevelt won't sit by forever. I've been just as guilty about it as anybody. Maybe more so. The point is that while the Olds was in the garage in San Marcos getting fixed, it began to seem to me that it's one thing to sit around and spout about what the British ought to do, or what the French ought to do, and how things ought to be, and another thing altogether to put some muscle behind your words. So I made the decision to come on up here to Canada and see what I can personally do to help win this damned war. With that idea in my mind, and once the Olds was fixed again, I struck out right up Highway 5, which if you look at a map, splits the United States right down the middle. It took me most of six days hard driving. I made some wrong turns, and the highway petered out a few times, but eventually I crossed into Canada.

To make a long story short, I tried to join the Canadian Air Force but they wouldn't take me. They've signed some kind of an agreement with the USA that they won't recruit Americans into their military forces. After all those days of driving, I nearly lost my temper over it, but one of the men at the recruiting station in Winnipeg took me to the side and told me that there are ways around the Neutrality Act (that's what the Agreement's called), and he gave me a name and a telephone number, and with a wink sent me on my way. I stopped at the first phone booth I came to and made that call.

The number the fellow gave me was for a hotel in North Dakota. I was supposed to ask for a man by the name of Mr. Howard. It was all like something out of a Cagney movie, and I felt a little bit leery about it at first. This fellow named Howard told me I was going to have to cross back into the States and that I should come to Fargo and meet him at a particular hotel. By then I was pretty riled up, felt like I was getting the run-around, but I had made up my mind and had come all that way, so I drove the 220 miles back to Fargo, North Dakota.

Mr. Howard was waiting for me at the hotel just like he said he would be. He was a bald little fellow with a nervous habit of scratching at his sideburns. By the time I got there, he had picked himself raw and was bleeding down one side of his face. He said he had just about given up on me, and had nearly packed it in that morning. Hadn't dawned on me till then that he'd been waiting *around for just me. I had sort of figured there would be a line of us fellows.*

Anyway, he asked to see my logbook and when I showed it to him, all of the sudden he couldn't do enough for me. He said they didn't usually get men with as many flying hours as I've got under my belt. He took me to supper downstairs in the cafe and got me a nice fat steak along with a bottle of the reddest wine you ever saw. Terrible stuff, but he sure seemed to like it. The best part of the whole deal was he paid for everything, including my room.

Turned out Mr. Howard is an old warbird like Sterling, from the last war, and now he works for the Clayton Knight Committee recruiting American pilots for the RAF—that's Royal Air Force, in case you didn't know.

The next day he drove me out to an airfield where I flew a Taylorcraft tandem trainer with him in the observer's seat. You probably don't realize it, but it's the same plane I flew for Sterling, or almost the same, which means I was already familiar with that type. So we did a couple of circuits and I greased it both times. It was all a test to make sure I knew what I was doing. He seemed satisfied, told me I would be amazed at all the doctored logbooks he'd seen in the past few months. That night he made some phone calls, and the next morning, bought me another steak for breakfast and put me on a train bound for Ottawa. He paid for all that, too.

So, unbelievable as I know it probably sounds, I have signed on with the RAF. They have me in what they call a refresher course. Some other guys from the USA here, too. One is from Del Rio. We even know a couple of the same people. There's another fellow from Utica, New York, another from Lansing, Michigan, and one from Gallup, New Mexico. See, I'm not the only one with this same bright idea.

They're giving us a lot of classroom work in navigation and meteorology, and I'm learning Morse code. When I'm through here, providing I don't wash out, I'll be in the RAF with the rank of

Pilot Officer, which is equal to a Second Lieutenant in the U.S. Army Air Corp. So how do you like that?

There is no place for personal belongings around here so I had to sell the Olds. Mr. Howard took care of that for me, and he'll be sending the money to Aunt Dellie. Let her know I plan on writing to her, too. Tell her I'm OK. I wish all of you could see it here.

Mild days and cool nights, like Texas at her best in early Spring. This has got to be the cleanest place on earth, and everybody is so dern friendly. Makes you feel right at home.

I know this is all probably a little too much for you to take with one swallow, Papa. It's almost too much for me, too, but every day I'm more and more sure I've done the right thing. Eventually the USA will have to get into this war. It's only a matter of time. Once that happens there will be a draft. Mr. Roosevelt's already talking it up. With me in the right age group I would surely get plucked up pretty quick. This way at least I can choose how I'll spend the war— in the air where I know a little bit about what I'm doing. Truth is I have about decided I might just be cut out for military life and didn't know it till now. If you think about it from my standpoint, I believe you'll agree, that for once I've used my head about something.

Your son,
Lange

P.S. Tell Gabe I sure am sorry I won't be there in October to help him work calves. Choke Hargrove is going to be sending you my last paycheck. Take it against what I owe you. I'll get the rest of it to you as soon as I can.

~

September 10, 1940
Dear Ding,

I am writing to you because I cannot wait for your papa to get around to it. He is still trying to figure out what is a Cagney movie. And I have something I want to say. As you should well know, even without me telling you, I have always felt by you as if you were my own son. Your Uncle Daniel, rest his soul, thought the world of you, too, as does Gabriel. In fact, all of your family members have always adored you especially much. You are our little Ding. Now, I know you are not that anymore, we all realize this, but I think it would break everyone's heart if something should happen to you. That is why I must beg of you, dear nephew, to please reconsider this decision you have made to join the RAF. You say you believe that our own country will have to get involved in the war in Europe sooner or later, and I know you are thinking of your sister's children when you say that. But the point is, dearest boy, America is NOT in the war yet and it is NOT your responsibility.

If you need money to get back home I will gladly send it. I know now I never should have given you all of those letters to read, I will always rue that day. I had forgotten what a sweet, sensitive soul you are at heart. We just can't risk our Ding to the RAF. Tell them you have made a mistake. We will repay your Mr. Howard all that he spent on you. If necessary, I will write to him. After we get you safely back home, we will all help you to get a new start in whatever you decide you want to do. Only please come home at once.

Your devoted and most concerned,
Aunt Dellie

~

October 1, 1940

Dearest Aunt,

By the time you get this letter I will be on my way to England. Once I get there and have an address I will send it to you. It touches me that you are fretting so about me, but rest easy. I am doing just fine. The instructor had a talk with me yesterday. He told me that normally somebody my age would automatically go on to multi-engine school to learn to fly bombers or get posted to ferry duty. You see, dear aunt, by RAF standards, I am an old man. But he marked me for single engines, and I tell you, I couldn't be happier. This is exactly what I had hoped for. I can think of nothing worse than having a whole crew on board for me to worry over. This way I will only have to worry over myself, and I have already been doing that for twenty-six years! So be happy for me because truth is, I think deep down this is just what I have always wanted to do.

Two of the other Americans that were in our class didn't make it. The one from Del Rio washed out last week on navigation exercises. The fellow from Michigan spun in on a botched landing. He's in the hospital with a lot of broken bones but it could have been worse. They'll send him home when he gets out. So, that only leaves me and Jim Hiller. Jim is the farm boy from Utica I told you about. He is a top-notch pilot. He's going on single-engines, too. We're hoping to get the same OTU once we're in England. OTU stands for Operational Training Unit. Everything is abbreviated in the RAF. OTU is where we'll learn combat tactics and military procedures. It's going to be different than any kind of flying I've ever done before, but I think I'm ready for something new. I feel like the luckiest fellow alive.

Your nephew,
Lange

CHAPTER 5

"Sunny's Kids"

"JUSTINE"

SEPTEMBER 1940

My sister Nina holds my hand as if I am still a child. She is always in a hurry wherever we go but especially when we walk to the village on Mondays. Monday is when they post the new lists at the Prefecture of Police. In this village the building serves as the *hôtel de ville* and anything else that has to do with government and authority. It is not anything like Paris here. It is not as well-run, and the people are country people. Nina says they are not stupid. They simply are not as worldly as people in the city. I try to go along with her on that, but I think I still see a lot of stupidity around me. I dread having to start back to school in this place.

When we near the building Nina lets go of my hand and rushes up the steps to crowd around the other women gathered there. All of them are scanning the new lists that are posted along the outside wall. Two of the others are also pregnant, but Nina seems somehow so much more so. This is because she is usually so trim and beautiful. She is still beautiful but hardly trim. She has begun to waddle like one of Mémé's old geese.

While she searches the list for Emile's name, I stand at the edge of the steps leaning against the building out of the sun. Down the street there is a knot of German soldiers around the back of a lorry. We have only just begun to see a few soldiers here. A man in the back of the lorry fills the soldiers' tin cups from a large urn. Once they have their cups filled the soldiers move over to the sidewalk to drink their coffee. They are all young and dressed in the field gray. I don't know what the different patches and insignia on their uniforms mean. One of them is blond and fair, and he catches me looking. I move back a step so that I am hidden behind the edge of the building. When I peek out again, he is still looking my way. He smiles and makes a cuckoo face. I laugh and cover my mouth as I step back again to where he can't see me.

We are supposed to hate them. Two months ago, we ran all the way from Paris down here to the edge of the Morvan just to get away from them. Emile's *grand-mère*—we call her Mémé—has a farmhouse here. When the war started Emile gave Nina instructions to come here if anything should happen so that he could find her. Well, we are here and so are the Germans, but Emile is nowhere to be seen.

"Come on." Nina catches my arm and pulls me from beside the building. The blond soldier is still looking my way. So is the friend standing with him now. I return his look. He touches the bill of his cap.

"Stop that," Nina says to me in French. "Ignore them."

The soldiers watch us go. They seem sorry. They seem friendly. It's against the law to show them any hostility.

"Emile isn't on the list?" I say.

She shakes her head sharply as we cross the street. She shows no emotion, but I know it is a blow to her every Monday that passes without news of his whereabouts. It would be easier on her, I think, even to know if he has been killed.

The last we knew Emile's regiment was near the Ardenne. It's all a mystery to us what happened there. We don't know if his regiment was overrun or if they surrendered. Emile's cousin, Gaston, is also missing. Nina would tell me if Gaston's name was on the list, so I assume by her silence that he is not there either.

Since we are in town we do Mémé's shopping. She needs sugar, flour, salt, and some other things. We queue up with other shoppers, and by the time we get to the counter the grocer has already run out of flour. He takes our ration tickets and hands over the other things on our list. Nina tries to argue with him about the flour, but he turns away from her.

The farm is a far walk from the village, and on an uphill grade. I wonder how much longer Nina can make this trip on foot. She breathes hard and has to make several stops. I end up carrying most of the groceries.

"I like the name Bernard for the baby," I say because talking about the baby is the only thing that makes Nina happy these days. "I looked it up in Mémé's book and it means strong as a bear. And bright."

"Bernard's a German name. I want my baby to have a French name. Or an American one." She says all of this in English which confuses me for a moment. It is something she has done more and more often since Mama died. Mama used to speak English with Nina and I think she misses it, fears she may lose it if she doesn't use the language sometimes. I have already forgotten a lot of my English and have to think for a while to understand what she has just said.

When we round the final corner, Peter is there waiting for us. He signs to Nina—"What did you find?" Or more exactly just *What find*? We understand his shortcuts. She shakes her head. He gives me a questioning look and takes the bags of groceries from me.

I tell him we saw some German soldiers. He is interested in this, I can tell, but his hands are full, so out loud he says, "Where?"

I answer him with my hands. Our brother Peter is deaf. He was born deaf. And not just hard of hearing, but profoundly deaf. In Paris he went to a school for the deaf, and there he learned to read lips and to speak a little, although his voice sounds odd and draws attention from strangers. Peter is also very handsome. All of my Parisian friends begged to be introduced to him, but the strain of having to learn sign was too much for any of them to become a serious girlfriend. One by one they drifted away without breaking his heart too much. Peter yearns, even more than I do, to go back home. He has always yearned for something more. I think of how lonely it must be for him to be away from all his deaf mates from school. Of all of us, I think he is the most alone here.

At the farmhouse, Mémé is canning sweet mirabells we picked from her orchard last Sunday. We have been canning fruit for the past two weeks. Before that it was beans and tomatoes from her garden. She says that the last time the Germans came, hunger came with them, so this time she is determined to be prepared. We spend all the rest of that day canning along with her.

Now that we are on German time it gets dark before six. Mémé lets us turn the generator on each night for an hour so we can hear music on the radio. Peter, of course, doesn't hear it, but it doesn't stop him from trying to dance with us anyway. He laughs his wild laugh and bobs up and down around us. I am a good dancer, and so is Nina. She and I do American dances like the jitterbug to some of the fast songs. After a while, she is out of breath, but for a few minutes she seems to have forgotten about Emile. Once we shut off the generator the silence is suffocating.

When we first got here I liked the idea of living with candles and oil lamps, but now I find it tiresome. The light is not good enough to read by or to do much of anything for that matter. We all trudge upstairs early to our beds. Mémé has already been in her room for a while. On the landing we say goodnight with our hands. Once the generator is turned off Nina makes us all sign. She says that way we will keep from waking Mémé, as if the radio and the noise of the generator itself hadn't been enough to keep Mémé from her sleep.

Peter loves it when we all talk only with our hands. He has the most nimble, expressive hands. For a few moments the ballet of hands continues on the landing, and then we all kiss and hug goodnight. Peter turns for his room; Nina and I to the one we share.

At night is when I miss Paris the most. It's hard to go from living in the loveliest of cities, the most modern and sophisticated, to living like this, with the dirt and insects of the country farmhouse. We have to dust off our feet before we can get into bed. When I complain Nina says, "You're just spoiled."

"Well, I don't see why everything has to change just because the Germans have come." Emile's mother and father, François and Clothilde, have already gone back to Paris. I wonder why we can't go back as well.

"You know why. Because I promised Emile that if the Germans broke through I would come here and wait for him."

I want to tell her that I don't think he's coming, but I don't dare.

She blows out the candle flame, and I feel her settle into the bed. After a few seconds, she says, "Besides, I don't think I could make that trip again. I believe this baby is going to come early. I have not felt right for the last two days."

"Have you told that to Mémé?"

"No. It's only a feeling."

"Well, don't have it in the bed tonight."

She giggles, so I feel safe, too. It feels nice to laugh together. She clutches my hand under the covers.

"I have been missing Mama lately," she says.

"Me, too."

"I think it's because of the baby. I'm not scared but I wish I had someone I could talk to."

"What about Mémé?"

"She's too old. I ask, but she gives me old wives tales." She squeezes my hand. "If something happens to me, Justy, you must take care of Peter. Even though he's older than you. It will have to be you."

"I know that. But nothing will happen to you."

"But if something does, you have to be Peter's ears. Will you promise me, Justy?"

"Nothing is going to happen to you," I say again. I am not in the mood for serious talk. Everything is always too serious lately.

But Nina keeps on. "Please, say that you promise."

"I love Peter. Why do I have to promise?"

She lets go of my hand. I feel her readjust herself in the bed. It seems to take her a great effort. "Why are you such a hard head?" she says, but I do not answer her.

On Saturday morning Nina goes into labor. I try to stay in the room with her, but I cannot watch her suffer so much. Mémé says the baby is turned wrong. She tucks a kitchen knife between the mattress and the springs to cut the pain in half. I do what I can, fetching towels and water, bathing Nina's forehead while she strains, but I have to keep leaving the room. It is too much for me. Peter disappears from the house, and I wish I was a boy, so I could go, too. I remember our conversation in the dark room. Somehow she had known the baby would come early. I pray she does not die. I stand outside the door and listen to her screams and think that she must be dying right then. I cannot see how anyone could live through such pain. Not her. Not even the baby. I sit on the floor and cry hard for her.

Then Peter comes hurrying up the stairs. He has a doctor with him. I scramble to my feet, amazed that Peter has worked this miracle. The doctor pushes by me and into the room, and in a minute Nina's screams end. This terrifies me even more, and I try to open the door, but Mémé shoves me back. Peter takes me by my shoulders and turns me to him. Our eyes meet silently. We stand locked together outside the door and wait.

Finally, the strangled cries of a newborn baby come. I lift my head to listen. Peter signs at me frantically. I tell him, "A baby is crying." He smiles, but I am still afraid for Nina. I have not heard her voice in a long time.

Mémé comes out of the door. She holds a baby wrapped in a blanket. "A tiny girl," she tells us. Peter hugs me in joy.

"What about Nina?" I ask for both of us.

"She is sleeping now. She will be fine." Mémé holds the new baby. A squeaking noise comes from inside the bundle of white blanket.

I want to cry again. From relief and because the baby is so tiny and sweet. Her face looks purple, but she moves her head and her fingers clutch out at the air. Mémé gives the baby to me. I worry I will drop her. She is soft and squeaks.

Mémé touches Peter on his cheek. "You are a good boy," she says to him clearly and slowly, so he can read her lips. He bends his cheek down for her to kiss him. Mémé is especially fond of our Peter.

I WALK ALONE to the village on Monday to read the list posted at the Prefecture of Police. Neither Emile nor his cousin Gaston are listed there. Nina has named her baby Joie. I think how it is sad that Emile does not even know he is a father. The father is the one who is supposed to register the new baby at the mairie, but I go inside to do it for him. A picture of Hitler hangs on the wall inside the doors. He looks angry in the picture. I cannot help but stare. It is the first time I have seen his picture hanging inside a public building.

I have to show the authorities my identity papers and answer questions about my mother being an American. The man at the desk seems confused by this, but finally he begins to fill out information about the baby. Joie Lia Monnier. I write it out exactly the way Nina instructed. When I leave the mairie, I have Joie's certificate of birth. I resist the urge to give a Nazi salute to Herr Hitler as I pass the stern picture of him. Some people might think I meant it.

On the street, the canteen lorry is where it was parked last

Monday. Soldiers are grouped around it getting their tea and coffee. I recognize the same blond soldier who smiled at me before. He smiles again and even raises his hand in greeting, as if we are acquainted. Perhaps I look a second too long at him before I lift my chin and continue across the street. From the corner of my eye I see him following me. I quicken my stride. He quickens his as well. My heart beats loud in my ears.

"Mademoiselle," he calls out. His accent is terrible.

I do not know why I stop walking. I know I should pretend not to hear him, to ignore him the way Nina has preached. But there is the slim possibility of trouble if I fail to stop, so I do. He comes closer, smiling. His friend is coming behind him. He says something in German to his friend, but keeps his smile focused on me.

The friend speaks. "He says to tell you that he is Dieter Gaertner." The friend's French is understandable at least. Even so, he seems about to break into laughter. Dieter Gaertner growls out something else but keeps smiling at me. The friend translates again. "He wants to know if he can kiss your hand." No sooner does the friend get this said than he bursts into laughter, which he tries to stifle. Dieter Gaertner's face flames, but he does not laugh along with his friend.

I look straight at them both, give a haughty shake of my head to keep the hair from blowing into my eyes, and lift my hand like a queen. The blond soldier removes his cap, clicks his heels, and bends at the waist to plant a dry kiss on the back of my hand. It all seems very funny, and I nearly laugh, but then I remember myself. I glance towards the Prefecture building. Two of the women on the steps watch us. Quickly, I drop my hand and pull away from the two soldiers.

"Wait! Please!" Dieter Gaertner says in his awful French. This time I do ignore him and nearly run for the hill that leads to Mémé's farmhouse.

"He wants to know your name," the friend calls, but I keep

going. I pray the two women on the steps do not know Nina well enough to tell her what they have just seen.

I kick at a stone lying in the center of the road. It slides straight ahead of me, so I kick it again. I wonder if the solders are still back there watching me. I imagine that I can feel their eyes boring into my back. But I don't turn to look.

PART TWO
Per Ardua Ad Astra
"THROUGH STRUGGLE TO THE STARS"
(MOTTO OF THE RAF) NOVEMBER 1940

CHAPTER 6

"The Train"

Lange used the men's room at the Chester train station to finish up his morning ablution—a word he had learned from his flight instructor. It meant combing down his hair with water, touching up the rough shave he'd given himself back at the air station. The facilities at Hawarden had been thrown together at the last minute and so none of the buildings had hot water. There had been no shower facilities nor a mess hall. Every evening the trainees were bused to another base close by for supper, and twice a week, for a shower. Hawarden had one usable hangar and flat ground, and that had been good enough as far as the Air Ministry was concerned.

He wasn't sorry to be leaving OTU behind, but he was apprehensive about what lay ahead. Like it had been in Ottawa, things at OTU were hurried up. They'd been told from the outset it was an eight-week course that they were going to do in three weeks or less. It all depended on how the war was going, and it wasn't going too well. The RAF needed fighter pilots and needed them quick.

After twenty-five minutes on a Miles Master, Lange had flown his first Spitfire. He hadn't even had the chance at a walk-around before the ground crew was shoehorning him into the cockpit and the instructor was hollering things at him:

"Just let her sort herself out on her own. She wants to fly." A pat on the shoulder. "You're ready for her. You wouldn't be going up if you weren't."

Lange felt like he'd been shot from a cannon. The airplane was stiff on the ailerons, but fingertip sensitive on the elevators. He barely touched the control and almost flipped over on his back. A far cry from Choke Hargrove's Flying Jenny, that was for sure. Exhilaration hadn't overcome the jitters until he was well up in the sky, doing a split-S and roll high over the Welsh countryside—a little kid with a new, 350 mile-per-hour toy. And it landed like a dream, wheels kissed the ground twice and it was done. By the end of that first flight, he had lost his heart.

In the men's room mirror, he straightened his tie, flicked a speck of lint from the wings on his tunic—they made him feel important, those embroidered wings. A Spitfire pilot. He hoped he could do it, that it was in him somewhere—courage. There was no way to tell, just by studying his reflection in the mirror. He was smart enough to know that pretend dogfights with training mates or shooting at seagulls off the coast of Wales were not the same thing as combat. But there was no turning back now. He'd come this far, made it through Primary and OTU without washing out, and he hadn't embarrassed himself too much either.

He shrugged into his greatcoat. It was damned cold in November in this country. He settled his service cap on his head, took a last look at the Pilot Officer in the mirror, that stranger. In his pocket he had a thirty-six-hour leave pass, a railway travel voucher, and his orders posting him to an operational squadron based near London. He only wished Jim Hiller from Utica was going with him. But he and Jim had parted company three weeks ago when Jim got sent to Lincolnshire to learn to fly Hurricanes. Lange lifted his kitbag from the lavatory and went out to catch the train that would take him to the war.

~

FIVE MINUTES after the train got underway, a woman fell onto his lap. She was attempting to stash her belongings into a spot in the baggage rack above him when the train jarred over a rough patch on the tracks. Lange had been staring out the window, thinking that it looked a little like Texas out there except for the rain and the sheep, and he didn't notice the woman until she landed on him, face to face. He got an elbow in the collar bone but he instinctively grabbed to catch her, otherwise she might have gone sprawling out into the aisle.

She clutched at her cap, regained her balance. "Sorry," she said, then the train jarred again, and he had to catch her a second time. "Oh, sorry. Sorry," she said. "Blast this damned train!"

By then he was laughing. "You'd better just sit down." He slid over to the seat by the window, giving her the one she kept falling into.

The train lurched yet again, and again she grabbed her cap. She was wearing some kind of uniform, a shade darker blue than his. Everybody in this country was in uniform but he recognized the gold wings on her tunic. They were identical to the wings on his except where his said *RAF* hers read *ATA*.

"You're a ferry pilot?" he said, automatically. There had been a ferry pool at Hawarden, so he recognized the insignia, but he hadn't seen any women pilots there, just busy older fellows going in and out of a two-story building.

"Yes," she answered. "And you're a Yank."

"Well...I'm an American. But I can guarantee you there's no damn-yankees in my family."

She was blond, a little older, or maybe the uniform made her look older. Straight teeth, downturned nose. She wore a little makeup, pink on the apples of her cheeks, but he could see pale freckles underneath. Startling blue eyes. Good-looking, if you liked the type. Personally, he had never gone for vanilla ice cream blondes.

She stuck out her hand. "Mackie MacLeod," she said. "From Canada."

He shook hands. "I didn't think you sounded British."

"And I didn't think you sounded real. My family spent winters in Florida every year, but I never heard syrup like you've got. Where did you get that drawl?"

He wondered if he should feel insulted. Only a couple of days before, the bartender at Chester's Blossom Hotel had told Lange his accent was impossible to understand.

"Texas," he answered.

"Well, I declare." Clearly, she was mocking him. She fingered out the lapel of his greatcoat to peep underneath at the wings on his tunic. "Another proud member of the Royal Texas Air Force, I see. Now, ain't we lucky."

He bristled, thinking he could've just let her fall on her ass in the aisle. She didn't seem at all grateful. "I did my primary training in your country."

"Do tell?" She was still at it, and she thought she was clever, too.

"Yeah, and turns out I had to come all the way to England to meet my first smart-ass Canadian."

A single laugh erupted from her, loud enough to draw the attention of the other passengers. She covered her mouth and raised her eyebrows at him. Her fingernails were clean and buffed but not polished. A gold ring with a single ruby-colored stone was around her third finger, right hand.

"Apologies. Really bad day. Can we start over?" She stuck out her hand. "Mackie MacLeod. Third Officer, Air Transport Auxiliary." He shook her hand. "And your name, Texas? Are you going to tell me your name?"

"Oh...Lange. Lange DeLony."

"Is that French?" She finally pulled away her hand. Before he could answer, she asked, "Just out of OTU?"

He nodded, smiled. She was a fast talker.

"God, not dimples, too," she said, also smiling. She had on pale pink lipstick. "I feel better about the war already."

THEY ATE lunch at the station cafe in Crewe. The train to London was running late, and she kept getting up to go out to the platform to check on the arrival board. By then, he couldn't help but notice the swizzle in her walk and how well she filled out her uniform, the shapely pair of legs inside her dark military-issue stockings, black seams down the back. She helped pass time, kept his mind off tomorrow and reporting to his new squadron. When she came back, he averted his eyes. Didn't want her to catch him ogling her like a fourteen-year-old.

"Everyone's talking about Coventry," she said. She reached for his pack of smokes—Players, harsh British cigarettes. He was going to have to ask the family to send him cigarettes from home. He struck a match and held it for her. She said, "They're saying it took a real pasting last night. That's what's causing this hold-up."

"The tracks got hit?"

She shrugged, blew out smoke. "It's nothing new. Sometimes I spend two or three days just trying to get anywhere. You'll see what I mean, once you've been here a while." She reached into her bag and pulled out a silver hip flask. She unscrewed the cap. "Scotch? You've got until tomorrow, right? This should help us get through the afternoon."

Strong stuff. Tasted like medicine. He was glad the flask was full. After two swallows he could feel it warming his bones. It made him friendlier.

"There was supposed to be a Maggie for me to take on from Hawarden." She sipped from the flask. "But it was gone when I got there."

He asked her how many different airplanes she flew as a ferry pilot, and that started a conversation, pilot to pilot, and one he'd never had with a woman. She pulled her logbook out of her bag, and he took it from her to flip through the pages while she talked. He had met a few lady pilots, but they had mostly been like one of the fellows, manly and rough. There was nothing rough or mannish about Mackie MacLeod. She flashed around her dainty hands as phrases like throttle tension, and rich or weak mixture, and variable pitch came out in a lilting, intoxicating voice. It had been a long time since he'd been with a woman. He wondered if he could get lucky with this one.

She told him about an aunt she had, with a country house in Cambridgeshire, and about her brothers, one in the ATA like her, the other a flight instructor back in Winnipeg. A family full of pilots. The ferry pilot brother was her favorite, though he could be "a bit of a bastard at times." Her mother had died of cancer when she was a schoolgirl.

"Dad lives in Winnipeg, too, with his young actress from Montreal. It's all tawdry and terribly fashionable. I don't see them anymore. Drink up, Texas, we've got a long way to go."

By the time the London-bound train finally arrived, his lips were numb and his ears buzzed. He helped her up the steps into the train, and then stumbled himself on the way to the saloon car, where they took a table and continued their drinking. They drained the last drops of scotch in her flask. He thought she looked a little bit tight herself. And somewhere along the way, she had become a whole lot more attractive, even being a pale-skinned, shimmery blond. Mainly, he couldn't get past those eyes, so big and round and bright blue. Little girl's eyes, except without the innocence.

He told himself he was just horny. Anything with a pair of legs would have looked good to him by then. The booze and anticipation of going operational had unfocused his mind. His eyes wandered down the curve of her neck, and further down to her bosom rounding out the front of her tunic.

"Are you listening, Texas?" She cocked her head at him.

"Yeah." He reached across the table and touched her index

finger, drew a line from her knuckle to the tip of her nail. "You were saying you need another drink."

"No..." Her hand pressed down gently on the back of his. "But I'll take one if you're buying."

Sure, he was buying. He reached in his pocket and got up for the bar. Had to save back enough for a hotel room for tonight though, or he'd be sleeping on a cold park bench somewhere. What the hell kind of signal was that hand press she'd just given him? Did it mean *no, don't touch me* or *watch this, I'm touching you back*? He didn't usually have to work this hard, but she was different. Not the usual honky-tonk babe waiting to get picked up.

While the bartender poured the drinks, Lange looked back at where she was sitting. She was watching him, too. He smiled. She smiled. He felt self-conscious, wondered if she was scrutinizing him the same way he'd been doing her a minute ago. He didn't know if women did that.

He carried the two drinks back to the table, sat down, tried to think with his fuzzy brain of something witty to say, something flirtatious. He scooted around a little closer to her, getting into a better position. She watched him, seemed curious, maybe amused. But then the train stopped and suddenly their attention shifted.

"Christ," she said. "What now?"

He pivoted around to look out. "Are we there?"

"No, we're in the middle of nowhere."

Outside the windows, it was still gray and dreary. The rain had let up, but it looked cold. When he turned back, she was at the other end of the saloon car in serious conversation with a train guard.

A man in a tweed cap at the next table said, "Jerry smashed up this bit of track again last night."

Lange wasn't sure if the man was speaking to him or just in general to the people inside the car. A murmured discussion began, which Lange had trouble following so he quit trying. He wasn't yet used to these British accents. He drank the rest of his drink and focused on Mackie as she came back to their table. She gathered up her bag.

"I'm walking from here," she said. "We could still be sitting here at midnight."

Lange set down his empty glass and stared at her. "You're walking to London?"

She gave him an indulgent smile. He half-expected her to tousle his head, as if he were a silly little boy. "Back to Tamworth. The trainsman said it's only about two miles back up the track. It was lovely to meet you, Texas."

"Wait. I'm coming with you." Lange stood up too fast. He had to clutch the edge of the table to regain his equilibrium.

"Poor thing," she said. "Did I get you drunk?"

"Not much." He grabbed his kitbag and anchored it over his shoulder.

She studied him for a second. "All right. As far as Tamworth and then we're parting company. I'm going to catch the Leicester line the way I should have in the first place."

He followed her through the car and off the train. Other people were getting off, too. They walked in patchy groups headed back for the Tamworth station, which they had just passed through a few minutes ago.

"I thought you were going to London," he said, when they were striding alongside each other. The train sat still on the tracks, hissing steam into the misty air. "What's in Leicester?"

"I'm going to see my son." She kept her face pointed straight ahead. "He lives with my aunt in Colesbury. You have to go through Leicester to get there. He's seven." Her breath made vapor as she spoke. She didn't have on a coat, so Lange took off his and tucked it around her shoulders. She seemed surprised. She folded the lapel closed at her neck. "Thank you."

Lange took her bag and threaded it over his other arm. It equalized the weight and he needed its warmth. He tried to keep his teeth from chattering. Damn cold country. If she had a son then she must have a husband. That thought hadn't occurred to him before. Suddenly, he felt as sober as Sunday.

"What's his name? Your son?"

"Given." She kept her attention on the track. "It's an old English name. I like a name that means something. He's my little sweetheart."

It seemed a lot farther than just two miles walking back to Tamworth. They had to stay off the tracks since in England the train tracks were electrified. Dusk began to fall. Mackie wasn't as talkative as she had been earlier, and he was struggling with a headache that had crept up on him. Nothing worse than a hangover after an early drunk. It had already been a long day and appeared he was in for an even longer night. Getting laid didn't seem to be in his near future.

Tamworth was easy enough to find. The tracks led them right to the station. She left Lange at the platform, just disappeared while he was looking around for the men's latrine. For a second, he worried she wouldn't come back and he would lose his greatcoat, which he already missed. But then he realized he still had her bag on his shoulder and knew she'd be looking for that.

When he came out of the latrine he saw her sitting on a bench beside the wall, out of the wind but huddled inside his coat. She didn't see him as he approached her. She stared down at the concrete, a gloomy look on her face. He sat next to her.

She gave him a tight smile.

"Here, take your coat. You're turning blue."

"No, I don't need it." He rubbed his hands together and tried not to shiver.

"That's chivalrous of you, Texas, but I grew up in twenty below. You're the one with the thin blood." She hoisted the coat over towards him.

He started to put it on. It felt warm from her body heat. "We can share it. If you don't think your husband would mind."

"What?" She squinted at him. "Oh." She forced a laugh. "Don't worry about that."

She helped him gather the coat over her right shoulder. He scooted in closer, keeping the other side of the coat tucked around his own ribs.

"The stationmaster said the last train to Leicester left ten minutes ago. Which means, I would have to go all the way back to Crewe and start over to get to Colesbury now. The train system in this country stinks." She raised her chin. "I'll try again tomorrow. Anyway, you need an escort to London." She held up two tickets. He took one.

"Do I look lost?" He tucked the ticket into his shirt pocket inside his tunic.

She laughed, more genuinely. "Yes, in a way, you do."

"I was top navigator in my class."

"Bully for you." She threw a playful punch at his chin, then gave him a quick kiss, right on the mouth. "There's no husband."

The kiss surprised him, renewed his hope. She was so close he could smell her perfume. Gardenia. Or maybe lavender. Something fresh and floral. "You're divorced?"

She shook her head. "I usually say he died fighting Franco. It sounds so heroic, don't you think? I even used to wear a wedding ring." She held out her left hand, fingers spread apart. "But I gave it up. Why am I telling you all of this?"

He shrugged. "You don't have to."

"Maybe that's why I am." She drew a breath. "We'll never see each other again, right?"

"It's a small country."

She smiled. "There's no husband." He watched her mouth move.

The sunlight had almost gone, and with the blackout on, no lights burned at the station except for some dim blue ones under the canopy near the ticket window. The sign on the platform said "Lichfield" but all the signs had been changed to confuse the Germans in case of airborne invasion. She was warm where her side touched his.

"Where are you staying?" Her breath whispered against his ear.

"Staying?" He reached to finger a strand of hair away from her lips.

"You have a hotel reservation in London, don't you? You won't get a room this late without one."

"Is it late?"

"It will be. There's still a hundred miles to go."

The bill of his cap bumped the bill of hers. She made a sound like "oops" and let out an awkward snicker. He turned his head to the side to keep it from happening again. She raised her face. Their noses brushed together. Both were cold. The moment their lips met, a train rumbled in on the tracks. Reluctantly, he let her go.

"That's ours," she said. He started to rise but she tugged him back. "Wait." She fished a handkerchief from her bag and wiped pink lipstick off his mouth.

CHAPTER 7

"The Cottage"

Mackie couldn't make up her mind whether to tell Pilot Officer DeLony about the cottage she shared with another ATA pilot attached to her same ferry pool. The cottage was located just outside London, near the air station at Wentworth that housed her ferry pool. She and her roommate, Phyllis O'Connor, had made a pact not to bring home any men. So far, she had held up her end of that pact, but she knew he wouldn't find a hotel room in London at this hour. She could just say goodbye, let him sleep on the street, and be done with him, or she could offer him a bed for one night. Phyllis was up north training and would never know the difference.

He was already asleep beside her. His head rocked on the linen-draped headrest with the rhythm of the train. She was glad he was asleep. It gave her a chance to sort things out in her mind before she woke him up. The next stop was the one they would need to take to get to the cottage—if she decided to take him there.

She held his service cap on her lap. It was spanking new, the visor crisp and unblemished. He'd been posted to an operational squadron at a forward station in Group 11, right up front where he would get shot at straightaway. That alone showed the desperation of Fighter Command, to post such a green pilot in the midst of danger. He probably wouldn't make it a month. She knew as well as anybody the statistics for fighter pilots. Seventy-five percent were shot down within their first two weeks.

Lord, but he was gorgeous. Tall and dark, with those lost puppy-dog eyes, lashings of Texas honey in his voice. He was way too young for her. She had always gone for older men, but he had been nice company. They'd shared some laughs. Clearly, he liked women, had been trying all day to seduce her, but he didn't act too in love with himself like some pilots she knew. He was a smashing good kisser. And gentlemanly; he'd given her his coat. Neil Bannion would have never even noticed she was cold.

She knew she was vulnerable, still smarting from the breakup with Neil, yet another married man who had decided against leaving his wife. Would she never learn? This morning, she had run into Neil at Hawarden. God, she hated running into him. He probably thought she'd come there on purpose. How was she to know he had been taken off operations and given a tour of instructional duty? He had acted pleasant, too pleasant, also distant, as if they barely knew each other, as if they hadn't been lovers—well, off-and-on lovers anyway—for the past eight months or so. She had hastily congratulated him on the new stripe on his sleeve and walked away.

Beside her, the Yank had started to snore lightly. Poor boy. Twenty-three, maybe. Surely not much older than that, despite the five-o'clock shadow sprouting on his Dick Tracy jaw. Twenty-four at the absolute outside. Sleeping like a baby. Nice, clean slope to his nose. Flat ears, a nick on the one nearest to her, some faded scar from childhood. He was exhausted, helped along by all the scotch he drank. Touching, to see somebody get blotto so easily and stay so friendly once he got there. She hoped that wouldn't change, but it probably would. He was a fighter pilot after all. They were guzzlers, the lot of them.

He was definitely too young. That was obvious enough. Not to mention the fact that he was another bloody fighter pilot. Best not get involved.

The voice on the Tannoy announced High Wycombe and Wentworth next stop. She sat up, pulled his coat closer around her, made the decision, and touched his arm.

"We're here, Texas."

He opened his eyes. They were wide and bloodshot, disoriented. The train had slowed to a crawl. She handed him his cap.

"It's our stop," she said

"This is London?"

"Close enough."

He rose like her obedient pet and followed her off the train.

THE COTTAGE WAS GLACIAL. Grip of winter taking hold already. She wasn't ready for it, wasn't one of those Canadians that loved cold weather. Escaping to Florida every November when she was a girl had taught her that winters didn't have to be iced-over rivers and snow drifts roof-high.

As soon as they got inside, the first thing she did was light the small furnace inside the fireplace. It began its confident little chug, puffing out smelly air, but the cottage wouldn't be truly warm until morning when she could open the blackouts to let in the sunshine. Provided the sun actually shone, which wasn't something you could count on in jolly old England. Not in November. There had been a drizzling overcast for days.

The Yank took off his greatcoat, laid it over the back of the arm chair. She had decided to give him her room and she would sleep in Phyl's. Maybe Phyl wouldn't get as upset that way, if she found out there had been a man on board.

"My roommate's on a two-week conversion course." She led him down the short hallway to her room, turning on the overhead. The fifteen-watt bulb glowed dimly. "She's transitioning to light twins. You can have my room."

She heard him drop his kit behind her. Her dressing gown hung on the back of the door. She reached for it and was looking for her slippers, when a pair of strong arms circled her waist from behind.

"Who are all the people in these pictures?" he said, against her neck.

His breath raised chill-bumps. He swayed her gently, to and fro. She leaned back against him, looked at the photographs lined up like soldiers on the dresser: Aaron standing beside his trainer back in Winnipeg; another with his wife and two kids beside Dad and his tart at Mum's family house in Florida. Adam behind his desk at the ferry pool; Adam in the cockpit of a taxi Anson. And then Given holding a cricket bat in Aunt Kath's garden; Given in his school blazer; Given wearing Adam's old flying helmet.

She turned around. He was standing so close there was no room for her to back away. She pressed her wrist to the place where his whiskers had prickled her neck. "Just for the record...I'll be thirty-two in January."

"No kidding?" He kissed her between her eyes. "What day in January? I'll send you a card."

"The eighth," she said, as his lips moved along her hairline, then down beside her ear. She shivered. He had clearly done this before. The dressing gown slipped out of her hands. "But the point is..."

What *was* the point? She struggled to collect herself. He kissed her softly along her brow, raised his face away, looked straight into her eyes. She looked straight back, fully aware of what would happen next. She couldn't say later, not even to herself, that it had only been a sudden weakness, a giving in. His deep, dark, bottomless eyes, the way his hard body felt against hers, what he wanted was exactly what she wanted, too.

Of course, she had known they might end up in bed—it was the reason for her indecision on the train. But what she didn't expect was that it would feel like real lovemaking. It was hungry and passionate, and, for her, powerful and emotional. His endless kisses, the magic in his hands—she got carried away, lost her inhibitions.

Afterwards, she lay in a dazed heap, wrung out, smitten, her mind free from lingering thoughts of Neil Bannion.

"Gee whiz," she whispered, louder than she meant to.

He pulled her backwards against him, spooning her into the curl of his body. His arm circled her. "I'll say," he whispered beside her ear. Then he got still, and in a minute—less than a minute—his breath came even and quiet.

A SOUND WOKE HER. A hollow thump, something falling on the floor or hitting the front door. It came from another part of the cottage. She roused from the pillow. The bedroom was dark, she was naked, and he was gone. It was almost as if he never had been there, a dream, a figment of her imagination, too good to be true.

The floor was icy on the soles of her feet. She scrambled around for her plum-colored dressing gown, found it on the rug. She didn't waste time hunting for her slippers but just bolted through the frigid rooms of the cottage, tying on the dressing gown as she went. His greatcoat was gone from the chair where he'd dropped it last night. Just before she opened the front door, she heard the far-off echo of the air-raid siren.

It was still dark outside. The frosty air bit instantly at her cheeks and then at her toes. Four steps out into the front garden, there he was. He had stopped to light a cigarette. She caught the tail-end of it, the brief flicker on his face from the match cupped in his hand before he waved it out. Moonlight peeped through black and blue clouds. He stood there, slumped inside his coat, kit bag slung over one arm, cigarette end glowing in his hand.

"Put out that light, mister," she said, half-teasing, half from habit. She pulled the dressing gown tighter, but her feet felt frozen on the garden stones. She marched a little to warm them. "You're leaving?" Her words misted out in front of her mouth.

"I heard the bombs and wanted to see what was going on." He sounded shaky.

She moved down the walk, peered around the lilac beside the front windows. Off in the distance the sky above London was ablaze. Searchlights battered the night clouds, coned a barrage balloon.

"The docks again. They hit there almost every night." She reached for the cigarette in his hand—thought of that hand on her body a few hours ago. "If the air raid warden sees you with this he'll have a conniption." She tamped the burning end out on the stone fence post. "You were leaving, weren't you?"

He took the doused cigarette when she handed it back, tucked it into his breast pocket. "I was thinking about all the trouble with trains we had yesterday, thought I ought to get an early start today."

"Not this early. The trains won't be running for hours. Come back inside where it's warmer."

He hesitated a moment, gave a last look at the distant city glowing on the horizon, then followed her back into the cottage. When she snapped on the sofa lamp he squinted in the sudden light. A frown line grooved his brow. Mouth seemed grimly set. After a couple of seconds, he dropped his kit at his feet and removed his cap.

"I couldn't have let you go off looking like that in any case." She took the cap from him. "You need a shave before you meet your new CO."

He rubbed his chin. "I was planning to do that at the train station."

"There's a perfectly good lav right down the hall." She pointed and laughed so he wouldn't think she was really scolding him. The laugh came out shrill and phony. He probably thought she was making up excuses to keep him there longer. She laid his cap down on the tea table. "I'm starving. Aren't you? I'll just pop into the kitchen and find us some..."

She didn't wait for him to answer before she ducked into the bedroom, glanced at the bed where he had unwrapped her like a Christmas package. She found her slippers, slid her cold feet into them. He was different this morning, kind of brooding and distant. Probably he already regretted last night? Probably he thought he'd have a hard time shaking her off.

In the kitchen, she lit the hob, filled the tea kettle and set it on the burner, and began a search through the cupboard for something to eat. There was nothing besides a few soda crackers and enough stale bread for two slices. From the fridge she grabbed the milk and a jar of jam. No butter, just a half stick of the vile un-rationed margarine Phyllis found last month at the grocer. She grabbed that, too.

The bread cleaved cleanly in two. She dropped the pieces into the toaster. She knew he had been trying to make his escape, despite his denial, and she caught him. Maybe that was how he operated, or maybe it was her age. Maybe he woke up, saw her beside him, and decided she was just too damned old after all.

The jam lid was stuck. She pried it open with the bread knife, spooned some into a shallow bowl. She raised her face to listen. He was so quiet in the other room, nothing at all like the merry fellow he had been yesterday. But yesterday he was trying to seduce her; today, challenge accomplished.

"I'd hardly call it a challenge," she mumbled, feeling her face get hot. She'd fallen into bed like a Piccadilly whore. She raised her voice, tried to sound more cheerful than she felt, "I hope tea's all right. I'm afraid there's not a drop of coffee in the house." She hoped he could hear her in the other room—if, that is, he hadn't sneaked off again when she wasn't looking.

"Tea's fine." His voice came from right behind her. She jumped, turned in time to watch him light the cigarette stub she had extinguished outside. He waved out the flame and laid the match down on the cabinet top, so the blackened end hung just off the edge. "Anything I can do?"

"Do?" Watching him mesmerized her for a second. She shook herself back to the present. "Oh…no. No, just sit down. Relax." She sounded too gay, too giddy, like some adolescent schoolgirl. She wished she could stop it and just be herself, but she didn't seem able to find herself at the moment. She felt her face flame.

She opened the drawer where they kept the ashtray, along with an array of other disorganized junk, matchbooks, receipts, a nail file. There was the white enameled cigarette case Neil had given back to her the last time they were together. She'd bought it for his birthday. Gold RAF wings embossed on the top. His wife had seen it, asked too many questions, he couldn't keep it. She shoved it to the back of the drawer, snatched up the ashtray, handed it to Lange.

She said, "Nothing in the house besides toast, I'm afraid. We really don't eat here very often."

He dropped the burnt match into the ashtray, dragged a chair out from the table, turned it around backwards, and straddled it. He'd left his coat and tunic in the other room. He hadn't shaved yet either. His blue-gray shirt was a rumpled mess; braces had a twist in them at the shoulder. She reached for the teapot and tried to pretend he wasn't there. In the corner of her vision he fidgeted, bounced one leg.

"First day jitters?" She measured two heaping scoops of tea into the diffuser. "I couldn't sleep for a week before my first day."

"I just don't want to make any mistakes."

"Oh, but you will. Best way to learn, those mistakes." She reached on tiptoe for two cups, two saucers. "Didn't you get fined at OTU? Surely?"

He let out a half-laugh. "Almost did. Once. Got stuck in the mud taxiing home." He straightened, the twitching slowed. "I'd seen this other fellow get stuck in the same exact spot. He tried to throttle out of it. Firewalled his engine and ended up standing his kite on its nose. Broke the prop right half in two." Telling this story seemed to calm him down. He started doing all the things pilots do when they talk about airplanes, physically showing her with his hands the way it had happened.

"Was he hurt?"

He gave her an impatient look, as if the thought of injury never crossed his mind. "No, he just released his harness and fell out on his head. But they really did stiff him for it. Lucky for me, I'd seen what he did wrong, so when it happened to me, I just cut my engine and got out. Let the ground crew tow the plane out of the mud."

She sat the cups inside their saucers on the table. "Hawarden's a quagmire."

"Old Flak bawled me out about leaving the plane, but he didn't fine me."

"Flak?" She didn't want him to stop talking. It had taken the edge off everything.

"My instructor. It's what everybody called him. The story was he'd run into a flak battery off the French coast. Kite was shot up so bad his ground crew didn't see how he made it back to base. They called him Flak after that. Flak Bannion, a real hard case, but he gave us some good advice. He was all the time writing these cornball phrases up on the board." Lange's hand spanned the space in front of him as if writing on a blackboard. His cigarette left a contrail of smoke. "'Aerial gunnery is ninety percent instinct and one percent aim,' or 'Fortune favors the brave, and those willing to learn.'"

"How Shakespearean."

"These Brits can get pretty wordy." He shrugged, reached over to crush out the cig in the ashtray. "He gave me an exceptional rating so I ending up liking him all right."

Flak Bannion. Old Flak? She'd never heard that nickname before, but she had heard the story that went with it, of that anti-aircraft battery on the French coast, heard it from Old Flak himself. No reason for her to be surprised that Lange should know Neil. Neil was instructing at Hawarden; Lange did OTU there. So they knew each other, so what? She changed the subject.

"You should let me iron your shirt before you go. You'll never pass RAF standards looking like that." She thought she sounded a little testy, so she softened her tone. "I can have it done in five minutes."

"You've already been too good to me, Mackie." He sounded like he did yesterday—sincere, charming, boyish. "I don't know how I'd have made it this far without you."

"I thought you said you were the top navigator in your class." She caught the kettle just before it started to whistle and poured the steaming water into the teapot to steep.

"I would've found my way to London all right, that's not what I was talking about."

Black smoke hissed from the top of the toaster. She grabbed the lever, accidentally touched the hot edge of the appliance, and burned her hand. "Dammit!" She stuck her hand in her mouth, grabbed up the knife, and started trying to stab the burnt bread slices out of the slots on the toaster.

Lange jumped up and, before she could think, yanked the plug from the wall. "You'll electrocute yourself like that."

He gave the lever a violent jiggle, but the toast still wouldn't budge, so he upended the whole thing over the sink. Two pieces of char fell out, hit the bottom of the sink, and exploded into a zillion black crumbs.

"Bloody damned English toaster," she said, as he set the toaster back on the cabinet.

"Let's see your hand." He picked up her wrist, uncurled her fingers. The heel of her thumb was red and starting to blister. "We need some butter to smear on that."

She shrugged, looked in his face. "War's on, as they say." He smelled like cigarettes, and starch, and Brylcream. "There's margarine in the fridge. Will that do?"

He unwrapped one end of Phyl's awful margarine sticks, picked up Mackie's hand again and touched the yellow margarine to the burned spot under her thumb. It felt cold and slick—provocative. God, was she going to go weak-kneed every time he touched her?

"Did your mother teach you this butter trick?" she said, with an uneasy laugh.

"My mother died when I was four." He let go of her hand. "There, that ought to help."

"How did she die?" Something they had in common, growing up without a mother.

"Spanish flu. I really don't remember her much." He laid the margarine down on its waxed paper wrapping. "Mostly what people have told me. She loved the picture show, dressed me in dresses, and combed my hair in baby-doll curls." He laughed, then went on. "She had a flowery apron. Kept a row of safety pins stuck through the bib. So they'd be handy, I guess. That's about my only real memory. They tell me she was a great cook."

He swept at the black bread crumbs around the sink. "This toast is a total wash-out." He picked up the bowl of jam, smile crept back. "But...we've still got this nice jam."

He reached for the spoon, scooped some out and made a big show of eating it. She smiled because he was so obviously trying to change the subject. So, he didn't like sharing much about himself. That was certainly a change from Neil, whose favorite subject had been himself.

"Apricot." Lange licked his lips, grinned. Those dimples again. He had one tooth on the bottom that was slightly out of line with the rest. She was grateful for that little imperfection. "Here, try some." He aimed the spoon at her mouth.

She dodged away from him, laughing. "No! Lange!"

He dropped the spoon in the sink. "So you *do* remember my name. I wondered."

"Of course." She touched her hair. She could just imagine what she looked like—an old hag with uncombed hair and freckles popping all over her nose. "You thought I wouldn't?"

"I didn't know. Everything was kind of, well...we did empty that flask."

She felt her face color again. "And today you're sorry?"

"I didn't say that." He swiped his thumb across the sticky place on his lips. "In fact, you can fall in my lap anytime you want to."

"I'll bear that in mind," she said. He was flirty again, had that sparkle in his eye. She ran her fingers underneath his braces, straightened out the twist. "I guess we should think about getting you down to the station in time for the early train."

DAYLIGHT CREPT around the edges of the blackout. The walls in the cottage were thin and she could hear the water running in the lav. She hoped the fickle water heater would work for him. As she put on her under clothes, she imagined the long, clean strokes of his razor as it peeled lather off his face. She did not want him to leave. One more day. She would take a half a day, or even a few more hours.

An idea struck her. A few months ago, she and Phyl and Adam had gone together to buy a little green car to putter around Wentworth. It wasn't speedy, but it was reliable, and anyway she wasn't looking for speed, not today. She wondered if the Morris was still where she'd left it with a full tank of petrol yesterday morning, parked outside the ferry pool. Most probably Adam had taken it over by now, but maybe, just maybe....

She went straight to the telephone, throwing on her tunic as she went. They'd had to have a phone installed so the station could reach them. She could hardly believe it when the connection went through on the first try. As Reggie answered the other end, she stepped into her skirt, zipped. Reggie was Adam's assistant, but he acted like a personal bodyguard. He was stern-voiced, fiercely protective of Adam and his position as commander of the ferry pool.

"The commodore's in his office right now," Reggie told her formally. "Shall I have him ring you a bit later?"

She glanced down the hall towards the lav door—water still ran. She balanced the phone on her shoulder and buttoned her blouse. "Do me a favor and go look out the window. See if the Morris is in the car park."

"It's there. I saw it earlier."

"Good. Tell Adam to just put the keys in the ignition. I'm coming to claim it."

As she hung up, the water stopped running in the lav. She went to the door, pressed her ear there, tucked her blouse into her skirt. No sound came from the other side. She gave the door a light tap.

"Listen, I've had a brilliant idea. I'm going to drive you to your posting. That way you don't have to worry over the trains running to schedule or anything. We just have to go pick up the car. The bus stops down the lane from here. It'll take less than ten minutes."

The door opened, and he stood there wiping his face with her linen towel. He had wet his hair and combed it straight back. He smelled luscious, clean, but she'd never got round to ironing the shirt, and it was wrinkled worse than ever. It was all she could do to keep her hands off him. She loathed the thought of letting him leave.

"I want you to have something," she said, feeling reckless. "To remember me by."

He stepped out of the lavatory. She hurried past him to the kitchen and flung open the drawer, fished around for the cigarette case, found it near the back. Two crumpled Players were still inside. She grappled them out, dropped them loose in the drawer, and swept away the tobacco crumbs. When she turned he was there, a frown on his face.

"I want you to have this." She held the case out at him.

"What's this? Mackie...you shouldn't—"

"You can't refuse a gift."

He hesitated, then took the enameled case from her, handling it almost gently, curiously. He liked it. She could see how his eyes coveted the RAF wings on the lid. He wouldn't give it the toss-off the way Neil had done.

"Give me your cigs," she said.

He withdrew the half-crushed box from his pocket. She took the case from him, laid it open on the table, and arranged his cigarettes one by one under the bronze holder inside. She snapped the lid shut and handed it back. "There. Now, you're a genuine officer in the RAF." She laughed.

He thumbed along the edge, opened the catch, snapped it closed again. "This is too much."

"No, it isn't." She nudged away his hand. "Take it. For luck."

He seemed about to say something else but then just smiled and tucked the enameled case into his pocket. "I guess I can always use some luck."

THE KEYS WEREN'T in the Morris. Not even after the phone call. She slammed the car door. "Damn Adam," she said, and then saw the apprehension on Lange's face. A Wellington roared off above them.

"Wait here," she told him when she could hear her own voice again. "This won't take a minute."

Inside the ready room, a couple of ferry pilots sat grouped around the coal-burning stove, drinking tea. She knew them both—Dolan and Harvey. She spoke, breezed by them. Harvey never quit working his crossword. Dolan nodded over his teacup.

Reggie wasn't at his post guarding Adam's doorway, so she was able to brush right into her brother's office without a fight. The office was small, little more than a supply cubicle furnished with a desk and a black telephone. "Car keys." She jiggled her hand.

Adam looked up from the routing schedules spread out on his desk. He shook his head. "I need the car tonight. You're supposed to be at Colesbury and I've made my own plans."

"What plans?"

"I'm taking Vivian into London." He stood, seemed ready for an argument. "There's a new jazz band she wants to hear."

"No problem. I'll have it back before tonight."

He stood there and looked confused. She loved to stymie his arguments. He frowned. "What are you doing here, Allie? Why aren't you at Colesbury?"

"God, Adam, you have no idea. I'm lucky to have made it with the trains...what?"

He had leaned around her and was looking past her now, through the open doorway. She turned, and there was Lange, out in the ready room, in conversation with Harvey and Dolan, sharing his cigarettes, displaying the enameled case, friendly, an animated expression on his face. She hadn't heard him follow her inside.

"Who's the pilot officer?" Adam's tone was smug. It goaded her. She could feel her hair roots. It was a bad sign to be able to feel your hair roots.

She reached to shove the door closed. "His name's Lange DeLony. I'm giving him a lift. He's been posted to Hornby Down and has to report this afternoon."

"And where did you find young Pilot Officer DeLony?"

"Adam," she warned.

"A simple question."

"I didn't *find* him. We met on the train yesterday." She saw the doubtful look Adam tossed her. She leaned her hands on his desk and gave him back a scorching one. "It was a bloody bastard of a day, Adam. Now, give me the keys and stop prying into my affairs."

"See, this is the reason you shouldn't be in my ferry pool. You wouldn't talk to your CO like that if he weren't me."

"I don't know. I might." She straightened, held out her palm, jiggled it more forcefully. "Keys."

Adam kept his arms folded and an asinine grin on his face. "Should I go out there and cold-cock Pilot Officer DeLony? Is there a reason for me to do that? Should I be worried about the family honor?"

Adam was in no position to tease her about this, not while he was as good as living with Viv Starger, whose husband happened to be off fighting the Italians in Egypt. Mackie sighed. "Don't be a pain in my ass, Adam."

He chuckled, stepped around her, moving past. "Such language. Let's go meet your pilot officer."

"Adam…" She reached to grab him, but he was already through the door, walking with purpose right across to Lange.

Adam had a commanding way about him; she watched Lange react to it, straightening. She was afraid for a second he was going to salute. They shook hands instead, formally at first, but by the time she stepped up to them, they were already chatting. Adam clapped Lange on the shoulder like an old pal.

"You didn't tell me he was a Yank," Adam said to Mackie. She glanced at Lange. He didn't seem insulted the way he'd been when she called him that on the train.

Suddenly she noticed Harvey and Dolan both staring with curiosity. No doubt they were wondering what Lange was to her and probably thinking she'd robbed the cradle. She wanted to say something to shut down the rumor before it got started. She knew she would get a first-class dressing down from Phyllis if she found out. Phyllis thought she knew all there was to know about unsuitable men.

"Long lost friend of the family," Mackie said to Harvey, who was the one most obviously eavesdropping.

"Right-o," he answered, but she could tell he didn't believe a word of it.

Then she realized that while she was busy worrying about gossip, Adam had spoiled her plans. Without mentioning it to her first, he had gone and offered Lange better, not to mention quicker, transportation—a Spitfire Ib going to the same airdrome as Lange.

Adam was saying, "Since you're headed that way, I could probably make a couple of phone calls and arrange for you to fly it there. That is, if the idea's acceptable to you."

A broad smile spread quickly across Lange's face. He said. "That'd be swell."

Mackie's heart dropped. "What Spitfire?" she said. "I didn't see a Spitfire." She bolted to the window, looked out through the slits in the blackout paper. Damn! There it was, big as life, a lone, war-weary Spitfire sitting exhausted out on the tarmac. "You're not sending him up in that thing. I've never seen such a clapped out, pathetic-looking kite in my life."

"Came in yesterday by mistake." Dolan eased up on her right. He bent to look out the window, too. "From Cowley. Adam's been trying all morning to fit it into the rounds. I would've taken it myself, but he's put me down for Abingdon today to pick up a Hurricane. So, it seems your friend has saved the day."

She turned to see if Dolan was being cheeky. Lange had gone off with Adam into the office. She could hear Adam in there on the telephone. She couldn't believe he had sabotaged her so quickly and so easily. She would never forgive him. Even more upsetting, though, was the look of absolute delight—no, relief—on Lange's face as they walked past her headed for the flight line. Defeated, forgotten, she followed them outside.

They met Reggie on his way back from some errand, and Adam was all business, barking instructions. Lange needed a parachute, a map, a flight-plan, petrol, a run-up. "Get the lead out!" he shouted, and Reggie quickened his step.

Lange paused long enough to thank her, as if the whole idea had been hers. She wanted to protest, to stamp her foot and demand that he forget the Spitfire and go with her in the Morris. Except...his eyes were tender, shining mirrors. "I had a lot of fun, Mackie," he said.

"Me, too." Although *fun* wasn't exactly the word she would've chosen. But she didn't think he meant to intentionally trivialize things. She walked a few steps with him. "I think I'm going to miss you."

He stopped and leaned to kiss her quickly on her lips. She shut her eyes and drew in the kiss like custard from treacle duff. This couldn't be all. It couldn't be.

"I thought your name was *Mac Cloud* when you said it that first time." He tapped her gently on the tip on her nose. "Like stratocumulus or cirrus filosus. I thought it was like that right up till I saw your brother's name on the door in there." He nodded towards the building.

She grabbed his hand, impulsively, and brought it to her mouth. He let her kiss his knuckles. She almost said the most bumbling, the most horrible, pathetic nonsense right then. Instead she managed to squeak out, "Look after yourself, hmm?"

"We'll keep in touch," he said and went smiling away from her, quickening his pace to catch up to Adam.

"Happy landings," she called, but he didn't appear to hear her. He didn't look back or wave either. She felt foolish standing there, wanted to cry. She gulped in air to keep from it, turned away.

She knew better than this—to get caught up like this. It was way too quick, too female, and he was too young, too handsome, too everything. Anyway, he would have broken her heart. That was certain. She told herself it was only a rebound thing, after seeing Neil yesterday. An impetuous little fling. She'd probably see his name in the papers in a couple of weeks, listed among the score of other pilots lost to the war.

Yet, she couldn't force herself to leave. She stood by the picket fence that surrounded the peri-track and watched him take off in the Spit. The plane flared upwards with zest and power. The instant he was airborne, the wheels went up. He banked right, on a north heading around the top of London. All of it done with style, as if he knew she was down there, still watching.

"Gee, thanks, Adam." She ambushed her brother as he came out of the hangar. "Thanks a hell of a lot for that."

"I got rid of him for you." Adam acted surprised to see her still there. "Last I heard, you were off fighter pilots."

"Well, that just shows how well you keep up!"

He frowned. "Nobody can keep up with you, Allie." He stuck his hand down in his pocket and came up with the keys to the Morris. He tossed them at her. "Here. Take your day off. Go to the flicks. Go somewhere, since you don't seem to be planning on Colesbury today."

She looked down at the keys, which she had caught automatically. Her face burned, the back of her neck crawled. She cranked back her arm and threw the keys as hard as she could right at Adam's head. They hit him in the chest instead, but she enjoyed the look of shock on his face.

CHAPTER 8
Letters

October 12, 1940

    San Antonio, Texas

    Dear Lange,

Thought you could use this extra money. We finally sold all the things Laura didn't want from the apartment. Just broke down this weekend and had a porch sale. So everything is finally taken care of. I thought it would be a relief to you to know. Although you will always put on the brave face—I know you, dear cousin—I am sure these many weeks have not been easy ones for you. You have had to learn the hard way that life's path is not always a straight one. But as they say: One door closes and another one opens. Seems like you have opened a new door all on your own.

We were up home for Sterling's mother's birthday last week, so of course we dropped in at Aunt Dellie's while we were there. She is still fretting over you, you know how she is. She read us parts of the last letter you wrote home. Be sure you keep that up. It puts her mind at ease to hear from you. Sterling tried to reassure her. He told her that while you might be reckless with some things, flying isn't one of them. She has the picture you sent her of you in your fancy uniform sitting right on the piano in the front room where nobody can miss it. Hubba, hubba, cousin. You sure do look all grown up. Try not to break too many hearts over there, hear?

Now, comes the serious part of this letter. I've wrestled all week with whether I should tell you this, but it is bothering me no end, so I feel like I should. Honey, Uncle Dane just isn't doing too well. Don't know if it's on account of simple old age, or if maybe he's had another little stroke, but he seems to be losing his grip on things. Half the time we were there he kept calling Troy Lee by your name, and the two of you don't look anything alike. Aunt Dellie says he talks to himself a lot and sits around in such a muddle so much of the time. For some reason, he seems to think you have gone off to France rather than to England to bring back Sunny's kids. He kept looking around like he expected them to be coming in from the next room or something. Of course, you can't understand half of what he says, but Aunt Dellie kept correcting him, then patiently translating for us, bless her heart.

Troy Lee didn't know how to act, or what to say. Poor guy always used to dote on Uncle Dane, do you remember? He always considered Uncle Dane like a substitute grandpa. Well, I know there isn't a thing you can do about it, but I just thought you should know the way things are so it won't come as such a shock when you do get to see him again, whenever that may be. Doesn't seem fair for it to happen to Uncle Dane. He was always so level-headed and spunky. I still treasure the little jewelry box he made for me when I was in high school. He was always so good at working with wood.

That's it from this end. Find some time for fun and sightseeing while you're over there. I always wanted to visit England and see some castles. You do it for me, okay? Don't try to be a hero, honey, you hear me? Sterling doesn't think I need to say that, but I decided to all the same. Remember this team is rooting for you.

Love from home,
Julianne

~

19 November 1940

Somewhere in England

Dearest Aunt,

Your package arrived here at my new station before I did. Thanks for the cookies, wool socks, and most of all, the cigarettes. I admit it surprised me when I saw them, coming from you, until you said in your letter that Gabe had sent them. Tell him thanks. Haven't seen a Lucky Strike since I left the States. It's not easy keeping my squadron mates out of them. I could probably use them as cash.

We have to be careful what we write so the censors don't make paper dolls out of our letters, so I can't say where I am exactly. It's too bad you never had the chance to come to this country. It really is like something out of a storybook. Houses still have thatched roofs, vines growing over the outside walls. People are about as friendly and good-spirited as they can be. I haven't been able to buy my own beer since I got here. Had one old lady just about cry telling me how much she appreciated that I would come from a country at peace to fight their war.

We've got fellows in this squadron from Australia and New Zealand, South Africa, Rhodesia, and one from Czechoslovakia, who happens to be my roommate, Joe. Most of us are replacements, which aggravates the heck out of our CO. He's a real go-getter type, hates having to train us new pilots. He keeps us in the air flying every day, battle drills and mock dogfighting. Sometimes I feel like I'm still in OTU, except that now it's all for keeps.

But I'll tell you, this being an officer business is all right. I can't walk anywhere on the airdrome without having to return a dozen salutes. First time I had a LAC—that's Leading Aircraftman— crack one off at me as I went passed, I just about fell off the sidewalk before it dawned on me that I should return his salute, so the poor fellow could relax and go on his way. Sure takes some getting used to, but I admit I kind of like it.

The other thing an officer gets is what they call a batman, which is a man-servant. One batman tends two rooms, so there's four of us Pilot Officers who share one old fellow named Pickens. Pickens is a civilian, but he dresses in a sort of uniform that he's put together on his own. He fought in the last war and has great respect for fighting men.

I'm sending you a check that came to me from Julianne. It's for the sale of the furniture and stuff out of the apartment in San Antonio. I owe Papa $50 and I told him I would pay him back so here it is. I don't know if I could have cashed the check here anyway, but I have signed the back. Did you know Papa carries around a wad of cash in his pocket? I don't consider that to be safe. Julianne says Papa's not doing too well. I would like to hear what you think about it. You are around him more than anybody. Please let me know something.

That's all for now. I'm worn out, can barely keep my eyes open. I promise to write again soon. Let me know about Papa.

Bye for now,

Lange

~

22 Nov 1940

Wentworth, England

Dear Lange,

Well, you should be sorted out by now and feeling a little more comfortable in your new digs. Hornby Down is an old station, a hold-over from the Great War, which I'm sure you probably know by now. Maybe one of these days, I'll pop over on a delivery there and say hello. In the meantime, I meant to give you my number when you were here, in case you would ever like to ring me for any reason. I forgot to do that before you left. Anyway, it's BQ-183.

That will ring at the cottage. They require us to keep a telephone there in case they need to get hold of one us in a hurry. I did enjoy meeting you and might fancy spending some more time. But at any rate, it's up to you, Texas, whether to phone. Best of luck, knock 'em dead, and all that rot.

Yours,
Mackie MacLeod

CHAPTER 9
"The War"

On the last Friday in November, after Lange had been with the squadron for three weeks and a day, the batman Pickens woke him at four-thirty, an hour earlier than normal. The smell of coffee came first and then Pickens's voice, "Come along, sir. You're on the board for this morning's show."

Lange opened his eyes, blinked. And then the batman's words registered. "You're joking."

Pickens smiled. "No, I saw it meself, sir. Pilot Officer DeLony, clear as day."

Lange was instantly on his feet. Pickens set a cup of coffee on the bed table. Dainty, dinky British cup consisting of about two swallows; Lange downed it in one.

"You'll be needing a hearty breakfast this morning. I looked in at the kitchen." Pickens folded Lange's pajamas into the bureau. "They'll be eggs and rashers, toast and chips. And beans, naturally."

Lange groaned, yes naturally. The English ate beans at every meal. Beans, beans, and more beans. Not that Lange had any special dislike for beans. It was just that beans had a way of repeating on you at 15,000 feet.

Over on the other bed, Lange's roommate, Joe Sokol, raised his head off his pillow. Sokol was a pilot from Czechoslovakia who had escaped to Poland when Hitler invaded, then on to France when Poland fell. He had managed to get across the Channel during the Dunkirk evacuation and had come to the squadron only a few weeks before Lange. Sokol's English was almost painful to hear and often incomprehensible, except when he spoke about the Germans. Then no translation was needed.

Sokol squinted one eye at Lange. "What are these noises?"

Lange continued to throw on his clothes. "I'm on the board."

Sokol rose onto his elbows. "You?"

Lange raised his chin to knot his tie. "I guess Morse decided I'm ready. Finally."

Pickens handed Lange his flight jacket. "I believe Mister Burnfield's leg was buggered by flak yesterday." Burnfield was one of the lead pilots in A flight. Pickens turned his attention to Sokol, "You have the morning off in case you'd care to sleep for another hour."

Sokol flopped back onto his pillow and pulled the blanket over his head.

Lange's heart banged in his chest. It was his first time on the flight schedule. He was relieved, tired of formation flying and firing at seagulls, but his stomach felt heavy, like it had dropped about two feet. No way he could eat anything. He rushed down the stairs and out the big front door of the Officers Mess.

Outside the cold moon was still in the sky. For a moment the smell of the night drove out the smell of dust and avgas that hung constantly over the airdrome. The drome was so close to the Thames it was often dogged by fog and mist. This morning the moon threw a band of light down through the buildings as he walked towards the waiting lorry.

Hornby Down had been bombed several times during the summer. Remnants of the damage were still evident. Sandbags shored up all the building entrances, paper covered the windows, and blast shelters lined the perimeter. One of the dispersal huts had been destroyed, bulldozed to one side, and a new Nissen hut put up on the site of the old one. A repair hangar had taken a direct hit, but work went on around the damage. There were two fractured Spitfires that had been shoved off the peri-track awaiting the metal recovery team. The field itself was a patchwork of filled-in craters that held water or mud, never anything less since the ground never dried out enough to harden.

Squadron Leader Morse was pacing in the ready room. The man never seemed to sleep. Lange was glad he'd chosen to skip breakfast and catch the early lorry. He was the first one there, which gave him a chance to study the map and the weather report from Met. On the duty board, "P/O DeLony" was chalked in at the bottom. Lange wished he had a camera.

Morse frowned and continued to pace as sleepy pilots trooped intermittently into the hut, but the CO said nothing, just tapped at his watch a couple of times, as if to move the hands around faster. "Dit-Dah" the fellows called him when he was out of hearing, the British version of "Dot-Dash" as in Morse code, but his real name was Desmond Morse III. He was demanding, sometimes abusive, above all, a perfectionist. He had come out of Cranwell, the RAF's West Point, but he was a fighter, had already shot down eleven German airplanes. He seemed ageless to Lange, had the permanent flyer's squint, pipe continuously smoldering on his desk. He had lost seven pilots in one day at the end of August. Lange's arrival had finally, belatedly, brought the squadron back up to strength.

Pickens was, as usual, correct with his information: Flying Officer Burnfield was no longer Yellow Leader. A flying sergeant named Chris Eggleston was put in his place. A sergeant leading three officers, but Eggleston had been with the squadron for nearly three months, one of the old-timers. Lange would fly Yellow Four.

"Well, bugger me," Pilot Office Tipton—Tippy as he was called —said when he spotted Lange. It was Tippy who had been the duty officer at the watch office the day Lange arrived and had shown him around the airdrome. He was a gangly fellow with white-blond hair and eyebrows to match, had a frail, nearly transparent mustache above his lip, a feathery handshake, and twinkling blue eyes. He'd just had his twentieth birthday the week before. "Not DeLony," Tippy said with a loud groan, grinning ear to ear. "That's the bloody limit, sir."

Lange laughed first, and the others joined in. The laughter helped ease the tension. Even Morse allowed himself a half smile, for a half second, before he told them where they were going. A routine convoy patrol up the Thames estuary. Nothing spectacular. Something Fighter Command had cooked up to protect against shipping attacks in the estuary and off the East Anglian coast. With the clearing weather, German fighter sweeps were expected.

Just before they left the dispersal hut, Morse pulled Lange off to one side. "Don't do anything on your own," he said, in a stern voice. "Stick with your leader and watch him. Do what he does but stay out of trouble. Is that clear?"

Lange took a deep breath, nodded. Morse gave him a tap on the shoulder. It surprised Lange, that tap, made him think maybe old Dit-Dah had a heart after all.

The ground crew helped Lange into the cockpit. The engine jumped, ground a bit, then caught, throated into a rumble that sounded like music to him. Body vibrating, he waved away the chocks and slid into line behind the others, taxiing down the tarmac.

The Spitfires took off three at a time. Lange managed that part just fine, didn't clip anybody's wings or ram anybody's belly, which was saying a lot since it was just barely light enough to see. He flew the bastard airplane nobody else wanted, the same one he'd ferried over from Wentworth, a war-weary crate with the letter "P" on the fuselage. The plane had two patches in the left wing, a chip in the rearview mirror, and that hasty letter "P" hand-painted behind the squadron designators and the RAF Roundel. After they'd been up a short while, the sun peeped over the horizon, a big yellow egg yolk that reflected on his spinning prop, turned it into a round copper blur whirling out in front of him. High, white cirrus smeared the upper sky.

Since he was the newest pilot, Lange was ass-end Charlie in the formation. He concentrated on doing everything Morse had drummed into him. He craned his head to look around every few seconds. He flopped Letter "P" like a fish on a trot-line. It wasn't easy to fly evasive maneuvers and stay in formation. He kept falling farther and farther behind, until finally, Sergeant Eggleston came over the R/T. "Bit less weaving about back there, Yellow Four. We need you to keep up."

After an hour and a half of flying up and down the Thames, they returned to base. Nothing had happened. No enemy sighted. Nobody fired their guns. The muscles in Lange's stomach relaxed. Suddenly he was ravenous, felt as if he could eat all the eggs, beans, and chips the cook could put in front of him.

AFTER THAT FIRST PATROL, Lange's name continued to come up on the board, and Pickens dutifully woke him before dawn. Day after monotonous day of flying uneventful sorties chased away the butterflies. Now and then something happened to cause a little stir: a pilot officer in Blue Section with mechanical trouble crash-landed in East Sussex. Tippy moved up to Blue Leader. Lange moved up, too, to fly on Eggleston's wing. Pilot Officer Gregory hit a barrage balloon near Southend. The pilot got out safe, but the aircraft was damaged beyond repair, so somebody had to bow out until a replacement plane was furnished.

He began to relax into guarding the convoys coming up the Thames, being part of the squadron. It wasn't long before he came to recognize landmarks around the south of England nearly as well as those he'd known in South Texas. His affection for Letter "P" grew. Secretly he christened it "Patches," even started to think of it as his kite and felt a twinge of jealousy whenever another pilot took her up. He could anticipate the way it would react on the controls, its tendency to list to port if left untrimmed. He knew its behavior the same way he might know a favorite horse's habit of balking over water or bolting at the sound of a car horn. He even found himself talking to the plane, giving it encouragement, calling it old girl, and patting it on the flanks once he was back on the ground.

At first the ground crew pretended not to notice his behavior. They were used to pilots with superstitions and peculiarities. But one morning, Sampson, the rigger said, "Ah, she's purring, she is, sir," as he came upon Lange rubbing his hand along her fuselage. "Had a bath and a good rest last night, and now she's bright-eyed and bushy-tailed." Lange shot the rigger a glance but there wasn't a hint of ridicule on Sampson's round face as he helped Lange shrug into his parachute pack.

Every night the German bombers came over the airdrome on their way to London. Just before they made their appearance, the station alarm would sound. The anti-aircraft batteries would kick up a racket. One heavy gun atop the water works shook the walls of the Officers' Mess. The pilots nicknamed that big gun Dolores. They made jokes and laughed about it, but sometimes Dolores kept the entire Mess awake all night.

Towards the end of November, the anti-aircraft gunners brought down a He-111. That night the Officers Mess erupted in cheers as the German bomber went flaming towards the center of the nearby village. The pilots raided the liquor closet downstairs and rushed outside in pajamas and overcoats to celebrate. Lange was right in the middle of the pack, caught up in the spirit of revelry. The ack-ack guns on the station were manned by a troop of Australians. That night the gunners carried their hero around on their shoulders until their commander came out to stop the ruckus. The base firefighters rushed off in a screaming roar to aid the local Home Defense in the village. The next morning, some of the pilots from another squadron went to town to inspect the damage and came back to report that the only decent pub for miles around had been demolished.

It didn't take long for them to find another pub—a rustic, beery, cavernous place called The Squeaky Door. The Door had a back room for games or for dancing to a raspy, dust-covered jukebox in a corner, and there were girls from the village with lean British faces, hard to understand accents, and overeager smiles. Tippy was girl hungry and not picky, and Sokol was a girl-magnet with his foreign flare and his sad-sack stories about his ruined home in Czechoslovakia. And Lange, well, he made out all right, too, but he was more particular. None of these girls interested him in a serious way. He had one thing on his mind and one thing only—to fly. And he was getting itchy to fight, to see if he could, if it was in him to shoot down another plane. He wanted to know if he had the stuff.

He still had the cigarette case Mackie MacLeod had given him. At first, he felt a little highfalutin using it, but then Sokol kept trying to steal it, and Tippy was constantly borrowing it to impress his girlfriends. Some of the other fellows seemed to covet it, too, so before long Lange felt proud to use it, to pull it out of his breast pocket and offer up one of the Luckies from Texas. He liked the familiar feel of the case tucked cool and flat inside his tunic pocket. And he started to think of it as his good luck charm.

Mackie had been high octane, and the timing had been just right to leave him with fond memories—end of OTU, the apprehension of going operational, and there she was, mature, compassionate, intelligent, a real knockout in bed. So if he was going to give anybody a call it would've definitely been her. She'd sent him her number. He still had it tucked away somewhere. A couple of times he started to call her, when he had a forty-eight-hour pass and was headed with some of the fellows into London, but something always stopped him—instinct or intuition, self-preservation or just a hunch he had that it might be a tad too easy for a woman like her to get under his skin.

～

EARLY IN DECEMBER the first no-nonsense call came from Control while Lange was up with the squadron. "Vector one-eight-zero. Angels twenty. Bandits twelve o'clock. Ten miles. Over."

Right away Morse's voice thundered over the R/T, "Full throttle! All aircraft, full throttle!" Morse, who was leading A Flight himself with B Flight behind and slightly below, swung his Spitfire instantly upwards. They were all expected to follow.

Lange's pulse quickened. He'd never used the emergency boost before. Never had cause to on standing patrol. He pushed the lever and the engine made a tortured scream. It bucked upwards like a horse spurred in the flanks. The red firing button looked grim and deadly uncovered. He switched the safety ring to fire, turned on the gun sight. An orange dot danced on the windshield. Inside his flight suit, rivulets of sweat began to trickle down his ribs. Beads of it gathered at his temples and pooled around his goggles. Oxygen switch on. Lange took a deep, trembling breath, kept his attention on Devon Eggleston to his right and on the rest of the sky around him.

Their course led them out over the Channel. The wrecks of airplanes littered the beaches beneath the cliffs. In the distance he saw land—the coast of France. Nazi Europe. A thought flashed of Sunny's kids down there. He remembered those newsreel images of Paris and the Eiffel Tower dripping with swastikas.

His attention focused on a bunch of flea specks below and slightly in front of the squadron, headed north. At the same instant Morse's voice came, "There's the bloody bastards! Let's get them!"

Morse's Spitfire went into a wild vertical turn, and they all followed him down onto that formation of flea specks. Black crosses on their tails came into terrifying focus. Lange held on with both hands, felt the "G" press his body into a sausage patty. His heart flooded his ears. Suddenly the German airplanes broke into a dozen whirling directions, swarming like hornets. He dove into them, swerved for one of them. Someone called out, "Behind you, Yellow Four! Break! Break!"

Yellow Four—that was him. He shot a glance at the chipped mirror just above eye-level. An Me-109 was closing in on him, little silver lights twinkling from both its wings. Tracer flashed past him. He pulled back on the throttle, jammed down the flaps. The violence of the maneuver caused such terrific "G" that everything started to go black. He fought it, his breath wheezing in and out.

His Spitfire skidded sideways and the 109 overshot him. As it passed overhead, a dark streak of black crosses slashed across his vision. He pressed his gun button. Nothing happened. The button was stuck. He pressed it again, so hard his thumbnail broke. The eight machine guns in his wings juddered the whole aircraft. He saw bullets arch out like tentacles and splatter the belly of the 109's fuselage, midsection to rear. A piece of the German's tail broke off. Then "P" bounced sideways as it hit the 109's slipstream. Lange wrestled for control, lost sight of the German plane. He rolled in a tight circle, came upright, ready for another firing pass but the 109 had vanished. He looked around him, nothing. The sky was empty. He was totally alone.

Solid cotton-wool clouds below—where had those come from? Buttery blue sky above. His legs trembled. Heart hammered in his ears. Sweat steamed on every inch of him. His flight suit was drenched. He couldn't seem to keep his feet planted on the rudder. His knees knocked together like maracas. The sky was so blue, so empty, just the roar of his own engine.

He battled for command of his nerves, pulled in a few deep whiffs of oxygen. He was all right. Still in one piece. He'd put some bullets into that 109. He'd seen them spray the fuselage. He wondered if it had gone down. He tipped his wing for a look below, but nothing had changed. Cotton-wool clouds. Empty sky. Same as before. Like it had been a dream.

Out on his starboard wing, a hole was drilled neatly through the middle of the red and blue Roundel—a perfect bull's eye—but nothing seemed damaged. He still had flaps and rudder. Gauges were all OK. Except as soon as he finished inspecting things, the engine started to run rough. Could've been his imagination, but in any case, he wanted to get home. He spread his knees to check the compass. East-northeast. Wrong way. He veered due north, switched channels on the R/T to ask for a bearing. His voice sounded like it belonged to a ghost.

The most beautiful thing he'd ever seen in his life was that airfield down below, camouflaged with painted-on hedges and meadows. He brought the plane in too hot, bounced the landing. Too much adrenaline. The ground crew waved him in. When he shut down the engine, they jumped on the wing to help him out of the cockpit. And he needed their help. His arms had suddenly turned to lead. He thought he might puke or pass out, maybe piss all over himself, or at the least, that his legs would collapse out from under him.

"You fired your guns, sir," Sampson said, excitement bubbling over. The seals on the gun ports were broken.

Lange found his feet. He noticed a second hole in the starboard wing, one he hadn't been able to see from the cockpit, near the wing-root. Another foot and the German's aim would've been dead perfect. Lange felt lightheaded, overloaded, like his body belonged to somebody else.

"The gun button's sticking," he said, remembering that half-second of terror before the guns began to fire.

The intelligence officer, Flight Lieutenant Webb, ran over with his clipboard. Later Lange couldn't have repeated whatever it was he told Webb. Once the combat report was typed up for him to sign, it read like something from a book he'd never seen. He'd been credited with a probable. Webb believed the observer liaison would confirm the 109 once the wreckage was found.

Morse said, "Well done, DeLony," and until that moment, Lange hadn't even been sure the CO knew his name.

For the rest of that day he felt sick and a little wobbly. He skipped supper in the Mess and beers in the bar later, even though Sokol and Tippy and some of the others tried to drag him out of his room for a round. Tippy suggested they go find themselves some village girls to celebrate, but Lange skipped that as well. Instead he wrote letters home.

He wrote to Papa and Aunt Dellie. He wrote one to Julianne. He kept the letters short, upbeat, lighthearted, positive. He wrote that he was doing swell. He hoped writing it would make it so. He didn't know what was wrong with him, or where the black disappointment came from. He had expected to be more courageous, to feel more victorious, but he knew if he *had* shot down that German plane, it had been pure reflex and pure luck, because the only thing he remembered for certain was that he'd been scared shitless.

HE TOOK to staying in at night, up in his room, or by the fire in the anteroom downstairs, devouring combat tactics in books he checked out from the station library. He didn't want to get caught from behind again, off his guard, with his pants down around his ankles. He eavesdropped on conversations between other, more experienced pilots in the Mess, listened as they told each other about near-misses they'd had, evasive action they took. He looked over his notes from OTU, absorbed his flight manual again, pored over his gun camera film, watched that piece of tail fin fly off the German plane at least a dozen times.

Christmas came, and nobody was given leave. Rumors of a German parachute invasion abounded, and London was still receiving her share of nightly bombing raids. So one of the hangars was turned into a ballroom, decorated by the station WAAFs. Announcements were mimeographed and posted all over the base. Sokol and Tippy invited their most recent girlfriends from the village. Lange thought of Mackie, wondered for a brief second if she would be able to come if he called her, or if she would even want to. A woman like that, why the hell would she want to come to some lame hangar dance? She had a kid somewhere to spend Christmas Eve with, and family besides.

So he talked himself out of it, talked himself out of the dance altogether, and went down to the deserted anteroom. He took his favorite chair by the fire. The orderlies had put up a Christmas tree in the corner, and it sparkled with tinsel. The sight made him a little bit homesick, and then Squadron Leader Morse walked into the room. Lange put down the book he'd brought with him.

"Ah." Morse was holding a drink in his hand, and by the looks of him, it wasn't his first of the night. The knot in his tie was loosened, his posture had taken on a slouch that wasn't usually there, and his face had a red glow. "DeLony, my American scholar." He motioned with the hand holding the glass towards the book on Lange's lap. "You know what they say: Beware the fighter pilot who would rather fly by the textbook than kick arse." Morse drained half his drink with one large swallow. "Why aren't you off with the other chaps? I appreciate your devotion to duty, but for God's sake, man, it's Christmas Eve."

Lange kept his finger at his place in the book. "I'll pass."

"On what? Christmas?" Morse sat down on the arm of the chair next to Lange's, tilted his head to read the title of the book. "Whatever it is you want to learn, I assure you, it's not in there." He finished off his drink, raised his voice. "I say, Woolsey. Another one in here, if you please. And bring Mister DeLony whatever he likes as well."

"Nothing for me," Lange said.

"Nonsense."

The orderly, Woolsey, a young fellow with a bright red thatch of hair under his side cap, came in with a bottle.

"This man needs a drink," Morse said in his CO voice, and Woolsey hurried off with a quick, "Yes sir." In a moment he was back with another glass, which he gave to Lange to hold while he poured.

"There. That's better." Morse raised his glass in a toast. "'This royal throne of kings, this sceptred isle...this blessed plot, this earth, this realm, this England...'"

Lange lifted his glass, too, and they drank. Lange almost spit his out. He had yet to develop a taste for scotch, and this was particularly vicious. "Jesus! Can't take much of that."

Morse took a big swig, swallowed easily. "You got your German," he said. "Observer corps confirmed this morning. The wreckage was found near Hythe. If the pilot survived he's skulking around in the marshes somewhere, spending Christmas in a farmer's oast house."

The back of Lange's neck crawled. He wasn't sure why. He sipped the drink, forced himself to swallow. "I sure would've rather seen the damned thing go down with my own eyes."

"Right-o." Morse gave Lange a rare smile, leaned over and clinked their glasses together. "When you got here I didn't think you'd last a week. I didn't believe you had the proper motivation. I'm still not sure what motivates you, but you can shoot at least." He waved the glass at Lange. "Here's mud in your eye."

Lange sipped again; he couldn't do more than sip. He marveled at the way Morse was belting the stuff down. "My old man and I used to shoot birds off the front porch," Lange said, for no reason, something to say, and he felt ridiculous as soon as the words were out. He sounded like a damned bumpkin schoolboy soliciting favor from the teacher, thumbs hooked under his overall straps.

"Ah, well, so you did. A bit of the same thing, isn't it? Except this time, it's a man instead of a bird, of course." Morse drained his glass and set it down on the table. "Another?"

Lange's glass was still full.

"Must catch up, old sport." Morse called for Woolsey, again. "Just leave us the bottle," he said once the orderly had poured another drink into Morse's glass. "Off you go," he said, shooing Woolsey away. "Best get to the ball before all the pretty WAAFs turn back into pumpkins."

"Thank you, sir." Woolsey set the bottle on the table and hurried off like he thought Morse might change his mind. Morse sucked noisily at the brim of his glass. Lange wanted to ask him about the first German he'd shot down, wanted some kind of reassurance that these mixed up feelings he had about it were normal. But he was still too intimidated by Morse to get that personal.

Meanwhile, Morse had gone wobbly. He couldn't seem to stay perched on the arm of the chair, and after a couple of near topples, took to his feet. A bit of booze sloshed out of his glass. He said, "I don't even like Americans really. Never have. Don't trust them."

"Yes, sir. You've told me."

"Oh, sod the sir business. How old do you think I am, anyway?"

Lange shook his head. "No clue."

"Go on, take a wild guess. You won't offend me." Morse held his glass, pointed with the same hand. "I know you're twenty-six. Bit old for this lark, if you ask me." Morse's smile turned almost savage. "You were born on July fourth, isn't it? American Independence Day, all that rot. Independence from jolly old England, come to that, and yet here you are, DeLony. What makes a chap like you want to come over here and muck about in our little war? Is it simply because you're keen on airplanes or are you a little bonkers?"

Lange laughed. He didn't think Morse was making a joke, but he couldn't help his laughter. He thought maybe the scotch was beginning to go to his head, too. He said, "Oh, you know, I heard there was thrilling adventure and sexy women, and tea and crumpets. Although...nobody ever said one word about Brussels sprouts and beans."

Morse frowned, stared for a second, and Lange waited, thinking maybe he'd gone too far, maybe Morse took his joke as criticism of dear old England. But the frown on Morse's face eased. He let out a low grunt. "Yes, Christ, those goddamned beans...." He reached again for the bottle, replaced the bit that had sloshed out of his glass. "March fourteenth is my birthday." He set the bottle back down. It landed unevenly on the table and warped around a couple of times before it settled on its bottom. "That makes me four months older than you. And *I* am definitely too hold for this fucking lark. Let's get the hell out of here, DeLony. The two old granddads, what do you say?"

He dug down in the pocket of his trousers and came up with a set of keys. Lange recognized them as belonging to one of the black staff cars parked outside.

"Can you drive?" Lange said. "I mean, should you..."

"I wouldn't pin my hopes on it," Morse answered, laughter overtaking him finally, but just for a moment before he righted himself. He gave his tunic a smart tug. "Stay on my wing, DeLony."

It wasn't at all the way Lange had expected the evening to go. Never would it have crossed his mind that he would go off anywhere privately with Morse.

They drove away from town, out in the woods, to one of those old estate houses that dotted the countryside. Lange had seen them from the air. This one had leaded glass in the windows and creeper vine covering a wall beside the door. A woman named Pauline let them in, took one look at Morse, and grabbed his arm. "Desmond, whatever are you doing here? It's Christmas Eve."

Lange stumbled in behind them, and it was like entering a different world: overstuffed furniture and knickknacks everywhere, homey smells, a Christmas tree with gilt-wrapped presents piled underneath, the warm glow of a fireplace, family pictures on the walls, soft music, sanity, peace. He didn't even know he'd been missing it.

Pauline was a girlfriend, or anyway, some romantic connection to Morse, clearly, by the way he kissed her. But she was also somebody's wife or had been. She wore a wedding ring. Lange followed them into a parlor where for the next few hours they sat in the overstuffed chairs, drinking more scotch, better-quality scotch, with music playing on the phonograph, eating delicate cucumber sandwiches and buttered muffins that a motherly housekeeper brought in on a silver tray. A blue haze of cigarette smoke haloed around them, and there was the blessed relief from the noise of airplanes and ack-ack guns. It turned into a Christmas Eve to remember because of that peace. Later, when he thought about it, he felt as if something had reawakened in him that night, something important that he had forgotten about himself. Something to do with home and hearth, with the civilizing effect of women. Something he realized he didn't want to live without.

TWO DAYS AFTER CHRISTMAS, he was shot down. It happened so fast he barely knew what hit him. One second, he and a German plane were circling, firing at each other; the next a sheet of flame leaped from the belly of his airplane. The cockpit filled up with white smoke.

He tore off his oxygen mask, ripped lose the cords connecting him to the R/T. With his left hand he whipped back the canopy, pulled the harness release catch, and with his right hand banged the stick forward with all his might. He popped out of the airplane like a champagne cork. He really didn't know how in hell he remembered, in his panic, to do all of that. Below him, the earth spun crazily. He caught a glimpse of Letter "P" streaming away in a cloud of black smoke, headed for her death in the North Sea. Poor old Patches. He felt for the rip cord and jerked it. The parachute blossomed out with a violent jolt to his groin where the rigging passed under his body.

He floated downward from twelve thousand feet. The flinty cold and gray silence engulfed him. As his thinking cleared he began to realize that he was all right, unhurt, lucky again. The cuffs of his tunic were a little singed, the tip ends of his gloves blackened, but the moisture that covered him was sweat not blood. Lately, every time he flew on ops he came away saturated with sweat. He looked down as the landscape of Kent came up to meet him. He tried to remember the drill. Limber up. Unlock your knees. Absorb the blow. Roll backwards.

The ground smashed upwards at him. He hit with stunning impact. It knocked a bolt of lightning through his head, like getting kicked by a mule. For a moment he couldn't breathe. He crumpled to the ground in a heap. The parachute dragged him fifty yards before he regained enough sense to dig in his heels and stop the forward motion.

He couldn't stand up—rubber knees again. He unclipped the shroud lines and just sat there. A breeze fluttered in from the direction of the sea; it smelled of the sea. It carried the parachute off a little way across the open field. He watched as a group of children from a nearby farmhouse started running out after the chute, saw a woman come out the back door and shade her eyes towards him. He reached into his breast pocket for the cigarette case, pulled it out and looked at it. *For luck*, Mackie had said when she gave it to him. He opened it, chose a cigarette, and tried to stop shaking as he watched the woman from the farmhouse hurry in his direction.

CHAPTER 10

"Colesbury"

The station van rattled to a stop in front of the cottage. "Thanks, Edie." Mackie popped open the door. "If Jerry invades while I'm gone, get one for me, will you?"

"Of course." Edie was no-nonsense. It was a kind of joke around the ferry pool, but she was always on time and ready to carry you wherever you needed to go. As the van drove off, it sounded as if it might collapse at the end of the lane.

Phyllis was already at home. The Morris stood in front of the cottage. It had been a long day for Mackie. She'd been from Luton to Cardiff to Sealand to Manchester where she'd had to wait for four hours for the Swordfish she needed to bring, along with another pilot, back to Wentworth. Now, she had just two hours to get cleaned up, pack, and catch the train for Colesbury. Aunt Kath promised to keep Given up late so Mackie could see him.

At the doorstep, she stomped mud off her flying boots and let herself inside. She tracked in mud anyway, so she took off the boots before she made a mess on all the rugs. Her toes ached. She wiggled them, realized she heard voices in the other room.

She pulled off her Irvin jacket as she went down the short hall, hung it on the wall-hook as she passed. Phyl was standing near the fireplace, already had the furnace going, glass of red wine in her hand. There was a mysterious smile on her face.

"Someone's here to see you." Phyl motioned with the glass towards the couch, and Mackie stepped further into the room. "I offered him a drink, but he turned me down."

Lange DeLony rose from the sofa as Mackie entered the room. He was grinning wide, looked almost bashful. There were lines and shadows on his face that she didn't remember from the last time. He was still gorgeous, standing there in his Class As. His service cap lay on the sofa, his kit bag on the floor next to his feet.

"Lange! Gosh!" She couldn't keep the surprise out of her voice.

"I probably should've called first," he said, and there was that Texas drawl. "I hoped it wouldn't matter."

Phyllis said, "I told him you were leaving for the countryside as soon as you got here."

Mackie pulled off her cap, drew her fingers through her hair, imagined what a fright she must look. She saw him glance at her feet with the thick boot socks on them. "Are you on holiday leave?" she asked him.

"You could call it that." He seemed positively ill-at-ease. She thought Phyllis must be the cause of that. She gave Phyl a pointed look.

"Well, I'll leave you two alone," Phyllis said, taking the hint. She walked haughtily from the room.

"Excuse her. She's not used to being polite."

"She told me you had an agreement about men visiting here," Lange said. "I'd forgotten that."

Mackie laughed and went a few steps towards him. "Well, as I said, politeness isn't one of Phyl's virtues. So, I suppose she knows now that you've been here before." She felt her face heat remembering his last visit to the cottage.

"I lost your phone number. I figured you'd spent Christmas with your son, but I thought I'd stop in and say hi." He reached for a box of chocolates she hadn't noticed until then. They'd been lying on the tea table. "Here. Maybe Given would like these."

"You remember his name." She took the box of chocolate. In the other room, she heard the wireless come on. A music program. "You Turned the Tables On Me" came blaring out mid-verse.

"Well." She smiled, taking him in again. Those dark eyes, like chocolate drops themselves. "You look as if you've tamed the wilderness."

"Maybe." He smiled back at her. "I had to bail out a few days ago and I'm still around to tell about it."

"Are you hurt?"

He shook his head. "Just my pride. Strained my back a little. Nothing much."

"Was it engine trouble or did you get shot down?" She combed absently at her hair with her fingers.

"Engine trouble. Caused by an Me-109. Old Patch didn't like the two slugs the Kraut put in her."

"Old Patch?"

"My kite. Number P. The one I brought in for your brother that day." He reached beside him for his cap, bent for his kit. He moved a little stiffly. She saw that now. She suddenly understood the weary look in his eyes. "I shouldn't have barged in on you," he said.

"I'm not rushing off this instant. Sit back down." He did. She sat beside him, slid the box of chocolates back onto the tea table. She said, "You're on medical leave? For how long?"

"Five days," he replied. "I remembered you had a birthday coming up, and..." He waved towards the box of chocolates.

She laughed. "I thought you said they were for Given."

"Him or you. Either way they were a good excuse for me to drop by." He started to get up again.

She tugged him back. "You don't need an excuse. Wait here while I get washed up. You're coming with me." She rose, smiled down at him. She really hadn't thought she would ever see him again. "It'll be fun. You can meet Given, and Adam might show up.

You remember Adam? Aunt Kath always puts on a bit of a splash for New Year's. I'd really like it if you would come, Lange. What else have you got to do?"

He didn't need much coercion. She could see plainly that he liked the idea of somewhere—anywhere—to spend his leave.

PHYLLIS DROVE them to the train station. Lange sat in the back seat, Mackie up front, trying to dodge the disapproving looks Phyllis kept giving her. When Phyl pulled to the curb, Lange got right out, and Mackie leaned to give Phyl a thank-you embrace.

"For God's sake, Mackie," Phyl hissed. "A Yank?"

"He's nice. Don't you think?"

"He does wonders for his uniform, if that's all you mean. Bit young, isn't he?"

Mackie got out, leaned in the window. "Toot-a-loo," she said, waggling her fingers. "Thanks for the lift."

She looped her arm through Lange's and they headed inside the station to wait for the train to Colesbury.

IT WAS one o'clock in the morning when Mr. Bailey picked them up at the Colesbury station. Patches of snow lay along the road. It was so cold in Aunt Kath's old Bentley that Lange's nose was running. He kept sniffling and reaching in his greatcoat for his handkerchief. He acted distant and peaky. She thought his jump had unnerved him more than he let on.

He leaned to whisper, "Who did you say this old fellow is again?"

"Mister Bailey. He's worked for my aunt for thirty years."

Lange nodded but still seemed twitchy and distracted.

"She's been here thirty years?"

"She married an Englishman. He died before the war, but she's English now or as good as after all this time." When they turned in the gate, Mackie leaned forward to speak to Bailey. "Was Given awake when you left?"

"Sorry, no. Master Given was long ago in bed for the night."

Despite the late hour, Bailey didn't seem to be in much of a hurry. He drove no faster than fifteen miles an hour, and she wished he would hurry it up. All day she'd been looking forward to seeing Given. No, all week. She'd found a set of small flying goggles; she wanted to give them to him to make up for missing Christmas. The goggles weren't a child's play set but were the real thing, a factory mistake. Given would love them. She couldn't wait to show him.

Lange whispered, "How damned rich are you anyway?"

She turned to face him. "What?"

He pointed out the car window. They had turned up Aunt Kath's front drive. The house loomed into view. She bent to see what he was seeing: Chimneys and gables all over the roof, dormers and multi-paned windows. She supposed it might look like a big fancy manor house in the dark.

"It's not as grand as it seems," she said, keeping her voice under Mr. Bailey's range of hearing. "It's old and musty and damp inside. Rats run in the walls. Besides it's Aunt Kath's house, not mine."

Lange snapped his fingers. "You're from Winnipeg."

"Yes...so?" She squinted. It was too dark inside the automobile and she couldn't see him clearly.

"It just dawned on me. I saw the factory when I was there. MacLeod Aviation. Is that you?"

"No. It's my father."

"You should've said something sooner, Mackie."

"Well, it never came up, did it? My father manufactures aircraft. Before the war, it was light and ultra-light. Now he makes twin-engine transports as part of his war effort, but none of it is mine. I haven't seen him in eight years. Didn't I mention that?"

Bailey stopped the Bentley at the front door. Mackie didn't wait for the engine to shut down before she was out of the car and running up the steps. She looked back to see Lange trying to handle their kits. He still moved stiff and carefully. She said to him, "Bailey'll get that."

And then Aunt Kath was there, wearing one of her frilly, old-fashioned dressing gowns. She grabbed Mackie in a quick, fierce hug. "I'm sorry we're so late," Mackie said. "The train was delayed, as usual. I've brought a friend with me. Is Given asleep?"

"He tried very hard to stay awake." Aunt Kath took both of Mackie's hands. "Introduce me to your friend, dear." She didn't seem a bit perturbed at the late hour of their arrival. She held her hands out to Lange, too, when Mackie introduced them. It was obvious he wasn't quite sure what he was supposed to do. He shook both Aunt Kath's hands at the same time. "Oh, he can be our dark-haired man," Aunt Kath exclaimed.

Mackie smiled at that, saw the confused look on Lange's face. "I'll explain later," she said and touched his sleeve. "I'm leaving you with Aunt Kath. She'll show you to a room."

She ran up the stairs and down the hall to Given's door. It was partly ajar. She leaned down to stroke his forehead. His sleep was so sound he didn't stir. She bent to kiss his cheek. Sweet, baby-soft and rosy in his flannel jimjams.

"Mummy's here, darling," she whispered.

He turned over and put his arms around her neck. He was getting so big and strong. He hugged her hard. "Auntie said you would be here directly." He had a perfect English accent and looked more like his father than he did her. She hardly noticed anymore. "I didn't want to go to sleep. I waited for you."

"I know you did, darling, but I'm here now, and we'll have a wonderful day tomorrow."

She sat with him until he went back to sleep, then crept to her bedroom. Mr. Bailey had laid her kit on the cedar chest at the foot of the bed. He had even hung some of her things away in the wardrobe. She got out of her uniform, hung it, too, although it was beyond salvation with wrinkles over every inch. Her nightgown was draped on the bed, which was turned down for her to climb right into the covers. Good old Mr. Bailey. He was everything: chauffeur, butler, valet.

Quickly, she unpacked the gifts for Given—the goggles, a handful of chestnuts, some hard-to-come-by toffee, peppermint rock, a small book of poems by Robert Lewis Stevenson. Given was reading quite well already. Lange's box of chocolates was in her bag, too.

After a few weeks had gone past and she didn't hear from Lange, she figured that was it, especially after the letter she'd written to him. That letter had taken a lot of nerve to write. She was surprised he remembered how to get to the cottage, as late as it had been, as sleepy and as sloshed as he was that night. And he'd even remembered her birthday was in January.

She pulled out the box of candy from her bag. He called the candy his excuse for dropping by to see her. So there had been plan-ning, deliberation. She tossed the candy on her bed, opened the wardrobe for her wooly wrap, stepped into a pair of slippers. The door squeaked when she opened it.

By then the house had quieted and gone dark. Lange would be in one of the guest rooms—the paneled room if she had to guess. It was Aunt Kath's favorite one for company use. Far east corner of the house, nice and away from everybody else.

Mackie crept down the hall, around the corner and to the end room. She hesitated outside the door. Should she knock? An image of him sleeping came into her mind. A yearning started in the pit of her stomach. She turned the knob soundlessly and eased into the room.

The fire in the gas grate gave off a flickering yellow light that bounced on the mahogany-paneled walls. She could see him clearly, snuggled down in the bed covers, but he wasn't asleep yet. He raised on one elbow as she moved up closer.

"It's me," she whispered. She stepped out of her slippers. "I wanted to look in on Given. I'm sorry to abandon you. But I see they got you settled in." She lifted her nightgown over her head and let it fall on the floor beside her slippers.

"Mackie...." He turned onto his back.

"Ssh." She slipped under the covers with him.

He seemed startled at first, but soon he responded to her lips. His warm, strong hands took hold of her, smoothed over her naked rump. This was what he wanted, too, she could tell. He had probably been counting on it. She pushed his undershirt up to his neck and over his head. There was a canvas brace wrapped around his ribs.

"Be still," she whispered and straddled his hips. His hands moved up her belly to her waist, held her there.

She awoke with a start, realizing that she was still in bed with him. She'd fallen asleep and hadn't meant to. He was curled against her, warm and just as delicious as she remembered. She managed to slip herself free of him and the bed covers. The fire was long out, and the room was cold. Around the heavy draperies Aunt Kath used as blackouts, day was already dawning.

The robe and nightgown lay on the floor where she'd dropped them, cold from lying there. She hurried them on. The doorknob clanked; hinges rattled. Everything in this old house squeaked and clanked and rattled. She watched the bed. He didn't waken. Poor boy.

Out in the hall, she pulled the door closed behind her, turned, and almost collided with Aunt Kath. "Oh!" She gathered the front of her robe together. "I was just seeing if Lange was up yet."

"Nonsense, Allison. You weren't in your bedroom an hour ago when Given awoke."

"You checked?"

"Of course not. You're a well-grown woman. Your business is your own. I confess I don't understand the ways of modern romance. Things are a world away from when I was your age." She took hold of Mackie's chin. "But what matters is that lovely glow on your face."

Mackie relaxed. "Do you know how much I adore you, Aunt Kath?" She pressed her aunt's palm to her lips.

"Yes, yes. Now go get dressed and join Given in the kitchen. He's excited over the goodies he found in your room."

Mackie raced around the corner and back to her room. All the gifts she'd brought for Given, and laid out on the dressing table last night, were gone, including Lange's box of chocolate candy. She threw on some clothes, blotted a little powder on her cheeks, stared for a moment at her reflection, searching for the glow Aunt Kath mentioned.

She daubed a drop of perfume behind each ear and leaned in close enough to inspect the fine crow's feet at the corners of her eyes. He was twenty-six. She'd weaseled it out of him last night. Five years younger. Was that too much? It was borderline, but not as bad as it might have been. It didn't seem to matter to him. Hadn't he gone to the trouble to find her? Was it just for sex? Was that all he wanted? But for that, he could have any girl. There were legions of pilot-parasites setting traps all over London—all over England, for that matter.

She shut her eyes. *Stop it, just stop!* She was always reading in too much, complicating everything. They enjoyed each other's company. Wasn't that enough? She took a deep breath, opened her eyes again.

"There's a war on," she said to herself. "Pull yourself together. And quit looking so damned besotted!"

CHAPTER 11

"A New Year"

Given was a quiet little boy, in some ways seemed older than seven, very proper, very English, as dark as Mackie was light. Seeing the son made Lange mildly curious about the father. She hadn't really said much about it, just a casual dismissal of the subject on the train that day.

He hadn't slept well, had the fire dream. The dream began innocently enough. He was back in Choke Hargrove's Flying Jenny, only too high up, dancing through cotton candy clouds, tasting the air and the butterscotch sunshine flooding down on him. Then an ominous feeling began to move in, caused him to dread the next cloud...and suddenly the plane was on fire. He had startled awake, found Mackie snuggled against him. She didn't waken, so he settled back on the pillow, but that made twice since the bail-out he'd had a nightmare like that, a nightmare that didn't finish before he woke himself from it.

Mackie and her aunt were off in some other part of the big house seeing to dinner preparations. There was going to be a party to celebrate New Year's Eve. Lange was a little uncomfortable at the thought of a party with people he didn't know, but he'd been among strangers for the past six months, so one more night couldn't hurt. It was better than hanging around the airdrome or spending money on a cheap hotel in London. Sightseeing might have been nice, but he didn't really have the cash for much once he paid his mess bill every month.

He focused on the boy and the train set he said came from Santa Claus. He was a serious little fellow, in his sweater vest, short pants and knee socks, flight goggles positioned on top of his head. He was intent on his train and had no attention to give to conversation. Lange had already made a stab at a question or two to get something started, but he got only one-word replies, each of them followed with the obligatory "sir" until Lange felt he was back at the airdrome talking to Pickens or one of the ground crew.

He didn't have much experience with kids. He and Becky had talked once about starting a family, but she hadn't been ready, so he wasn't either, and the marriage started coming apart shortly afterwards. Seemed she'd had a change of heart, though, with that Sullivan fellow from Arkansas. Not that he gave a damn. He barely thought about all that anymore.

He sat there smoking, staring around at the aunt's parlor. It was a swank place, overloaded with little do-dads, lots of delicate china, heavy tables with fringed lamps, reminded him a little of Christmas Eve with Morse, although not quite as lavish as that big mansion had been. Mackie's aunt apparently had a fondness for brass—brass fire irons, brass candleholders, brass curtain rods. The walls were covered with paintings suspended on long cords from oak picture rails—some sourpuss fellows, some hunting scenes with lots of hounds and horses, along with one black and white photograph of Winston Churchill by itself above a console radio, as if the aunt wanted to be able to look her prime minister in the face when he spoke to his country.

A vision of Papa and Aunt Dellie and Gabe came to him, gathered around their radio waiting for news. He wondered what they were doing at that exact moment. He had been thinking about them quite a bit, but he figured it was probably the holidays working on him. According to the mantle clock it was only eleven, which would make it about five in the morning back in Texas. No doubt Papa would be awake, and Gabe would already be out checking cattle. Daylight would be breaking.

"Sir," Given said, his voice startling Lange out of his reverie. "Do you think you could hook up these cars for me? I can't get them to stay together."

There was a brass dish in the shape of a maple leaf on the table to Lange's right. He crushed out his cigarette. It looked like an ashtray; he hoped it was one. His back didn't feel as stiff today. He attributed that to Mackie's magic last night. The brace the doctor ordered him to wear made it hard to bend. He knelt on the floor by the boy and his train set.

"Let's see." He took the two train cars from the boy's hands.

"They're supposed to connect right in here." Given's little finger pointed.

After a moment of inspection, Lange saw the connectors. The set was metal, heavy enough to stay on the track. There was a ramp and a bridge, a tunnel, and the boy didn't seem to have any of it put together yet. "Flying Scotsman" the carriage car read. There were pink lamps in the Pullmans, and a conductor, passengers, and a lever on the bottom that made the engine whistle sound. When he was a kid he would've traded his left eye for a model train set like this one. He snapped the couplers together.

"Thank you." Given set the cars on the track, gave Lange a quick glance. "Do you fly Ansons like my Uncle Adam?"

Lange picked up the smoker car. There were tiny people inside all the windows. "Have you heard of a Spitfire?"

The boy's eyes lit like prisms. "The Mark One or Mark Two?"

Lange chuckled. Obviously, the boy knew more than Lange thought. "Mark One. But we hope to get some Mark Twos pretty soon."

He handed the smoker car to Given. He seemed to have the

hang of the connectors now. Lange leaned to fit the tracks onto the tunnel piece.

"You want to be a pilot?" he said to the boy.

"Yes, sir." Another coupler snapped together in Given's small hands. "But I might want to drive a lorry. If the war's still going on when I'm old enough."

"God forbid," Lange mumbled.

Given sat back on his heels and looked squarely at Lange, as if seeing him for the first time. "Do you know Tom Mix?"

The boy was so earnest, Lange had to bottle his laughter. "No, but I have a cousin who's an awful lot like him."

"Does he ride a horse?"

"Like a Comanche."

Given squinted at the word, obviously confused, so Lange explained about the Comanche, how they were the horsemen of the Indian tribes. He couldn't tell if any of it registered.

"I ride," Given said. "Do you?"

"A little bit," Lange answered, remembering when he was a kid, streaking barebacked through the countryside, a wad of old Dunny's mane in his hand for a bridle.

"I have a Welsh pony," Given said. "His name's Blin, which Auntie says means Troublesome, but I don't think he's one bit troublesome. We can ride later, if you'd like."

Lange was just about to reach over to tousle the boy's head, when Mackie's aunt swept into the room, like a grand duchess, which she might have been for all Lange knew. "I see you two are getting acquainted," she said.

Mackie came in the room next, dressed in a soft gray sweater and tweed slacks. He'd never seen her in civvies. He liked how she'd done her hair, without all the curls and foo-foo.

Given sprang to his feet. Lange came up slower, favoring his back a bit. "Mister DeLony's a Spitfire pilot, Mummy."

"Is he?" Mackie grinned.

"Yes, and they're going on Mark Twos pretty soon." The boy was almost breathless.

"Good heavens." The aunt put her hand to her heart, looked at Lange and then Mackie. "I think he's found a new hero. Won't Uncle Adam be jealous? Come along, young fellow. Time for your lunch. Take your friend into the garden, Allison. It's a lovely day."

Mackie gave Given a quick hug as he went past her, turned to watch her aunt take him off into another room.

"Swell kid," Lange said.

"I've never seen him talk so much to someone he's just met." When Mackie turned back to face Lange, there was no mistaking the pride beaming on her.

"Your hair's different," he said.

"Just brushed it out." She clasped her hands together behind her back, as if she were hiding something. He thought about last night, how good she had felt, and how willing. Hell, she'd been the one to start it. That surprised him a little. And now, this morning, she seemed, for some reason, ready to blush and act shy. "We can go outside and scout around if you want."

He cocked his head. "So it's Allison?"

"Yes, well." She doubled her fist at him. "Nobody but family calls me that."

"It's a nice name. You should hear what my family calls me."

"I'd love to," she said, guiding him into another part of the house. They went through a vestibule and stepped outside onto a stone terrace. He let her lead the way.

"I've got this scar." He touched the notch in his ear. "They had to use an instrument when I was born."

"Forceps." She nodded. They dodged around an arrangement of concrete furniture, and went four steps down into the lawn, brown and thatched with winter.

"So Papa called me Ding. It caught on with the family. I can't get them to stop it either."

They walked a little way down a stone path. She stopped,

turned to look at him. "Ding! That's a horrible nickname for a pilot."

"That's what I say!"

She looked him in the eyes. Sure enough, a pink blush started at her hairline and completely encircled her face. Freckles spattered across her nose. He felt like he could read her mind, and she was thinking about the same thing he was. He slipped his hand around the small of her back, thought he might give her a little kiss, but she curled away, took him by the arm and pulled him down the path.

The outside air had a chill in it. Humidity clung like fog to the trees. The grounds they walked through had once been a well-kept English garden with trimmed hedgerows and rounded trees, but the whole thing had fallen into disarray. Overgrown bushes intruded on the footpath. One hedge had completely enveloped a statue of a wood sprite.

"Aunt Kath's gardener joined the army," Mackie explained. "She hasn't found anyone to replace him. She thought about a Land Girl, but she doesn't really qualify as a farm."

They went through a gate, the wood pulpy from years of wet weather, and followed the footpath past winter-bare trees. Stone steps that looked as if they had been in place for centuries were set into the inclines and swales. Mackie threaded her arm through his and matched his steps. He didn't know where they were headed. He just walked along with her.

"Aunt Kath tells me people are talking about invasion again," Mackie said. "Predicting Hitler might try to disrupt New Year celebrations with bombers and airborne troops."

Lange glanced at the sky. Concrete gray. Eight tenths overcast. "I don't think they'll cross the Channel in this weather."

"Are we in for bad weather?"

"Is there any other kind in this country?"

She laughed. "It can be quite lovely in summer."

"I'll believe that when I see it."

"You'll have to come back in the spring. There are roses everywhere and lilacs. You can't tell right now but it's beautiful in the spring."

They came to a wooden bench beside a tree, and she sat down, patted the spot next to her. He sat. They were on a rise overlooking an open meadow. She told him about landing a Magister there once.

"But I wouldn't recommend it. Lot's of stones in that meadow. I nearly tipped it on its nose." She laughed, glanced at him. "How's your back?"

"Better." He gave her a smile. There came that blush again.

He kept her arm threaded through his. They huddled close. He was wishing he'd bought his overcoat. She fingered the single stripe outlined on his sleeve, raised her blue eyes to his. He touched the tip of his nose to hers. She smelled like perfume.

"Will you be all right?" she said. "Your nerve, I mean."

"Oh, sure," he said, quickly. "Get back up on the horse...." He swallowed. His mouth felt dry. He looked away. "Tell me about Given's father."

"Well...there's nothing much to tell. He was one of my father's test pilots. Back in Winnipeg. As far as I know he's still there. His name was—is Eugene Marchand. He was married. I didn't know it, but when I found out I didn't care."

He glanced at her. She kept her face turned away but he thought he saw a tear slip down her cheek. He wondered if it was because she still felt something for the guy or because it was a hurtful memory.

He squeezed her hand. "Everybody's got things they regret."

"I don't regret it. I have Given." Her voice lightened.

"Does he know about Given? This test pilot fellow?"

"Well, of course, he denied everything. And my father believed him over me." She let out a hollow laugh, choked on it, sniffled. Another tear slid down. "Oh, for pity's sake." She swiped at her face. "I don't know what's got into me. I'm over all this, I really am."

He shook out his handkerchief, gave it to her. She blew her nose.

"So you made a break for it and came here," he said. Sounded familiar. Same thing he'd done. He took a deep breath.

"Aunt Kath took me in. Given was born a few months later, at Peterborough, just up the road. When war broke out, Adam came to England, too. End of story. Aunt Kath's been like a mother to me, to all of us. She really has been."

"I have an aunt like that, too. Aunt Dellie. My second mother."

"Good old aunties," she said.

She sat there for a moment, her head against his shoulder. A grey squirrel ran across the open meadow, raced up an evergreen. It was too chilly for sitting outside, but he didn't want to move. She felt warm, and plain good, next to him.

"What about you?" she said. "Why on earth did you get involved in this war? You could be back with your family in Texas."

"Don't think that hasn't crossed my mind." He reached in his pocket for the cigarette case. When he pulled it out, she straightened, laughed in surprise.

"Well, I guess it hasn't brought you any luck, has it?" she said.

"Oh, I wouldn't say that. I'm still here. That's lucky."

He offered her a cigarette and took one for himself. Stick matches and dry boot soles were hard to come by in England, so he'd bought a little Swiss box lighter off one of the ground crew. He held the flame for her. When she'd lit her cigarette, he lit his. He blew out the smoke. It was immediately lost in the hazy sky.

"I guess I was kind of aimless," he said. "Figured the RAF or somebody could put me to use. I've been flying since I was fourteen."

"That's all there is to it?"

He laughed. "Well, I don't like the Nazis."

He reached his arm around her again. She was soft and dainty but kind of fragile, too. Like somebody needed to protect her. He could tell she liked him, maybe a little too much. He liked her, too. Maybe too much.

He kissed her temple, decided to tell her about Sunny's kids—

Nina, Peter, and Justine—how they were still in France, how his sister, Sunny, had died suddenly a couple of years ago. He told her how Papa and Aunt Dellie had tried to get them out of France when the war started, and how Nina, the married one, had turned down the offer. "Nobody knows what's happened to them since the krauts invaded."

They sat in silence for a moment, smoking. She sank closer to him. "So? Are you planning to win the war by yourself?" she said.

He chuckled. "You sound like my cousin Julianne."

He drew her to him and kissed her. He had been wanting to for a while now. It felt sincere and important, that kiss. She kissed him back, and it started to get heated like things seemed to do between them.

But then Given came running up the pathway towards them. Mackie broke away, even sprang to her feet as if to hide the fact that they'd been kissing. Lange doubted Given could have cared—he had an announcement to make: "Aunt Kath says it's time for grown-up lunch."

They ate lunch in a room the aunt called a sunroom, even though there wasn't a drop of sunshine in the sky. The kitchen cook brought out dainty sandwiches, and some small sausages, hot tea bread. He ate with gusto and hadn't realized he was hungry. The aunt relayed news she'd heard on the radio. Thirty-seven U-Boats had been destroyed in the Atlantic since the first of December. She poured sherry into cut-crystal glasses, and they made a toast to victory in 1941.

After lunch, Mackie and her aunt disappeared again, more party preparations. Lange helped Given finish off the model train set. The mechanism to sound the tunnel whistle gave Lange trouble, but he finally figured it out, and by then, he realized he had stopped feeling awkward and out of place. He and Given talked like old friends.

The boy wanted to know about Texas and growing up on a ranch, so Lange told him stories about fishing in the creek with Papa and punching cattle with Gabe. Before he knew it, the afternoon had flown, and party guests began to arrive.

The first guests were some nearby neighbors, a middle-aged couple, properly English. Then came an older, more talkative couple. Next, a widow lady and her niece arrived, and another old gentleman, with a briar pipe and a fob in his vest, who took right up with Lange, bragging on the RAF, slapping his shoulder with lots of "Ruddy good shows." Most of the rest of the conversation was a blur. More sherry went around the room.

About eight o'clock, Adam burst in, with bottles of champagne. For a few seconds it was all hugs and greetings. He had a wrapped gift for Given, which the boy took and immediately began to rip apart. Adam's eyes shot round and landed on Lange. He came forward, hand out.

"Sis didn't tell me she was bringing her golden boy. Sorry, mate. I don't recall the name."

"DeLony." Lange thought Adam McLeod might squeeze his hand in half. *Golden boy?* What in hell did *that* mean? He thought it might be an insult, but he wasn't sure.

"So it is. The Yank that's not in the Yank squadrons." Adam was talking about the so-called Eagle Squadrons made up of American volunteers. Adam didn't have a trace of British in his voice. He sounded like he was from Michigan or Minnesota.

"So, where's the sherry?" Adam boomed and leaned down to look Given in the face. "Did Santa Claus drink up all the Christmas sherry this year?"

"Thank you for the lorry, Uncle Adam." Given held a blue trunk with RAF painted on the side. It had a tandem wheel trailer, just like the truck the crash crew drove back at the airdrome.

With Adam's arrival, the whole party changed tone. He took charge of the conversation and of the liquor cabinet, switching right away from sherry to whiskey, pouring all around the room. He knew everybody, called them by name, and he was obviously popular among the guests.

In a while, the party drifted into the dining room. A big chandelier hung from the ceiling, snow-white tablecloth on the long table, paw-footed chairs. The aunt directed everybody to the seats. She put Mackie next to Lange, with Given on the other side of her. At each place, gold-rimmed China plates were stacked one on top of the other: dinner plate, salad plate, bread plate, this much, at least, he had learned from Thursday formal dinners in the mess. A red linen napkin, folded into an unidentifiable shape, perched on the top plate. There were several sizes of forks, two knives, two spoons. Glasses went up; they gave the "Victory in '41" toast again.

It was a feast, beef roast done rare, crispy light Yorkshire pudding, mashed potatoes, the dreaded Brussels sprouts, and sticky toffee pudding. He watched Mackie chase one Brussels sprout around her plate, then stab it with her fork. She caught him watching, leaned in closer to him and whispered, "Thank you for helping Given with his train."

"My pleasure." For a moment, their eyes locked.

When dinner was over, the party moved back into the front room. Adam kept pouring, "Another splash?" Bailey kept the old gramophone cranked, and a few of them danced, Lange with Mackie. Adam with the aunt. There was a lot of laughter and talk. Just before midnight, Adam uncorked the champagne. By then, Lange was three-fifths to the wind and struggling to hide it. Off in the distance, fireworks sounded, or maybe thunder. The party was singing, everybody kissing everybody else, and hugging. Someone started "Auld Lang Syne." The whole room took it up.

Lange kissed Mackie too long in front of her family. Then her aunt was dragging him by the hand out the back door, giving him some odd instructions he was too drunk to understand. He kept asking her, "What? What? Say that again, please." And then he was wandering alone out in the dark and the cold. He realized what he'd been hearing wasn't fireworks. Distantly, to the south, there were continuous lightning flashes and the low, menacing, echo of heavy guns.

He reasoned he must have been kicked out of the house for kissing Mackie. The aunt had probably been scolding him, but he couldn't leave without his kit, which was still in the upstairs bedroom. He went around to the front door and heard someone calling him from behind. Mackie ran towards him, laughing.

"I think your aunt hates me," he said.

"No, she doesn't. Here." She stuck a piece of bread and a holly branch in his hands. He stared at both his hands, trying to make out what he was holding. He thought he must be asleep and in the middle of some oddball dream.

"You're our dark-haired man, darling." She pulled at his arm. "First footing, and all that rot. Aunt Kath's big on tradition. Come back inside now."

"First what?"

"Footing. First Foot. Out with the old year and in with the new. Come along, darling. It's symbolic. You'll see."

He motioned with the crust of bread at the flashes through the clouds off in the distant south. He felt unsteady. "Sons of bitches."

She stopped, looked with him towards the rumbling. "Must be Cambridge."

They stared off together for a moment, then she took his arm. The bread crumbled in his hands. When he stumbled back inside the house, everybody jumped out and clapped, dazzling him in the doorway.

Later, in bed, she tried to explain it all to him—a silly old British tradition. "First foot. Symbol of good luck for the New Year. The first person across the threshold—the dark-haired man, that's you, darling—represents the New Year coming in the door, bringing bread so there will be plenty to eat all year, and greenery for long lives. There were some other things you were supposed to bring in, but we didn't plan it out very well." She giggled.

"What other things?"

"Coal. And money." Her giggle turned to a full-throated laugh. She stifled it.

"Screwy damned English," he mumbled, tucking her next to his chest. He kissed her behind her ear. "Thank you for today," he whispered.

"My pleasure," she whispered back.

ON THE THIRD morning in Colesbury, he caught the train back to the London, then on to Hornby Down and the airdrome. He was ready to get back on ops, felt like he'd licked the willies. He owed that to Mackie. She'd helped him through it. He wondered if she knew that.

When he walked into his room, Pickens was there, tidying up. "Back so soon, sir?" he said.

"Happy New Year, Pickens."

"Same to you, sir. Did you have a good leave?" Pickens took Lange's kit and his overcoat.

"Yes, thanks."

Pickens brushed lint from the overcoat and hung it away in the wardrobe. Lange watched him and realized he didn't know anything about the man personally.

"Are you married, Pickens? Do you have kids?"

"Oh yes, sir. Coming on twenty-two years now. Got three kiddies. Two girls and a boy. All but grown, now."

Lange sat down on the straight chair, unbuttoned his cuffs. "I was married. I don't think I was any good at it."

Pickens chuckled. "Well, it's not really hard, sir. You just let them tend to you. I find a woman likes to tend to things, the kiddies, the house. Keeps them busy and happy."

In a moment, Pickens brought in Lange's mail, along with two pair of spit-shined shoes, Lange's and Joe Sokol's. There were two letters from Aunt Dellie, one from Julianne. He thumbed them open, one after the other, carried them into the sitting room, eased into the stuffed chair, and read about home.

CHAPTER 12

"Sunny's Kids"

"PETER"

1 January 1941—

Today I found this notebook in Mama's trunk. In it she had written birthdays and death days. My father was born on 8 February 1899. He died on 28 April 1926, when he was twenty-seven. Today is Mama's birthday. She would have been forty. My father was gassed in the last war. It weakened his lungs so TB could set in. TB took Mama, too. I miss her every day.

My birthday was 4 December, but everyone forgot about it except for me and Mémé. Nina remembered the next day, but that was too late. I had already turned eighteen. My sisters are busy with other things. Nina has her baby, Joie. Joie cries all the time. This is not because she is ill. Mémé thinks she is just spoiled. To me the baby always looks to be laughing except that tears have begun to show up on her plump cheeks. She has black hair like Emile. I think her eyes will be black, too, but right now they are blue, although not as blue as Nina's or Justine's.

My eyes are brown. My hair is dark but not black. My face is square. I would like to grow a mustache or a beard, but I think my sisters will laugh at me. I am going to write in this notebook in

English. I am afraid I will forget how now that Mama is not here to help me remember. So I will use this notebook to keep in practice.

Justine has a boyfriend. She thinks nobody knows but I have seen them together. I think I should tell Nina, but I would not like to get Justine in trouble. He is a German soldier. He is blond, tall, and clean. He wears the uniform of the *Wehrmacht,* but he is only a private. He has a friend who acts as lookout when he and Justine are together. The friend makes hand signals when a superior officer is coming. One day I will wait for Justine after she meets her boyfriend. I have questions she will have to answer.

Here are the other things I found inside the trunk:

1) A single blue baby boot. It is tiny. It might have belonged to a doll. Or perhaps to me.

2) A packet of dried-out chewing gum. It smells of mint. It came from America.

3) A cigarette lighter that says FIRESTONE TIRES on the side. This surely came from America, as well.

4) A black case with a war medal that says VICTORY. This belonged to my father. Mama showed me this medal when I was small.

5) A stack of photographs of people I do not know. Perhaps our relatives.

6) A diploma from Dr Laurent's School for the Deaf in Paris. This is mine.

7) A barrette of cloisonné. If there is an English word I do not know it.

8) A bundle of handmade birthday greetings to Mama from me and Nina and Justine. They are crumbling to bits.

9) A typewriter eraser. The brush is frayed.

10) An electric torch with G.M. DAILEY 117TH SUPPLY TRAIN scratched into the side. Also my father's. He was a soldier in the Great War. I will keep the torch. Maybe there are batteries for it at M. Caullireau's store. I might use the cigarette lighter, too, if I can find fuel for it. All fuel is restricted now. I

have been stealing some of Nina's cigarettes when she is busy with Joie.

12 JANUARY—

I caught Justine with her German. His name is Dieter Gaertner. He is nineteen, which I told her is far too old for her. She has to break it off with him. I told her I am the man of this family now and she must do as I say. She said—you are a pighead, Peter—and walked away from me. Maybe she said bighead, sometimes it is difficult to read Justine's lips. So I threatened to tell Nina. Justine does not want me to do that. Nina hates the Germans. They still have not posted Emile's name on any of their lists. We don't know if he is dead or a prisoner-of-war or if he is in England with de Gaulle. I choose to think of him in England.

14 JANUARY—

Justine says that she told her "friend" that they could no longer meet. I do not believe anything she says. She has always been the one to do wrong things in this family. Mama called Justine full of life. Mémé calls her a fancy pants. Mémé is beginning to learn to sign. I can read her lips but she does not always understand me when I speak. Sign makes things easier for me. Lip reading tires me.

18 JANUARY—

Mémé helped a tramp today. He came to the door begging food and she gave him eggs and bread. He said he was a soldier afraid to turn himself in. Justine told him that it was all right now to give himself up to the Kommandant and nothing would happen to him. He smelled like *merde* and looked to be a hundred years old, but turned out to be only three years older than me. He went away with his eggs and bread, and I do not think he will turn himself in to the

Kommandant. Mémé was upset by the man and Justine says she hopes he will not come back again.

25 JANUARY—

I shared a cigarette with the man I mentioned before. His name is Dilane Bastian. He comes from the Oisne but cannot go home. It is too dangerous to cross the country without papers now. He told me about the day the Germans overtook the army in Sedan. He hid in a wheat field. He said men were dying all around him. Airplanes were bombing overhead. He said he was frightened and just kept running until there was no more gunfire.

I wrote Emile's name on a slip of paper, but Dilane does not know of him. All Dilane wants is to go home, but I can do nothing to help him. I cannot even talk to him much. I wish I could speak better. Nina says I must do more of it, but I don't like the looks people give me. Even Mémé flinches from me. I let Dilane sleep in the barn. Nobody knows he is out there. I think it will be all right for a day or two. He has nowhere to go. In the morning I will take him some bread and perhaps some cheese. I left him my electric torch, but I hope he will not use it much. Batteries are hard to find, and the light might draw the attention of Mémé or my sisters. Anyway, it belonged to my father and it is nearly all I have of him.

30 JANUARY—

All is well now with Dilane Bastian. He has found another place to stay. I am relieved. With him in the barn I became aware of all the Germans we have here now. I don't know why they bother with this tiny place on the map, except perhaps because we are so close to Dijon. It seems to me that there are more Germans here now than there are people in the village. Dilane has learned of some other French soldiers in hiding out in the Morvan. They are planning to try to get to the Southern Zone some way and then to Algeria. He went to join them. He said he did not want to get me in trouble because it is a crime to harbor soldiers from the French or British armies. I did not think of it that way, as harboring anyone. I was only feeding a hungry man. But he is right about the crime of it. There are signs posted in the village that clearly state who are our enemies now.

Nina has been talking of sending Justine to the Lycée Dijon. Justine has always been smart in school, but she does not want to go to Dijon alone. I would go with her but, Mémé needs help with this farm. I am not much good at it, but I am better than nothing. Besides there is no money for the Lycée, and that is the fact of it. The last letter from the Monniers in Paris came with half as much money as they have been sending. Nina is talking about trying to find a job doing something in the village.

5 FEBRUARY 1941—

I have been thinking of writing to our *grand-pére* in America. It is possible that he would send us money. I do not know for sure if a letter would get to him or not. We have heard nothing from him since we came to Bourgogne, and we often had letters from America before the war. Letters from the Monniers are often cut to ribbons from the postal censors. We have what we can grow on the farm, and Mémé keeps chickens, but we have nothing for fuel or things we cannot grow. We have not had a meal with beefsteak in months.

Yesterday I asked M. Caullireau if he could hire me to work. I wrote it all down on a paper, and Justine went along with me in case M. Caullireau had questions he wanted to ask of me. She told him that I am good at reading lips, but I think he will not hire me because I am deaf. Mémé says no matter, she needs me to milk the cow and till the garden, but I would like it better if I could earn money.

~

9 FEBRUARY—

Justine is still seeing her Fritz. I suspected it all along. She is headstrong and will not listen to me when I tell her she should end this with him. Yesterday I caught them in the field behind the farmhouse. If Nina had looked out the window she would have seen them there for herself. I went out of the barn to shoo him away with my hands and arms as if he were a wayward pig! He was startled by me, and my actions worked. He left in a hurry. For my efforts I got a slap in the face from Justine. She has never struck me before, and it hurt so much I had to go to the barn until it stopped. I did weep a bit, but I would never let anyone see that.

23 FEBRUARY—

Today is a joyous day! Nina received a letter from Emile! It was six months old and had been all over France. Also it has been heavily censored, but it is proof that he is still alive. Nina has been delirious with happiness all day long, hugging me four times at least. Emile is a prisoner-of-war in Saxony. He tried to write more of his whereabouts, but Saxony is all that got through the censors. Nina has had an atlas out today looking for Saxony. He was defeated and taken near the Marne River last 11 June. He has been a prisoner for ten months, and still he is not on their list at the government offices. We are going to have a celebration tonight. We only have a little fuel left for the generator, but Mémé says Fire It Up! She is happy to know that her grandson is safe. She has already wrung the neck of two chickens. We will eat hearty tonight.

Joie has started to crawl, as if she knows she will see her papa someday and wants to grow up fast for him.

20 MARCH—

Nina is twenty-one today. At least she is not a widow. But she will not celebrate. She says she will not celebrate anything at all again until the Germans are no longer in France.

30 MARCH—

For a long time, I have not written much in this book. I have been too tired. M. Caullireau has hired me to work in his store and I have had to learn what he expects of me. He is a shy man and never speaks much, but he keeps me busy until dark every day. Some of his customers dislike me. They refuse to believe that I can read their lips, and they act surprised when I bring them what they ask for. It makes some of them angry. They accuse me of pretending to be deaf, so I will not have to serve the Germans in their army. Other customers are very kind and give me small tips for my help. I hope M. Caullireau will notice the kind ones and not pay attention to the grousing of the others. I need to make this money. It is much help at the farm.

Nina, too, has gone to work. The owner of the *pâtisserie* put her in the front serving his sweets. Nina is very pretty, and she is friendly to people. She will be a success in her job.

Justine continues to shun school. Mama would be so unhappy with this. She held high standards for Justine, expected her to be a doctor or a lawyer or some other high profession. Instead, she has turned out to be slothful. Mémé complains that she does nothing but lie around reading Hollywood movie star magazines all day. They are all old magazines from America and worn out around the corners. When Mémé confronts Justine, she claims to be looking after Joie and has no time for other chores. Joie, though, has turned out to be a good baby. She sleeps often and plays alone quite well. I do not know what can be done about Justine. When I asked about her Fritz she said that he has been transferred away from here and for me to stop worrying over her business.

~

31 MARCH—

I found Justine crying in her bed just now. She says she wants to go home. She hates it here in the country where everything is so dirty and where she has no friends. She hates having to wash her feet before she gets into bed at night. She wants to go live with the Monniers above their bakery in Paris. I wonder if they will take her. I plan to write a letter to them, but I am not sure of how to word my request. She will be another mouth for them to feed, but perhaps they can put her to use in the bakery. I think she would go to school if she was back in Paris. It might be best for all concerned. But then who will look after Joie? I think it is too much to ask of Mémé. She is an old woman. I will speak to Nina about it when she comes home from work.

1 APRIL 1941—

There was a terrible row here last night. It is hard to be the only man amongst all these females. Justine and Nina were screaming into each other's faces. I stopped watching for what they said and took Joie out in the night air. The nights are beginning to get mild. Her body was tense, and she had been crying for a long time from the way her chest jerked. She hung onto my neck as we walked into the fields. Poor Mémé, left in there with the two of them. I had a cigarette in my pocket that M. Caullireau had given to me when I left his store. I used my father's lighter and leaned on the gate with Joie in my arms to smoke. It was the only peaceful time for me last night. Joie fell asleep on my shoulder. Now, today no one is speaking. It is not necessary to be a hearing person to know when anger has won.

20 APRIL—

Today is Herr Hitler's birthday. I did not know this until one of the *Waffen SS* came to tell M. Caullireau to close his store. It is a national holiday and must be observed with reverence. There are penalties for not doing so. M. Caullireau sent me home with four boxes of cigarettes. I smoked half of one box before I got there. There are ten in a box, so I am turning into quite a smoker. They no longer make me dizzy, but they give me a nice calm feeling inside. I like using Papa's lighter but have just about run out of fuel for it once again. The fuel is rationed and in short supply, so I may not get anymore for a long time. M. Caullireau says cigarettes will soon be rationed as well. The flame on the lighter is already down so low it is hardly bigger than a bean, but it burns very blue.

Part of my job at the store is to sort out the billets for Mme. Caullireau. She then sends them to the *mairie* and the government replenishes the store's stock based on the billets. These are the things that Caullireaus sells that are now rationed:

1) sugar, which we rarely have in stock.

2) coffee, which is the same as sugar.

3) cooking oil

4) salt

5) soap of all kinds

6) wine, except that we are in *Bourgogne* so wine is not essential here. We have plenty.

7) cheese

8) jam, of course, because it contains sugar

Each person may have 500 grams of sugar per week, but we never have enough to supply that to everyone, so their billets become useless. They may have 300 grams of coffee, but the same goes for coffee. People in this region do not care for tea, nevertheless, it is also rationed. Every week something new seems to be added to the rations list so by tomorrow this list will be obsolete.

21 APRIL—

The German soldiers shot up the village square last night. They were celebrating their Führer's birthday and were issued beer from their headquarters. It got them all on a drunken rampage and now M. Caullireau has no front window on his store. I spent the entire morning boarding it over for him. He is old, and he is not tall so he could not do the job himself. He swept up the broken glass while I hammered up the boards. There were broken bottles out on the front walk and in the street as well. Someone smeared boot black on the door of the church. Everyone used the day cleaning up the village.

2 MAY—

The Monniers have finally replied to my letter. They are unable to take Justine to live with them just now. I carry this news home with me and have kept it a hard secret. Justine has become very sullen and I do not know how to break it to her that she must stay here in Garance with us. Nina will be home in an hour, and I will talk it over with her first. Joie takes so much attention now I think it is probably for the best, but I know Justine will not see things this way. Perhaps if we all save as much as we can she could go live in Dijon and attend school there. We have some hard choices to make.

10 MAY 1941—

I saw Dilane Bastain today. He is much improved. He is living in a small village eight kilometers over the mountain and is well-dressed, clean-shaven, and in good spirits. He goes by the name of Pierre-Marceau now. Pierre is my name in French. He has learned a little sign from his new priest. He said that knowing me has made him want to learn. This pleases me. We stood at the side of M. Caullireau's store and smoked cigarettes. He showed me a gun he hides in the pocket of his coat. He got it from a German officer in a restaurant toilet. The officer laid the gun on top of the rubbish cylinder while he relieved himself, and Dilane stuck the gun into his own pants without anyone noticing. There was a commotion later, but he managed to leave the restaurant without being searched. It was very daring of him, I think, but I wonder where he will get bullets to fit it. He has two in the chamber and likes flipping them in and out. He hates the German *salauds*. He says he plans to shoot one of them as soon as he gets the opportunity. It feels good to finally have a friend, although Dilane is a hearing friend, and that is very much different from what I am used to. I have had no friends at all since we left Paris.

16 MAY—

Today Justine is sixteen. She would like to be twenty-one and able to leave here without asking. The past months have been diffi-cult for her, I think. She is still hurt by the Monniers' refusal to accept her into their home again. We lived with them for a while after Emile left for the front, but I suppose it would be too hard on them now with the rationing and the shortages. Despite Nina's oath not to celebrate anything while the Germans are here, she made Justine a cake. It was the most delicious thing I have ever tasted. Mme. Pompon who owns the *pâtisserie* helped Nina find all the ingredients for the cake. I suspect, but do not know for sure, that some of the items were black market. Mme. Pompon is not the sort who would do without just because of German laws. Mémé sewed a new dress for Justine. Mémé has been working for weeks in secret. Justine looks very pretty wearing it. The blue flowers match her eyes. I gave her the cloisonné barrette from Mama's trunk. Justine recognized it and cried when she saw it. She has worn it in her blonde hair all today. I think it was a good birthday for her.

It is hard to believe that one year has already gone by since the Boche invaded France. How much has changed since then, and none for the better.

19 MAY—

Dilane says it is unnatural for Frenchmen to live under the thumb of another government. French people are meant to be free. He says it is what our ancestors fought for. I told him I do not really have any French ancestors but he would not listen to that. He said, *this is your country, too. And it is your war.* He has made me think. He has found a bicycle for me so that I can come to his village over the mountain. He lives with a woman there. Her name is Marielle Audan. Her husband has been listed as missing for more than one year. She has a daughter Lorna who is nice to look at although she is far too young and skinny. We talk to each other with pencils and paper. She calls me L'Abbe after Abbe Charles Michel de L'Eppe who invented sign language in France. Not many hearing people know of this, so I think she must be quite smart.

When I got back to the farm Nina was angry with me. She called it worried not angry, but she was shouting. I could tell by the look on her face and how wide her lips parted with each of her words. It does no good to shout at me, but I let her do it anyway. It must make her feel better, or perhaps foolish in the end. Mémé gave me extra bread and cheese for supper. I think she likes me the best. I like her too. I have realized that I no longer yearn for Paris the way I used to do. Mémé's cow does not scare me anymore. I like the fur and hay smell of her as I lean my cheek against her warm side to milk her. And I can wring the neck of a chicken almost as well as Mémé does. Our mama was a farmer when she was a young girl, so I think I have inherited this talent from her. The worst part of being here has been watching Justine change from the silly laughing schoolgirl she was in Paris to the sad one she has become.

Today Joie took her first wobbling step on her own.

2 JUNE 1941—

Dilane has found more bullets for his gun so now he can practice his aim. He showed me how he can shoot plums from a rock wall. We go into the Morvan to do this practice. He let me shoot at one of the plums. The gun felt hot and heavy to my hands. It jerked my arm when it fired. Dilane has already picked out the German he wants to shoot. He is the officer who frisked Dilane and two of his friends outside a cafe for no reason except that they were three men standing together. Dilane had his papers in order. Even though they are false papers, I have seen them, and they look real. If the *Boche* knew he was an escaped soldier he would be in prison the same as Emile. The government keeps promising that the soldiers will be returned to us, but nothing happens. Marielle Audan has been told that they were sent to work camps and that the *Boche* have no intention of bringing any of the prisoners home. I think Nina has been told this as well. She carries a long face now.

Lately, I am the only one who ever plays with Joie. She lets me hold her tiny hands and walk her around in the kitchen yard. She wants to chase the chickens, but she cannot run yet. She tries to crawl after them, but they scatter. I think I will not fire Dilane's gun again.

15 June—

A British airplane came over the farm today. It was flying quite low and nobody knows what it was doing. I think it might have had bombs. There were swellings underneath the wings. I could feel the vibration of the engines as it passed overhead. Mémé was frightened and ran into the woods. Justine went with her and cried for a long while after the airplane had gone. She said the sound of the motor reminded her of the days on the road here from Paris. But Nina's face was happy for the first time in a long while. She said she hoped the bombs were for Petain. This is a dangerous thing for her to say. My sister is very brave. She went to the *mairie* today to find out how she could send packages to Emile. They told her it might be possible. She is to go back tomorrow.

~

19 JUNE—

Today I had to appear before the Prefect to prove that I am deaf. They are beginning to register people for work in Germany, and they wanted to send me there. I don't think they believed that I was deaf because I work in M. Caullireau's store. Nina had to do a lot of talking, and she showed them my papers which prove I am disqualified. They call it disabled—hors de combat. I had my diploma from the school in Paris. They bent their heads and made serious faces and did a lot of secretive talking with their backs turned to us, and then they let us go. Nina held onto me all the way home. I think she was much more upset than she showed. Damned German bastards!

22 JUNE 1941—

The *toqué salaud* Herr Hitler has betrayed Russia! Today he sent his Panzers and his Luftwaffe to attack Stalin's armies. I hope the Bolsheviks kill them all!

27 JUNE 1941—

I think I am in love with Lorna Audan. I don't care if she wears eyeglasses and is a hearing girl. Dilane teases me about her. He calls her bug-eyes, but I think that is not at all funny. To me she is beautiful. I like her little hands and tiny wrists. She has become quite good at finger spelling. I think she is much too young, but my heart will not listen to my thinking. In five more months I will be nineteen. Lorna is one month to her fifteenth birthday, but she is small for fifteen. I would like to kiss her, but I cannot bring myself to even hold her hand in mine. Dilane tells me that women don't like a shy man. But I am more than shy. I am deaf. Deaf, deaf, deaf. *SOURD-MUET!!* It seems to matter more to people here than it did in Paris.

1 JULY 1941—

I do not mind being deaf. It is peaceful. Sometimes I do hear things. Certain things. Very low rumbling sounds or perhaps they are only vibrations from the earth. They are my earth sounds. I am used to them and usually pay them no mind. I believe I feel them as much as I hear them. It is as if I am connected to something deep inside the world.

Lorna tries to explain to me the way things sound. Mama taught me that sound was like color. The wind is blue. Rain is silver. Thunder is dark purple. I believe I can nearly hear thunder. Lorna is pink. I think of her when I see something pink. She does not love me. She loves someone named Thierry who lives in Angers. Her mother plans for Lorna to one day marry Thierry of Angers. Dilane tells me not to worry, he will find someone better suited for me. I can shoot a bottle off a tree stump with a single bullet, now. Dilane says he will find me a gun of my own. I have put Papa's Victory Medal underneath my vest, pinned over the heart of my shirt.

2 JULY—

Lorna came to Caullireau's store. She had false sugar billets. I could tell they were forgeries, but I gave her the sugar. When she left the store, I tore up the billets. Mme. Caullireau will have to account for them, so I will put my own in the drawer tomorrow. For now, I hope no one will notice the short change. I worried over this for the rest of the day. Mme. Caullireau asked if I was feeling ill. I shook my head but thought better of it and excused myself from work for the rest of the day. Instead of going home, I walked over the hill to see Lorna. I planned to act very strong and scold her for coming to my store with her false billets. I wanted to be angry, but she had a good reason for wanting the sugar. There are children at her church who have been orphaned by the war. She plans to make cakes for Bastille Day and take them to the orphans. I cannot help but love her.

CHAPTER 13
Letters

8 *July 1941*

    Upavon, Wilts.

    Dear Lange,

    Hello from Wiltshire! Found out yesterday morning that I was being sent away for a conversion course on single-engine fighter types, Hurricanes first and then Spitfires. The ATA has finally decided to let us girls get in on the fun. About time, too. We want to see what all the fuss is about. This means it's possible one day I'll make a delivery to your station and we can get up a little dogfight. Maybe I'll even let you teach me a thing or two.

    I caught part of your interview on the BBC. Had just landed at Kemble and was waiting for the taxi back to Wentworth when the broadcast began. They played it over the Tannoy. Didn't recognize you at first, but then it dawned on me—Say, where had I heard that Texas drawl before? Well, you certainly spoke about the war with stubborn conviction. The bit about Hitler being doomed, well, that caused the whole hangar to erupt in cheers. You convinced me, too. Didn't realize you had such a passion about it. Perhaps you have a calling for this sort of thing, eh? Ever considered a career in politics? By the way, congrats on the new stripe. Much deserved, I'll bet.

Hope you like the scarf. It's only partially silk, but it should be enough to keep your neck from chaffing. All that twisting and turning, just try not to unwind your head while you're at it. I think I would miss your head if it were gone, although it might scare the bejesus out of the Germans to see you flying along sans your head.

OK, now this letter has deteriorated into the ridiculous. Sorry. I just wanted to let you know where I was in case you try to ring me. You can even write to me here. That would make me very happy. You can send care of ATA. They have put us in gloomy barracks and I desperately need some cheering up.

No doubt, you have noticed by now that I enclosed a couple of photos. The one of me is the "official" ATA snap. Hope you don't mind much me sending it. You don't have to hang it above your bed or anything. The other one is self-explanatory, you and Given putting together the train set at New Year's. He asks about you all the time, now. Think you were really a hit with him. Maybe we can get you back to Colesbury one day soon.

Do write to me, Lange. It's going to be a long two weeks. As soon as I'm out of here, shall we try to meet somewhere? I should have a forty-eight once this is over. Let me know what you think of that idea.

Kisses,

Mackie

P.S. Please miss me a lot. I miss you.

1941 July 10

Dear Mr Delony,

I heard you on the BBC and was quite taken with the reasons you gave for wanting to join in the fight with good old England. Would that we had the foresight to see the Nazi menace and recog-

nize it in its evil as early as you have done. I congratulate you on your youthful wisdom.

During the last war I knew a Yank pilot myself. He also came from Texas. I wonder if you are possibly acquainted with Harold A. Kellman? He was wounded in battle in France and was put in hospital in Paris where I worked as a Red Cross nurse. We got on famously. I remember him as brawny in build but rather ruddy, a quite pleasant demeanor. He was released on a day when I was off duty so I lost contact with him. When I heard you on the BBC say that you hailed from Texas, I simply had to write to you to ask if, perchance, you or any member of your family were familiar with my old friend. Not likely, I realize. I believe Texas is as big as all Great Britain. You sounded so much like him. I could almost believe I was hearing him speak.

With prayers for your continued safety, and with gratitude for your service to the King, I am

Your faithful servant,
Mary Alexander Brooks

~

12 July 41

Dear Flying Officer D'Loney,

You don't know me so let me first introduce myself. My name is Audrey Paxton. My sister is Melanie. She and I listened to you on the BBC. We decided on the spot that we simply must write to you and give you our thanks for helping keep us safe from the Nazi Germans. Since you are an American and have no obligation to fight Jerry, we found it touching that you have left your comfy home in Texas all for us. My sister and I feel a special kinship with Americans. We have a third cousin who is an American and lives in Newark, New Jersey. We have never met him personally, but he is an admired member of our family. He sends cards at Christmas from Newark. Melanie and I are hoping one day to visit him in

America, perhaps when the war is won. It gave us such heart to hear you say the war will surely be won in the end. Is Newark anywhere close to Texas?

We are hoping that you will answer this letter and tell us all about America. We simply adore warm weather and have thought we might like to one day go to Texas. In fact, if you like, we could meet you in London for tea or perhaps the cinema, and you could tell us about Texas in person. Do you like the cinema? There is a dance club around the corner from where we live. Soldiers and mili-tary men go there quite often. We have danced with some of them but never with an officer in the RAF. Do you like to dance?

If you think that you would like to meet us in London reply by post with the time and place, or you may telephone either my sister or myself. Our number is VI.5986. We will try to be vigilant about answering the telephone, but if a man's voice should answer simply hang up.

It would be a treat for us to receive a letter from you. We hope you will write to us.

Yours sincerely,
The Paxton Sisters

~

9 July 41

For F/O Feelony

Sir:

We do not need you here fighting our bloody war. Didn't need your lot in the last one either. Do you think an Englishman can't hold his own against the likes of you? Americans are a bastard race. We don't need you mixing with our ladies, creating more bastards. We don't need you seeking adventure in our skies. Ain't your bloody war, mister! And if it was, we'd bloody well have lost the bugger by now. Go back where you came from. We can take care of Hitler on our own.

(unsigned)

~

15 July 1941

Somewhere in England

Dear Folks,

Hello from Jolly Old England! What I should say is Jolly COLD England. It rains 185 days a year, and stays cloudy for 100 more! Been here now through just about all the seasons and haven't warmed up yet. It's still cold enough for longjohns and sweaters, even in the middle of July. Never thought I'd miss the hot Texas weather, but I surely do.

Thanks for the boot socks, Aunt Dellie. They came just in time. My old ones were getting a bit more air-conditioned than is to my liking. The ones they issue to us are so thin you have to wear two pair to do any good at insulating your toes. And believe me, as chilly as it is on the ground, multiply that times 100 at 25,000 feet. I still love it though. Nothing quite like climbing a mountain of cloud and going over the top. Makes you want to go on up and see what the moon's made of.

Guess this is a good place to set the record straight about the squadron I'm in. Don't listen to Sterling. He doesn't know what he's talking about this time. I am not, I repeat NOT, in one of the so-called Eagle Squadrons, the all-American squadrons. There are lots of others like me who are mixed into one of the regular RAF squadrons and I like it the way it is, wouldn't want things to be any different. For one, those American boys in the Eagle Squadrons all have to fly Hurricanes. Nothing wrong with a Hurricane. It's a sure enough hot airplane, just not quite as hot as my Spitfire. I see those pin-up Eagle boys when I'm on leave in London sometimes. You might recall me talking about a fellow I came over here with, Jim Hiller from Utica. He's in one of the Eagle Squadrons, and he likes it just fine staying to the rear. Me, I want to be up where the action is. Had one of their COs try to recruit me on a recent foray into London. We were staying at the same hotel and met for drinks in the bar. Felt like a Grand Slam hitter being scouted for the Cincinnati Reds. Told him thanks but no thanks. I'm happy as a clam right where I am. We finished our drinks and toasted London, so no hard feelings.

Glad to hear Papa's up and about. Made me a little homesick hearing about y'all having that fish-fry. Never knew anybody that could catch fish like Papa. When I was little I used to think he could call them in like calling ducks in to a stock tank. The minute you hear this war is over and won, you tell him to start sacking them up because I want a repeat of that meal you described, with all the trimmings. What I wouldn't give right now for a big batch of hush puppies and cole slaw. Maybe some peach cobbler thrown in with a big gob of vanilla ice cream on top. Haven't seen a dish of ice cream since I've been over here.

Did a little radio interview the other day. They sent a couple of us fellows out to London to meet the BBC. We had just had a nice row with a German bomber that worked out to our favor. I got a little promotion out of it, too.

Well, guess I ought to close this one down for now. Duty calls— in this case, sleep. Thanks again for the socks. Always nice to get a little touch of home.

Lots of love,
Lange

~

16/July

Dear Mackie,

I like your idea of getting together in London. I should be up for a 48er on the 26th. Think you can swing it for then? We can meet at that same place again, The Whitehorse. I'll buy you a drink to celebrate you becoming a hot new Hurricane pilot. I'm having a hard time picturing you in one. Why, I bet your feet don't even touch the rudders, do they? I'd like nothing better than to take you up on that dogfight, you just say the word. And I promise not to go easy on you either. Although I have to admit, it would be a hell of a thing for me to shoot down my own best girl.

Thanks for the scarf. I feel just like the Red Baron wearing it, or maybe Rickenbacker. Too bad the Spit has a closed cockpit and the thing can't trail out in the wind the way it really ought to. I'm glad you heard me on the radio. Hope I didn't sound like too much of a bumpkin. You wouldn't believe the mail that's come here on account of that little interview. Most of them are so damned nice. But I don't know when I'll find the time to answer all of them.

I like the picture of you. It's cute as a flop-eared hound, as we would say back in Texas. I'll put it next to the one of Given from New Year's. Say, when did you take that one anyway. I don't remember you pointing a camera our way, you sneaky thing. My bedside table's starting to look like a photo gallery.

More another time,

Lange

P.S. If you get to the Whitehorse before me, wait for me in the pub. If I get there first, I'll do the same. Save me lots of kisses.

CHAPTER 14

"*Falling*"

Late in August, Lange led the squadron for the first time on a Rodeo—code name for a fighter sweep across the Channel. Squadron Leader Morse had gone off on a visit to Group and left Lange in charge. He felt a little on edge about it—taking ten fellows up through heavy cloud cover. Two of them were new—young and green. One he'd never even spoken to for more than a few seconds. He really didn't want to get to know them. They were too rosy-faced, too wide-eyed eager, too in love with the thought of being fighter pilots, and too many just like them had already come and gone through the squadron. They had lost three on a Rodeo last spring: Stanley, Bassey, and Lowe. Another new fellow named Gregory had lasted two months before he crash-landed near Ramsgate. You had to give the new fellows a chance but not get too attached. They might not be around for supper.

As the squadron broke through the heavy overcast into brilliant sunshine, Lange saw Joe Sokol keeping station to his right; on his left, Devon Eggleston, who had won a recent commission from Flying Sergeant to Pilot Officer. Both of them old hands. Both leaving ten thousand feet of contrail. Seeing those two helped his confidence. They rose in formation, and he relaxed, began to feel like the lead goose in a migrating flock of geese, all of them swaying gently in the thermals. When he turned, they turned. When he throttled up, they throttled up. He had to resist the urge to make a game out of it; he couldn't keep the jackass grin off his face.

Leading the squadron, he took them out over Dungeness to the edge of the French coastline. He knew the new boys wanted some excitement. He knew they would be disappointed, or anyway they would say they were, when they didn't meet any enemy aircraft. But he was elated. Nobody lost, one sortie under the belts of those new fellows. Both of them looked like they were just out of the cradle. Arriving at the dispersal huts, he could feel their respect, as well as the chummy pat on the shoulder from Sokol, the "Well done," from Eggleston, as if Lange himself were personally responsible for the lack of German activity in the sky.

However, a few days later, when the squadron escorted twelve Blenheim bombers to France, they weren't so lucky. Morse was back from Group and leading the squadron, when Devon Eggleston caught some flak near Boulogne. Sokol swore he saw Devon bail out, but nobody could confirm it. That night at mess, all the fellows were gloomy and quiet. It had been a while since they'd lost one of the old timers. They didn't perk up until a week later when Morse gave them the news from HQ that Eggleston had been picked up and now resided at a German prison camp somewhere in Nazi Europe. They all stood around the bar and toasted Devon, and then they shot down a Heinkel the next day in his honor. It was a squadron effort. They came upon the bomber below and to the left, just asking to be attacked. Everybody took a pass at it. The He-111 went down flaming, shedding skin and parts, until it winged over and dived into the sea.

On September 8, another squadron mate was lost—one of the new fellows—out around Gravelines. He'd last been seen chasing a Me-109 inland at zero feet. Lange didn't learn the fellow's name until he was gone. Frank Pullman. Even Morse, who had a photographic memory about most things, had to refer to his roster when he sent Lange off on funeral detail. Lange had drawn the short straw. He hated having to walk slow and solemn behind the coffin, trying to stay dry-eyed through "The Last Post," the British military dirge as mournful as "Taps."

Funeral detail brought with it a day off, and Lange telephoned Mackie to see if she could meet him in London. They had a regular hotel, The Whitehorse, a few blocks from Victoria Station. They'd found the hotel one night back in the spring when they were tired of taking in the town and feeling lusty. The Whitehorse was clean, but mainly it was cheap, since after paying his mess bill and tipping Pickens, he was always close to broke. There was a little pub in the basement—handy for air raids—and an ungodly number of stairs to climb to get to number seventeen, one of the least expensive rooms at the top where they could look out the narrow windows and watch when the bombs fall across town.

The first time they came to The Whitehorse, the only rooms available had been on the top floor. The landlady, Mrs. Ingersoll, was reluctant to rent them since the top floor was exposed to bombs, but Mackie made up lie on the spot about them having just the one day and nowhere else to go, and the woman had capitulated. Mackie signed them in as Mr. and Mrs. Rushford, and that was the way they had signed in every time since.

Number seventeen had everything they needed—an ashtray, a couple of glasses for the scotch in Mackie's silver flask, W/C down the hall that was all theirs since they had the whole top floor to themselves. There was a washbasin in the corner, white sheets, dark brown dresser with a broken latch, their own refuge from the world, where they could hole up and make love all night.

She was easy company, Mackie. She laughed a lot, and it didn't hurt that she had that big pair of sparkling blue eyes, or those legs, that sexy swish in her walk.

If she got there first, she would wait for him in the basement pub. Other times, when he arrived first, he would pace with a cigarette out on the walk in front of the hotel. If she arrived by train, he would be there to meet her as soon as she turned the corner from the station. If she came in the little green Morris, he would hop in and help her find a parking slot. But either way as soon as she was there he found that his mood lifted instantly.

The day of funeral detail, she beat him to the hotel and was already down in the pub on a stool at the bar, with a captain in Royal Army green leaning next to her. She had a smile on her face that caused a stab of annoyance to shoot through Lange.

"Saved by the RAF," she said, as he walked up.

The army captain had clearly been drinking a while. He wobbled and held onto the bar.

"Is this fellow pestering you?" Lange wedged himself between her and the captain and took her arm.

The army captain mumbled something, cursed at the RAF for stranding the boys back at Dunkirk. Mackie rolled her eyes and slid off her stool.

A hand clamped down on Lange's shoulder. "I say, old chum, I caught this bird before you did. Piss off."

Lange shrugged out of the captain's grip. "You can see she was waiting for me," he said, trying to sound cheerful.

"He's feeling no pain," Mackie said, half mouthing the words.

The hand clamped again on Lange's shoulder, harder this time. The captain slurred, "You glory boys can't have all the girls. This one's mine."

Lange turned to stare into the captain's face. He had a wide gap between his front two teeth. Lange thought he might like to make that gap wider. "Take your hand off me, and if you do that again I'll cold-cock you."

"You just try that, you goddamned Yank," the captain snarled and puffed out his chest.

"He's drunk, Lange. Come on." Mackie tugged at Lange's arm.

When the idiot grabbed at Mackie, Lange's ears started to ring. He clutched a fistful of the captain's tunic, backed him into the bar.

"Take it outside, boys," the barkeep said.

"All right, you sonofabitch...." Lange shoved the man towards the door. A table skidded out of the way. Lange turned the captain around and kept shoving him in the back, thinking that he would march the guy out of the pub before any real harm was done.

"Let it go, Lange," Mackie said behind him. "He's just drunk."

As soon as they stepped through the door, the captain dodged out of Lange's grasp and sucker-punched him on the side of his head. He wore a finger ring that cut Lange's cheekbone.

"Goddammit!" Lange charged him, gave the captain a quick left-right to the gut that doubled him over. Before he could recover from that, Lange threw a left upper cut to the captain's jaw. The fellow staggered back, and Lange started to go at him again, but Mackie had followed them outside. She grabbed at Lange's elbow.

"Stop it! Stop it this minute!" she said. "What are you doing? Lange?"

His fists relaxed. He straightened but kept his eyes on the captain, who righted himself, pulled down on the hem of his tunic. He bent to swipe his cap up off the pavement. He looked dazed, spat out some curses, and headed off down the street.

"What was that all about?" Mackie said, watching him go.

The astonishment on her face registered with Lange. He felt a little astonished himself and shaken. "He was a smart ass," he mumbled.

"He was drunk."

"Why were you talking to him anyway?"

"There was nothing to it. Let's go upstairs. I have the room key."

When they got to the room, he loosened his tie and sat down on the bed. He was still rattled and over-stimulated. His cheek throbbed. He hadn't resorted to fisticuffs since grade school. The anger had washed over him like a case of hives. He rubbed his knuckles; they felt bruised. Sonofabitch had it coming.

Mackie poured an inch of scotch into a glass and handed it to him. He took it. She automatically clinked her glass to his, the way they usually did, but he didn't feel much like toasting. He took a long, settling drink.

"I thought you were my girl." He wiped his mouth.

"I am. You know that." She kicked off her shoes, pulled her tunic off, too. She dipped a corner of her handkerchief into her glass.

"Then why were you flirting with that sonofabitch?" he said.

"I wasn't flirting. He came over and started talking to me."

"You were smiling at him."

"No, I wasn't. He was drunk. That's all." She sat down on the bed and reached with her handkerchief to dab some blood off his cheekbone. He flinched. The place felt touchy. The scotch on the corner of her handkerchief burned.

"Who else are you seeing?" He didn't even know why he said it, it just came out. But as soon as it did, he realized he wanted the answer.

"What? Why are you acting like this?"

He moved her hand away from his cheek. "I don't want to share, that's all. And I won't be made a fool of either."

"Nobody's going to make you a fool. What's wrong, darling? Was it a friend you buried today, someone you knew well?"

"I didn't know him at all."

She took his glass, set it on the dressing table, then straddled his lap. She kissed his forehead, his lips, and started unknotting his tie. He pulled her against him, kissed her neck, sank his nose in the perfume behind her ear.

Making love was the healing balm, like putting horse liniment on sore muscles. Afterwards, naked and under the covers, they shared a cigarette. The earlier tension was gone. She talked about Given having trouble with a bully at school. Adam thought the kid needed boxing lessons. Now, she teased, maybe Lange should be the one to give the boy those lessons. "I had no idea you were such a brute." That coaxed a chuckle out of him. And then she told him about Phyllis, who had a new fellow. "Surprising since she's been so notoriously anti-man." Mackie went on to tell him about the airdrome at Wentworth getting bombed last week. Luckily, she had gone off on a delivery, an Anson Tutor she had taken up to OTU, so she wasn't there.

She was always talkative after lovemaking. He liked the sound of her voice. As he listened, his eyes followed the gas line that ran along the edge of the ceiling. It turned a corner above the bed and piped down to the radiation heater they had to feed with coins to keep the room warm. Sixpence for an hour. With the sun on the descent the room had already started to chill.

His mind drifted to another time—San Antonio. Downtown on one of Sterling's errands, making a bank deposit, then on to meet Becky for lunch. He saw her through the drugstore window, sitting at the soda counter, face to face with some stranger, heads bent together, talking privately. When the soda jerk brought their Cokes, the stranger paid. Becky took a sip through her straw. The stranger moved back her hair, hooked it behind her ear, lingered a little too long, too familiar. The sight kicked Lange in the gut. He turned and walked away—walked away before he saw more. She never asked him why he missed their lunch date, and he never mentioned it either. *Because he didn't want to know.* So he could keep on lying to himself, pretending nothing was wrong.

The memory tangled a knot in his throat. Absently, he pulled Mackie tighter, grazed his lips along her hairline. "I was married," he said softly, against her temple.

Her conversation stopped. He felt her body stiffen. She rose from his arms.

"You're married?"

"I was."

"Was? Or are?" Her voice had gone higher-pitched.

"She was killed in a car wreck."

Mackie stared at him. Her mouth dropped open, just a little, enough he could see her sorting through his words. He didn't want there to be any pity in that stare.

"Stop looking at me like that," he said. "It wasn't how you think. We had already split up."

"No...I just..." She fell back on the pillows to stare at the ceiling instead, the same way he had been a few moments ago. "I can't believe you're just now telling me this?"

"I didn't want to talk about it." His throat felt dry. He swallowed. "I still don't."

"When did all this happen?"

"Before."

Silence settled between them. She sat up on her knees, pulled the covers around her shoulders. She looked at him, waiting for him to go on. He didn't. "Am I allowed to ask questions?"

He searched her face, saw her confusion. He didn't want to spill out all the gory details, maybe spoil what they had. He'd already said too much. More than he ever meant to.

Traffic noise came faintly from outside. One of them was going to have to get up, close the blackouts, feed the heater. For a moment, he felt paralyzed. The silence continued, threatened to grow.

Finally, he threw back the covers. "Let's go find something to eat," he said, springing out of the bed. "Maybe a nice steak at Carlinder's."

She stayed still. He felt her eyes follow him as he went to shut the curtains.

"Come on," he said, buttoning his pants. "Get dressed. I think I could eat a horse."

"Lange?" She tilted her head at him.

"Just get dressed, Mackie. Let's go have a nice supper."

THERE WAS NO MOON, sky as black as coyote scat. They ate a steak at Carlinder's, even danced to a couple of songs the band played, but it was hard to retrieve the old lightheartedness. Walking back to the hotel in the blackout, he stepped off an unseen curb and cracked his eyebrow on a crossing stanchion. She fussed over him, completely bloodied her little lacy handkerchief. Back at number seventeen, she scrubbed the blood out of his tunic. She had some headache tablets in her bag and he washed them down with the scotch. She thought he should go have stitches. He wished like hell he could go back a few hours and start this day over again.

The next morning, he woke with a cracking headache. He had a black eye, either from the army captain or the traffic stanchion, he wasn't sure which. Mackie was in a hurry to leave, had to get back to her ferry pool. They skipped breakfast, said a quick goodbye at Victoria station.

When he got back to the airdrome, he took some ribbing from the fellows about his banged-up face. They said things like how he should try sleeping with a woman instead of a gorilla for a change or that he ought to think about selling ringside tickets next time. Morse inspected the black eye and grounded him. "Precaution. In case your sight's been affected." Lange knew his sight hadn't been affected, but each day the bruise seemed to darken and spread until it made a semicircle under his left eye that curved up over the bridge of his nose. There was also a little bulbous knot on his brow where the stanchion had made contact. In a couple of days, the knot went down, but the bruise began to turn colors—blue to green to black and several shades in between—before it, too, started to fade.

Over the next two weeks, even after he was back on duty, up on patrol, or out on cockpit alert, he found himself thinking about Mackie—hearing her laughter, some witty something she'd said, the way she had looked at him when he told her about Becky. He thought there was a pretty good chance she might not want to see him again, and the more he thought about it, the more he knew he didn't want to lose her.

He tried to call her on the mess phone. He gave the station operator the number, listened to that fast, double, English ring. He imagined the telephone in the little cottage, sitting in the alcove in the hallway, Mackie racing to answer. But it rang on and on, so he finally hung up.

It was complicated, all this love and romance stuff. And how did you know anyway if what you felt was love? With Becky, it had been so instant, all mixed up with lust and the age he'd been. With Mackie it was more comfortable than that, more gradual. Maybe he only liked her a hell of a lot, he didn't know. She made him feel good, like he mattered, like he was the most important person in the room.

The first time his call went through, he got the roommate. Phyllis told him that Mackie was working, held up by bad weather at Kinloss. Disappointment followed him for the next couple of days.

Jerry came over one night, and as soon as the ack-ack guns went into action, everybody ran for the shelter. Once the raid stopped, the station commander gave anybody who wasn't already busy, a shovel to help fill the craters in the runways. Lange felt like he was back home mucking stalls for Gabe. The big gun, Delores, had bagged a Dornier. It went down in a field five miles away. Some of the fellows took a staff car and came back with the swastika off one of the fins. The metal shears they used left sharp edges, but they nailed it to the wall in the Mess bar.

The third time Lange telephoned Mackie, nobody answered at the cottage, so he asked the operator to connect him to the ATA pool at Wentworth. After getting handed around three times, Adam MacLeod finally came on the line. "She's gone to Colesbury," he said. "You can telephone her there."

They talked a little about all the recent bombing activity, small talk. When Adam gave Lange the number, he penned it on the back of his right hand. As soon as he hung up, second thoughts crept in, so he let one of the other fellows have the phone.

He didn't really have anything to say to her, no news, no leave, no real excuse for a phone call. He just needed to hear her voice, to make sure nothing had changed between them, and he wasn't even sure he would know just by talking to her on the phone. So he joined Tippy and Morse in the bar and had a beer. Drank that one pretty fast and had another. They played a round of snooker, drank another round of beer. He kept glancing at the number written on his hand. Pretty soon one of digits had smeared. If he was going to make that call, he decided he better do it before he sweated the whole thing away.

Mr. Bailey answered. Lange thought about hanging up right then and there, and if he hadn't already spoken to Adam earlier, he might have. But Mackie was bound to find out he had called, so he went ahead and asked, hesitantly, for her. Mr. Bailey's starched voice said, "I believe Miss Allison may have retired for the evening."

Lange checked his watch. Eleven-thirty. He hadn't realized it was so late. Noise from the anteroom came down the corridor. The fellows were still horsing around, getting loud and rowdy. "Tell her...just tell her I called—"

"Lange?" Her voice came in his ear. "Lange, what is it?" She sounded sleepy—and alarmed. He hadn't meant to alarm her.

"Nothing. I didn't realize it was so late."

"Are you all right? Where are you?"

"Down in the anteroom. It's loud in here." He scanned his mind for something to say. This had been a mistake. "We had an air raid," he told her. "The gunners got a DO-Seventeen."

She was quiet for a second. "And you're OK?"

"Yeah. Oh yeah." He closed his eyes, imagined her face: little freckles across her nose, clear pale skin. "I should have a forty-eight in a few days," he said.

"I don't know if I can get loose. I'm on leave right now."

"Try, baby." He heard the crack in his voice, and thought he was finally losing it. There was a long pause.

"Are you drinking?"

"Not much." He had an urge to say something else, but he couldn't form the words. "Tell Given hello."

"Are you sure you're all right, Lange?"

"Yeah, yeah. I just wanted...I didn't realize it was so late."

"Get some sleep, darling."

"Good idea." There was a prolonged silence. He thought the line had gone dead. "Mackie?"

"I'm here. What is it?"

"Nothing. OK. See you soon."

"I'll do what I can about getting leave."

He pinched the bridge of his nose. "You're still my girl, right?"

"Lange? Has something happened?"

"No. Everything's OK. I just wanted—" He grimaced. "Don't give up on me."

"What are you talking about? That never crossed my mind."

"OK then. All right. Good night."

"Good night, darling. Sweet dreams."

He hung up.

What in the hell was all that all about? She must think he was off his beam, or drunk, calling so late and without a damned thing to say. And he almost made some grand declaration—almost. Came within an inch of it. A lot of people threw words around easily, but he had never been one of them.

"Enough of that nonsense," he said, sounding like Morse. Last thing he needed was a pair of baby blue eyes in his mind all the time. "Jesus Christ, get ahold of yourself," he muttered, as he took himself up to his room and to bed.

DURING THE NIGHT Pickens shook him awake. "You're wanted downstairs, sir. In the Mess Manager's office."

"What?" Lange bolted upright. "What time is it?"

"I'm afraid it's two a.m."

Lange jumped up. His first thought was Mackie, thinking she must've tried to return his call, to find out why in hell he had called her for no reason. He almost went out the door in his pajamas, strictly against mess rules, but Pickens had his shirt and trousers already out of the closet. He got dressed quickly.

A fellow from one of the other squadrons sat at the desk, manning the Mess Manager's post, a South African fellow named Vandusen.

Vandusen picked up the black telephone on the desk, spoke, then covered the mouthpiece. "It's the cable office," he said, holding out the phone for Lange to take.

"Flying Officer DeLony?" the WAAF on the line said. "You have an overseas cable here. Should I send a courier with it or shall I read it to you?"

"Go ahead and read it." His heart started to thump.

"All right. It's come from Texas. Signed by—it says Aunt Dellie?" The WAAF hesitated, then in a strong reading voice, "'Your papa has had another stroke. He is in Austin hospital. Critical condition. If possible, come home right away.'"

Lange's throat closed. He swallowed hard. "Thank you," he said to the WAAF.

"You're welcome, sir."

He handed the phone back to Vandusen, but that was the last deliberate thing he remembered doing that night.

PART THREE

Family

NOVEMBER 1941

CHAPTER 15

"*Stroked*"

Dellie nervoused around the house, checking on her big supper a dozen times, a feast. Dane could tell from the heavy smells that came from the kitchen and from how long she had been in there—since noon. Dellie had never been much of a cook. When she still had a husband taking care of her, she always had household help, some woman from town, a Bohemian or a Pole, who could wield a frying pan the way a good farmer wields a plow. Since the Depression struck, Dellie had made do with a pile of cooking books, and since June, with her new Chambers range.

Gabe'd had good luck with his calves this year, raked it in at auction. Cattle hadn't brought ten dollars per hundredweight since the Twenties, and the first thing Gabe did with all that money was buy his mama that Chambers. Had it freighted in from Austin. The day it arrived, Dellie said everybody at the depot admired it and stood around watching as Gabe and his cowhands unloaded it from the flat car. It had taken them half an hour just to get the thing up the back-porch steps and installed in the kitchen. Ever since then Dellie had been using them all—Dane, Gabe, and all his hands—as her guinea pigs, fixing suppers that sometimes weren't even edible. Occasionally when she wasn't paying attention, Gabe's camp cook, old Cipriano, would sneak some stew or red-hot chili in for Dane. Just thinking about Cipriano's chili made Dane's mouth start to drool.

The next time Dellie came through the front room she had a smudge of flour on her cheek. She had it all over her apron, too, and seemed unaware of it. She grabbed the cup towel on the table beside Dane's chair and wiped his mouth. He smelled the rose water on her wrist. The broach Ding had sent her from England last Christmas was pinned to her collar, a set of pilot's wings that matched the pair he wore in the picture in the walnut frame on the mantelpiece. She laid the cup towel back down, then went over to the front window, fingered back the curtains. Sunlight slanted down on her face, illuminated the cross-pattern of wrinkles on her cheeks—baby sister. He could remember the day she was born. Where had all the years gone? Nobody had warned him they would rush by so fast.

Dane sat slumped in the wheelchair and watched her through hooded eyes. His mouth hung slack, but his mind wasn't gone, just a bit addled. That last spell had been a whopper, left him half-dead again—over half—and before it happened he had nearly gotten back the full use of both his hands. Not anymore. This one had come on all of a sudden, on his way down to the creek. October was a fine month for crappie. Eyes failed him. Balance failed him. Next thing, he was on the ground. The whole memory of it was hazy.

Dellie came back over to where he sat and bent down to look in his face. He knew what she was seeing. He'd caught his own reflection in the hall-tree mirror. Was not a pretty thing to behold. Drooping jowls, sallow flesh, one eye bulging out, mouth wizened up. Overnight he had turned into a wrinkled up old wreck of a man.

"Maybe we should put you on a bow tie," she said. "What do you think? It's a special day after all. You want to get a little dandied up for it?"

He stared at her.

She went to the sofa table, got the scrapbook she'd been keeping, and brought it back. "Here. You look at this while I go find a tie for you to wear." She balanced the scrapbook across his knees, open to the page with the latest clippings. Dane's eyes bobbled down to look at it.

There was Ding in his fancy uniform, didn't even look like himself. "Hometown Hero" the headline read. Dellie was constantly sending the Bastrop paper news of Ding. Dane couldn't focus on it. The words jumped up and down. Sometimes things changed colors on him. Other times he had specters running across his eyes—once a little black mouse, but more often a moth fluttered around the edge of his vision.

"Flying Officer DeLony Speaks On Radio." A picture of Ding inside an airplane; this one clipped from *LIFE Magazine*. He wore a leather helmet like he was about to go out for a touchdown pass—save for those goggles raised round his forehead like a second set of eyes. One time, Dane had caught a catfish with a third eye. Some kind of deformity, he reckoned, caused when the creek flooded all the pastureland. Later, once the flood waters receded, cow dung had clabbered the creek.

Another clipping came unstuck and fluttered down on the floor beside the big wheel of Dane's chair. He tried to lean for it, but it was no use. He peered over the arm at it down there. Another picture of Ding, this time full-length in his flying get-up. Looked like an overstuffed scarecrow with rain boots on his feet. Damned cigarette in his hand, halfhearted grin on his face. Couple of other boys standing with him. Cigarettes dangling off them, too— scrawny, frosty-looking foreign boys. You would think all those boys had to do was pose for the camera and smoke.

In a little while, Dellie came clunking down the stairs. She had on her church shoes, and they made an awful racket. He wondered if she realized how loud they sounded. She bent down to retrieve the fallen clipping, stuck it in the crease of the scrapbook. The tie she'd picked out for him had to be the worst one in his drawer. A loud yellow thing with blue stripes. He didn't recall it, thought she might have given it to him for a birthday one year. It fit so tight it choked off all his air. His mouth fell open, gasping.

"They should be here by now." Dellie loosened the tie a notch. "I hope the train wasn't delayed. I thought I heard it while ago, didn't you?" She peered directly into his face. "One is yes. Two is no. Remember what the nurse told us?"

He blinked twice, humiliated by having to answer with his eyelids. What would happen when those went, too? He imagined his eyeballs would dry up and he'd go blind. He wished somebody would put a gun to his head. No, he took that back. His own papa had done that, found out he had the cancer and blew his brains out. Chickenshit bastard.

"There now. How does that feel? Looks real nice. Yellow has always been your best color, brother." She admired him for a second or two. He wished she wouldn't be so cheery. She drove him plumb crazy with her constant cheeriness.

She bustled over to the window and pulled back the curtain again. From that window you could see a far piece down the road. He wondered if Gabe had got around to clearing his fences yet. It had been a wet summer, and last time Dane saw the fences on the road, they were covered with rose hedge and bindweed. Would make for good bird hunting but the cost came in poor road visibility. Gave coyotes a place to hide, too. When they were hungry, coyotes could take care of your calves in a heartbeat. Wreak havoc on Dellie's chickens, too.

Dane could feel drool rolling down his chin again. Nothing he could do but let it roll. Pretty soon it would be all over the clean tie. He tried to say something. He sounded like a grunting monkey. It got Dellie's attention, though. She hurried from the window over to his chair.

"Oh dear." She dabbed at his slack mouth with the cup towel.

"Here. See if you can hold onto this." She fingered the towel into the claw that was his hand. "I bet you can if you try hard enough, and then maybe you can raise it to your mouth on your own."

He just stared at her. If he was going to try dabbing spit from his mouth he'd do it without her scrutiny. She put her hands on her hips and frowned at him.

"You old goat, I don't know why you're acting so hateful today. Your son's coming here to see you. I hope you understand it hasn't been easy on him getting here. He had to come clear across the Atlantic Ocean, dodging those German U-boats and who knows what all else." She went back to her vigil at the window. "Don't forget, he's a war hero, now. The *Advertiser* says he left England with three victories against the Germans. Now, what did I do with that paper?" She juned through a stack of magazines and papers on top of the piano nobody knew how to play. Only thing that piano was good for was as a catchall. She gave up on her search, went back to worry the window. "I wonder what could be keeping them? I'm sure that was the train while ago. Didn't you hear it?"

No, he hadn't heard it. He had enough trouble focusing his mind on swallowing his own spit, let alone listening for trains. The scrapbook started to slide towards his knees.

Dellie backed away from the window. "I suppose that means he's killed some folks. I hate looking at it that way, but I suppose that's what they mean when they say *victories*. I have a hard time imagining our Ding...well....But the Germans did start it after all. Seems like they're always starting it over there." She fanned at her face. "I sure wish they would hurry. Supper's going to be bone cold."

She scampered off towards the kitchen as if her thoughts had reminded her of the meal cooking. He heard some pans banging, the squawk of the oven door opening, slamming shut again. Drool rolled from the corner of his mouth. His fingers closed on the handkerchief, but he couldn't get the damn thing to go up to his mouth.

It quivered up about two inches, no more. The scrapbook slid off his lap and hit the floor. Clippings scattered all over the damned place.

A moment later he heard Gabe's pickup popping over the new gravel the county had spread outside on the road. Dane's eyes shifted to the front door. Too late. All he saw through the screen was a swirl of dust. And then Dellie came running in from the kitchen.

"Is that them?" She jounced into the room, straining to look out the windows. She tripped on the scrapbook, bent to scrape it all together in a heap she shifted over to the sofa table. Outside two car doors slammed, one after the other.

"Lord." She yanked the apron off over her head, wadded it up, and stuffed in under a sofa cushion. She grabbed her Brownie box camera off the top of the piano, hurried to Dane's chair, and started wheeling him towards the front door, even though it would be unlike Ding, or Gabe either one, to come in the front way. She dropped her Brownie camera on his lap, and he managed to clutch at it with his hand-claw and the cup towel. The wheels of the chair balked at having to roll over the high pile throw rug. She shoved and tugged.

"Where y'all at?" Gabe's voice came from the kitchen way. Sure enough, they had come in the back door.

"In here," Dellie hollered. "Oh..." She manhandled the chair around to face in the opposite direction she had been trying for just as Gabe stepped into view, carrying a thick white duffle bag.

"Well, I got him," he said, and then Ding came grinning out from around Gabe. He had on a dark suit, cut in an odd way at the waist and with more lapel on it than fellows around here wore. He was mean-skinny, must've lost twenty pounds.

Dellie left the chair and ran over to hug Ding. They gripped each other tight. Gabe flopped the duffel bag on the floor beside the wheelchair. The bag was stuffed so full it looked like a boxing dummy. *F/O C.L. DELONY* was stenciled on the canvas.

"Hello, old man," Gabe said to Dane. "She been bossing you around all evening? Sorry it took us so long. There was newspaper reporters and camera men, and I don't know what all at the station. They been hounding poor Ding since he landed in New York City. Half the town showed up to welcome him home."

Don't he look skinny? Dane wanted to say it but he couldn't make a sound. He willed his shaking claw-hand to raise, with a little nudging help from Gabe, to dab his mouth with the cup towel. Didn't want to be drooling spit in front of his only son. *The war hero.* Gabe caught the Brownie before it bounced off on the floor. He set the camera on Dane's table.

There was a smaller bag made of leather slung over Ding's shoulder. Looked like he had come to stay a while. Dellie was battling tears and losing. "I thought he'd be wearing his uniform," she said, loud. She swiped at her cheeks. "I wanted to make a picture of him in his uniform."

"It's against the law for him to wear it in this country, Mom," Gabe said. Apparently, he'd already learned this information for himself.

Ding said, "It sure feels funny being out of it, though, I'll tell you that."

And then he looked at Dane. He dropped the dark shoulder bag on the floor next to the white duffel bag, leaned on both the arms of the wheelchair. It tried to roll but Ding steadied it, then squatted down on his haunches.

"What the hell did you do to yourself this time, Papa?" After a second, he leaned forward and planted a kiss on Dane's forehead.

The kiss shocked Dane to the core. For one thing, it wasn't natural for one man to kiss another, not even a son and a father; for another, Ding never had done that before. And his voice didn't sound right either. He was stretching out words in a way he didn't used to do, clipping off others kindly short. He had a grease-pencil thin mustache above his lip, hair grown long and combed straight back off his forehead, wearing that peculiar suit with those wide lapels, carrying a sissy little shoulder pouch to boot. They'd turned him into a Limey, that's what they'd done. His son had become a goddammed Limey.

CHAPTER 16

"Compassionate Leave"

"He scared the hell out of us," Gabe said. "Out of me anyway." In the halo of light coming from inside the house, Gabe's face looked lined and worn, more worn than Lange remembered. "When I came upon him lying there...."

Gabe stopped and sucked at his teeth. It was a habit he had always had, when he was thinking on something. When Lange was little, he'd tried to copy that teeth-sucking thing. Also, spitting. Back then, he had idolized Gabe. Gabe had taught him to rope a horse, throw a calf, wrestle a steer, to smoke, to cuss, and a lot of other things.

"He was a sorry sight," Gabe went on, "I'll tell you that for sure."

Lange pushed his empty juice glass towards Gabe for a refill. Good old Kentucky Tavern; it sure went down smooth, especially compared to all the scotch he'd been drinking for the past year. Gabe refilled his own glass, too. A little bit of whiskey sloshed out. He licked his thumb and sopped up the spill. They were sitting on the back-porch steps. Crickets throbbed in the darkness.

"Heaved him up over Wahoo's back," Gabe continued. "Carried him that away to the house. Had a time of it. They sent an ambulance from Bastrop. Took him from there to Austin. And of course, Mom went with him. She stayed up at the hospital day and night. Till I finally got her a room at the Driskill so she'd rest. We'd just brought him home the day before you called from New York." Gabe raised his glass, bumped it against Lange's, then drained it in one gulp. Lange knocked back the contents of his glass, too.

The whiskey had already started a rosy glow. He was glad. It helped chase away the old ghosts threatening to haunt him again. Hard to see Papa all bent and withered in that wheelchair, drooling out one side of his mouth. Aunt Dellie had arranged her sewing room as a bedroom for Papa, so he could be downstairs, now. Lange had carried him in there to bed, carried him like a baby and tucked him in like one, too. He knew it galled Papa, he could feel it in the stiffness in Papa's spine. He thought about how much Papa always hated to get sick, never trusted hospitals and doctors, said doctors were no better than horse thieves and lawyers.

Lange reached into his pocket for his cigarette case, flipped it open, took out one. He'd already filled it up with Luckies, did that at a New Jersey newsstand. They were the first thing he'd wanted when he hit American soil; second thing was a hamburger.

The cigarette case made him think of Mackie. He hadn't had a chance to say goodbye to her or even tell her he was leaving. As soon as Morse had come through with compassionate leave, Lange had hopped on the first ship that gave him a berth.

"Let me see that thing." Gabe grabbed the cigarette case, turned it over, ran his finger along the bronzed edges. He let out an admiring whistle, pressed the latch, took out a Lucky and gave Lange a sideways grin. "I bet you get laid every goddammed night. Don't you?"

Lange muffled a laugh. Better subject. Eased the ghosts. He tucked the case back into his shirt pocket. "I do all right. How bout you? Still seeing Miss Chase?"

"When the occasion arises." Gabe struck a stick match on the heel of his boot. He held the match cupped in his hand, lit his cigarette and reached to light Lange's. "Which ain't nearly often enough."

Lange stuck the end of his cigarette into the flame, pulled it to life, blew out a stream of smoke. "She still got all those cats?"

Gabe choked on laughter, coughed out the smoke in his mouth. "Which kind of pussy cat do you mean? The feline variety or the female?"

"Either." Lange laughed, too. "Or both."

Gabe grabbed the bottle of Kentucky Tavern by its neck and poured more whiskey into Lange's glass, topped off his own. "Oh yeah. She's still keeping the cathouse, both kinds. Yessir, she sure is. Got a couple of hootchy-kootchy dancers, now, too." He set the bottle on the step between them. "Why? You think you might want to go over there while you're here?"

Lange shrugged, then he shook his head. Last time he'd paid a whore he'd been all of sixteen, as horny and awkward as a young buck, with a hard-earned five-dollar bill in his pocket. The idea of it now didn't do much for him.

He tugged at his collar, drank down the whiskey. Compared to England, the weather was warm and mild. Mid-November night— soft breeze, great big sky loaded with stars. He took a deep draw on the cigarette, leaned back against the next step up. This was how he remembered it, what he had been homesick for, but now that he was here he felt like a completely different person. Suddenly, memories were lurking too close again, creeping up on him—Becky, Papa, the little kid he'd once been, lonely and scared all the time. Of what, he didn't know now. He tried to shake off the strange feelings, stretched out his legs on the steps below, pointed up at the sky.

"Now, that's what I call a sight." He drew his finger around Cassiopeia, then Orion and the Great Square of Pegasus. "The sky never looks like this in England."

Gabe looked up, too. "Black as a bull's ass, ain't it?" He flipped his cigarette out into the yard. Sparks scattered like fireflies. "Rained the whole goddamned time I was in Europe. Used to worry about my toes webbing up. Everywhere was just godforsaken mud. Sticky, rotten mud you couldn't scrap off. Nothing worse than French mud."

"Except English mud," Lange said.

They laughed and passed the bottle again. The whiskey was quickly going to Lange's head, which was just where he wanted it. He took another deep drink.

"How the hell do all those people put up with the rain and foul weather?" Gabe finished off his glass, wiped his mouth on his sleeve. "Letty liked the heat. I expected her to bitch about it when she got here, but she never did. She always said she liked being warm to the bone."

"Letty never bitched, period," Lange said.

"Nope. She surely did not."

Letty was Gabe's war bride. He'd brought her home from France. She had been kind of pretty but mainly so sweet and soft-spoken that everybody loved her right away. She died in childbirth, along with the baby she'd been trying to give to Gabe.

Lange reached for the bottle. He didn't want to think about dead wives. And he didn't like the melancholy tone he was hearing in Gabe's voice either. Lange wanted to get drunk, howl-at-the-moon, dance-on-a-table-top drunk. He wanted to forget about Papa, shrunken-up and beaten in that wheelchair.

"I met a woman over there." Lange decided to just swig from the lip of the bottle. To hell with those little juice glasses. "She's the one gave me that cigarette case. Said it was for good luck. So far it's worked pretty good."

"Damn you, you little pissant. Give me that bottle before you drink it all." Gabe swiped the whiskey away from Lange's hand, made a big show of wiping off the opening, used his finger and his shirttail, running it down inside after cooties. Then with a sly grin, he took a direct swig from it himself.

"What kind of woman is she?" Gabe said.

"Regular kind," Lange answered. "Two of everything."

That struck Gabe funny again, and he spewed the swig he'd just taken. Lange laughed, too, which kept Gabe's laughter going on longer. Soon they began to get downright silly, laughing over nothing, going past the buzz and descending into real inebriation. Much better than melancholy, better than remorse. Lange didn't really want to talk about Mackie. He had mentioned her to change the subject, and it worked. Gabe upended the bottle into his mouth. A few more big swigs like that, and he'd be ready to howl at the moon, too.

By the time the bottle was empty, Gabe had decided a visit to Miss Chase was long overdue and a damned good idea, and he didn't care to hear any objections from Lange. After that, things began to blur one into the other: An argument over who should drive the pickup truck, which ended in the decision to ride horseback instead. Then trouble with getting two unhappy, rudely awakened horses caught and tacked up. Lange hoisted himself into the saddle all right but was grateful for the horn to grasp hold of and balance himself. He didn't know which horse he was astride, thought it was a bay named Daisy, but he'd been gone a while and Gabe surely did have some new horses. Lange glanced over in time to see Gabe fall all the way over and off his horse, Wahoo. Gabe landed so hard and lay there so long, that Lange finally quit laughing and got down to check for injuries. The horses both made a quick exit out the rear door of the barn and back into their starlit pasture.

"Ribs gouging you anyplace?" Lange said.

Gabe pushed himself up to a sitting position. "If they are I can't feel them." He took the hand Lange offered, rose shakily to his feet, dusted himself off. He said, "I believe I'll just head on to bed, if it's all the same to you."

"Suits me, too," Lange said.

"We'll get them damned horses unsaddled in the morning."

They limped and staggered their way back to the house, held

onto each other to keep their course steady, and parted company at the upstairs hallway.

"Good having you home, little pardner," Gabe mumbled, before he disappeared into his room.

Even with the whiskey swirling through his veins and the room spinning, Lange stayed wide awake. Bed was too soft, the room too bright without blackouts over the windows to block the starlight. And it was too quiet. He'd gotten used to ack-ack guns rattling on all night, airplanes taking off and landing. The drone of crickets, the whine of peace and silence, kept him tossing till daybreak.

AFTER BREAKFAST, despite a roaring hangover, Lange carried Papa out to the fishing hole. Papa's gear was all still there, straight chair, fishing rod, worm can, tackle box. He sat Papa down in the chair. Two weary eyes started shining, went to flitting around. Lange squatted down in front of him.

"You sit tight, Papa," he said, as if the old man could get up and walk off. "I'm going to find us some crickets, and we'll see if we can't catch us some perch. All right?"

Papa's eyes came around to rest on Lange. There was a troubling ache in those eyes, or maybe, Lange thought, he was reading in something that wasn't there. He thought about the letter he'd had from Julianne saying Papa had been suffering confusion about Sunny's kids, had the idea Lange had gone over to France to look for them and bring them home to Texas. He wondered if he ought to bring up the subject, if that could be what was worrying Papa or if bringing it up would only torment him more.

Finding a few crickets should've been easy enough, seeing as how they'd kept Lange awake all night, but they didn't seem in such abundance in the light of day. Finally, underneath a fallen willow log right beside the bank, Lange hit pay dirt. He baited a cricket onto Papa's hook, threw the line out, and wedged the pole in Papa's hands. There was a little bit of a grip there, in those old curled fingers. Papa knew what was happening, Lange was sure of it. He knew they were fishing, and that Lange was there with him.

The sun rose higher in the sky. Lange sat on the bank and carried on a one-sided conversation. Aunt Dellie had said Papa understood every word, so Lange told him things about the past year in England, about Lord Haw-Haw, the traitor Englishman who broadcast on German radio, how he seemed to know everything about the RAF even before the pilots did, and how they laughed and made fun of him. He talked about high altitude flying, how unstable the air felt above 30,000 feet, like you might just fall right out of the sky, how the controls on the plane get sluggish and balky, and your voice comes out high-pitched and squeaky from the top of your throat. He told Papa about the weird beauty of making vapor trails, the stuff billowing out behind you like long, frothy cloud fingers, and going to the picture show, singing "God Save the King" after the movie ended, and about walking all through the Tower of London and hearing Big Ben toll, about double-decker buses and riding on the wrong side of the road.

Papa didn't catch any fish, but he seemed to enjoy being outside in his familiar spot. Anyway, his eyes shone a little clearer. So the next morning, Lange took Papa back to the creek again. This time Lange came prepared with worms he'd dug out of the mud inside the old spring house. He baited a worm three times around Papa's hook and sat on the bank to smoke. Papa held onto the fishing rod better than yesterday, and stared out at the water like he expected a fish to strike any minute.

Lange was tired, exhausted from tossing a second night in the soft, quiet bed. He needed a good, hard RAF mattress, besides which, he was having strange dreams. War dreams mixed up with being a little boy and with Mackie and London and flying out over the white chalk cliffs. It had taken sixteen days at sea, plus three more by train to get to Texas, and after just two nights in Aunt Dellie's house, he was already homesick for England. God help him, he even missed the war. He missed Mackie. He didn't want to admit it, had purposely been trying to ignore it, but there it was. She'd wedged herself good and deep under his skin. And he hadn't even told her he was leaving.

A few meditative minutes passed before he started up another one-sided conversation like he'd done yesterday, just to fill up the silence at first, but before he knew it he was talking about the war, telling Papa about shooting down Germans, recounting aerial battles he'd had, and about beating up train yards. He even found himself bragging about the day he'd led the whole squadron. He told about how he and Joe Sokol had blasted the JU-88 out of the sky, and he went so far as to recount almost word-for-word the radio interview the next day with the BBC, before the sickening realization came to him that he was trying his best to impress Papa. He didn't know why he was doing it, but he recognized it, and suddenly felt small and foolish—an eight-year-old boy back from his first dove hunt, begging Papa to notice all the birds he'd brought home in a tow sack, or flying his first solo, buzzing low over the pasture so Papa couldn't miss that it was him up there, flying by himself. Doing something grand and glorious. He remembered the shaking fist Papa held up at him that day. Not at all proud, just angry as hell that Old Bossy had been startled by the noise.

The sick feeling in his gut shut him up. He stared at the fishing line in the water, the little rippling circles growing outward from the cork, like a target, a bull's-eye, an RAF Roundel. Silently he questioned why he still felt the need to prove himself to Papa. A useless and asinine need. How much more did he have to accomplish before he could feel valuable, significant, respected? Why did approval have to come from someplace outside himself? And when, he wondered, would he ever get past all this senseless crap?

Papa's rod bent double and the cork disappeared underwater. Lange sprang up to haul the fish in, but Papa had already pulled back on the rod, just enough—it clearly took all his strength—to set the hook.

"That's it. That's right." Lange reached around Papa to steady the rod. "You got him, now."

He placed his hands around the two old, liver-spotted hands already grasping the rod with all their might. Undeniably Lange could feel some strength stirring through those hands, and it occurred to him, just for a brief second, that maybe Papa was trying to prove something, too.

"YOU BEING HERE IS SO good for him," Aunt Dellie said. She was fixing lunch—chopped ham sandwiches with dill pickles, tomatoes, and sliced onions. She had the radio on, turned low, but on as usual. "He enjoys you so much. Always has." She picked up a can of pork and beans. "Before this last spell, your name was on his lips an awful lot. 'Wonder what kind of supper Ding's sitting down to right now?' he'd say, or he'd wonder about the weather where you were. He pored over your letters and clippings."

Lange cracked a tray of ice cubes and chuckled to himself. There she went again, living in her fantasy land. She had always pretended the relationship between him and Papa was something it wasn't. Lange dropped the cubes into six glasses and watched her struggle to open that can of pork and beans. She was starting to get old, too. He took the can opener away from her, punched into the can lid, and started sawing around the rim.

"Over in England, they eat these things for breakfast," he said.

"Oh my." She pulled down a blue bowl from the overhead cabinet. "Things must be desperate."

"No. Well...yeah, they are sort of. But mostly I think they just like eating beans for breakfast." He dumped the beans into the blue bowl, shook out the four or five that stuck to the bottom. "The food over there's not like here. We eat pretty good at the Mess, compared to the civilians, but it's all just different."

Aunt Dellie poured tea into the glasses. She said, "I can fry up some potatoes real quick if you'd rather have them."

"That's OK." He gave her a kiss on top of her head. She was always thinking about others, always reading everybody's mind. Tending to everybody. He thought about what Pickens had said about women. He went to the sink to refill the empty ice tray, stuck it back into the little freezer section of the icebox.

Aunt Dellie cut a lemon into wedges. She met his eyes for a moment. "Gabriel says you have a girl over there."

Lange let the door to the icebox fall shut. Good old big-mouth Gabe, and dear, sweet, nosy Aunt Dellie. He thought about Mackie, tried to picture her standing here in this kitchen. The image wouldn't focus. "Well, she's thirty-two, if you want to call that a girl. She's a ferry pilot for the Air Transport Auxiliary."

Aunt Dellie placed lemons in a saucer. "What does a ferry pilot do?"

"She takes new planes from the factory to the airdromes. Or brings repaired ones back from the maintenance stations. The ATA pilots have to be able to fly anything, just by reading a book."

"Just by reading a book? Well, I'll be. She must be smart. How did you meet her?"

He thought about the day Mackie fell into his lap on the train, about drinking from the flask of scotch in her bag, sharing his great-coat on the bench at the depot...that first kiss, the unexpected roll in the sack. He should've known right then he'd get hooked on her.

Band music came on the radio, and the announcer introduced Glenn Miller's Orchestra. "Moonlight Serenade." Lange turned up the volume. "Care to dance," he said, holding out one hand to Aunt Dellie.

She laughed, wiped her hands in her apron. "I can't dance to this kind of music."

"Sure you can. Music's music."

He pulled her in his arms and she lifted her head, regal and proud. She had been the one to teach him how to dance, box step, but that was years ago and probably the last time they'd danced together. She felt awkward, a little clumsy, and kept tittering with embarrassed laughter, until they finally fell into step at the end of the number. When it was over, he bowed from the waist and kissed the back of her hand. Tears sprang to her eyes, and he hadn't meant to cause that reaction. She wiped them away with the hem of her apron.

"Why don't you come on home for good, Ding? Just stay now you're here. What's the worst they could do to you if you didn't go back?"

"I can't do that, Aunt Dellie. I've got to go back. I want to go back. I made a commitment. Not just in my head, but on paper, too." Jazzy music came on. He reached to turn the volume back down. "This is home. It always will be, and I love it here. I miss everybody, but there's things...I don't know...stuff—all kinds of stuff tied up with all this, and I don't have that over there."

He saw her face change, sadden. "What *stuff*?" She emphasized the word.

"You know. Me and Papa. Me and Becky. Just stuff."

He took one of the lemons off the saucer and squeezed it into a glass of iced tea. The lemon smell broke the air. Sweet, cold *American* tea. With lemon. His mouth salivated at the mere thought. He took a long swig, savored it, wallowed it around in his mouth. Aunt Dellie was watching. He smiled at her. "You have no idea how good that tastes."

She arranged the sandwiches, and the glasses around the table. "She's English? This girl?"

He decided he would just let her go ahead and use the word *girl*. It was easier. And he should've known she wouldn't drop the subject easily. "Canadian. She sounds kind of like she's from Boston or somewhere up north." He took a handful of forks out of the drawer.

"Well, it's no wonder you like her so much. If she flies airplanes and all, you must have the same outlook. I bet she's the real reason you want to go back."

The kitchen table was bathed in a flood of honeyed light from the windows. He started laying out the forks. He didn't want to say anything else. Let her think what she wanted to. Damn Gabe, repeating what had been said in confidence, not to mention drunken confidence. Talking about Mackie to anybody felt odd— and good—both at the same time. Maybe Aunt Dellie was right: maybe Mackie was part of the reason.

He looked out the window over the sink and saw Gabe coming up to the porch, followed by Shorty and Tom Brophy, his two most trusted cowhands, all of them stomping cow shit off their boots.

Lange went into the other room. Papa was asleep sitting up in his chair. For a second he looked dead, and Lange's heart went to his throat. But as soon as Lange reached to straighten him, his eyes fluttered open.

"Come on, old man." Lange gave Papa's shoulders a pat. "Let's go eat some ham sandwiches."

After lunch Lange went out and worked with Gabe, strung fence on one of the far pastures, rustled some loose cows. It had been a long time since he'd worked so hard. His hands blistered, even inside leather gloves. His back and legs ached, knees had strawberries from gripping the saddle. He cut his arm open when a length of barbed wire popped back on him. Gabe teased him about going soft.

Lange came in that evening sunburned, covered in dust and blood and cow piss, too exhausted for anything beyond a bath and bed. Aunt Dellie forced him to eat. She piled his plate with food and told him how much Gabe appreciated the help, while Papa slumped there in his chair, slobbering potatoes and peas down the front of his shirt. Lange was sure there was a gloat on Papa's face. Nothing had ever tickled him more than to see Lange covered in grime and worked to a nub.

THE DAYS WENT BY: five days. Seven. A kind of routine settled in. Fishing with Papa in the morning. Working with Gabe the rest of the day. The work made him feel like he was contributing some-thing to the family besides just his presence for this short while. Aunt Dellie planned a big Thanksgiving dinner, invited all the extended family. She had let everybody know that Lange was home for the holiday.

Julianne and Sterling arrived by car; Troy Lee came later, flying Sterling's brand new Piper. "He wanted to show off for you," Julianne told Lange, as they were going out to the east pasture where the little airplane had come down. She had tight hold of Lange's hand. "Sterling's been a nervous Nelly all week about this."

"Nervous over which one? The Piper or Troy Lee?" Lange asked, with a brittle laugh.

The plane was a beauty, yellow-green stripes down the fuselage, white sidewall tires, a solid teakwood joystick. And Troy Lee had grown a mile, just wanted to talk flying, had a zillion questions about the Spitfire, about flying for the RAF, about dog fighting. He told Lange he'd decided to go into the Navy when he was done with high school. Navy pilots didn't have to fool with so many regula-tions, and he liked the idea of hot-dogging off the deck of an aircraft carrier.

He reminded Lange of the new sprogs that came from OTU to the squadron, ready to knock the world out of the sky. Most of them ended up in the graveyard or at the bottom of the English Channel. He was afraid the same thing could happen to Troy Lee. After one short joy ride Lange was convinced of it. Troy Lee did just about all the things to an airplane he shouldn't. Lange didn't say anything, but Sterling came fuming out as soon as the Piper touched ground to tear a strip off Troy Lee right there.

"He's reckless, isn't he?" Sterling said, walking with Lange back towards the house. Troy Lee had retreated red-faced to join Julianne on the back porch.

"Maybe having me in there with him just shook his confidence," Lange said.

Sterling shook his head. "He could be a good flyer if he'd learn not abuse the machinery."

Lange could well remember Sterling riding him in just the same fashion for "abusing the machinery." He would have a wall-eyed fit if he could see the things Lange did in his Spitfire.

"Try to keep him home as long as you can," Lange said, and gave Sterling a slap on the shoulder just as Aunt Dellie came to drag everybody up to the house for pictures.

After the first one or two with the whole group, she begged Lange to go in and put on his uniform. "We all want to see you in it," she said, and the others joined in with the cajoling. Try as he might, he couldn't get them off the subject, so finally he gave in and when he came downstairs wearing his RAF blue, Gabe was right there to throw out a loud wolf whistle.

"My, my, ain't he purty," Gabe said, and Lange felt like a first-class idiot.

"Ding's got an English girl over there. She flies airplanes, too. Just like he does." Aunt Dellie said it like an announcement. "Isn't that wonderful?"

Lange groaned and shook his fist at Gabe, who grinned and skulked off towards the back door.

The whole day had an unreal, carnival feel to it. The entire Williams family came from over the county line, caravanned in three automobiles, laden with cakes, sweet potatoes, and store-bought bread. Julianne's two older daughters came with their husbands and kids. Lange didn't know any of them all that well anymore, which only added to the surreal quality of the afternoon.

A baseball game got going out in front of the house; out the back, Troy Lee was giving rides in the Piper. Inside the kitchen the women were all stepping over each other and chattering like black birds going to roost. And in the middle of it all, there was poor Papa, parked in his wheelchair, looking alone and abandoned, a rock in the rapids, disrupting the flow around him.

A piss smell rose from him. As soon as Lange noticed it, he

rolled Papa off into the room Aunt Dellie had set up for him, closed the door, poured water from the pitcher into the bowl, and wet a rag. Papa laid there silent with his eyes closed while Lange cleaned him up, changed his pants and wiped up the chair. Lange thought Papa was just pretending to sleep to avoid the humiliation of it all. It occurred to him that humiliation was the word he'd been looking for since he'd been home.

"There's no use in beating the devil about the bush. I think I know what's eating at you," Lange said, as he put a pair of clean socks on Papa's feet. "One of these days the war's going to be over, and when it ends, we can get Sunny's kids and bring them here. Provided they want to come."

Papa's eyes opened.

"But I did not go over there with them in mind." Lange tugged down on the hem of Papa's pants leg. "I want you to understand that, once and for all. I had my own reason, and it didn't have anything to do with that, you hear me?" Papa's eyes kept staring. "Anyway, Papa, you know me...it's not in my nature to be a hero."

He dropped Papa's foot on the bed, stood over him. Papa's eyes followed his movements.

"You'd probably rather stay in here for a while, wouldn't you? Get out from underneath all that commotion out there in the house."

Lange studied Papa's face. He wished he knew how much the old man understood. Their eyes stayed connected.

"I wish...Papa, I wish I knew what the right thing to say to you is. I just never could figure it out. But I'm going to keep on doing what I'm doing. That's all I can tell you. And you keep on trying to get better." He reached to draw the quilt up over Papa's legs. "Take a nap, now. I'll wake you up for turkey."

A WEEK LATER, aboard the ship going back to England, Lange wished he'd said more to Papa. Something more meaningful and heartfelt, something that might've made a difference. Those few words said there in Aunt Dellie's made-over sewing room, could easily turn out to be the last he might ever speak one-on-one to Papa. He wished he'd spoken them with more eloquence, more importance. He wished he'd had the nerve to say I love you. But that wasn't the kind of family they were.

Halfway across the Atlantic Ocean, nearly back to England, a news dispatch received over the ship's R/T was posted—along with all the other daily news—on a bulletin board in the passenger lounge. It said:

"Japanese Attack Pearl Harbor, Hawaii"

"The American battleships *Arizona*, *California*, *Oklahoma*, and *Utah* were sunk. *U.S.S. West Virginia* settled in shallow water, *U.S.S. Nevada* run aground. Also damaged in attack were the American battleships *Pennsylvania*, *Maryland*, *Tennessee*. The U.S. destroyers *Cassin*, *Downes*, *Shaw*, as well as the minelayer *U.S.S. Oglala* were sunk or damaged. In all, about nineteen ships. Three thousand casualties estimated, nearly all American servicemen and civilians. Roosevelt asks Congress for a declaration of war against the Empire of Japan."

CHAPTER 17

"Sunny's Kids"

"NINA"

"To hell with de Gaulle!" This is what my brother shouted at me, in English, in his thick, unformed speaking voice. I don't know if he realized he was shouting. Some people think he sounds retarded or weak-minded when he speaks aloud, but he is neither. He is, in fact, one of the most intelligent people I know, except he isn't acting intelligent about this.

He brushed me aside and streamed out the door with his long stride, not looking back. He carried a rolled-up blanket under one arm and a sisal sack slung over his shoulder. The heavy sweater and coat he wore made him seem bulky, but I know he is skin and bones. There is never enough to eat anymore. I can feel Joie's ribs when I bathe her.

For a few seconds, I watched Peter's back, then I ran after him. "Come back here! Peter!"

He couldn't hear me, of course. So I charged forward, bursting out in front of him. He had to sidestep to keep from tripping over me. I signed at him furiously.

Don't go! Don't leave us alone, Peter! What will I do without you? I need you!

He averted his eyes and kept walking, but I had slowed him down. I stayed in front of him, shuffling backwards. I put my hands on his chest to stop him altogether and took hold of his chin. I made him look at me. This is what Mama always used to do, since he was a small child. He palmed my hand down from his face.

"Go home, Nina!" Since he can't hear himself but only goes by the vibrations his voice makes in his throat, he often roars—enough to unsettle the person he is talking to, but I am used to it.

He started away from me, and I grabbed at him again. I caused the bedroll to spurt from under his arm and land on the ground. He slammed the sisal sack down by his feet. He gave me a backwards push with both his hands on my shoulders. He gave me another. And another. Small, firm pushes. And then he let fly with his hands, too close to me at first, threatening, moving me back. Peter's hands are much more eloquent than his voice.

Don't try to stop me, Nina. I have made up my mind and there is nothing you can do to change it. Dilane is waiting for me by the road. You go back inside the house and tend to Joie. What kind of a mother are you to leave your small child untended? You know where you are needed, and I know where I am needed. His hands beat at his own chest.

"Peter, please. I'm begging you." I clutched at his elbows and spoke into his face. "Do not let Dilane talk you into this—"

His hands interrupted me. His face had gone to harsh lines. *Peter is no longer my name. I have told you this. It is L'Abbe now. I will not answer to anything else. L'Abbe!*

We stared at each other. Peter's breath was coming hard. After a few seconds he bent for his bedroll and his sack. I grabbed at the sleeve of his coat. He raised his eyes again to my face, settled the sack on his shoulder, and watched my mouth.

"Please, listen to me," I said, "it's too dangerous for someone like you. You could get killed."

That could happen anywhere. It is a dangerous world. Then

aloud in French, he said, "*Mon pays, ma guerre.*" Which had become like an anthem to him and his friend, Dilane Bastian.

It's something hard to argue against. *My country, my war.* I feel the same way. But it's different for me. I'm older. I have a husband who is a prisoner in Saxony. I feel personally dishonored every day that I see the soldiers in the streets in town. Peter is my sweet, laughing brother. My special one. We had, all of us, always coddled him, protected him. Mama will blame me for letting him go. It's the first thing I will have to answer to her for when we met again one day.

But there was nothing else I could do or say. I stood and watched him to the bottom of the hill, where it planed out on a level to the hedges around Mémé's farm and continued down to the road. My dear—my amazing—brother. His country, his war. I spit on the ground. I spit on the day Dilane Bastian appeared at Mémé's door. I spit on the influence he has on Peter.

Dilane's figure, small and dark, appeared in the waning sunlight beyond the hedges. He had his motorbike, the one he keeps hidden at his girlfriend's house, the one he steals petrol from the Germans to fuel. I heard the motor cough to life, watched Peter climb on behind. It was a daring way for them to take off—loud and defiant —into the wilderness of the mountains to join the communists. I pictured them even after they were out of sight. So bold, so full of self-righteousness.

"Mama!" Joie's voice called to me from the doorway. She has begun to talk. She can say Mémé, and *Oncle Peter*, and *Tante* Justine. She loves animals and says *vache, petit chat, poule, le chien,* and *papillon.* There doesn't seem time to teach her English, too. Mama would be unhappy with me for that, as well.

I swiped tears from my face and turned to go back into the house. I guided Joie inside out of the cold, damp air. It seemed to have a stranglehold on me, this cold, damp air of the countryside. How I long for spring, but it is still months away.

~

SINCE PETER HAS GONE everything is falling apart, and I don't seem able to hold it together anymore. I think back to this time two years ago: Emile had come home for Christmas, home to our apartment in Paris. We lived two buildings away from his parents' bakery. I could walk there every morning in time to open the front doors. The Monniers were up and had been at the ovens for four hours already, but I would stay late so they could leave for dinner and go to bed. I closed the shop each evening. And Justy was in school, excelling at her studies. And Peter was at his school for the deaf, teaching the younger children by then. And we were going to win the war. The Germans didn't really want to fight us or the British. It would all be over by summer.

Well, it was. But not how we expected.

I THINK Justy is in trouble. She's working for the banker and his wife in the village. She tends to their three small children. She has moved into their house. And there is a German officer billeted there, too. The postal clerk has seen them walking together along the canal. First it was the blond private, now it is this German officer. I don't understand why she is drawn to them or how she can even look at them in that way. They disgust me. I feel physically ill each time I see them loitering around the stores or packed into their lorries.

She has begun to wear her hair piled up and lipstick on her mouth. Her dresses all fit too tight. She isn't even eighteen, but she looks much older. She has become secretive and I can't talk to her. She tells me to mind my own business and not to butt into hers. She tells me I have already ruined her life by bringing her to this horrible place. She says she hates me and will run away like Peter if I push her too far. I don't know what to do, so I do nothing.

Mémé has grown weary and worn in the year and a half since we came to live with her here. Her joints are rheumatic and she chews bark from the poplar to soothe the pain. She can no longer churn the milk from the cow, so I do it in the evenings when I come home from Pompon's sweet shop. This is hard for me, too, because I'm tired in the evenings and Joie wants me to play with her. She needs to play—she's only a baby.

M. Caullireau came looking for Peter. He asked me when he could expect Peter to come back to work. He had Peter's wages, which he gave to me when he saw how little we have and how cold the house is. I've gone to the tracks to pick up coal like the other beggars in town. This house is so old, the walls and windows are sieves. I sleep with Joie next to me and underneath four blankets. Mémé takes the cot beside the kitchen fire where Peter used to sleep. He is a constant worry to me. I worry that if the Germans don't kill him, the cold in the mountains will. I worry that Dilane or the others they have joined will take advantage of his disability. I worry that if something happens to him I will never, ever know. I feel old and used up with so much worry.

I pray to Mama. I tell her I don't think I can handle another day. I don't have her strength. I think of how she must have suffered when our father died. He was so young. Both of them were so young. And I am young. I have had no word from Emile in nine long months. Inside myself I can no longer say with certainty that he is alive.

THE NIGHT PETER finally came to the house, rain was falling. It had fallen all through the day and didn't stop with sunset. Fat, round drops floated heavily down to cover everything in water.

A friend came with him. A friend named Lothaire. I know this is a nom de guerre the same way that L'Abbe is for Peter. Lothaire calls Peter L'Abbe. They sat at the table and devoured the goat cheese and flat bread Mémé warmed for them. I opened a bottle of wine. I felt so happy to see Peter I couldn't stop hugging and kissing him. He smelled bad and had grown a patchy beard on his chin. He had cut the fingertips out of his gloves and once he had eaten his fill, he signed ebulliently with me, as if he were ecstatic to be with someone who understood his hands again. He had so much to tell me.

He had been on a wild boar hunt. He was the one to fire the killing shot. He showed me the gun stuck inside his belt. It looked like something pieced together from two guns, or maybe three. The handle was long, and the barrel belonged to a pistol. One end didn't match the other. I tried not to show my alarm at the sight of a gun stunk inside the belt of my sweet, peaceful brother. Lothaire shook his head and touched the barrel, directing the gun back into Peter's coat. I took heart in that. I hope perhaps this Lothaire will look after my brother and not let anything bad happen to him.

I begged them to stay the night, but Peter wouldn't have it. The friend, I think, would have stayed. He looked longingly at the fire where Mémé's bed was made. Peter kissed both my cheeks, held my face, and looked down into my eyes.

"Do not worry for me," he said, aloud and in English.

I KNEW EXACTLY the day I became pregnant with Joie—or anyway within three days. Frosty December, that first year of the war. Emile was home on Christmas leave before being sent up to the front. We stayed in bed for most of those days. His mother was jealous of the time away from her. We had been married for only six months, and half of those six had been spent apart. Emile was a quiet lover, a romantic lover, whispering to me through it all.

His mother didn't want him to marry me. Because I was American. Because I'm not Catholic. Neither of those things bothered Emile. In fact, it made me more appealing to him. He called me his American heathen. I think he was even a little disappointed when I decided to convert. I began to learn catechism and began sleeping with him almost simultaneously. We didn't think about possible consequences or the sin of it. Now, every night I pray for him to stay alive, to come back to me and to the daughter he's never seen.

I haven't heard from him in so long, I wonder, have I done the wrong thing coming here to Mémé's farm? Justy is lost to me. Peter is living in the depths of the woods with the communists. I have found copies of their newspapers with his things. I have seen Justy in town on the arm of her *Wehrmacht* lieutenant in his *feldgrau*. Nothing is as it should be anymore.

THE WEATHER HAS WORSENED. Last winter was the coldest I ever remember, and this winter promises to be even colder. For two days the hill down to the village is so slick with icy rain, I can't get to work. All day, Mémé, Joie, and I huddle around the kitchen fire. We are down to burning planks pulled from the barn fence. All the food we have to eat is some thin leek soup and stale bread.

On the third day of this bad weather we hear the sound of an automobile coming up the hill. It stops outside the house. I get up to see who it is just as Justy bursts in through the front door. She's wearing a heavy coat I have never seen. It has an ermine collar. She carries a basket with loaves of bread protruding from their wrapping. Behind her comes her tall, green-eyed lieutenant. When Mémé sees him she automatically gasps and clutches Joie close to her bosom. Mémé remembers two other wars full of German enemies. The fear stays in her eyes.

Justy's face is pink from the cold outside and from good health. She seems to have grown by two inches, until I notice the high-heeled boots on her feet. They are ringed with ermine as well. She puts the basket on the table but neither Mémé nor I pay attention to the food. Our wary eyes stay on the lieutenant. He takes off his cap. Up close I can see he is, perhaps, a little shy.

"This is Archie," Justy says.

"Archie?" Mémé answers, in astonishment. The name is inconsistent with the formality of what we know of soldiers in the *Wehrmacht*.

"Lieutenant Hoefling," Justy says.

The lieutenant dips his head. He takes a step forward for my hand, which I don't know whether to give or not. In my confusion, I let him take my hand.

"Pleased to meet you," he says in near-flawless English, with another small bow of his head.

"Archie is from Linz," Justy says. She is already unloading the basket onto the kitchen table.

Archie brightens. "Do you know Linz?" he says to me.

I shake my head.

"It's on the Danube. Archie talks about the Danube constantly," Justy says. She has brought more than bread. There's a jar of mustard, some corned beef, onions, cabbages, rutabaga, a regular cornucopia.

Archie says, "I will bring in the rest."

"The rest?" I watch him go back out the door. The cold air blows in behind him. "Justy," I say with amazement. "Where did all of this food come from?"

"I told Archie I was worried about you and Mémé and Joie up here in this weather, and he said we would bring you some things." Justy smiles. "He is a supply officer."

Mémé has risen to inspect the bounty on the kitchen table. She touches the bar of soap to see if it is real, picks it up to smell.

"Any news of Peter?" Justy asks, almost whispering.

"No." I won't tell her he's been here. Not with Lieutenant Hoefling just outside the door.

"I'm worried about him as well, you know," she says.

"Please don't take your lieutenant looking for him, Justy."

She frowns at me. "I would never do that, Nina. But if I did nothing would happen to Peter. Archie is a good, kind person. He would not let harm come to my brother."

"He's a soldier in the German army."

"What of it?"

If she doesn't understand I see no point in trying to explain. "Does he know you're an American?"

"Of course. He loves me."

"Oh, Justy." I want her to face reason. "They're taking Americans away. I heard it from the priest. One of the spa hotels in Vittel has been made into an internment especially for American women." But Justy turns away from my warnings.

Archie comes into the house with a canvas sack. It's filled with coal. He goes to the fire and begins to feed black chunks into it. I look at Mémé. She watches every move the lieutenant makes. Joie stuffs bread into her mouth. I find a butcher knife and saw open a can of peaches. I take out a slice and give it to Joie. Within one minute she has peach syrup smeared all over her face.

TWO NIGHTS later I'm awakened by a loud rap on the kitchen door. Mémé sits up on her cot, but I motion for her to stay still. I've left Joie upstairs warm in my bed. The person at the door is Peter's friend, Lothaire. He is agitated, tells me he needs me to come with him. Someone is hurt.

"Is it my brother?" I ask.

He shakes his head. He waits while I put on warm clothes. I gather what few medicines we have on hand. He has a horse. I have never ridden on a horse. He says it is the best way to travel in the Morvan. He helps me up onto the horse, ties on my bag of medicines, and then he climbs up and settles in front of me. He tells me to reach around him and shows me where to grip the saddle. Even with gloves my hands are soon numb with cold. I duck my head against the wet wind that blows.

We are a long time on horseback. I think how Lothaire must trust me, not to blindfold me for the journey. I begin to hope I will see Peter, at least. It's colder on the mountain and inside the cover of trees. Just as I begin to fear we're lost, we come to a low, shambling hut, almost buried in this dense section of this forest. Smoke puffs out of a stovepipe in the roof. Without a word, Lothaire takes me down from the horse. He hands me my sack of medicines. His lips are pressed grimly together.

Inside the hut a moaning boy lies on a pallaise. The floor of the hut is earth, but some straw has been strewn around. The boy is thin and gray. He's shivering and gasps for breath. I feel helpless as I kneel beside him.

"What's wrong with him?" I ask.

"He has been shot."

"Where?"

Lothaire pulls back the blankets and I see the dressing wrapped clumsily around his hip. It is soaked through with dark blood.

"Who is he?" I ask.

Lothaire shakes his head and doesn't answer me.

"Is my brother involved in this?" I ask.

Lothaire looks directly at me. "No."

I do what I can with the little I have. I wash his wound with the antiseptic I have brought. It is a deep wound. I think the bullet might still be inside. The boy needs a doctor. I think shock has taken hold of him. When I say so, Lothaire again shakes his head. Together we get the boy to drink some water. Lothaire takes more blankets out of a trunk, and we spread them over the boy's small body. This seems to make him more comfortable or else he has gone into deeper shock. He stops gasping and trembling so much.

"How old is he?" I ask.

Lothaire glances again at the boy beneath the pile of blankets. "Fifteen."

"Did you shoot him?"

"No!" He barks it at me, so I understand he's tired of my questions. I huddle nearer the fire. "I cannot take you back tonight," he says finally. "I won't leave him alone again. Get some blankets from the box. Fix yourself a bed."

"I have a daughter waiting for me to come home."

"We will go in the morning."

I hesitate, feel a little desperate, but there is nothing I can do. I could never find my way back on my own. I go to the box. Inside are several more ragged blankets. Full of vermin, I'm certain. I take a couple of them over near the fire, opposite from where the boy lies. I spread down the blankets and sit once again.

Lothaire shakes a cigarette at me. I nod, and he uses a stick from the fire to light mine and also one for himself. It has been several days since I've had a cigarette to smoke. It makes me light-headed. I brush away tobacco crumbs from my lips.

He digs out a bottle of cognac from his coat, pulls the cork, and takes a swallow of it. He wipes his mouth and holds out the bottle. I hesitate, then reach across for the cognac. It's sweet and hot at the same time.

"Did the boy run away from home?" I ask, thinking of Peter.

"What home? The Germans have taken our homes, all of us." Lothaire raises the bottle once more and drinks. Then he tucks it back into his coat. "He is my brother."

My hand goes to push back my hair. I don't want to appear too surprised. Lothaire doesn't look like the kind of man who would have any family.

"You don't have anyone you can take him to?" I ask.

"No one I claim." He scratched at the fire with a stick. "They're all traitors. They believe in Petain and Laval's lies. They care only for peace. I say to hell with peace."

He sounds like Peter. I wrap my arms around myself. The fire begins to warm me. "Was he shot by Germans?"

Lothaire stares into the flames. Firelight dances on his face. He doesn't answer. "I shouldn't have brought you out into the cold night."

"He needs a doctor."

He shook his head. "He is in very much trouble. Even if he lives now he will die anyway."

His eyes are watery, and he suddenly seems gentle. I wonder who he was before the war. He is sad and angry all at once. It steams from him.

"Where is my brother?" I say.

Lothaire shrugs. "In the mountains."

"You're alone here?"

He stares at me for a second and nods towards the pallaise. "Except for him."

"My husband is a war prisoner. Did my brother tell you?" I don't have any reason for saying this, but I know I won't sleep if I lie down. A little talk—even with Lothaire—is better than none. "Since the defeat. He's somewhere in Saxony."

"They've probably shot him. They're shooting fifty prisoners a month because there's no food."

A chill shivers over me. His words slap me and bring up a tear. I lift my chin. "I don't believe that."

He throws the stick into the fire. "I'm going to sleep now."

I watch him spread a blanket down beside his brother. I lay on my palliasse and listen to the fire crackle and the walls breathe. The wind whistles outside. The sound of it makes me cold.

I wonder if Emile *is* dead. Could it be true that the Germans are executing our men? I close my eyes and try to picture Emile's face. It will not come. I'm losing my memory of him.

It's hard to relax enough in the strange hut to find sleep. I toss most of the night. Once or twice I hear Lothaire stirring the fire. Deep sleep finally takes me into its fog.

In the morning, Lothaire's brother is better. He still has fever, but he can lift himself onto one elbow to eat the rabbit meat Lothaire has roasted for our breakfast.

"This is the angel who saved you," Lothaire says to his brother in an angry voice. "Tell her *merci*."

"*Merci*," the boy says. He has a timid voice. I know I was not the one who saved him, but all the same I'm grateful that he is better.

Overnight, the storm has cleared. Lothaire takes me back to the farmhouse the same way, on the saddle behind him. The whole forest drips. Limbs hang low and soggy from the trees. We dodge through them and go slowly down the mountain.

"I'm in your debt," he says to me after he helps me off the horse. "For saving Alain."

So, now I know his brother's name. "If you want to repay me, then watch out for my brother," I say. "I know he's brave. I'm proud of his bravery, but I'm also afraid for him."

"He's a strong man. And smart enough to be afraid on his own. He doesn't need your fear, too."

I want to say that he is not a man yet. Something stops me. "I couldn't bear to lose him. Will you take him some food? Will you do that much for me?"

He nods. He waits while I go inside the house to gather as much food as we can spare. I select things from Justy's soldier. I would rather pass it on than eat it myself. I carry the parcel of food to Lothaire. When he takes it from my hand, he smiles. It's the first smile that has crossed his face. "*Adieu*," he says.

Work tires me more than usual. I trudge home in the gloomy dusk. The days have begun to shorten. Ever so slightly, by only minutes, but I can feel the difference in the light. The rain has made a muddy streak down the side of the hill. Leaves cover the ground. Birds have disappeared, and the world has turned brown and gray. I picture myself growing old and ugly, waiting for this war to end and Emile to come back to me.

Just as I top the hill but before the farmhouse comes into view, someone jumps me from behind. Before I can find my balance a pair of hands spirit me off the path and into the broken woods at the edge of Mémé's land. I struggle against the attack. I open my mouth to yell but the hands whirl me around. Lothaire is laughing in my face. I almost don't recognize this smiling man.

"You were afraid," he says, pleased with himself.

I put my hand to my chest, gasping for breath. My heart is wild in my chest. I shove him away from me. "That was not funny."

Again, he laughs. "You were walking so carefree. You should watch yourself closer." As if by magic he produces a packet of Gauloise, an entire, unopened packet. "*Voila!*" He is smiling. "A gift."

I want the cigarettes. I almost reach for them, then pull my hand back. He forces me to take them.

"You saved Alain," he says. "These are from him."

I look at the packet. It has smudged handprints on the front. "If you took the packet of food to my brother, then I have already been paid."

"And now you have been paid again. You want to smoke one?" He twirls a single match between his first two fingers.

"I'll save them for later." I'm thinking that Mémé would like to have one as well.

He stops smiling. He watches me put the cigarettes into my coat pocket. "I am Michel," he says. "I thought you must have heard Alain use my real name, so I will tell it to you. Michel Garrity."

I shake my head. If Alain said this name I never heard it. "I don't want to know who you are."

He continues anyway. "I come from a village near Saint Quentin. I have another brother, Nicolaus, who is a soldier in the German Army and a traitor to his country." He spits on the ground. "Alain was protecting me when he was shot. I didn't know he had bullets in his gun. I believe he killed a soldier. I saw the man fall. Blood...." He makes a motion that tells me the soldier bled a lot.

"Why was he protecting you?" I back away from him. "What were you doing?"

He straightens, raises his face to study me. "Stealing dynamite."

I take in my breath. "Why are you telling me this?"

"Because I want you to think well of me."

"All I want to know is if my brother is OK, and if you took the food to him."

"Yes," he says. His gaze on me is too bold and too direct. "He says you shouldn't worry over him, he has plenty to eat. His only concern is that there is no man to work on this farm and to protect you and your *grand-mère* and your daughter. So I offer my services. I worked many farms near my village."

I study his face. He seems sincere. It isn't what I expected from him. "Lothaire, I..."

"Michel," he corrects. "I insist. I owe you my brother's life."

"Where is your brother?"

He looks further into the woods. His eyes are soft and intent. They frighten me. I follow his gaze and see finally, Alain wrapped in a blanket, propped against a tree.

"I can do many things for you. I can milk and feed and plow and reap. Please, if you will take Alain until he is well."

"Hide him, you mean?" I say it softly but with firmness.

"Yes."

I stare into Lothaire's—Michel Garrity's—eyes. They are hazel, honest, desperate, and hopeful. I think of Mémé and wonder if she will agree to it. I glance again at the pitiful boy wrapped in the blanket. My heart beats quicker. I feel dizzy.

"You must promise me that you will not let anything happen to Peter. If you promise me that, I will hide your brother. But only until he is healthy again."

He grabs me by my shoulders, dances me around, takes my hand and kisses all over my knuckles. I have never seen a man act so foolish. He grabs my face and kisses me on the forehead. He hugs me and lifts me off my feet. For a moment, I allow it, even welcome the comfort of strong arms around me, the longing that rises inside of me.

"No," I say, and push away from him. "Please, I am a married woman."

"Forgive me, but your husband is dead." He speaks with such certainty.

Tears gush to my eyes. They surprise me with their speed. I can't stop them. Dismayed, I watch him run into the woods to gather his broken brother in his arms like a child.

CHAPTER 18

"*Landings*"

Mackie caught a crosswind bringing the Spitfire in for a landing, flared out, and took a big bounce on touch down. She managed to wrestle back control. Personally, she didn't understand all the fuss about these Spitfires. She much preferred the wider-spaced, more stable undercarriage of a Hurricane, but she had learned not to voice an opinion unless asked. The mere mention that their beloved kites might be less than perfect caused all hell to break among fighter pilots.

The ground crew took over as soon as she pulled to a stop. She checked in at the Watch Office, signed off on the Spitfire, asked where she could find the Eagle Squadron that had just been posted to this station. Butterflies had already started.

She knew he was here. Adam had found out that much this morning, which was the reason he gave her the chit for the Spitfire. His friend at Uxbridge had telephoned with the news that Flight Lieutenant DeLony had returned from his compassionate leave. *Flight Lieutenant.* He had been posted to a new squadron—the second of the all-American squadrons that had recently been formed—and given a promotion. Fighter Command had begun to gather all the nationalities together: Czechs with Czechs. Poles with

Poles. Americans with Americans. Everything would probably be changing now that the United States had come into the war. But for now, he was here at this base. She knew he was. She could almost feel his presence as she rode across the airfield with the WAAF driver, who said Lange's squadron was now on stand-down. They'd been on Ops all morning. The woman thought he might be at the Officer's Mess.

"Kin to you, is he?" the driver asked.

By that time, Mackie was in a state, sweaty armpits, dry mouth. She shook her head, but of course the WAAF couldn't see that. "Not hardly," she managed.

"I know how that is," the woman said. She was in her early twenties, flat-voweled Shropshire accent, bright flame hair underneath her cap. "Mind you don't get too attached. You know these fighter pilot types. I taxi them to dispersal every day. Honest girl doesn't stand a chance with their likes."

Mackie made some lighthearted comment, something that meant nothing and that she forgot a moment after she spoke.

She wouldn't have been here at all if Adam wasn't pressuring her. He'd moved into the cottage after Phyl left for White Waltham to be near her sweetheart and after Viv Starger's husband had come home from the Mediterranean. Having Adam as a roommate was like having a guilty conscious nagging at you all the time. He knew too much. No way to keep it from him, not with him underfoot day in and out.

This morning, he called her into his office, shut the door, said in a conspiratorial tone of voice, "He's back. He's been posted to North Weald." And then he had handed her the chit for the Spitfire Vb. The flight took half an hour, mainly because she'd had to fly through the industrial haze over the Midlands.

The WAAF driver pulled up outside the Officers Mess. It was a brick building with lots of cross-taped windows, an attic cupola, vines, now defoliated, growing all over the face. Mackie stared at the sandbagged front door.

"Well, here it is, ducky. Just go on up and ask for him."

"Yes. Thanks." She got out of the vehicle. No sooner had she closed the door than the WAAF was driving off in a cloud of exhaust smoke.

Mackie stood there on the lawn, uncertain and ready to change her mind. She'd been inside an Officers Mess many times before. They were all alike—quiet and dignified by day, boisterous and busy by night, black leather armchairs and sofas, clubby crests and aircraft artifacts on the walls, cozy fire no doubt roaring in the anteroom.

She stood there trying to buck up the courage to go inside. She wished she'd had a chance to comb her hair, to wash the flying grime off her face. She smelled like aviation fuel, and her uniform was rumpled and grubby. The thought occurred to her that she should've asked for the driver to take her to the WAAF house where she could've spruced up her appearance. She had some essentials in her overnight bag. When she heard the automobile pull up behind her she had the ridiculous idea of hitching a ride somewhere, anywhere besides where she stood.

Two officers got out of the black staff car, and one of them—God, she felt she might faint—one of them was Lange. He had an extra ring round his sleeve—flight lieutenant. He outranked her, now. Automatically, she turned in the opposite direction, away from the Officers Mess, back towards the Watch Office.

She couldn't go through with it. Just seeing him changed her mind—busy about his business, living a life totally exclusive of her. Adam was wrong. This was wrong. If Lange wanted to see her he would have telephoned. Chasing after him did nothing but make her feel degraded.

"Whoa, there. Whoa, whoa!" A pull on the strap of her bag whirled her around, and there he was. Dimple in his cheek, that crooked front tooth. He wore his side cap cocked at a natty angle. "Jesus, Mackie, I thought it was you."

"Oh!" was all she managed before the bear hug took her breath away. Her face pressed against the rough wool of his uniform. He smelled like cigarettes and washing powder. She went as soft as porridge.

"What the hell are you doing here?" He sounded pleased, kept that big smile on his face. He held her at arm's length. "Did you know I was here?"

She nodded, swallowed. "I heard you were."

"I just got back from the States."

"I know."

"You do?" He let go of her arms.

She glanced towards the staff car parked in front of the Mess. The other officer was waiting on the front stoop. She said, "I tried to reach you. I rang the old station. They said you had a family emergency."

"Papa had another stroke. A bad one this time. They didn't think he was going to make it. But he pulled through." He bent to look closer into her eyes. "Hey, I'm sorry I didn't call you before I left. I should have done that. I didn't think about it till I was already gone."

She touched his sleeve. "Flight Lieutenant."

"Yeah." He laughed, bent his elbow to show off the new ring on his cuff. "Can you beat that? I think it's because I'm an old guy. All these other sprogs are still wet behind the ears."

"I think it's more than that."

His eyes traveled over her. "So, you're working?"

She nodded. "I just brought in a Vb." A partial lie. She was here to see him. Period.

"That one's got to be for us. That wasn't you just now, who came in so low? I knew they shouldn't give a woman a Spitfire to fly." He grinned and took her arm. "Come on in. Are you in a hurry? Do you have time for a drink?"

She tried to hang back. "No, I really..."

"We'll go someplace else then. I just have something I need to do first. Come here. I want you to meet Jim Hiller. He was with me in basic at Ottawa. He came over with me, and now we're back together in this outfit. You'll like him."

She didn't like him or dislike him either. She had no opinion whatever about Jim Hiller. He was simply an intrusion, and today she had no patience for meeting new people.

Lange left her standing in the foyer with this Jim Hiller person. He told her where he was from. Went in and out of her brain instantly. He offered her a smoke. She took it. He told her that the squadron was transitioning from Hurricanes to Spitfires. She already knew that. He said they'd been transitioning off one aircraft and onto another ever since the squadron was formed. He thought that was a funny statement and laughed at his own wit.

She watched for Lange to come back downstairs. The grandfather clock against the wall startled her when it struck the half-hour. She wondered when, or even if, Lange had intended to ring her. She hated being the one to seek him out. She had tried to tell Adam it was not a good idea.

When Lange came down he had changed into his service cap. He was still adjusting it on his head. He smelled of fresh shaving soap. He put his hand on the small of her back and guided her out to the staff car, opened the passenger side for her. Jim Hiller came out, too, waved, and said goodbye—these damned friendly Yanks. Mackie thought she probably wouldn't recognize Jim Hiller again if she saw him on the street.

Lange drove the car into the village. He said he didn't know much about the surroundings yet. He'd only arrived two days before. It was a mild day for late December, yet the sky still had that gloomy winter cast.

She had never ridden in an automobile with him driving. She hoped he wasn't this reckless in the cockpit. She couldn't concentrate, couldn't take her eyes off the road for fear she'd get thrown out as they careened around curves, going way too fast for the narrow streets. She pulled her eyes off the roadway and watched his hands resting lightly on the steering wheel. Long fingers, sharp knuckles, a splash of dark hair. She had almost forgotten how lovely he was.

He told her about the voyage back from America. He'd been on a converted freighter with about a hundred other RAF and Royal Navy. They had a U-boat scare out in the middle of the Atlantic, and the convoy had veered so far north they started seeing icebergs. He told her about his father in a wheelchair, and about how the United States coming into the war had changed his view of flying with an Eagle Squadron. This new bunch needed flyers with combat experience, so here he was. Didn't hurt that the posting came with a promotion. He would lead B Flight, and she detected pride in his voice.

For once, she let him do all the talking. He seemed different, more animated, happy, and it didn't add up, not with a father direly ill and his country now at war. Yet there was no mistaking his smoother brow, the sincere laughter, the attitude altogether easier than she had ever seen with him. Maybe, she thought, he was simply well-rested, with that six weeks of vacation from the war. Whatever it was, with him so good-humored, she found she couldn't even keep up a pretense of anger at him for going away without a word.

The Tally-Ho was a simple, plain establishment. It would have been so even without the sandbags and shuttered windows. Its proximity to the airdrome made precautions necessary, but they added to the gray austerity of the exterior. He opened the heavy strap-hinged door for her and held her hand as they went into the bar. It was empty except for a bored barkeep, who rose expectantly as they entered. The smell of old stale cigarette smoke and stout lingered in the air.

"I'm going to ask if there's a room available," she said and quickly, before he could get the wrong idea, added, "I need a bath and a change of clothes." In her overnight bag, she had a sweater and skirt, fresh knickers, a makeup kit. Once she had washed up, she would feel better, more in control.

Lange gave her a bewildered look. "You don't have to go back today?"

She shook her head. "There's nothing for me to ferry back."

She left him confused and waiting at the bar while the keep drew off two pints from the taps.

The desk clerk did have a room available. The way the woman said it, with such enthusiasm, Mackie felt certain there must be several rooms available. She took the key to number eight, end of the hallway, up one short flight of stairs. Extravagant private bath attached to the room, faded floral counterpane on the bed, clean but old. The room smelled musty, faintly of the stale cigarette aroma from the pub below, and also perhaps a bit of damp mold. Wind-up alarm clock on the night table, an ashtray. She could see a small garden through the window slats.

She dropped the overnight bag on the dresser, checked her face in the small mirror above the basin. Dreadful. She soaped away the surface grime. She reached to turn on the bathtub taps, unbuttoned her tunic, and before the hot water arrived, she heard him knock at the door. She went to answer.

He held a pint of beer in each hand. "Extra bitter," he said, smiling. "Good old warm English beer."

She took one of the glasses from his hand, returned the toast he offered. Their glasses chinked flatly as was their habit. She took a sip. It tasted strong. A pair of aircraft flew over, single engines from the sound. The Tally-Ho was in the flight path. The walls shook. She took another sip of the beer.

"I didn't get the room to sleep with you." She said it evenly.

"I figured you were mad at me."

"I'm not mad, as you say. I'm just..." She shrugged, shook her head.

"I should've called you," he said. "It happened so fast. What can I say, Mackie? I'm a bastard at heart."

"I don't believe that." She put her hand flat on his breast bone. "Not at heart."

He caught her wrist, chased her lips, kissed her, sweetly and tenderly. She almost spilled her beer. He took her glass and set his and hers on the night table, sat on the edge of the bed and pulled her onto his lap. The water was still running in the tub. Clearly, he didn't believe she meant what she said about not sleeping with him. He was already trying to make love to her.

"I missed you," he said. "I was going to call, I really was. I just haven't had the time yet." His eyes were sincere. "I'm happy as hell to see you."

"Is this some kind of Texas snow job?" She shoved out of his lap. "I'm going to take a bath."

"I'm coming in, too."

She turned to stop him. "No. I mean it, Lange. You're not going to seduce me. I know you think you can—"

"All right. OK. Go get dolled up. I'll take you out to supper. I don't know my way around here yet, but we'll find some place."

She left him talking and went in the bathroom. "I'm locking the door," she said, loud enough so he could hear her. She undressed, left her dirty uniform in a pile, and eased in the tub. The water was only tepid.

"I could scrub your back." He sounded like he was right outside the door. She imagined him leaning there.

She smiled. "You could have dropped me a postcard, too."

"Yeah, you're right. But I figured I would beat it back."

"Sounds like another excuse."

She finished bathing, thought about stalling longer, but got out and dried off. The towel was as thin as paper. She realized she had left her overnight bag on the dresser beside the bed. She muttered "Damn" to herself and pulled her slip back over her head. When she opened the door, he was standing right there, leaning against the jamb, as she had imagined.

"Have you punished me enough yet?" He touched her arm, rubbed his thumb over the ball of her shoulder.

"I'm not trying to punish you." She stepped out of his reach.

She couldn't think straight with him trying to make love to her every second. "I have to talk to you. And then if you still want to, you can take me out for that nice dinner."

He reached for his beer. His eyes traveled over her length. "Is that what you're wearing?"

She didn't laugh, although she knew he was fishing for one. He could never stand for them to get too serious.

"I'm pregnant."

There. She said it. Straight and simple. She hadn't prettied it up the way she planned in her mind, but just put the words out there, between them. Let him wrestle with it the way she had been for these past weeks. She sat down on the bed, traced her finger over one of the faded roses on the counterpane, looked up at him again, watched the beer glass come down from his lips. Utter surprise washed over his face for one second, then quickly ebbed. He set the glass down on the table beside her glass.

"How long have you known?" He sounded calm, not the reaction she had expected.

"Officially, for three weeks. But I think I knew it before you left."

"Why didn't you say something?"

"I almost did. That night you called me so late. But you sounded like something was wrong. Besides, I didn't want to do it over the phone." He was looking at her intently, but she still couldn't read anything in his expression. "Adam's given me the sack, of course. Today was my last day. That Spitfire...well, that was the end of it."

She had the urge to cry, felt her bottom lip tremble but quickly willed it away. Partly, it was relief. She was glad this much, at least, was behind her. Holding in this secret all this time had taken a toll on her. Only Adam had guessed, and then as her CO, required her to get a medical exam.

"It's due in June," she said, "in case you were wondering."

His chin raised. He looked contemplative, doing the math, she supposed. He sat down beside her.

"One of those nights at The Whitehorse." He picked up her hand, turned her palm up like he was going to tell her fortune. "Seems like we should've known when it happened, doesn't it? Bells should have rung, sirens gone off, something."

"It doesn't work like that," she said.

His eyes warmed on her. "You were all the talk back home."

"Me?"

"I mentioned you to my cousin Gabe, and before I knew it, my aunt was telling everybody I had an English girl waiting for me that I had to get back to."

"An English girl?"

He shrugged. "People hear what they want to hear." His thumb rubbed back and forth over her palm. "I've got a forty-eight coming on the seventh. I was going to try to see you on your birthday anyway. We'll have to make it fast. No time for a real honeymoon, but I reckon we've had our fair share of those already."

Her breath left, momentarily choked her. "No! Absolutely not! I am not asking you to marry me!"

She started up off the bed, but he grabbed her and pulled her back down. "No, I'm asking you. And I don't want to argue about it."

"I thought you should know, that's all. I'm not trying to force you into anything."

"You're not forcing me. Truth is, I was coming around to it anyway." He lifted her hand to his lips, kissed her palm. "You love me, don't you?"

The question stopped her. Her eyes touched his. Her resolve fell away. She nodded. "Yes. Yes, I do." She reached around his neck and kissed him on the mouth.

He laughed, squeezed her tighter. "All right then. It's decided."

～

"WELL?" Adam said, when she phoned him from the corner news agency to tell him she wouldn't need the taxi Anson to pick her up. She'd left Lange in room eight, naked and fast asleep. She would wake him when she returned so he could get back to the airfield. There wouldn't be time for that nice dinner after all.

"He says we're getting married," she said into the telephone, loud because of the airplanes coming over.

"I thought he might."

"No, you didn't. You thought he'd given me the push."

Adam's chuckle came through the line. "So, you snared your golden boy after all, did you?"

"Don't be so cynical. I'm dreadfully in love with him, Adam."

"I know you are."

"I guess the wedding will be in a couple of weeks. You'll be there, won't you?"

"I wouldn't miss it."

"Good. I need somebody to give me away."

"I'll be there."

"OK. Well...happy landings," she said.

"You, too."

"Adam?" she said, before he could hang up. "Thanks for making me come tell him."

"I thought he should know. He's not Eugene, Allie. Different day. Different chap."

CHAPTER 19
Letters

10 January 1942

Dear Folks,

Got back here 17 December. That was some hairy boat ride. I'll tell you about it sometime. On the twentieth I was posted to a new squadron with lots of fellows I already knew from training days. So you can tell everybody that I'm officially an "Eagle" now. I know I said I would never make the switch, but they didn't give me much choice, and I feel good about it, especially now with the States in the war. So far there's not much that's different over here, but I expect that will change soon. We had a visit from a USAAF bigwig. He says we'll all be given a chance to make the shift, but the details haven't been worked out yet. Until then we're to sit tight in the RAF.

Now for my big news. Hold onto your hats for this one. I got married. She's the gal all of you were whispering about while I was there, the Canadian named Mackie. Actually, she's got a good old-fashioned name, Allison Loretta MacLeod—well, DeLony now. The wedding was two days ago at her aunt's big country house. Mackie wanted to have it on the back terrace but it was raining cats and dogs—this is England after all—so we moved it inside halfway through the vows. Both of us got soaked, so there was a time-out for drying off. Didn't seem to help me any. I'm sick with a head cold as I write this to you. My CO gave me a couple of extra days to celebrate so we've gone to [censured] (Oops! Probably shouldn't put that in a letter.) Anyway, Mackie's nursing me with Beecham's Cure All and some sort of smelly liniment. She's gone right now to look at an old castle down the street from our hotel. Left me tucked in bed so I thought I'd write to you.

It was a nice wedding, a real war wedding. Lots of my old flying buddies came. Jim Hiller stood up with me, remember I've mentioned him before? Mackie's brother, Adam, gave her away. She said she would send pictures once she gets the film back from the developer. By the way, she has a son (more on this later), and he was our ring bearer. Although it wasn't much of a ring he had to bear. Whole thing hit me sort of blind side, and I found myself flat broke as usual. Fellows in the squadron came up with the dough, and I managed to get something to put on her finger thanks to their efforts.

Suppose I ought to tell you Mackie's expecting in June, which is the main reason for the big hurry. Hope this doesn't shock you too much, Aunt Dellie, but after all, we're both of us grown-up adults. Besides which, you'll probably be able to tell it in the pictures she's sending. She's slender and dainty so she's already showing a little bit. I keep pinching myself about it. Never thought much about fatherhood before, just figured it wouldn't happen to me, so chose to get on with life and not think in terms of future generations. But now all that's changed. It's like somebody threw a switch in the middle of the game and everything I thought I knew went blank. I hope I'll be good at it. I know I sure am excited about it.

Said I wanted to tell you more about Given, Mackie's son. He just turned eight a few months ago and is as dark and quiet as his mother is blond and lively. You just have to be around them for ten seconds to see he adores her. He's a swell little Brit, has the pure accent and manners of a regular English gent. I think we're going to get along just fine. He's already asked if I would come to his school and tell his schoolmates about being a Spitfire pilot. Mackie says she thinks he just wants to show off. I said I'd do it, of course. Score some brownie points. See? Fatherhood is already upon me.

While we're on the subject of young Given, I sure would love to teach him how to play baseball. He would see right away how much better of a game it is than this silly cricket stuff they play over here. If you happen to come upon a small-sized baseball and bat, send it to me, and I'll pay you back once the war's won.

Now that I've dropped this bomb on you, let me back up to just after I hit the shores of England and got my new posting. This squadron hasn't been around but for a few months. They have been well trained and I'm happy to be with them. But they've been used until now as a sort of replacement squadron, filling in holes in other squadrons, so they're short of men with any combat experience. The CO from my old squadron was sent over there to shape them up, and he put in a request for me to come as soon as I got back. To sweeten the deal a little they made me a flight lieutenant, which is the same as a captain in the USAAF. I've decided that the trick to making rank in the RAF is just to stick around long enough, and pretty soon somebody notices you. But the best thing is this squadron has just made the switch to Spitfires, so Morse has sort of made me chief bottle-washer when it comes to instructing on the new aircraft. New for them, not me. All these boys are just as game as the old bunch. In a way, maybe even more so since Germany has declared war on the United States, now. Everybody wants to do a good job and help out the old USA any way we can.

Well, that's about as many bullets as I should fire at you in one letter. Excuse the rambling. Think the Beecham's has gone to my head. Take care of each other. I believe I miss you all the worse since I was there.

As ever—

Lange

~

January 15, 1942

Colesbury, England

Dear Mr. DeLony and Family,

It seems we are part of each other's family now, and as such, I thought I should take the liberty of writing to you myself, so that you might know a little bit about your new daughter-in-law's background. She is the daughter of my dear departed sister, Ireni. My sister and I were born into the Graham family, but Ireni married a MacLeod, which explains Allison's maiden name. The MacLeods, of course, hail from Scotland, but more immediately from Manitoba, Canada. I never had children but married an Englishman before the Great War and have been living in Cambridgeshire since then. I lost my husband in 1933, and shortly thereafter, Allison arrived. She and her son, Given, have been a Godsend to me, as is, Allison's older brother, Adam, who also is a frequent visitor here. They have all of them quite completed my empty life.

You may know Allison as Mackie. As the only girl with two older brothers, I believe she imagined the name would make her seem as tough and resilient as her brothers. I assure you, she is lady-like and quite lovely despite her fondness for this man's game of airplane flying. I prefer to call her Allison, which is the name my dear sister gave to her when she was born.

She and your dear Lange are a very good match. They seem to most enjoy each other's company and are constantly joking with each other and laughing. Given has stars in his eyes over Lange, and so I am confident they will have a happy life together, the three of them. It is my most earnest wish that we could have had both of our families together for their wedding. It was small but lovely. Some of their friends from their flying squadrons were here for the ceremony, and the vicar from the town came out to recite the vows.

I do hope that this note from me will ease your mind of any worry you may have for the kind of family dear Lange has married into, and that you will be as happy for them both as I am.

Most sincerely,
Kathlyn Townsend

~

February 5, 1942
Colesbury, England
Dear Papa DeLony, Aunt Dellie and Cousin Gabe,
I hope it's OK for me to call you all by those names. Lange speaks so often about you that I feel I should know you all already. I'm enclosing some photos from our wedding. I'm sorry for the poor quality. Film in England is hastily developed since the war, as is everything else really. The one of Lange and I is probably the most self-explanatory. The one of the larger group may stump you, so I have penciled names gently on the back of the snap. Most of the men are from Lange's squadron. These chaps really pull for each other and have a great time teasing each other and making light.

It was a wonderful wedding. My Aunt Kath held it at her house in the country. Somehow, Aunt Kath managed to have a cake, although I still have no idea how she managed it with the rationing on sugar, butter, and eggs in place. The day was every-thing I could have wished for, and so much more. It's hard to believe that it has already been a month ago. I have to keep pinching myself. To think that in the middle of this wretched war, on this little island so far away from both of our native lands, Lange and I would find each other and have so much in common. I cannot begin to explain how much I value him and love him. I hope that you like the photographs. I will write again in the near future.

Ever yours,
Mackie DeLony
P.S. Has Lange told you yet about his DFC? It was just

awarded to him last week. I know you are as proud of him as I am. I hope I didn't just spoil a surprise.

~

February 20, 1942

McDade, Texas

Dearest Lange,

Guess it's time we all dropped the "Ding" for good and ever, but it won't be easy so forgive us if we slip up now and then. Flight Lieutenant DeLony sure sounds noble. You must be doing something right to get so many promotions. Congratulations on your marriage, too. Don't suppose I need to say you sure surprised us with that one! Funny thing is a letter came from your bride today, too, along with two pictures of your wedding. Brought a tear seeing you so happy. Gabriel joked that you looked like you had just swallowed a whole bottle of castor oil, but he just wanted me to tell you that to get your goat. I set the pictures in front of your papa and he just stared at them for the longest time. He is getting so much better. I think it was your visit that pulled him through. I will go to my grave believing that.

Mackie a darling letter, told us all about your wedding day, and also about you winning a DFC. Gabriel read an explanation of it from our Encyclopedia of Universal Knowledge. It said this is a medal given for "acts of valor, courage or devotion to duty whilst flying in active operations against the enemy." Mackie didn't explain what you won it for, but I hope you will fill in the blanks. We think it sounds very impressive and I want to know more about it, dear, if you can tell us. I know you are limited by what can be written to us, but I certainly hope you are not in any danger in this job of flying for the RAF over there. It sounds a little scary to this old lady.

Have you decided where you will live once the war is over? My fingers are crossed that it will be right here. We have that house

Gabriel and Letty lived in just sitting vacant since he's moved in here with me. He was talking about hiring a ranch manager and letting him use the house as part of his pay, but I will squelch that idea right quick if you think you would want to live there. You know you would be more than welcome. Just keep yourself safe and come home as quick as you can. I have always hated wars, but this time is different. We were attacked on our own soil in such a cruel way!

As you can well imagine your letters are the only good news we have had since Pearl Harbor. The whole country is in an uproar, and now that the Japanese are swarming all over the Philippines, I guess we can expect more of the same from them. Gabriel does nothing but sit in front of the Philco to listen for more war news. Julianne says Troy Lee is already threatening to quit school and join the navy. She says even Sterling is itching to get into it. He went over to Randolph and volunteered his services as a flying instructor. Can you beat that? I walk around here all day long with my heart in my throat.

I've started putting together a package to send to you all. Thought Mackie's aunt might could use some sugar. They haven't started rationing here yet, although everybody thinks it will happen soon. We did without in the last war, and we can do without again. Lucky Strikes for you, of course, even though you really should cut back. They are so bad for your health, but I don't suppose a young man your age thinks about such things, does he? Gabriel has dug out your old baseball bat and ball and says he will look for a glove small enough for an eight-year-old boy's hand. Will get them all off to you next week. What can I send Mackie? Oh, I guess I'll think of something. The enclosed check is a wedding gift for both of you. Do with it what you want. Maybe supper out on the town and a picture show. Do you ever have time for silly things, too? Hope you can easily cash the check or exchange it for guineas and pounds or whatever they call their money over there. I'm so confused by it.

Still nothing from Sunny's kids. I suppose that we are official enemies of France now, so I don't watch for anything to come in the mail any more. I hope and pray they are safe and sound and have not suffered too many hardships under the thumb of Herr Hitler.

Well, this old lady has rattled on long enough for one letter. We love and miss you and can hardly wait for the day when we are able to meet your new family.

Many hugs from,

Your Aunt Dellie

CHAPTER 20

"Honour and Hope"

The briefing room was situated in a Nissen hut. From the ceiling hung a clanging furnace that belched out a skunky smell and didn't do much to warm the early morning air. Rows of chairs faced a raised platform and, behind the platform, just below the recognition charts of German aircraft, a map of England covered the wall. On the map was a maze of pins with a red string linking various airfields around London to one larger pin at Canterbury, the rendezvous point. From there, a single red string traced out all the way to Boulogne, round that pin, and back to England.

Up on the platform, the station commander, with the endless stripes on his cuffs and gongs on his chest, said the same thing he said each time: "Well, chaps, this is the day we've all been waiting for."

Lange tuned out. He looked down the line at the pilots in B Flight—*his* flight. Jim Hiller sat on his right and seemed to listen intently. Jim was a Flying Officer now and Lange's Number Two. Next to Jim was Tom Donaldson, nicknamed Alabama since he hailed from Tuscaloosa. Donaldson looked half-asleep. To Lange's left was Toady Cooper, North Platte, Nebraska, a skinny fish-faced

guy who liked to drink lemon squash. Toady's cheeks looked perma-
nently puckered from the sour cocktail. On the other side of Toady,
Butch Sawyer and Rory Kosak were whispering, half laughing.
Lange felt compelled to send a nudge down the line. The pair
looked across at Lange, then quickly up in time to hear the station
commander say, "...so give them a good show, lads. Hit them hard,
and good luck to the lot of you."

Then it was Morse's turn. What Morse had to say would be
more important than what they'd just heard from the station
commander, so Lange focused his attention: "A Ramrod. Twelve
Bostons. Twelve-thousand feet. Close escort. Keep a watch out for
the Abbeville crowd. Press tits at forty-five minutes past the hour
and synchronize watches to the clock on the wall. That's it then. Off
you go. Watch your tails."

Chairs scraped back. Flying boots clomped on the floor.
Conversation stayed light but fraught with nerves. The transport
idled right outside the hut. Lange climbed in. The others climbed in
behind him. The driver, a plump WAAF with dyed red hair, took
them to the flight line.

They climbed past fair-weather cumulus, and then
everything—the narrow streets, the hedgerows—fell away and
became miniature. They lifted into the blue, kept in echelon to the
rendezvous where they picked up the bombers. Two other flights
from different stations arrived. Lange's bunch stayed on the
bottom. No bogies over the Channel. Clear sky. Just after they hit
the coast of France, black flak began to blossom up around them.
The closer to the target they got, the hotter the flak.

And then the controller came over the R/T reporting forty plus
bandits approaching from Abbeville and another thirty-plus
twenty-five miles dead ahead. Lange looked to see if his flight was in
position. Hiller was tucked in nice and tight under his wing in the
number two spot. He worried that Sawyer and Kosak were too far

out. He wanted to holler at the bombers to drop their goddammed bombs, so they could all get the hell out of there. He glanced behind just in time to see a bunch of 109s slice into the flight. "We're getting bounced!" he said. And that was almost the last clear thought he had.

A grinding bang came from his rear. His plane shuddered violently, threw him backwards. Immediately its nose pointed heavenward. He wondered briefly what had happened to Jim and the others, just as his airplane flopped over on its back and started to spin.

For ten thousand feet his altimeter unwound as he was thrown around the cockpit like a rag doll. He fought against blackout, tried to recover the controls, but everything felt frozen stiff. Well, he thought, if he blacked-out at least he wouldn't see the impact. So this is how he would die. He thought about Mackie, saw her face, her swollen belly. Tell the baby his daddy loved him.

A voice came, vague and faraway. He couldn't hear over the screaming engine. And then, "Good Christ, Lange! Open your hood!"

Jim's voice in his ear snapped Lange from his torpor. Everything was upside down. He unlatched his seat belt. The Perspex came open easily. He pulled his heavy feet up off the rudder pedals and launched himself out into nothingness. For a second, he thought the airplane would fall into him, but the wind took him out of range. To hell with counting to ten. He jerked the ripcord and the chute stopped his fall with a bang, swung him wildly. He looked down and saw the Channel coming at him. At least he wasn't over Nazi territory. Eighty yards away the Spitfire made a huge splash going in.

He remembered to flex his knees this time, but he still hit the water harder than he expected. The cold of it shocked him like a jolt of electricity. He felt that familiar stab of pain at the base of his spine. He went twenty feet under before his downward momentum was checked by the dinghy inflating. They'd only had the dinghies for a couple of months. They were like sitting on a brick, and he had complained just like everybody, but now he welcomed the yellow raft. When he surfaced, he gasped for breath and got a mouthful of the sea.

Swells, larger than they appeared from above, tossed him around like a popping cork, insignificant, invisible. He wallowed himself in over the side. A gush of water came in with him. He tried to roll over on his back without turning the dinghy over with him. It was an unstable little thing.

Overhead, an airplane circled, made a low pass. Jim Hiller, taking a bearing. "I'm right here!" Lange shouted, as if Jim could hear him, then raised his hand out of the water to let Jim know he was OK. Lange watched Jim's Spitfire get up altitude and swoop around, taking up the whole sky with his turns. He wondered why the damned fool didn't go home. This had to be Nazi waters. There was nothing Jim could do, but he kept on stooging around. He had to be running short of juice, but still he stayed up there. Lange began to watch with fascination. His teeth chattered uncontrollably, but his attention stayed on Jim's Spitfire. The sonofabitch could sure enough fly. The beauty of the swanning aircraft mesmerized him. He almost expected Jim to start doing Immelmann turns and aileron rolls.

After a while, the cold settled into his bones, and he felt almost warm. The swells had a soothing rhythm, like swinging in a hammock. He thought he could probably drift off if Jim would stop buzzing him, taking his attention with the flash of wing so close overhead. Then Jim's kite would dash off to the south some-where, and Lange would think—*Wrong way, you crazy fool! England's north!* But in a few minutes, Jim would be back again, plunging down so low Lange thought a wave might leap up and snatch the Spitfire out of the sky.

He wondered if he had begun to hallucinate. Even lying back in the dinghy, he was drenched with water that washed up over the sides. He'd heard how cold the Channel was, but he never imagined it would be like ice. He thought he might have frostbite on his hands. He couldn't feel them anymore. And one of his flying boots was gone. He could still move his big toe but it was numb. His eyelids had swollen nearly shut from the salt in the water. He rubbed at them but that only made it worse. He had no idea how long it had been since he bailed out. Felt like hours, but it might have been only been a few minutes, too. The wildness of it out there distorted time.

He felt sleepy and at peace, a reaction, he figured from the adrenaline he'd expended in the fall. He daydreamed, thought about Mackie again, always Mackie, imagined her with their baby, and that coalesced into a mental picture of his mother. God, he hadn't thought about his mother in years. She wore a soft blue apron, those safety pins stuck through the bib. And earrings. She wore little silver stud earrings, and she smelled like baking bread.

A great farting sound startled him so badly he nearly capsized the dinghy. He craned around, saw a huge boat bearing down on him. He braced for the crush, prepared to hold his breath going under, hoped the propellers wouldn't tear him and in two. Instead, a pair of strong hands seized him from the dinghy and wrestled him on board with the help of a grapple-hook sort of thing. Gaffed him like a game fish. The sailors slapped at his back. Two sailors mummy-wrapped him in a scratchy blanket. A third gave him a generous tot of good, strong Royal Navy rum. It bit his throat but cleared his head. He couldn't stop trembling, teeth and bones rattling.

The rescue ship had already caught another fellow, a flying sergeant from a Hornchurch squadron. They snagged another one, a pilot officer from Biggin Hill, a real lace drawers snot, who pretended that a "brolly hop" into the Channel was nothing for him. The three of them lay quivering in the blankets, like three beached whales. They accepted one tot of rum after another from a seaman in a silly white hat. By the time they reached shore, Lange was stinko. So were the other two. They hung onto each other and sang like the best of pub pals.

They were delivered by bus to the Air Ministry office at Portsmouth, poured into dry uniforms that didn't fit, and slopped onto a train bound for London. At Victoria station, Lange awoke with the worst cracking hangover he'd ever had in his life. He felt as if he'd been hit between the eyes with a 50-pound mattock. The other two fellows were nowhere to be found.

He got off the train and telephoned the squadron office. Morse already knew what had happened. Jim had landed and written a report. Lange reckoned he owed Jim his life. Morse said, "Take some time, Lange. Go see your wife. Be back by tea tomorrow."

At King's Cross, Lange telephoned Mackie. He wanted to tell her he was on his way. He still had the headache. The telephone operator made the connection for him, and the line began to ring. It rang on and on. He checked his watch, but the dunk in the Channel had stopped it cold.

No answer on the line. Unusual for Bailey, at least, not to be there. The operator came on and with her starchy voice said, "There doesn't seem to be an answer, shall I keep trying?" He could barely hear her for all the noise in the train station. He said no and hung up.

He thought about the motorcycle he almost bought last month. A fellow in one of the other squadrons had posted a notice on the board in the mess. But before Lange could make up his mind, a pilot in Kip Shaker's flight had snapped it up. The fellow offered to rent the motorcycle to Lange, but Lange wasn't piled up with money like most of the other fellows. His paltry wages had to go for necessary things, like his mess bill and trips to Colesbury. And he had a family to take care of, now.

At Euston Station he tried calling her again. Still no answer. He thought they might have gone to a picture show, or maybe to Kathlyn's Red Cross meeting, or who knew where. He took a seat on a bench to wait for the train. There was a delay sign posted on the board. Always delays. He drummed his fingers on his thigh. He was keyed up, a reaction from the rum maybe, or more probably from the bail-out. His headache had turned to a dull pain behind his eyes.

A sandwich board man walked by advertising the station cafe's menu: clangors and pork pie. The place was packed with people in uniforms of all kinds—regular uniforms like Army, Royal Navy, RAF, RAAF, and RCAF; women in uniforms, too—WAAF, WRENS, NAAFI, and ATS. The war had taken over everything. Walls were plastered with posters:

"LET US GO FORWARD TOGETHER!"
"CARELESS TALK COSTS LIVES."
"BACK THEM UP!"
"BUY WAR BONDS."

It suddenly hit him that he was sick and damned tired of this war. Heart in his throat out there swishing around in the Channel. How many more times would his luck hold out? Nearly two years of it already. Did he have another two years left in him? Three? Four? How much longer could this rotten war go on?

Everybody had believed with America in it the whole thing would be over in three months. But America was too busy in the South Pacific now to pay much attention to anything on this side of the world. And America wasn't ready for war, not on the scale it needed to be. There wasn't much of an army, and there sure as hell wasn't an air force. He had seen a few of the American airplanes sent over through Lend Lease and there wasn't a one of them he would trade for his Spitfire.

A faint, feeble cry reached through the racket of the station— the voices, shoes scraping as people walked by, the lady announcer on the Tannoy, trains huffing at the platforms. He thought he was hearing things, but the cry came again. More of a squeak than a cry. A baby piglet? A tree frog? He peered under the bench. A few cigarette butts. Wads of paper. He listened harder for the sound. When it came again, he followed it towards the phone booths.

Then he saw it. Wedged in between the wall and the end phone booth in a three-inch wide crevice—a scared, hungry, miserable little orange-and-white tabby kitten. It squirmed backwards out of his reach. He went down on both knees.

"Come on out of there, little fella. You can't stay back there." He baby-talked it up to the opening of the crevice where he could nab it by the scruff of its neck. It wiggled and tried to fork him with its needle claws. He opened his coat and dropped it inside next to his chest. The needles went into him through his shirt and under-shirt. The kitten mewed and trembled there. He talked softly to it, and it hid its head under his arm.

The kitten was still there inside his coat when he boarded the train. It stayed there, purring, then sleeping quietly, throughout the ride to Colesbury. It gave him comfort for no reason, except the feeling he'd saved something.

At Colesbury, the stationmaster poured the kitten a saucer of milk. The kitten lapped up the milk until its sides bloated out.

"Come all the way from London with him you say?" The stationmaster was an old man, weary-faced. His voice was soft and shaky. Lange had come to Colesbury so many times by then, that he and the old man were regular pals. The stationmaster stroked the kitten's head. "Rare beautiful he is, isn't he?"

"I'm bringing him for my wife's son." Lange cleared his throat, corrected himself. "For *my* son."

He gave the stationmaster a cigarette and used the phone in his office. There was still no answer at the house. Evenings were staying light longer with double-daylight savings time, but he knew it would be dark by the time he made it all the way out there on foot. And it had been a hell of a day already. He didn't relish the thought of a long walk. Even in May, a chill came into the air as soon as the sun went down. Lange thought of the frigid water in the Channel and shivered.

"I'll fix you right up." The man had a gleam in his eye. He set the kitten down on a chair, where it promptly began to clean its face. When the man came back, he was wheeling an aged bicycle. "Just bring her back to me when you come tomorrow."

Lange held the kitten inside the breast pocket of his coat and pedaled the stationmaster's bicycle all the way to the big house three miles outside town.

Nobody was home. The Bentley was gone from the car shed, but they had left the kitchen entrance unlocked. There was a pot of soup on the stove. Left over from supper, he figured. He realized his stomach was grumbling. He set the kitten on the floor and fired up the burner on the stove to heat the soup. It was a carrot and cabbage concoction that smelled foul but he dipped his finger in for a taste, and it was palatable. A half loaf of cottage bread under a cloth lay on the table. He tore off a hunk.

He found the whiskey in the room they called the study. He poured two fingers into a glass and swallowed that quickly, enjoyed the burn of it as it went down. It took away the chill, and pretty soon, the headache, too. He poured some more. The gloominess that had crept up on him during the trip here began to subside. He wondered where they could all be, and after it got dark, he began to get a little worried. And lonely. He hoped they weren't gone someplace overnight. He hated the thought of spending a night by himself in this big, creaky house.

He gobbled down a big bowl of the hot soup, sopped it up with bread. He let the kitten lick the dregs. It was a cute little thing. *Rare beautiful*, the stationmaster had said. It had a kind of golden hue in its coat, eyes to match. It rubbed against Lange's ankle. He scooped it up and carried it with him into the study. He poured himself another drink and sat down in the easy chair. The kitten went around sniffing everything. It poked its head into nooks and crannies, batted at a fuzz ball under the sofa.

He didn't intend to fall asleep. He'd wanted to be awake and waiting, a surprise, when Mackie came home. But the whiskey, the soup, the train ride, the after-combat letdown, all of it worked against his wishes. Kathlyn said she thought there was a burglar, all the lights on, no blackouts pulled across windows. She said she would've waited for Bailey to come in first except Given went bounding inside ahead of her.

"It's just Daddy, Auntie. Can't you smell his cigarettes?"

It was Given's voice that woke Lange. He came up blinking, feeling out of sorts, suddenly in need of a bath and a shave. The whiskey had left a bad taste in his mouth. He tried smoothing out the creases in his uniform.

"Look! A kitten!" Given had spotted the tabby. He went immediately to capture it, his little face aglow. "Can I keep it?"

"I found him at Euston station," Lange said.

"What's its name?" Given hugged the kitten. It began to crawl up to his shoulder. Given's eyes squinted in a giggle.

"That's your decision, buddy. Name it anything you like." Then Lange noticed the distress on Kathlyn's face. "I hope you don't mind, Kathlyn. The poor thing was starving."

"No. Not at all, dear. It's a relief to find you here." She set her handbag on the sofa, and that was not at all like Kathlyn. She was one who believed in everything in its place, and the sofa wasn't where she normally dropped her purse. "I was going to telephone you anyway. It's good you've come. Allison's having a little trouble."

"Trouble?" He was wide-awake now, alert. He sat on the edge of the sofa. "What kind of trouble?"

"We had to put her in hospital. In Peterborough."

He was up and out of the room before she could say more. He found Bailey and took the keys to the Bentley, his heart a knot in his chest. He was nearly running.

AT THE HOSPITAL too many memories seized him—starchy nurses, the carbolic and disinfectant smell, Becky's mangled face, limp body, how she had lain there, looking dead before she was.

He eased onto the hard chair beside Mackie's bed and for a second stared at her while she slept. Here he was again. Powerless. He took her hand. The nurse had told him they'd given her something to help her sleep.

"Mackie," he whispered. His thumb rubbed at her wrist. "Honey, it's me."

She rolled towards him, and for a second it surprised him that she responded. She smiled sleepily. "Darling." She grasped hold of his hand. "How did you know I was here?"

"What the hell happened?" he said.

She kept smiling at him. "They gave me something, and I thought I was dreaming. But it *is* you. Right here."

"Kathlyn said you had some kind of trouble."

Mackie pressed the palm of his hand to the mound of her belly. The drowsy smile stayed on her face. "Did she tell you it's twins?"

"Twins?" His voice rose louder than he meant for it to. Other patients were asleep all around them. She touched a finger to his lips. "No kidding?" he said, quieter.

"Two heartbeats. No wonder I'm such a mountain."

She laughed and he rubbed her belly, thinking about twins. It was a startling thought. Twins had never occurred to him as a possibility. Julianne's daughters, Troy Lee's older sisters, were twins. Maybe twins ran in his family.

"This morning," she said, "I thought I was in labor. I had a few pains, and then there was some bleeding."

"Bleeding?" His smile left quicker than it had come.

"Oh, you know, just a little bleeding. The doctor says this load is too heavy for my body." She kept her hand on top of his. "He wants to keep me here, on my back."

"For how long?"

"I guess until they finally decide to come. I'll probably deliver a little early, that's what he thinks. But he says the longer we can keep them in there the better off they'll be. The babies. Doesn't that sound funny, darling? Babies, plural. I was just getting used to the idea of one baby and now I find out there's two. We're going to start right off with a whole real family, aren't we?"

He pulled her hand to his lips and kissed her fingers. The idea of this whole, real family moved him unexpectedly. Twins. Plus Given. And Mackie. Maybe tomorrow he would feel burdened, but now, holding her hand, he thought he might burst with pure joy.

He didn't trust it, this kind of happiness. It was the sort of thing that seemed meant for somebody else. He wasn't sure if he should give into it, let it take over, in case it turned out to be fleeting.

She linked her fingers inside his. "Are you OK? You're not up for leave yet, are you?"

He started to tell her about nearly drowning today, but then thought, *what the hell*. He cupped her hand inside both of his. She was warm, soft, his wife. "Twins," he said again. "How about that."

She squeezed his fingers.

TEN DAYS LATER, early on the first of June, Mackie delivered two tiny girls. The doctor said they were not identical, which was probably a good thing with sisters. The first one came a little after midnight; the second was born seven minutes later. Tiny, perfect little babies. One with darker hair than the other. One a little bigger. Mackie named them Honour and Hope, in that order. She did it before Lange could get to the hospital, but he didn't think he would've changed their names anyway.

He handed out cigars to everybody in the squadron. "Only one?" Jim Hiller said. "For twins, it seems like we ought to get two." Lange handed him another. Jim took it, slapped Lange on the shoulder. "Congratulations, Pops."

CHAPTER 21

"*Dieppe*"

As soon as she saw the headlines in the morning paper, Mackie was frantic with worry. There had been an assault on a French port, and she was nearly certain Lange had been involved in it. "500 Fighters Sweep French Coast" one headline read. He had to have been in it. Besides, she'd had a bad feeling for several days. She always got a bad feeling when she didn't hear from him for a while. Not that he would've been able to tell her anything. She was sure he probably wouldn't have, but just hearing his voice would have made a lot of difference.

What she knew about Dieppe was that it lay across the Channel on the French coast and that it was a resort town with a casino and beachfront hotels. Anyway, it had been all of that at one time. After yesterday's raid, and after two and a half years under the Nazis, there was no telling what the place looked like now.

Another headline: "Big Raid On Dieppe May Initiate Second Front." Mr. Bailey and Aunt Kath were delighted with that one. They talked with glee all morning about the idea of a second front. Almost all anybody talked about anymore was a second front, just as if there wasn't already a second front in Egypt. But as Mackie read the details of the Dieppe raid, it didn't sound as if a second front or anything else had been accomplished besides the loss of a lot of pilots and Canadian soldiers.

The BBC said the fighter coverage assisting the raid had been excellent. Preliminary losses were ninety-eight fighters with thirty pilots safe. Those numbers hardly soothed Mackie. That meant sixty-eight pilots were either killed or taken prisoner. Five words repeated in her head: *Please, let him be safe.*

She waited for as long as she could stand it, then mid-afternoon she telephoned Lange's squadron. Lange was flying out of Southend, now. She didn't know the person who answered the squadron phone, that day's duty officer. He said his name but he had such a deep southern accent she could barely understand him.

She asked for Lange. Said she was his wife, still not used to the sound of that. Her voice was shaky and impatient. She couldn't help it. A thump came from the telephone, so she thought the connection had been broken, but then the southern drawl was back on the line. "Ain't here. We reckon him and coupla fellers wandered over to London. Be back in a day or so."

She let out her breath and hung up. She stood in the hallway, staring at the telephone. Thank God, thank God. That meant he was OK. Just in London. Back in a day or so.

Her eyes wandered to the window. She could hear the babies in the garden where she'd left them with Aunt Kath. Hope, fussy Hope, who cried the loudest, always hungry, always wet, always needing extra attention. She looked back down at the telephone, Aunt Kath's old candlestick phone.

London? What was he doing in London? He wasn't up for leave. The normal schedule was twelve days on, two off. It could vary, if things were hot or if the squadron was short-handed. But he'd just mentioned two new pilots he'd been busy training, and he'd only been gone for four days. And now—now, he was in London?

Normally, he would telephone if he went into London, so she could meet him there. Aunt Kath would insist on it. She would mind the babies, as long as Winnie was there to help. Winnie was the new housekeeper, an older woman from up north whose husband was in the local home guard.

Hope was in the throes of a squalling fit. Mackie glanced through the window and saw Aunt Kath wiggling a pink rattle over the perambulator, trying her best to quiet the screaming Hope. Winnie was tending to Honour, who was at least quiet if not asleep. They were hungry. Mackie had come in to get their bottles, then got sidetracked by her worry.

All of a sudden, she felt ill. Her head ached, stomach queasy. For a moment, she thought she might faint. She sat down on the hall bench, bent forward so her head was between her knees. She felt the blood rushing to her face. Usually he would call if he went to London. She could meet him at The Whitehorse, like before. They had continued to check-in as Mr. and Mrs. Rushford. It was romantic, secretive, the top room, the lovemaking. If anything, it was more intense, their lovemaking. Especially now, away from the babies and Colesbury. What was he doing in London without her?

The garden door opened, and Aunt Kath looked inside. Hope's wailing came sharper, almost painful. "Allison, we can't get her to shoosh. I think she wants her mummy. Are you all right, dear? Is it Lange, have you heard from him?"

She sat upright, wiped her face with both hands. She still felt woozy. "He's fine. He's in London."

"Are you going?"

Mackie shook her head and pulled herself up from the bench. "I'll get their bottles."

Aunt Kath followed. "What in the world is he doing in London?"

Mackie shrugged. "I'm just glad he's tucked away safe." She tried to sound like she meant it. She *did* mean it. Only she wished he would telephone. Just to tell her himself that he was there and thinking about her.

"Who would have ever thought we would be saying that:

Tucked away *safe* in London, of all places?" Aunt Kath removed the bottles from the warming pan on the stove. She shook milk onto her wrist to check the temperature and handed the bottle to Mackie. "Poor dear. You're getting a permanent fret line between your brows, aren't you?"

"I'm not fretting. Now that I know he's OK. I am not fretting."

"Good. That's the spirit. Stiff upper lip. No other choice."

Mackie wiped the bottles off with a towel. A pot of soup simmered on the stove. The smell of it turned Mackie's stomach, carrots and cabbage again. A little bit of stringy meat. Endless cabbage soup. Shortages were beginning to get severe. It had been over a month since there had been an egg in the house. Aunt Kath was talking about, God forbid, taking up the raising of laying hens.

A tear slid out onto the tip of Mackie's nose. She caught Aunt Kath staring at her. Annoyed, she knuckled away the errant tear. "I know what you're thinking and it isn't so. You think I'm too dependent on him. You think it will devastate me if something should happen..." Mackie choked on that last word and couldn't get out any more.

Aunt Kath moved to put her hand on Mackie's shoulder. "I had so hoped you would be happy once you were married. Two beautiful new babies, a husband who dotes on you."

"Dotes on me?" Mackie pushed at her hair, trying to regain her composure. "He doesn't dote on me."

"Of course, he does. It's plain as day. Now, try to smile, dear."

Aunt Kath handed Mackie a handkerchief. It smelled like lavender. She blew her nose. She knew she was a pitiful mess. She could not be a pilot's wife and fall apart like this.

Winnie came in carrying Hope. Big tears wet her long lashes. Mackie lifted the baby from Winnie's arms. "There now, darling." She patted Hope's little back and watched Winnie hurry again to the garden for Honour.

It took a while to settle Hope down enough so she would take the bottle. Three months old, and she already had such a temper.

Mackie murmured to her and kissed her head. She looked like her daddy. They both did but Hope the most. Dark hair, blue eyes, but they weren't going to stay blue. They would be chocolate candy drops like Daddy's eyes.

Bailey had brought down Given's old cradle from the attic and set it up in the kitchen. Both babies fit in there together. They liked to sleep curled up one to the other, like kittens. Gently, Mackie rocked the cradle. Honour fell right back to sleep. Hope whimpered, thumb in her mouth. Mackie reached to pull out that thumb, but knew in a second it would be right back in Hope's mouth. A test of wills, and Hope was winning.

Aunt Kath took the lid off the soup pot, stirred, and made some suggestions to Winnie. Aunt Kath's long-time cook, Imogene, had left six months ago, claimed she needed to move in with her old mum in Manchester. The Jerries had turned their attention to a munitions factories there, and Imogene's mother lived too close. Until Winnie came, Aunt Kath had taken over the kitchen, and she was finding it difficult to relinquish control.

From a distance, a faint little roar began and quickly grew stronger. Mackie looked at Aunt Kath, who stopped stirring the soup. The sound came closer, a low flying plane. Mackie's heart raced.

"Oh my." Aunt Kath's hand went to her chest. "Should we go down to the cellar?"

"That isn't a bomber. Listen!" Mackie rushed out of the kitchen, down the hall, and to the garden door, peering through each window she passed. She stepped out onto the terrace, shaded the afternoon glare from her eyes, and watched a Tiger Moth circle the south meadow. The little gray bi-plane was down to two hundred feet, already in landing approach.

She dashed across the garden, watching as the Moth came lower. Lange! She could see him clearly in the open cockpit. She stumbled a couple of times, righted herself, kept running. When the little plane was ten feet above the meadow he stalled the engine. It dropped neatly to the ground. That was one way to avoid the rocks that studded the meadow.

By the time she got to the clearing, he had climbed out of the back cockpit. He unharnessed his parachute, tossed it onto the empty front seat, and jumped to the ground. He wore his flying boots, a completely rumpled uniform. He looked ragged, had a bandage on his temple just below where he'd stowed his goggles atop his forehead. He walked towards her, opened his arms out wide, and she raced into them.

He squeezed her so tightly, she almost couldn't breathe, but she didn't care. He swung her around in a half circle, then put her down. "My God, you *were* in it, weren't you?" she said. "That business across the Channel?" He kissed her between the eyes and didn't answer. "What happened here?" She touched the bandage. He winced, ever so slightly, laughed, pulled off his helmet and goggles.

"Had a little run-in with my gun-sight," he said.

A mental picture of that came into her mind. She knew what it meant. "You mean you crashed?"

He shook his head. "Forced landing. Broken crankshaft. The field I picked wasn't as smooth as it looked."

She waved at the Tiger Moth. "How did you come by the kite?"

"Borrowed it. I hope Kathlyn doesn't mind."

"She thought we were being bombed."

They walked arm-in-arm toward the house. She wouldn't ask him about the newspaper headlines. If he wanted to tell her he would. Meanwhile, she could piece together what had happened. He'd taken a hit, maybe anti-aircraft, enough to break the crankshaft on his aircraft. He had managed to make it back to England. The plane was probably a total wash-out, and he was lucky not to have more than a cut on his head. She suppressed the shiver that raced through her. They were flying him too much, using him up. The fatigue on his face was clear to see. He needed a good long rest.

"I have to be back day after tomorrow," he said, almost like he read her thoughts. She nodded and squeezed his waist. She had to pretend not to worry. For him. And for her.

WHEN LANGE WAS THERE everybody scurried around him like he was the king. Even Marmalade, Given's cat, purred around Lange's feet. Aunt Kath made him sit at the head of the table and had Winnie serve the soup on the best china, which they had mostly dispensed with using these days. Lange ate the awful cabbage soup with enthusiasm, as if it were some delicacy from the Savoy chefs. It was almost as if he thought he had to entertain them, telling little stories about life in the RAF, keeping it light, away from any combat. To listen to him, one would think his squadron did nothing but frolic around the airdrome all day. He always brought along a little something: A sack of flour this time. Last time he'd brought onions. As usual, he mesmerized Given with just his presence.

She'd never seen Given so madly enthralled with anyone. He already called Lange Dad, followed him like a puppy, chattering nonstop, about his baby sisters, about school, about airplanes. He asked Lange questions she could have answered, probably had answered in the past, but nothing held any worth for Given unless it came from Lange's mouth.

They went out to let Given sit in the Tiger Moth and stayed until nearly dark. Then Lange sat with the babies, both of them, in his arms, and they looked as content as two peas snuggled in there. Everything, and everybody, was all right when Lange was there.

Later, when she finally had him all to herself, she made him sit on the edge of the bed while she massaged his feet. Gradually the story came out. His squadron had been there, just as she suspected, at Dieppe. They weren't allowed to make outside calls beforehand. They all knew something big was up, but they didn't know what until the briefing. His flight had gone on three sorties and shot down nine German planes. But they had lost some pilots, too. One taken prisoner, two killed in a mid-air collision. All the pilots in his flight came in OK, to his relief.

She poured him a glass of whiskey from the bottle she brought from downstairs, took a sip herself before she handed it to him. "And this?" She touched the white bandage on his head. "How did this happen?"

He grabbed her fingers. "I told you. I hit the gun-sight."

"You crash-landed somewhere."

The meek smile he gave told her she had guessed right. "Beachy Head. I bet I didn't clear the cliffs by more than six feet. Bellied in on one of those grassy hills right there. Soon as I jumped out, the damned thing caught fire. But I rescued my logbook."

He laughed. She didn't. It wasn't funny. "You and your bloody damned logbook," she said, as she unknotted his tie.

"Long as you walk away life is good." He took a big swallow of whiskey. "I was in London all morning."

"Oh?" So the southern drawl on the phone had been right after all. She pulled her dress over her head. He watched with interest.

"Signed up with the US Army Air Force," he said.

She stopped. "I thought you hadn't made up your mind about that."

He shrugged, reached to rub up her hip. "They offered me captain's pay. It's about three times what the RAF's giving me. Plus ten thousand dollars life insurance. I couldn't turn that down."

"I suppose not." She tugged his braces off his shoulders, handled the drink glass for him while he freed his arms. She gave him back the glass and started unbuttoning his shirt. He didn't have on an undervest. Just his RAF ID discs around his neck.

"Stretch out," she said. "I'll massage your back."

"I've got a better idea." He dropped his drink on the table and tugged her onto the bed, pushing her slip up to her waist. "Give me a kiss, woman," he said, snuggling into her neck and rolling her underneath him.

~

IN THE MIDDLE of the night one of the babies cried out. Mackie threw off the covers and got out of bed. She fumbled in the dark for her robe, found it and put it on, then realized Lange was missing. The bedroom door stood wide, and the crying had already stopped.

Moonlight leaked in around the makeshift blackout panel Bailey had tacked over the high window above the hallway. Mackie moved in the darkness down to the next room, which they had fixed as a nursery. Lange had drawn back the window curtain and stood there in just his baggy underpants. He held Hope tight against his cheek, talking to her in a low voice, showing her the moon. One chubby arm bobbled out, almost as if she reached for the sky. In the crib, Honour slept soundly.

"Why didn't you wake me?" Mackie said in a low voice.

Lange turned. "She just needed her diaper changed. She's happy now."

"You changed a diaper? Good Daddy." Mackie rubbed up his back to his shoulder. She could feel the knots of tension there. He didn't sleep any better than Hope did. Not even lovemaking helped him relax.

"There's a sight," he said, nodding at the window. "Look at that moon."

She wound her arms around him. It still felt good to have her hands on him. She wondered if she would ever get over that. Hope's little fist paddled down on her mummy's head. "At Wentworth we would've called that a bomber moon."

"It's probably wrong of me to say this..." He patted Hope's bottom, and she laid her little head on his shoulder. "But I believe these are the two pretties babies I've ever laid eyes on. Does that sound too much like bragging?"

Mackie gave a laugh. "No, I agree." She eased Hope out of his arms. "Let me see if she'll go to sleep now."

The baby squirmed for a bit, but Mackie stood over the crib and patted her until she quieted. She tiptoed from the room, left the door ajar. Lange was already in bed when she got back. She snuggled in after him. He put his arm around her, and she hugged up to his side.

"You know what I had at the American headquarters today?" he said. "A Coke. Icy cold. Best damned thing I've tasted in two years. Funny thing is, the US Air Corps wouldn't have had me two years ago. Guys like me...the whole squadron is guys like me that couldn't have made the grade, too old or with eyesight that's not up to snuff. Now they're acting like they're afraid we're not going to come in. So they gave me a Coke and a Parker Brothers pen to sign my name, and a hundred and fifty bucks for new uniforms. I go for my physical next week."

She couldn't tell if he was happy or not. Somehow his tone didn't sound exactly happy. There was a note of fatalism she couldn't identify. She had been hearing it from him a lot lately. She rubbed his chest, the patch of fine hair there.

"I'm going to have to get used to saying Captain DeLony," she said. "Sounds odd."

"I want you to think about taking the kids to Texas," he said. "Aunt Dellie's already told me we could have the bunkhouse."

She kissed his shoulder. "We're perfectly fine right here."

"I'm not sure about that. Don't believe that crap you read in the paper. We got licked yesterday. There were fellows down by the hundreds on the beach. Looked like piles of driftwood down there. My flight went over there three times ourselves, and we just couldn't do much. It was a Canadian show. I guess you knew that."

"Yes, I knew it." She put her arm across him. He squeezed her closer.

"What about Texas?" he said. "Let's talk about that some more."

"I'm not going, Lange. I wouldn't be able to stand being so far away from you."

He got quiet for a little while, and his grip on her loosened, but she knew he wasn't going to sleep. She wasn't sleepy anymore either. She was thinking about him crash-landing at Beachy Head, about piles of Canadian soldiers like driftwood, and sipping an icy Coca-Cola through a straw.

He said, "You are planning to live with me in Texas? Once this is all over?"

"Is that what we're going to do? We've never really said, have we? I thought it might be bad luck to talk about it."

"Except I think I need to talk about it."

"I thought we might stay here. In England. Maybe we'd open a little flying school. Something like that. If you can settle down to such a slow pace."

"But not in England. That sky we just looked at? That's how the moon looks in Texas all the time. Big and clear. Doesn't rain every damned day."

"You sound homesick."

"Maybe. Truth is, this is going to go on for a while yet. I don't see a quick end. And I really need for you to promise me you'll go to Texas if something should happen."

"Darling, you're scaring me." She wished there was a light on, so she could see his face.

He rubbed her shoulder, tightened his grip. Yesterday had clearly rattled his nerves. She wanted to say something to reassure him but anything that came to mind sounded pathetic and trite, and she battled her own worries every day. She held onto him, maybe too tightly, until she felt his body begin to relax.

"Your flying school idea sounds kind of cute," he said. "I could teach them how to shoot down Nazis, and you can teach them dead reckoning."

"In Texas?" she said, glad for the easier sound in his voice.

"Yes, in Texas."

"Whatever you say, captain."

He grunted a laugh and rolled over to his side. She hugged up to his back, kissed his shoulder, and tried to will herself to sleep.

~

A COLD RAIN LASHED DOWN. End of September, summer long gone. The wind blew fiercely for several minutes, and when it slacked up everything was soaked: her hair, her shoes, stockings. Good stockings were hard to come by these days, and now these were thoroughly soaked from the knee down and beginning to droop. She drew her coat tighter around her and wondered about the musical instruments in the band out there on the parade grounds. Didn't the horn flare of the tuba act as a conduit for the rain water? For a moment, she pictured rain draining through the bell of the tuba and into the player's mouth. The thought made her laugh, a dry laugh, and then her tears resumed.

RAF Debden. She'd flown in here herself a few times. It was always rain-soaked. Situated just far enough inland to catch the seaborne clouds from the Irish Sea, the North Sea, and the Channel. Today, they all seemed to collide right over the parade grounds. Debden was notorious for rain delays. Thinking about it made her yearn for those days of flying for the ATA.

They looked fine out there, the three Eagle Squadrons, standing at attention as the American anthem played, lined up in neat rows in their RAF blues, soggy from the rain. The wing commander and the air chief marshal each gave a long-winded address. Once the "Star Spangled Banner" began and the American flag was run up the pole, the sky really opened. It seemed portentous in some way— an end to something besides the obvious. So he would be flying for the USA, now. How could that change anything between them? Logic wasn't at work. She was too emotional. It didn't take much to bring on tears, something far less dramatic than a military band and a changing of the flag.

Her raw emotions were her first clue that she was pregnant again. Such a careless thing to be in the middle of a war, with two babies at home barely four months old. Lange didn't know. She thought she would break the news once this ceremony was done.

She had put it off because, well, it was an embarrassment really. It was reckless and ridiculous, this mad passion she had for her husband, standing six rows back, third from the left, at attention, saluting his country's flag as it went up the pole.

He had told her not to come today. "It'll be one of those stupid hooplas the British love so much. Don't waste your time, honey." But she wanted to be here to see the official change over. It meant a lot to him, even though he pretended otherwise, as if it was just the pay rise and the benefits that had lured him, nothing at all to do with national pride and patriotism. She supposed this would be his last time in RAF blue. From here out it would be the US Army Air Corps "pinks and greens."

They were planning to meet afterwards, at the mess, which was open today to the public, friends and family. The America press would be there. Mackie didn't know what to expect of that, so she'd worn a gray striped suit she'd had since before the war, a box hat with a piece of veiling in case of photographs. But her entire outfit was wet and sopping, despite the brolly she clutched tightly in her hand. She had already turned the veiling back over the hat and out of the way, and now wished she hadn't worn a hat at all. She was glad she hadn't brought Given, as much as he had begged to come. He would have been soaked through, at risk of catching cold, and he didn't need to miss school.

As the squadrons marched by the review stand, a voice behind her said, "Mackie?" Then more insistently, "Mackie MacLeod? Is that you?"

She turned, and with shock and horror, saw Neil Bannion standing right behind her. He had squadron leader stripes on his sleeves, sandy hair curling out from under his service cap. He looked dapper, elegant, even in the rain. Their time together came back in a flash.

"It is you," he said, smiling. "What in devil's name are you doing here? You're not in uniform." His smile cleaved deep creases in his cheeks. "Are you going to the luncheon? Come along, I'll walk you over."

"No, I…" she stammered.

"You're not going? Are you here for someone?"

People had begun to move around them. She realized the ceremony had ended. The crowd surged away from the parade grounds, everyone heading towards the Officers' Mess.

"I'm here for my husband." She held up her left hand, so he would see the gold ring on her finger. Lange wore its mate. She started to move away.

"You got married? That's bully." He took her arm. "You're not going to walk away, are you? We're old friends, aren't we, Mackie?"

She smiled, calmed herself. "Lovely to see you, Neil."

"Yes, it is. Quite." He put his hand on the hollow of her back, as if to start her walking. "Did you leave the service for this bloke? Good heavens, he's not a Yank, is he?"

As if on cue, Lange walked up. To Mackie, he said, "I thought I'd take you over." Then he looked at Neil, smiled, gave a salute, put out his hand. "I recognize you, sir. You were my flight instructor at OTU."

Neil furrowed his brow at Mackie, shook Lange's hand. "Right-o. I believe I do remember you," he said. "From Texas, isn't it? Looks as if you've done quite well. I'm delighted to see that."

"You've met my wife Mackie?"

Neil turned a brittle smile on her. "How do you do," he said and held out his hand.

She wanted to shrink into the ground. So Neil was going to play it that way. She shook hands awkwardly and watched the two of them, so cordial and familiar.

The rain picked up. She mentioned it. The three of them began to walk briskly. Lange led the way. She had hoped to leave Neil on the parade grounds, but he kept up with them. She splashed through a few puddles, doused her shoes and stockings even worse. Lange kept hold of her arm, steering her towards the Officers Mess.

Lange and Neil kept up a solid run of easy-going conversation all the way to the front arched doorways of the mess. She could tell Lange was pleased to have Neil's company, but she kept trying to think of some way to shake him. The three of them went up the steps and inside. There was a crush of people in the entry hall. They threaded their way through to the anteroom. People milled about in there as well. The noise level was too high for any possibility of conversation. Relieved, she couldn't see Neil anymore and hoped he'd got lost in the crowd.

Lange leaned in close to her ear. "Follow me," he said, and pulled her by the hand through the crowd, across a corridor, and into the dining hall. The tables were set up in long rows. Placemats bearing the RAF Insignia, "*Per Ardua Ad Astra,*" the crown and eagle lay on the table in front of every leather-bottom dining chair. Chandeliers overhead put a golden glow on everything. A fire roared in the fireplace at the far end. She held onto Lange's hand, admired the lovely room.

A camera flash popped in her face. She realized with dismay that Neil had caught up to them. He and Lange were talking to the photographer and a reporter, explaining how Neil had been Lange's OTU instructor all that time ago when Lange first arrived in England. It was going to be a long ordeal, this luncheon. There were reporters from *Life Magazine*, and *Time*, and all the major American newspapers, as well as the BBC. Even she was interviewed briefly by one reporter. He wanted to know who she was married to and seemed interested to hear about her service in the ATA, but then he switched tactics to learn more about Lange. She tried to remember how many sorties he had flown. She didn't have exact numbers, and what did it matter anyway? Too many, that was the answer, but of course, that wasn't what the reporter wanted to hear.

Finally, the luncheon was called to order by one of the commanders, and as the cacophony subsided, everyone took seats at the tables. She was dismayed when Neil sat on the other side of Lange. No doubt, Neil reveled in all the limelight, he was that sort. She couldn't believe, now, that she had once thought she was in love with him. She hadn't known back then what being in love even meant.

The food was better than the average wartime fare—a joint of beef, fresh vegetables. Conversation was social and pleasant, although she spent more time talking to Jim Hiller, across the table, since Neil completely dominated Lange. Her trepidation at first seeing him had turned to annoyance.

Once the plates were cleared, the wingco and air chief marshal had more to say. Then came the new American commanders, two generals and some other American big shots. Cigarettes were lit, ashtrays passed around, coffee was served. People chuckled politely at the half-witted jokes from the dais. And she almost missed it when Lange offered Neil a cigarette from the case she had given him, the same case she had also given to Neil.

She heard Neil's voice, "I had one exactly like that once upon a time." He leaned forward to look at Mackie—a brief glance, nothing much, except it was enough to let her know he remembered the cigarette case. She held her breath. "Well, maybe not exactly like it," he went on. "As I recall, mine had a bit different clasp." He pulled out a cigarette. "Thanks, old boy."

Lange snapped the case shut. Her face was hot, ears rang. She reached for her clutch, opened it, rummaged around for her dignity. She couldn't stop her eyes from roaming past Lange down to Neil. Had he just done something gracious? Even gentlemanly? For her sake?

Unreasonable, inappropriate tears welled. Fighting them back, she pulled out a handkerchief and snapped shut her clutch, left it lying in her lap. At the same moment, Lange glanced away from his conversation, smiled at her, and under the table, gripped her cold hand in his warm one.

CHAPTER 22

Letters

October 17, 1942

   Colesbury, England

   Dear Papa, Aunt Dellie, Gabe, and all,

   Lange sends his love. He is very busy with the new squadron, learning the US Army Air Force way, and getting used to having two sets of wings on his uniform. And I'm getting used to him in his "Pinks and Greens." Gabe may know why the uniform is called that, but just in case, it's because the tunic is olive drab and the trousers are a kind of a beige color that looks a little pink in certain lights. It's really the winter dress uniform, and, of course, he looks fantastic in it. I have enclosed his official US Air Corps snap and also a newspaper clipping from the change-over ceremony that was given by the RAF when the Eagle Squadrons transferred. The paper did a little interview with Lange I thought you might enjoy. The newspaper picture of the ceremony is grainy, so I took the liberty of circling Lange so you would know which one is him. It was a lovely event, and I have wished practically every day since that I had let Given attend with me. The weather was quite horrid, but I think it might have been worth a sore throat or congestive cold not to have to hear over and over how disappointed he is that he wasn't there. Have I mentioned that Given absolutely adores Lange? Doesn't everybody?

I have also enclosed another snap of the twins. They keep their mum busy. They're growing so fast, trying now to sit up on their own. I really don't know what I would do without all the help from Aunt Kath. Two babies are quite a handful. However, whenever their dad is around, all they seem to do is sleep, so he thinks I'm exaggerating, of course, when I complain.

I was wondering if you happened to have any pictures of Lange when he was a boy that you wouldn't mind sharing with me? I would love to know more about him then, what he was like as a child, etc.

Our weather here in the Fens has got quite cold now. Seems the wind is blowing down from Scotland. They're saying that it will be a hard winter. I am certainly not looking forward to that. I'm not one of those Cannucks that likes snow and ice. Had enough of that when I was a girl, thank you very much. I look forward to coming to Texas and meeting all of you in person one day. I feel as if we are already family.

Ever yours,
Mackie

~

November 14, 1942
McDade, Texas
Dear Mackie,

Thank you so much for the news clipping and pictures, and for the letter. We do so enjoy hearing from you. It's hard to imagine the weather already being so cold. We are having mild weather here, and before long it will be Thanksgiving again. It's hard to believe that this time last year, Lange was with us. On his visit he spoke of you, which we all thought was peculiar for him, until we got news the two of you had married.

Please send a picture of Given. We would so much like that. Does he get one taken in school or anything? We can just hardly wait to meet you and Given and get our hands on those precious baby girls. To think our dear little Lange had to go all the way to England to find his purpose. It is still so hard for me to imagine him flying a fighter airplane and shooting down German airplanes out of the sky. My grandnephew, Troy Lee, has done his best to try to explain exactly what goes on in this flying war, but it is just more than my mind can absorb.

You asked about Lange as a boy. I will tell you he was always a joy to me. He stayed at my house an awful lot growing up and became like a second son. He was always helpful, especially to Gabriel, never was a nuisance or a complainer, and was just full of curiosity about everything. I have sent you a picture of him when he was about eight years old with our dog, Ben. Lange just loved that old dog and taught him to do lots of tricks. He was never a child given to sadness, although I reckon he had plenty of cause to be. The only time I ever knew him dragged down low was when Becky died. But I guess going off to join the Royal Air Force was his way of getting past that. I sure am glad things turned out so well for him. I worried for a long while after he first left.

Truth is, I would be lying if I said I don't still worry quite a bit. Especially when we hear news on the radio about how the war is going over there. They have us saving tires and tin for the war effort. I have a load of those things ready to take to the collection center up at Bastrop.

Mackie, thank you for writing to us. It is good of you to do that. I am so grateful to you for giving our boy new life. You are already precious to us, and we don't even know you yet.

Many hugs,
Aunt Dellie

~

January 5, 1943

Colesbury, England

Dear Aunt Dellie,

I cherish the photo you sent of Lange with the dog. I can see so much of our girls in his eyebrows and the shape of his face. I showed the photo to Lange when he was last here on leave, and he said he remembered the day that picture was taken. He said he and Ben were sitting on the porch step in back of your house. I think he got a kick out of seeing it again.

Thank you also for giving me a little insight into Lange's boyhood. I knew, of course, that he lost his mum when he was young, the same as I did. I think losing our mothers when we were young was one of the first things to connect us. Losing Becky must have been devastating for him, too. He hasn't spoken much about that, or at all, really, so all I know is she died in a car wreck. I hate to bring up a touchy subject so maybe you could enlighten me a little further. He did tell me about his sister, Sunny, of course. Losing her was probably hard for him as well.

Did I forget to mention in my last letter that we will be welcoming another addition to our family in May? I hadn't got back my figure yet from the twins, and here I am in smocks again. This is absolutely going to be it for us. Four children are quite enough, and we can be content with our little family as it will be now.

I look forward to hearing from you. I hope that Papa is continuing to do well.

Ever yours,

Mackie

~

February 12, 1943

Dearest Mackie,

Thank you for the sweet Christmas picture of the five of you. I took it to Bastrop to have it enlarged and framed. Now it sits on top of the piano in the front room. I find my dear brother staring at it often. He is finally beginning to recognize his son in it, but I still have to remind him who the rest of you are. I think he's overwhelmed by the change in Lange. He does look so grown up, and my goodness, such a big, growing family! What a handsome young man Given is, and congratulations on the new little one coming in May. That sure is welcome news.

I hope I didn't open my mouth about something when I mentioned Becky in my last letter. We never did think she was the right girl for ~~Ding~~ Lange, but of course, we didn't wish for anything bad to happen to her. They were just so young when they got married. The car wreck was a tragedy. There was another person killed, too. Ask Lange to explain it all to you. I would hate to mess up the facts. I'm sure it is natural for you to want to know everything about your husband, especially in your situation, the two of you coming from different countries and backgrounds and all. My Gabriel brought home a bride from the last war, and dear Letty never got tired of looking through my old photo box. As for me, I grew up less than a mile from my late husband, so there were never any gaps to fill in for me.

Keep writing to us. We can hardly wait to get your next letter.

Many hugs from,

Aunt Dellie

~

21 May 1943

Somewhere in England

Dear Folks,

I know it's been a long time since I have written to you. I apolo-

gize for that. Not only have I been busy, but I guess a little lazy too, since I knew Mackie was doing the letter-writing for all of us. My bet is she writes a better letter than me anyway.

Last Sunday, 16 May 43, our little girl, Susannah Faire, was born in Peterborough, England. She weighed 7'5 or half a stone, as they say here. She has blond peach fuzz on her head and right now looks a little bit like Papa! I finally got to see her this morning—a brand new little person. She looks huge compared to how tiny her twin sisters were when they were born. Her mama is doing fine, too. I'm sure she'll be sending you pictures of little Susie as soon as she's able to. Can you believe it? Two years ago it was just me, and now there's six of us!

Everything else is all right. I wish I could say that the war will be over by autumn, but I think there's still a lot of work to do. The damned German show no signs of giving up. I suppose the same could be said now of the Japanese, too. I sure am happy to be flying for the good ol' USA. Hard to believe it's already been seven months ago we made the change. It was a relief when the mess switched over from British rations to American rations, I will tell you that much for sure. I was getting pretty tired of beans and Brussels sprouts.

We have been transitioning to a new US aircraft, the P-47 Thunderbolt. It's a big monster compared to the Spitfire. Feels like there's room to square dance in the cockpit. One day when I went out to the flight line, my ground crew had a big surprise waiting for me. During the night, they had painted Cpt. C.L DeLony on the upper fuselage, and in fancier writing, GUNSLINGER underneath. I got a laugh out of it, but I'm not usually the kind to much like that sort of thing, especially since some of the other guys fly the plane as much as I do. But anyway, I'll send you a picture of it, or have Mackie do it when she gets back on her feet.

By the way, thanks for explaining to her all about Becky. I had only told her a little, just never did get into it much. But after your letter we had a long talk, so now it's out and she knows everything there is to know. You can skip this part when you read this letter to Papa. He's always thought this sort of stuff was chickenshit.

Don't have much else to say. Still learning a lot.

Much love,

Lange

PART FOUR
Wild Blue Yonder

OCTOBER 1943

CHAPTER 23

"Rhubarb"

It was the old bus run: Ostend to Ghent. A Rhubarb: strafing mission, targets of opportunity. Lange's flight had made this dash dozens of times before. Hit the port. Go in low over the rail yard; get under the guns. Cause some hell; tear up tracks. The weather had been stinking since mid-October—fogged in. The boys were all itching for action. Seven miles west of Ostend, Lange spotted an airfield he remembered hitting before. Light flak. He-111 bombers parked in dispersals, just as he'd been hoping. Ducks in a pond.

He took the fellows down to treetop level. They went screaming in at 400 miles per hour. Lange's gunfire walked across the turf and sprayed into one of the bombers. He gave it a long blast, looked back in time to see it explode in a cloud of flames and black smoke. The other boys in his flight got in some hits, too.

When Lange brought the flight up, just as they were gaining altitude, a gaggle of Me-190s jumped them, coming out of the sun. The big, heavy P-47s were slow to climb, but Lange firewalled his engine, got the drop on one of the 190s, turning right instead of the expected left. The 190 lined up in his sight, and Lange let him have it. Hits danced up the 190's wing, flashed into the fuselage. He did a quick one-eighty, ready to go again, but saw the pilot bail out. The 190 augered into the ground from six hundred feet.

The P-47 Thunderbolt was a big bruiser. Brawny as hell and loaded with firepower. At first, Lange hated it, but every battle in it gave him more confidence. He went after the 190 dogging Jim Hiller's tail. Shell casings clattered against his windshield from the 190's guns. Lange gave the German plane a burst in the ass, took off part of the rudder. He skidded to starboard to cut off his turn, just as a huge bang jolted the T-bolt. It came from out of nowhere, and sounded like a stick of dynamite hit the nose of the fuselage. His heart jumped. The plane pitched sideways. A split-second later, a falling 190 flamed across his vision. Hydraulic oil poured out of the cowling behind the propeller and blacked-out his windshield. The engine vibrated hard. He throttled back, but the T-bolt sounded like it might shake apart.

He was grateful to his crew chief for screwing on a Spitfire rearview mirror. He could see behind him at least, and through the sides. He knew his plane wasn't going to take him back to England. He had to make a decision. Adrenaline flooded through him.

"I'm bailing out, Jim," he said into his mic. But almost as soon as he said it, he realized he was too low to bail out, and he didn't have enough power left to climb. He would have to find a place to belly in; the T-bolt was failing fast.

With no more contemplation, he started searching for an open field. There were lots of small fields and lots of trees, but nothing looked long enough. He still had pretty good speed and somehow the prop still turned, but the engine coughed and juddered violently. He squinted through the murky, oil-covered windshield, spotted a field of beets up ahead that looked long enough. As soon as he saw it, he shoved the stick forward, and at 170 miles per hour, laid the P-47 down nose first in the field. He held the stick forward, as the plane plowed through the soft field, tearing up beets, metal screaming, earth flying. The impact slung him around the cockpit. Uprooted beets drummed against the fuselage like stones.

Just before he hit the tree line, he kicked the right rudder hard and covered his face with his arms to keep the gun sight from knocking him out. He'd learned that lesson at Beachy Head. He grabbed the bar on the canopy and braced for impact with the trees. Just before the plane hit, it looped around, tipped up on its nose, and dug in. It seemed for a moment as if the Thunderbolt planned to stand there on its nose, but after a long pause, it flopped back on its belly with a huge thud and a sigh.

By then, the plane was smoking so he only had a moment to collect his wits. He reached to shove back the canopy. It wouldn't budge. He tried again. Nothing. Panic grabbed him. He imagined his feet were burning. He braced both boots on the instrument panel, grabbed the bars of the canopy, and heaved with all his might. The canopy screeched open a foot and stopped. Hard as he tried, he could not get it to move another inch. So, he shrugged off his parachute, flight jacket, the .45 he worse strapped to his ribs. He left the parachute in the cockpit, but threw out the jacket and .45 wadded together, threw them out through the one-foot opening. He squeezed himself up. Shoulders didn't want to push through. He closed his eyes and heaved himself out through the canopy. As soon as he was out, he jumped down on the wing, gathered his jacket and the .45. Smoke poured from the cowling now. Poor old Gunslinger. It had saved his life, but it was done for.

He jumped down from the wing, looped the .45 back over his head, and stuck his arms back into his jacket. Part of his flight suit had ripped when he pulled himself out of the cockpit. There was a nine-inch gash in his left calf, and his flying boot was quickly filling up with blood. One of his gloves had a slash across the palm. All five fingers were still there. He wiggled them to make sure. The adrenaline slammed through him, made him feel a little sick and wobbly.

He glanced around to get his bearings. He knew he was in Belgium—German-occupied Belgium. It wouldn't be long before they would be hunting for him. Somebody had surely seen him go down, heard the crash-landing. He raced for the trees.

In a few seconds, his flying boots were caked with mud. He thought he heard someone holler out and quickened his pace. Just as he got into the trees, up ahead of him a man appeared, an apparition in coveralls, carrying a long-tined hayfork. Lange stopped, crouched, then started to veer off, but the man waved for Lange to follow him. He had a friendly expression on his face, but it flashed through Lange's mind that the man might want to turn him in to the Germans. The Nazis put bounties on downed airmen. Stories had circulated through the mess. But he didn't have a better plan, so he ran towards the man.

When he got close enough, the farmer rattled off something—it sounded French. All Lange caught for sure was the word *"Boche."* The man indicted that Lange should follow him, so he did. From the direction he had just left, a big fireball *whomped* and filled the sky—the P-47 exploded in flames. Smoke billowed high into the air, thick and black enough to be seen through the trees and for miles.

That caused the farmer to pick up his pace. Quickly, he guided Lange through the woods. The smell of the pasture drifted off the man, a pungent, warm smell, like sun-dried grass and earth. Following behind the man, Lange felt like he was running on mud blocks his boots were so caked. The farmer gestured wildly at him to hurry.

They broke into a clearing. There was a huge pile of manure, a hay wagon, and some white flop-eared cattle in the clearing. Lange started for the wagon, but the farmer shouted. "No!" Excitedly, the farmer gestured towards the manure pile. Right then, Lange heard an automobile engine. The farmer waved his hayfork toward the manure, so Lange stopped thinking and dove into the pile, burrowing under like a mole. He felt the farmer arrange the dung back over the tunnel his body had made going in.

He lay there, as still as possible. Air roared in and out of his lungs. He'd been around plenty of cow shit in his life. He had stepped in it, had it squirted on him working cows with Gabe, had even tossed it around like horseshoes, but he had never been buried in it. The smell was familiar, marshy and rich. It was hot and getting hotter by the second.

He heard the farmer's nonchalant singing. Then other, louder voices came. German voices—at least, they sounded German, guttural and sharp—but he couldn't really be sure. The talking went on for several minutes. Lange's heart pounded so loud he thought it might give away his hiding place. A thought of Mackie and the kids flashed through his mind. God, he didn't want to get picked up by Germans and spend the rest of the war in a POW camp. At least he was in Belgium. He stood a better chance in Belgium.

The Germans and the farmer seemed to be in an involved, urgent discussion. Lange couldn't tell how many different voices there were—at least three, he thought, counting the farmer. The voices came fainter. He figured they had probably gone to inspect the burning T-bolt. He thought about the long gouge in the farmer's beet field, hoped the farmer wouldn't turn him in. It took a great effort to remain still. The heat from the manure pile became almost unbearable.

After a few minutes, the voices returned. The vehicle engine fired up and pulled away. The farmer began to sing again. The song sounded shakier than before. His voice grew softer, closer. In a few seconds, the tines of the hayfork prodded him. He rose from the shit pile, felt like the dead rising from an unholy grave. The farmer waved Lange to follow again and to hurry.

THE FARMER'S teen-aged daughter kept trying to talk to Lange. She tried it in what he thought was French and then in what sounded like German. She kept trying until he made it clear he couldn't understand either language. So she started repeating the same thing over and over, and it finally dawned on him what she was saying, "RAF? RAF? RAF?"

He smiled, hoped he looked friendly. "No." He shook his head. "USA," he said, patting his own chest. "American."

The girl smiled, nodded.

Across the room, the farmer's wife fussed and fumed. She was clearly unhappy about the downed flyer in her kitchen. The farmer sat humped over a heavy table with his hands clasped, not answering. He seemed to have shrugged off all responsibility for Lange in the face of so much anger from his wife. Lange didn't blame him. He knew it was dangerous for them to help him. He wanted to apologize for having ditched his plane in their beet field.

The girl said something to the wife, and the older woman wrapped a chunk of cold sausage in brown bread. With reluctance, she handed the food to Lange. Then she began trying to shoo him out the door. He got the message and rose to leave. The daughter followed him outside.

Rain and fog had moved in, weather just like in England. A zippered pouch on the leg of his flight suit held a bail-out kit. There was a silk map in there, along with a compass and some other survival items. He reached for it, but the pouch that held the kit was torn open and empty. He supposed the kit had gone up in flames with old Gunslinger.

The girl exclaimed and he jumped, but she had only spotted his bloody leg. She tugged him towards a ramshackle barn. It was beginning to get dark. Inside the barn was so dim he couldn't see a thing for a moment. As his eyes adjusted, he bit into the sausage and bread. He hadn't had anything to eat since preflight breakfast.

The girl indicated to him that he should sit on a wooden box, and when he did, she inspected the gash on his leg. She motioned for him to stay and left the barn. With her gone, he felt alone and on edge. He wished that at some time during his life he had thought about learning to speak a foreign language. There had been a language card in the bailout kit, too, along with some German money, all things he would need to evade back to England.

In a short time the girl returned. She brought a worn blanket, a stub of a candle and some matches. She also had a bottle of yellow wine, which she handed to him. She cleaned his wounded leg with a pail of water and a rag. The water stung and made him shiver with cold. With the caked blood washed away, the wound didn't look so deep.

All in all, he felt he had been lucky. His situation would have been far worse with a serious wound. While the girl wrapped his left calf with a cloth bandage, he drank the wine straight from the neck of the bottle. It was raw and sour, but it was wet, and he needed something to steady his nerves.

With the candle lit he saw that the building was more of a storage shed than a true barn. She indicated that he could sleep there, and that he shouldn't burn the candle except when necessary. At least, that's what he thought she meant. It was like playing a game of charades, gesturing at each other.

"You don't speak any English?" he said. "Not even just a tiny bit?"

She gave him a blank look. She was about sixteen, had a thick braid of blonde hair hanging down her back like a piece of rope. Her face looked strong, too. He more than liked her; he probably owed her and her father his life.

"Well, I don't speak any Belgian either," he said and took another long swig of the sour wine.

She glanced at the door as if to make sure no one was coming, and then she reached into a pocket in her skirt. She brought out a single, much-handled cigarette and offered it to him. At that moment, he wanted to hug her. He used the candle flame to light the cigarette. It was harsh and burned quickly, but he pulled every last whiff of tobacco smoke deep into his lungs. God only knew when he would have another.

It was a rough night. The gravity of his situation settled heavily on him. He sat in the dark with the blanket wrapped around him, shivering, and listened to mice skitter all around him. He thought he should stay watchful in case there was a search party. The rain came harder, and he was thankful the shed had a good roof. He doubted the Germans would prowl around out in a downpour. Maybe they thought he had burned to death in the crash. He drank the entire bottle of wine. After a while, it began to taste better and he appreciated the mind-numbing intoxication it brought.

His mind stayed on Mackie most of the night. He wondered if she knew yet he'd gone down. He pictured her with their babies and tried to calculate how long it would take him to get back to them. He knew Ostend couldn't be far. If he could find a boat, hell, he would row back to England. Or maybe he could make his way to Calais and steal a plane. There was an airfield there. He had escorted bombers there many times before. From Calais it was only about twenty miles across to Dover. Eight minutes by plane. There had to be some quick way for him to get back.

Before daylight his friend with the rope of hair came again. She brought a torn-off hunk of bread and, wrapped in an oilcloth, two tiny pickled eggs the size of guinea eggs. The eggs were sour and tasted off, but he felt it would be rude to refuse her so offering, so he gobbled them down without much chewing. He figured he would need every ounce of energy they might provide.

She watched him eat, then produced another one of her mangled cigarettes. He lit it and took a long, appreciative drag, smiled and offered her a drag, too. She accepted, but kept a watchful eye on the door to the shed. Rain no longer pounded on the roof.

As he finished the cigarette, a commotion sounded outside. The door burst open. Lange jumped to his feet expecting German soldiers. He had already reached for his .45 before the girl jumped up, too, and began to chatter. Two scruffy fellows stepped into the shed. One motioned for the girl to quiet down. The other one kept his attention on Lange.

The one in front said, "You! Come wiz us."

Lange took his hand out of his pocket. "You speak English?"

"Little bit," the first one answered. "Come wiz us." He nodded at the other one, who stepped forward and took the .45 from Lange's pocket. And the gun was gone—as quick as that.

They didn't give him a chance to speak. He didn't say goodbye to the girl or thank you to the farmer. Without one wit of courtesy they escorted him out of the shed and away from the farm. He prayed they were friendly, but he hadn't liked the scared look on the girl's face, or the way one of them kept shoving him along.

They came to a wagon so old the wood sides looked petrified. The quieter one of the two men, the one who had done the shoving, ducked Lange into the back and piled a lot of beet sacks on top of him. The two of them talked for a long while, and then he felt some more things piled on top of the sacks, weighing him down. After a while the wagon began to move, at the slow pace of the dark draft horse harnessed to the wagon tongue.

Again, Lange thought about the bounty for downed airmen. It had been a frequent topic around the fire in the mess. Just a couple of months before, one fellow in another squadron had managed to evade back to England. Lange wished he had paid more attention to how that pilot had done it. He considered throwing off the scratchy beet sacks, hopping over the side of the wagon, and sprinting off on his own. At one point, when the wagon slowed, he almost did just that. If he had been able to speak the least little bit of the language, he would've felt he stood a chance of getting back to England on his own. As it was, he figured he had no choice but to try to trust the rugged fellows driving the wagon.

CHAPTER 24

"Missing"

Mackie looked at the clock. She hadn't heard from Lange all day yesterday. She hadn't heard from him today yet either. While one day without a call wasn't all that unusual, two days would be, and when the clock slipped past noon, she felt the first pang of worry.

She thought she and the children should move closer to the airdrome, maybe to Cambridge, where she could keep better track of what was going on with his war. Maybe if she were close enough, she could get over this constant concern for his safety. But of course, he had nixed it before she could come up with a more convincing argument. The airdrome was a target, and he didn't want her or the kids anywhere near a stray bomb. "Besides, Given would have to change schools. Bad idea, honey," Lange said.

He wanted her to take the kids to Texas straight-away. He had started talking about it constantly. If he'd had his way, they would have been on a ship weeks ago. The fact that ships were being sunk all over the Atlantic didn't seem to filter into his determination. He wanted them out of reach of the war. And maybe he was right. Maybe she wouldn't fret so much if the war wasn't all around them. She didn't know which would be better. Or worse.

For most of the morning she was swamped with the children. At six-months, Susie was teething and fretful. The twins were rambunctious. In the last few weeks, it seemed they had gone from crawling to standing on their feet to walking full steam. Poor Marmalade the Cat stayed hidden under the bed most of the time, until they all went down for naps. Then he would creep out to see if it was all clear. Thank goodness Given was in school. One less to worry over. Sometimes she felt guilty she hardly had a moment to give him anymore.

She left Winnie in charge in the playroom and took Susie down to the kitchen for a three o'clock bottle. When she heard the automobile coming up the driveway, she thought at first it was Bailey, fetching Given from school, but she soon realized it was too early for that. She carried Susie into the front room to peer out the big window.

A Jeep had turned in the long driveway. Lange had come home a Jeep before, and her heart leaped as she hurried for the door. Susie fussed at the interruption to her bottle and clutched a handful of Mackie's hair. It wasn't Lange driving the Jeep.

Jim Hiller stopped near the front steps, pulled the hand brake, and got out. She stepped through the front door. She cradled Susie against her shoulder, and waved, but her pulse had already quickened.

Jim looked smart in his uniform, silver lieutenant's bar on his service cap. His face was serious, grim. She drew in a weepy, anticipatory breath, and hugged the baby closer to her as he approached.

"Jim," she said, going down the steps. "What a surprise." She heard the faint crack in her voice.

He palmed off his cap. His hair was sandy brown, close cut. He had an honest face. She had never really noticed before. Susie studied him, trying to decide if the man in the uniform was her daddy. When he got within four paces he stopped, seemed to gather himself, but didn't speak for a second.

She took a backwards step. "Jim, I don't think I want to know why you're here."

"First of all…" He held up his hand as if to quiet her growing panic. "…he's only listed as missing."

"Missing?" The word spurted from her mouth. She felt like her heart stopped.

"Near Ostend."

"Belgium?" Her throat clamped shut and she gasped a little. "Did he bail out?"

"Yes."

"You saw it with your own eyes?"

His gaze left hers, came quickly back, but she saw the hesitation. "He said to me, 'I'm bailing out, Jim.' He said it that plain and calm."

She felt dizzy, nauseated. She shoved Susie at Jim, barely noticed how stunned and confused he looked as he took the baby. Awkwardly, he wadded Susie close in his arms.

Mackie knew she had to sit down before she fell. She groped for Aunt Kath's fancy wrought iron porch settee. *Breathe.* She sat heavily, took her head in her hands. Everything was spinning. She tried to focus on a broken elm twig between her feet.

"We got bounced," Jim continued. "And then we got split up. Lange shot down two of them. I saw that much. One of them was on my tail. After that I don't know. Butch Sawyer got one upstairs, and we think it must've clipped Lange's plane."

"It knocked him down?"

"No. I think it got his prop. He said, 'I'm bailing out, Jim,' as clear as that. And then I lost him."

She looked up. Obviously, Jim was struggling with this, too. She saw the grief and guilt, Lange's words echoing in his mind. She swallowed, gathered some control. "Was he on fire?"

"I don't know."

Susie squirmed, began to fret, reached for her mummy. Jim juggled her and his cap. Mackie stood up, took Susie from him. She complained about being manhandled. Mackie patted the baby's back.

"Thank you for coming all this way to tell me, Jim," she said and wondered where the brainpower to conjure those words had come from. She felt foggy.

"You'll be getting official notice," he said, "but I knew you would be wondering, so I came…"

"Yes. Thank you."

He looked at the cap in his hands, then at her. "He had enough altitude to make a jump. I don't believe for one second he didn't make it down."

"But you didn't see his chute?"

"No. I'm sorry." He looked at his feet, shook his head, reached to give Susie a pat on her little back. She whined and twisted from him, grabbed a handful of Mackie's blouse.

Mackie watched Jim walk back to the Jeep. Later she thought she probably should have asked him to stay for dinner. He had come so far, just to personally deliver the horrible news. But she didn't feel able to be a good hostess, to make nice and pretend that this day was the same as yesterday. She stepped into the foyer and Aunt Kath was there, about to come out to see what was happening. Mackie took one look at Aunt Kath and nearly collapsed. Susie wailed. Aunt Kath pulled the baby from Mackie's arms.

SHE GAVE herself an hour to weep and mourn privately in her room, and then she put a call into Adam. When he came on the line, the words spilled out of her all at once. She managed to get them all said without sobbing. No more time for that.

"I just feel like I should be doing something," she said. "Maybe I could fly over there. Unofficially, of course."

"And do what, Allie? For gods sake! Have a look around? There's a war on."

"I'm a civilian. Don't I have a right to know what's happened to my husband?"

"He's missing in action. That's the end of it. You're not an idiot. You know what you're talking about is unrealistic."

She drummed her fingers. "What about MI-Six? Don't you have a friend there? Maybe they would know something?"

"Be patient. That's all you can do now. I know that's hard for you."

She put her hand up to smooth her hair. She couldn't stop shaking. "What if he's dead, Adam? Will they tell me that? Will I get his body back? What happens if he's dead?"

He didn't have an answer. He asked to speak to Aunt Kath. It had finally begun to sink in. Lange was missing, knocked out of the sky. He had bailed out over enemy-occupied territory, fate unknown. And there wasn't one bloody thing she could do about it.

Aunt Kath went up to check on the children, made sure all was well with Winnie in the playroom. When she came back downstairs, she poured Mackie a glass of sherry and sat with her in the drawing room. Mackie thought something stronger was surely in order but sipped at the sherry anyway. She repeated everything Jim Hiller had said for the second time to Aunt Kath, and then they sat in silence. She was glad Aunt Kath didn't offer any platitudes—none of that "Keep calm and carry on" crap. Mackie decided she would telephone the airfield tomorrow, speak to Lange's CO, find out anything else they might know. At least it would make her feel as if she were doing something.

She trudged up to bed, practiced in her head the questions she wanted answered. She stood at the window and watched the light go out of the day. She was so absorbed in her own thoughts, she almost missed the feathery rap on her door.

"Mummy?" She turned from the window just as Given eased into the room. He wore his jimjams. She didn't even remember when he'd come home from school, or seeing him at all since break-fast. She held out her arms, and he came into them.

"Darling." She hugged him tight.

"Is Daddy dead?" he asked in a quiet voice.

"What? Oh, gosh, no." She held him at arm's length and saw the fear on his face. "Something happened to his airplane and he had to parachute out of it. But he's only missing."

"I thought I heard you say on the telephone he was dead."

"Oh, darling, no, I didn't say that. I would know if that were so, and I don't believe it."

"I don't either," he said.

She backed up to the bed and sat, pulling Given with her. "Jim Hiller said he shot down two more Jerry fighters."

"Confirmed?"

She let out a light laugh and tucked Given's head under her chin. His hair smelled like a bird's nest. She kissed his forehead. "You should go to bed now."

"If they're confirmed that will make five with the USA and five with the R.A.F. Daddy will be a double ace."

"You shouldn't be so concerned with all that." She moved his hair back and rocked him against her. "Daddy wouldn't like it."

"I know. He says it's war. He says it's not pretty. Not like in the movies. He says there's no theme music."

She forced a laugh, for Given's sake, for hers. She could hear Lange saying that. She studied Given's face for tears, didn't find any trace. She struggled with her own.

"You can climb into bed with me for a bit." She lay back on the pillows and he crawled up beside her. She put her arm around him and held him tightly to her. "Tell me about school today."

It was good to listen for a while to his schoolboy adventures, to hear his little voice in her head, to clear out all the other confusion for a time, so maybe she could sleep, or think about something else at least.

CHAPTER 25
"*Shuffle*"

During the long days, Lange played solitaire. He tried once to teach the old grandmother poker but gave up because of the language problem. He managed to teach her to shuffle the cards, but that was all. With simple things they could communicate just fine. She would make the motion with her hand to her mouth, and he would nod if he was hungry. Sometimes he just talked to her anyway, and she always appeared to listen with great concentration. During air raids, he comforted her, attempted to explain that it was Americans or the RAF—he could usually tell by the sound of the engines—and that the bombing raids were necessary if the Nazis were ever going to be defeated. In the kitchen, she allowed him to sit at the table with the deck of cards. The Jack of Spades was missing, but he had learned to do without it. He tried to play poker by himself but somehow it wasn't the same when you knew the contents of the other hands.

Things got better when the baby was awake. It was a happy baby and liked for Lange to get down on the floor and play itsy-bitsy spider and pat-a-cake. He sometimes pretended the baby was Susie, except this Flemish baby was a solid, pink-cheeked boy named

Anton, and he was five months old. Anton liked for Lange to rock him to sleep.

The rocker was the most comfortable chair in the house. Sometimes he sat awake at night after the house was quiet and dark, rocked, and thought about the day he went down, what he might have done differently. If he had throttled back, pampered the engine, could he have crippled home to England? If he could go back and correct certain things, would the outcome have been any different? He couldn't come up with a definite answer. He knew he was lucky to have landed in the beet farmer's field.

The fellows with the old beet wagon had turned out to be the famer's nephews. They had carried him to a horse stall where he had slept in hay and woke up itching with lice. There had been a brook or a river running nearby. The sound of the burbling current had helped him sleep. They brought him other clothes to wear, a pair of nut-brown trousers that were too short at the bottom, a white shirt that fit if he kept the sleeves rolled, and a gray striped vest. They hadn't been able to find shoes to fit him, so he still had his flying boots. He didn't know what they did with his uniform, and it worried him. The evasion lectures MI9 had given instructed all downed airmen to never give up their uniform, but the farmer's nephews hadn't given him a choice. He still had his metal dogtags, but if he should get caught, that was all the proof he had of being in the USAAF.

The nephews had taken him to a rendezvous outside a country inn and deposited him into an automobile with Tatania, baby Anton's mother. She was the first person who could speak enough English to tell Lange where he was, how many people were sympathetic to the Germans and how many were not. If Tatania had a husband Lange never saw him, just the old grandmother, the baby, and Tatania herself, day after endless day.

Tatania had never helped a downed Allied airman before. She worked at a sidecar factory in Jabbeke, which was the reason her uncle, the beet farmer, had turned Lange over to her. There were people at the factory who she claimed were trying to help her decide what to do, how to get Lange safely back to England. No mention was made of the word underground or the resistance, but he knew these were the people she was trying to reach. He also knew it was dangerous for her and her family. From what she said, half the people in Flanders would not cooperate with the German authorities. The other half—she called them the Black Belgiums for their soulless hearts—they were ready to work for the Germans without regret. These people posed the most danger. She had to proceed with caution.

The house was in a small village a few miles from the city center. Tatania rode a bicycle into Jabbeke every morning and returned close to dark. She nearly always brought a sack of food when she came, help she said, from some of her co-workers, who voluntarily contributed to the family larder. Rations were meager, but the old grandmother was a superb cook and managed to make even the most unappealing meals taste delicious.

In the evenings, they listened to the BBC. When it was reported that the RAF and USAAF had launched an all-out, 800-aircraft, bombing assault on Berlin, they celebrated with scratchy radio music. Lange danced with Tatania and the grandmother, and even with baby Anton, who squealed with delight.

During all this time, Lange never felt threatened. He hadn't even seen a German soldier up close, and the family did all they could to make him comfortable and welcome. But after several weeks cooped up inside with the baby and the grandmother, he got restless, increasingly impatient with how slowly things were moving. He could almost imagine spending the rest of the war right there in that little house near the train tracks, and that idea was unacceptable.

Mackie and the kids dominated his thoughts. He daydreamed about them, tried to picture what they were doing while he played another endless round of solitaire. He longed to be able to get word to Mackie that he was all right. He knew she would be worried. He wanted her to know he was trying to get back to her. He thought about just walking out the door, go it alone out there among the natives. Maybe he could find the underground on his own. Deep in his conscious, he knew that was an idiotic idea, but the inaction almost drove him to give it a try. He started to plan. He kept going back to the idea of hijacking a plane he could fly back to England. He longed to be a part of those big raids that came over almost daily.

Finally, before he was driven to something rash, Tatania came home early, with more than a sack of food. She brought a man named Roland. He was a friend, she explained, even though they didn't seem to know each other well. Roland was in his mid-twenties, thin, with large gray eyes. He wore a porkpie hat and spoke English with almost no inflection in his voice, as if he had learned it from memory, syllable by syllable.

"Are these the only shoes you have?" Roland said, without a smile or a handshake.

Lange looked down at his flying boots, nodded. Tatania said something in Flemish to Roland and quickly disappeared into another room.

"We will be going on a journey," Roland said. "You must talk to no one. Pretend you are not with me. When we walk, walk behind me. If anyone should speak to you turn away, or pretend to be deaf and dumb. Do you understand this?"

Lange nodded. "Can I ask, where are we going?"

"To the train station." Roland handed Lange a ticket. It was printed in Dutch. The word *Brugge* was plain enough.

Tatania came hustling back with a pair of black trousers. She had the baby on her hip. "These are maybe longer," she said to Lange. "They will cover the boots better. Anton wishes to say goodbye to his American friend."

Lange took the baby in his arms, and felt sentimental for a second. Just nerves. He kissed the baby's forehead, and Anton let out a big chuckle.

"We must hurry." Roland looked at his watch.

Lange went into the tiny room where he had been sleeping, and changed into the black trousers. He wondered briefly where they had come from, if they had belonged to Anton's father, and where he was now. The trousers were snug around the middle, but they were considerably longer. They covered the uppers of his flying boots. The dark brown leather still seemed to him to stand out, but there was nothing that could be done about it. He had to have something on his feet.

Roland gave him a critical once-over. "I am afraid I must ask you to empty your pockets."

Reluctantly, Lange did as he was asked. It was the end of the line for several items he hated to part with, the beautiful RAF cigarette case from Mackie for one. He shouldn't have been carrying it with him in the first place, except that he believed in its good luck. He tried to explain to Roland its sentimental significance, but Roland tossed it onto the table along with Lange's cigarette lighter, his wedding band, wristwatch, anything that could identify him as an American aviator. He was allowed to keep his dogtags hidden in the heel of his boot but nothing else.

"I promise to send all of it back to you after the liberation," Tatania said. She gave him a swift hug.

The grandmother kissed him on his forehead, right above his eyebrow. She held his face, looked into his eyes, and said something. She seemed sad.

"She says pleasant journey," Tatania told him.

Lange walked behind Roland through the village streets to the train tracks and kept a distance to the rear as he had been instructed. A few people were gathered at the tiny railway station. It was hardly more than a small platform. Twilight was coming on and the temperature was falling fast. Lange yearned for his cozy A-2 leather jacket, but that had been lost to the beet farmer's nephews along with his .45. The gun might have made Lange feel a bit more confident, but the jacket, with its wool lining, would have provided more warmth than the thin overcoat.

True to his word, Roland didn't even make eye contact with Lange as the group of people waited for the train. A few more gathered before the train finally arrived, its headlights darkened to mere slits, and all the windows blacked out with paint. Lange got trapped in the surge for the door. Something poked into his back, right at the base of his spine—something hard and sharp, almost like the barrel of a pistol. He turned to see a little old woman prodding him along with her umbrella. Roland was not in sight.

Lange was rushed up into the doorway of the train and into the first empty compartment. The woman with the umbrella sat down right beside him. She was sour-faced, scowling, a Black Belgian he decided. He was relieved when Roland ducked into the compartment and sat on the opposite bench. He immediately leaned back against the seat and shut his eyes, which prompted Lange to do the same. When a German soldier sat down next to Roland and shook out a newspaper, Lange thought his own heart would leap from his chest. No conductor came through the car.

It was difficult to pretend to doze. He had an overwhelming desire to open his eyes and study the German—brown knee boots, red band around his cap. It was the first time he'd been so near the enemy. Clean-shaven, granite jaw. He wore a greatcoat, so Lange couldn't tell anything about the soldier's rank. The movement of the train seemed to add to the tension. Thankfully, it was a short trip, and in half an hour the train slowed and everyone in the compartment stood up. Automatically, everyone let the German go first. Even cool, collected Roland hesitated long enough for the soldier to depart.

Again, Lange followed Roland at a safe distance through the train station. The tickets, it seemed, were to be collected at a barrier, and when Lange saw this, he took his ticket out of the pocket of the striped vest. There seemed to be something causing the line through the barrier to clog. Immediately, Lange spotted three German soldiers at the barrier, checking passengers through. Panic gripped him. He had no idea what they were checking for, but he had nothing to show, no identity papers. He saw Roland pass through the barrier and then linger outside the station doors, a nervous look on his face.

Lange's stomach was in his throat. He didn't know what he should do. Press forward with the crowd and hope to pass through the barrier on sheer dumb luck, or make a break for it? What if they asked him a question? He couldn't speak a word of German or Flemish. He searched around him. There was no place to run. Soaked with sweat, he continued with the crowd. He could still see Roland loitering near the doors. As Lange moved closer to the barrier he saw that the Germans were searching cases and bags. Lange had no bag or anything at all except the train ticket. Sweat pooled at the back of his neck. The stout German on the left side of the barrier grunted, snatched the ticket out of Lange's hand, and gestured for him to step through. Lange nearly stumbled, his knees were so weak. As soon as he passed through, Roland began to walk. Lange followed.

Out on the street, he breathed deep. After a few blocks, he even began to gaze around at the buildings. He thought about escorting the bombers here to do their work, about the way this city looked from the air, with its winding streets and outlying factories just dashes and dots from 25,000 feet. There was no sign of destruction in the central part of the city where they walked. Streets were cobbled, buildings all intact and rising into the night sky.

When Roland turned a corner, Lange followed, and they turned several more times. It began to get dark, and Lange wondered about the curfews he had heard about in the occupied countries. Even London had curfews imposed. And it did seem that Roland picked up his pace. Lange drew the thin, ill-fitting wool coat closer around him.

The last street was a tree-lined avenue, and at the fourth house Roland motioned for Lange to wait at the bottom of the steps. The house had an ornate front door, two false wrought-iron balconies on the upper floor. Roland rang the bell. After a few seconds, the door half-opened and words were spoken. Then Roland beckoned Lange up the steps. Inside the entrance hall stood a small, well-dressed woman. She spoke in Flemish to Roland, seemed to admonish him to stay, but he clearly refused, shaking his head with an apologetic grimace.

When Roland backed away from the door, Lange realized that he had barely spoken to this strange, silent man, and that he would probably never see him again. He wanted to shake hands, but Roland was already leaving. Lange managed a feeble, "Thank you," before the door shut and he was alone with the small woman.

She introduced herself only as Sophie, no last name. She was middle-aged, wore her hair in a severe style caught back from her face, had an expensive strand of pearls clasped round her neck. She spoke flawless, British English.

"Have you eaten?" she said, and Lange realized he was starving.

She took him into a large dining room, sat him down at one end of a long oak table, gave him a German cigarette, poured him a large glass of brandy, and while he drank and smoked, proceeded to bring out the best meal he'd had since leaving England. There were lamb chops and a thick slice of ham, some kind of flat green beans, potatoes, a hunk of cheese that reminded him of the red-rind cheddar back in Texas, a slab of sourdough bread slathered with honey-butter. The hardships of the other people he had met here didn't seem to have touched Sophie.

When he had eaten until he couldn't eat another bite, she showed him up to a plush room with an old-fashioned featherbed like Aunt Dellie spread on her beds in winter. A pair of brown striped pajamas lay folded at the foot.

"You can wash in the W/C at the end of the hall. We'll talk in the morning." She smiled. "Good night, Captain DeLony," she said, and closed the door.

It unnerved him the way she said his name, like she had known him all his life. He couldn't remember having given her his rank. He didn't believe Roland had told her his name, at least not where Lange could hear. Everything about this place felt fishy to him.

There was real soap in the bathroom. A toothbrush laid out for him to use. There was a cup of lather and a cut-throat razor for him to shave. Since he was used to a safety razor, he had a little trouble making the straight razor work. He thought about sticking it in his pocket in case he needed a weapon, but left it lying on the edge of the basin. He dressed in the pajamas, sank into the cozy bed, and felt like he'd landed in a dream, or in the middle of a snare. Either way, he slept like he'd been drugged.

"You must answer these questions, Captain," Sophie said. Two men stood behind her. One of them leaned down and said something to her. She nodded. "We want to help you, but you have to understand, we have already risked so much just in bringing you here. Haven't you been treated well?"

Lange nodded. "I don't mean to seem ungrateful."

"I understand that you are wary, but we must verify your identity. We have had many traitors. We don't believe you are one, but we have to be certain. We have to know some particular things about you."

He looked at her, studied the two men standing there with her. One was tall and aristocratic. The other was on the small side, brawny, with wide, fullback shoulders. The second man was not as well-dressed as the first, but they both returned his look without swerving.

They could be Germans. They might be setting him up to turn him in. He had been treated almost too well in this house. On the other hand, he knew he would probably never make it back to England alone. He was in their hands. He had to assume they were friends. He didn't feel as if he had any choice but to trust them.

"OK," he said, with resignation. He saw the look of relief come to all three faces, especially Sophie's.

She sat down with a paper and a pen and wrote down all the answers he gave. They wanted to know which squadron he flew with, where he had trained, what type of aircraft he had been flying when he crash-landed, what was his mission, they wanted the name of his CO. He remembered from evasion lectures that he shouldn't ask too many questions of them to avoid provoking suspicions, but it was hard not to ask. He had things he wanted to know too, most particularly, if he was sure enough in the hands of the underground now?

It took three days for them to verify his identity. He wasn't sure exactly how they accomplished this unless they somehow had contact with the Allies.

Sophie broke the news to him. "You will be leaving here very soon." She gave a broad smile. He felt like he'd passed some sort of exam.

After that she became downright chatty, telling him all the answers to questions he had wanted to ask before. She explained that she was part of an organization that published a clandestine newspaper. Her husband had been killed in 1940 when the Germans invaded Belgium, and she despised the sight of them. Her group had connections to an escape line, and as soon as arrangements could be made, he would be going to Brussels to join them.

"There have been many infiltrators among them," she told him. "It's for their sake we had to handle you so carefully. You understand, captain?"

Elation overcame him. He thought about Mackie and the kids, good old England. Maybe soon. Maybe by Christmas he would be back with his family. He felt like he was on his way, now.

She gave him new clothes, including a pair of lace-up shoes that fit him perfectly. That afternoon she took him out of the house around the block to a photographer's studio to have his photograph made. She gave him a pair of glasses to put on for the picture. The glasses were blanks, had no strength in the lenses.

Later that evening, the tall swanky fellow, Gerard by name, was back with papers Lange would need to get him into France. He had been given a new identity. Léon du Bois. Sophie explained that he looked more French than Flemish and that the Germans usually spoke French less well. They had at first thought that he should be an agricultural worker after he told them he'd been raised on a Texas farm.

Sophie turned up the palms of both his hands and said, "But you have the hands of an architect."

He looked at his own hands and tried to decide what she meant. Regardless, in the place for occupation it said "*Architekt.*" They had put down his correct birth date, and everything was officially stamped. It looked authentic. Even the photograph looked real, a foreign stranger in black eye glasses. He hoped no one ever asked him to pencil-draw a building.

THE BRAWNY ONE with the powerful shoulders, Jules, escorted Lange to Brussels. They went by express train, and again Lange pretended to sleep the whole way. Unlike silent Roland, Jules sat right next to Lange and carried on animated conversations with other people in the compartment. Sometimes the conversation seemed to drift into disagreement, but good humor always came back into their voices. Jules had a braying laugh that was hard to ignore.

Lange let his thoughts wander back to England, to Mackie, the kids. He missed them terribly, and in this foreign country among people who didn't speak his language, he felt more alone than he ever had in his life. He didn't want to get his hopes up; there was still a long way to go.

It was already late December. He would have been taking command of his new squadron. He hadn't told Mackie he was tour-

expired or that he'd signed on for another one as soon as he learned he could make major if he stayed. He was afraid she wouldn't understand, but with the war still on, he didn't see himself going back to the States to do bond work or ride a desk while there were still ways for him to be useful in the air.

Now, he saw how selfish all that had been. He admitted to himself that he had begun to take unnecessary risks, to volunteer for the dangerous ops, to provoke the enemy. What had he been trying to prove? He should have taken a pass, gathered his family, and high-tailed it back to the States when he had the opportunity.

Once they reached Brussels, German soldiers were in evidence everywhere. They seemed to roam about at random, but mostly they kept to themselves. After the first few startling encounters, Lange began to relax about them. Jules walked freely and openly beside Lange, chattering away in Flemish when they passed other people. Lange liked him enormously, and believed in different circumstances, and without the language barrier, he and Jules might have been friends.

When they were alone Jules made a halting stab at a conversation in English. He spoke well enough for Lange to figure out that Jules was an automobile mechanic by trade, had a wife and four children. He seemed interested to learn that Lange had a wife and four kids, too. It gave them common ground for the walk to the apartment building twelve blocks from the train station.

It was a row of apartments, all of them connected, four to an entrance. Jules went into the third door and, once inside the foyer, rang a bell lined up in a group of other doorbell buttons. A woman's voice answered, and Jules said something sweet and low in French. Smiling, Jules winked at Lange as the woman's voice came on again. Jules led the way up the staircase. At the head and around one corner, a door opened.

The woman's name was Margot. She was young, petite, good-looking, the epitome of a French *mademoiselle*. She gave Jules a kiss on both his cheeks, did the same for Lange, as she pulled him into her apartment. Jules came inside, too, and Margot immediately opened a bottle of red wine. She poured four glasses, then with a coquettish smile, went to another door inside the apartment and knocked. Jules made a silly face at Lange, batted his eyes. Jules evidently thought Margot was swell.

"You can come out," she said, in her heavily accented English. She rapped her knuckles again on the door.

It opened, and out stepped a mangy fellow in baggy trousers, a short, corded jacket like a railway worker would wear, shirt and tie, a get-up as ridiculous as the one Lange had worn to Sophie's house in Bruges.

Lange almost laughed, but then he took a harder look at the fellow, and the shabby fellow gave a long, hard look back. Recognition hit them at the same instant.

"Jesus Christ!" Lange said.

The other fellow held out long, gangly arms wide to his side and came forward.

"DeLony!" Joe Sokol said, in his horrible, Czech-tinged English. "I am seeing things." He hugged Lange so hard Lange's feet left the floor. "You goddame bloody sonofbitch!"

"They know each other!" Margot said, clapping her hands with glee.

Lange couldn't wipe the smile off his own face. It was the best feeling he'd had in two months.

CHAPTER 26
"Sokol"

Joe Sokol had been shot down on November seventh off the French coast near Dunkirk and had been plucked out of the sea by a Belgian fishing boat. The fishermen had hidden him in their hold with their catch and off-loaded him at Nieuwpoort. They left him with an oilcloth slicker to cover his RAF flight suit and a pocket full of sardines. He had walked the ten miles to Ostend, arrived in the middle of a bombing raid, and been picked up by a policeman, who just happened to be an Allied sympathizer. Like Lange, he had made his way through a few safe houses before arriving at Margot's.

He had already been there for four weeks by the time Lange arrived. There had been a breech in the escape line, and the people were working hard to repair the gaps caused by several arrests. Sokol, however, didn't much mind the wait, since he had fallen in love with Margot.

Lange chuckled over this revelation. He remembered quite a few English girls who had been the object of Sokol's affection long before Margot. "This time is the real one," Sokol protested.

Margot seemed reluctant but also entertained by Sokol's blatant attempts to woo her, laughing as he followed her around the small apartment like a devoted hound dog. He helped her with domestic chores—washing dishes, cooking—all the while whispering sweet nothings to her in French.

His French sounded pretty good to Lange after his own poor attempts to make sense of the language. Mostly, though, it was good to have Sokol's company. They helped each other pass the time. Margot provided a deck of cards, but Lange didn't have any more success at teaching Sokol to play poker than he had with Tatiana's grandmother. The only card game Sokol knew was bridge, except he called it something else, and Lange was tired of it by the first week.

At the end of his second week at Margot's, two new fellows were brought to the apartment. They were a waist gunner and a tail gunner from the same B-17 crew, picked up near Antwerp. Stan and Ray. One came from Cleveland, the other from Omaha. They brought fresh war news and different stories to hear. However, the apartment was overcrowded with four men sharing one small room and two narrow beds.

Christmas arrived. Margot brought them two bottles of champagne she managed to acquire somehow. By then, it had been two and a half months since Lange's crash. With Christmas come and gone, Lange set a new goal of making it back to England by January eighth, Mackie's birthday and also their second wedding anniversary.

She was a constant, insistent worry to him, Mackie. What she knew, what she didn't know. He did not want her to give up hope. He hadn't given up. He wondered what was going on with the kids, what was going on with the squadron, the war. He was sick of playing cards, and of being cooped up with the other fellows in Margot's tiny apartment. He knew they all felt the same.

Tempers flared over nothing—the way somebody held their cards, or shuffled, or picked their teeth, or slurped soup. As the ranking officer, Lange found himself arbitrating more than he liked. He tried to encourage them to look on the positive side of their situation. They were safe, hadn't been captured or wounded. He didn't find it easy to stay positive himself.

January eighth came and went.

MARGOT LEFT THE APARTMENT FREQUENTLY, without an explanation to any of them as to where she went or when she would return. They assumed she had some sort of job and speculated about what the job could be with her inconsistent hours. She brought food she had scrounged around town from restaurants or from friends. She told them they needed good food to give them courage and strength to face the ordeal ahead. And that led to more speculation and discussion about what sort of ordeal she meant. Sokol thought they would be taken out of Belgium by a clandestine Lysander. Stan and Ray had both heard the Pyrenees would be their destination, where they could climb into neutral Spain. Lange didn't care as long as it was soon. He was closing in on three months on the dodge.

It snowed off and on the first few weeks of 1944. Usually at night, air raid sirens would pull them from their sleep, but they never heard any bombs. Once during the day, an armada of airplanes rattled the apartment walls. With sirens screaming, the four of them clustered around the small window in Margot's front room, and craned to see what was happening in the sky. The action was just out of sight—except for contrails and one glimpse of a fighter above 18,000 feet. Lange hoped it was one of theirs. One day bombs did fall and exploded off in the distance to jubilation among the four of them. They cheered and clapped each other's back, as if their team had just won the World Series.

On the third of February, Margot came back from one of her longest outings yet. She told them to gather their things. "Tomorrow you will travel."

Lange had nothing to gather, nothing but the clothes on his back, and even those weren't really his. But he was eager to go. Sokol seemed equally as eager. To be so in love, Lange thought Sokol left Margot behind mighty easily. The bomber boys were both white-faced as they filed out of the apartment behind their new guide, a man named Albert.

Before the war, Albert had been a stockbroker. He was straight-forward, spoke clear English, dressed a bit too dapper for his four motley charges. The day was rainy, more humid than cold. Lange perspired beneath the striped business suit he wore. His ill-fitting hat kept slipping down on his forehead. The eyeglasses pinched his nose.

They caught a streetcar. It seemed stuffed full of German soldiers. One of them rose to give Lange his seat, but Lange pretended not to see, so Albert quickly took the vacant seat with a casual, "*Danke.*" The German soldier moved to the back, as the noisy car heaved and rumbled over the uneven rails and through the streets of Brussels.

They got off at the train station and waited on the platform, each pretending not to know the other as Albert had instructed. But once on the train, Albert herded them together in the same compartment. He said, "At the last stop before the French border, you will leave the train and go to the left. Walk to the end of the platform, and someone will be waiting for you there. You have your documents, but it will be easier without going through border inspections. Watch me. When I stand up we will be at the stop. *Bon chance.*"

On the train ride, Lange fell back on the old pretense of sleeping so no one would try to speak to him. Just before the French border, at a station in Blanda, Albert stood up, and they all roused. They got off in single file, and as instructed, headed to the end of the platform.

A young boy sat astride a rusted bicycle. As soon as they made eye contact with him, he began to pedal slowly, deliberately glancing back to make sure they followed. Ray, the tail gunner, questioned whether the boy was the person they were supposed to meet. Lange shushed him and set out after the boy. The train began to move off —once again, no time for goodbye or for thank you. They left Albert at the station, calmly waiting for a return train to Brussels.

The boy on the bicycle led them through the little village. He kept glancing back at them, and Lange thought he acted too obvious. Anyone watching would find it odd that four men followed a young boy on a bicycle. They passed an obelisk memorial to the dead from the last war in a center plaza, a steepled cathedral, and a few old thatched houses, before the boy veered off the streets onto a well-rutted path through some woods. Once inside the cover of trees, the boy stopped the bicycle and left it propped against a poplar. He motioned for them to follow, and proceeded to lead them on foot.

Ray grumbled, "I don't like the looks of this."

"What other choice do we have?" Lange said, although he had been having the same thoughts. Behind him, he heard Sokol and Stan grumble, too.

The boy led them along a trail, which disappeared in several places beneath piles of fallen leaves and undergrowth. The ground was damp and spongy, the air thick and pungent with decayed leaves.

After walking for half an hour, they came upon a big draft horse tied to a stout tree. It was an unexpected sight and brought them to a sudden stop. The boy untied the animal, waking it from its slouch, and put the rope in Lange's hand. The boy said something. He was no more than twelve, small for his age and with an angelic face. He spoke directly to Lange, and Lange looked automatically at Sokol for a translation.

Sokol shrugged. "I don't understand Walloon."

The big horse had begun to try to walk away, and Lange held him back. The boy shook his head violently and reached to touch the rope in Lange's hand, forcing open Lange's grip. Sokol spoke to the boy in French. The boy spoke back. His dialect sounded different.

Sokol looked confused, pondering. "I think he says we are to follow the horse."

"Follow it?" Stan said and came out from behind Lange.

"Follow," the boy said, mouthing the English word carefully.

Sokol gave Lange a doubtful shrug. The horse was definitely trying to go, and he was strong enough to have his way. Lange held the rope and went with the horse. They all did. The boy watched, nodded encouragement, and turned slowly back through the woods.

The horse went at a walk, but a steady, driven walk, like he was pulling a plow. The bomber boys grumbled along behind. Sokol was smiling, about to laugh at the absurdity. Lange tried to keep the right amount of tension on the rope, enough to keep the horse from bolting away. He felt a smile grow on his face, too.

He was reminded of an old mule Papa had once tried to sell to a man who lived on the other side of town. All that mule's life, he had been part of a team, but Papa only wanted to keep the second mule. For a couple of weeks, every morning the mule Papa had sold would be back in its stall with its mate. Lange's job had been to drag that mule back to the man across town, until finally Papa was forced to admit defeat and refund the man's money. This horse seemed of a similar mind. It led the four of them through the forest and right up to the rear of a stone farmhouse where a man in tattered work clothes waited with a big open smile.

"Welcome to France," the man said in perfect English. He held his arm out wide and invited the four of them to come inside the house.

Lange hung back long enough to watch the big draft horse disappear through the open door of the stone barn. Back home, back in his warm stall.

Next morning—another hike; another train; new guides, a man and a woman, Georges and Celeste. Two more airmen dressed as workers—pilot officers from a Canadian Mosquito squadron— joined the party. One of the Canadian pilots was from Montreal and fluent in French. He smugly warned Sokol about his bad accent.

Sokol looked deeply offended. "He told me keep my mouth shut," he whispered to Lange.

Sokol seemed ready to start a brawl. Lange didn't want any trouble to brew, so when they boarded the train to Paris, he guided his friend to the next compartment down from the others. Best to keep space between them.

Once the train got underway, Lange settled in and watched the French countryside unroll—panoramic flashes of fields and trees, a chateau or two, rows of little houses. He read the names on the stations they passed, recognized some of them from sorties across the Channel. They were so close to England, he felt like he could smell it. Every town they went through crawled with German soldiers walking in pairs or standing in groups, many more than he had seen in Belgium.

He pretended to nap, and in truth, he was exhausted. The tension had taken its toll. After a while, the clatter of the tracks and the rocking rhythm of the train car lulled him into a deep sleep. He dreamed. It was that day on the train from Chester, when Mackie fell into his lap. She wore her uniform, ATA wings above the pocket, smile that rivaled the sun. He pulled out his RAF cigarette case which he wouldn't have had yet but the dream didn't care. He offered her a smoke. She asked him for a light. That was all—a simple, peaceful dream.

He came awake with a start. The dream felt so real, for a moment he expected to find her on the seat beside him. It made him long for her more than ever, the smell of her skin, the feel of her body. He wanted to share everything he'd been through with her: the beet farmer, the manure pile, the draft horse in the Belgian woods. She would never believe it. He could hardly believe it himself. But he was beginning to seem, after almost four months, like he might make it now.

He glanced across at Sokol, who was flirting with a couple of French mademoiselles. He was supposed to be a Dutch electrician, Guenther Vander Huull. His French didn't have to be perfect to beguile the ladies. Lange turned back to the window and continued to watch the long afternoon swing by.

AS THE TRAIN slowed into the Paris station, people moved into the aisles. Ahead, Lange's eyes found Celeste, or rather her black hat with the angled feather. Farther up, the two Canadians stepped into the aisle. He didn't see the bomber boys, but suddenly it seemed like the whole German army appeared from nowhere, swirling in from the front of the train, parting the crowd. One grabbed Celeste, another nabbed the Montreal pilot. The crowd began to rush for the exits.

Lange turned, seized Sokol's arm. Sokol had hold of one of the French girl's bag. He dropped it in the center of the aisle. Almost with one mind, they turned against the flow of the crowd. They bumped through the protesting people headed towards the far end of the car.

"In here!" Sokol held the metal lavatory door open. Lange started to go in, but one of the soldiers spotted them over the other passengers.

"Halt!" the soldier bellowed.

Sokol slammed the lavatory door. They charged towards the emergency passage at the same time, muscled through it, and leaped down onto the tracks.

"Halt!" came again from the rear of the train. They took off running.

Lange cut left behind the train. Sokol followed. There was no plan in Lange's mind, just getting the hell out of there. They had several sets of open tracks to clear before they gained the wall along the western edge of the depot. Lange ran for all he was worth. He braced for bullets to penetrate his back. He heard Sokol huffing behind him.

He hit the brick wall beside the tracks and started climbing straight up, like a monkey. He reached a hand to Sokol, and they dropped into an alleyway behind a line of buildings. They ran right, then ninety degrees to the left at the first opening. Sokol knocked a trash can over. It caused a loud clatter. They didn't speak. There was no time or breath for discussion. The only was sound was their feet hitting the pavement.

The passageway opened onto a narrow street. The uneven cobblestones made running difficult. Sokol grabbed Lange, pulled him left. Down the end of the street a black car came around a corner. Lange didn't know if it was after them or not, but he darted right, into an open door of a warehouse. Sokol followed. Two men in gray aprons looked up from their work. Without a word, they watched Lange and Sokol race by. Dead end. The engine on the black car hummed outside. Someone whistled loud. At the far end of the warehouse, a burly fellow in a black apron held open a metal door.

Lange sprinted that way. Sokol panted, "*Merci*." They banged through the door and out into another stony back passageway. Lange chose to go left in the same direction they had last seen the black car, banking that it had already moved on. Just before they hit the main street, Sokol spotted a slit through the walls of two buildings, barely wide enough to walk. They went through and burst out onto another cobbled street, avoided that in favor of yet another cutback through two buildings. It felt like they were running in circles.

It seemed to be an industrial sector, rows of warehouses and heavy buildings, few people on the streets, no cars. No place to hide either. They kept going, darting through any passageway they found. After several blocks, Sokol stopped, bent over held onto his knees. Up ahead there was a café and a shop with magazine and books out on a sidewalk rack. Civilization.

"Enough, DeLony. Nobody follows now." Sokol struggled for breath. He nodded towards the café. "Do you have money?"

Lange shook his head.

Sokol raised upright. His chest heaved. They had both lost their stupid hats. Lange had also lost his fake spectacles. He wondered what had happened to the bomber boys. He hadn't seen them leave the train.

"The American Air Force provides you with no money?" Sokol said.

"I lost my bailout kit when I crashed. Where's your money?"

"I gave to Margot." Sokol pressed his lips together. He had begun to get his breath. "So what do we do now?"

"I don't know. I could use a smoke."

Sokol laughed. He gave a longing look towards the café. "No money."

"Did you hear any shots?"

Sokol shook his head. He was getting back his breath. "Thankfully."

Lange nodded. His stomach rolled, legs felt like rubber. He still panted. "I have kin here somewhere."

"Kin?" Sokol looked confused.

"Relatives. Kinfolk. My sister's kids live here."

"Sister? She's here?" Hope was in Sokol's voice.

"She's buried here somewhere," Lange said. "Her kids are here someplace."

"In Paris?" Sokol laughed, grabbed the lapel of Lange's coat. "DeLony! Why you don't say so! Where? Where do they live?"

"I don't know." Lange squinted, tried to remember the address on Nina's letters to Aunt Dellie, those letters he had read the day of Becky's funeral, when in his wildest dreams he would never have imagined he would need to remember. He pinched the bridge of his nose. "Rue something."

Sokol let out a maniacal laugh. "Rue? That only means street, DeLony."

"Well. They own a bakery. They live above it I think. Monnier is their name." Lange spelled the name from memory.

A group of people walked by. Lange stopped talking. He automatically pressed back against the wall of the building. Sokol smiled at the people, nodded pleasantly. Lange realized his own sleeve was ripped, and Sokol had a bloody cut on his neck. They looked like beggars, or criminals.

"There are bakeries on every street," Sokol said.

Lange pressed his forehead, trying to picture those envelopes, the return address. It was a bad time, bad day. It seemed so long ago. But something nagged at the corner of his memory...there was some Texas connection.

"Uvalde, maybe," he said, in desperation. "Ruc Uvaldc. Uvalde Rue. No! Wait!" His mind clicked. He grabbed Sokol's arm. "Odessa. That's it. I know that's it. Rue Odessa."

"You sure?"

"I'm pretty sure. There's a town in West Texas, Odessa. I've flown over it. That name struck me when I saw it on my niece's letter. Rue Odessa. How do we find it?"

Sokol cast a dubious look towards the café. "We go ask. We wish for luck." Sokol's eyes shifted, narrowed, then widened in alarm. "Bloody hell!" he said.

Lange's heart lurched. The same black car from before, or one just like it, turned onto the street. Sokol bolted for the café. Lange chased after him. They barged in and a man, the owner or manager, yelled at them, threw up his hands. Sokol yelled something back and kept going. They barged through the kitchen. A girl jumped away from a sink. Sokol spoke to her. She pointed. They raced out a back door. The air in the alley stank like rancid grease and rotten food. The girl came out and ran behind them.

"*M'sieur*," she called, and chattered a few fast words at Sokol. Lange kept moving but the girl took the lead. She guided them into a courtyard, motioned them up a flight of stairs, and stopped at a door with a fancy glass-paned window. She knocked, then opened in the door.

Inside, a man slept on a daybed under a window. He roused when they burst in. Lange saw he only had one leg. The girl spoke, and the man reached for a pair of crutches.

"They will hide us," Sokol said.

"OK by me." Lange peered out the window, down into the courtyard. All seemed clear.

The girl showed them into a bedroom. The man stayed behind, standing with his crutches, one leg of his pants pinned in a deep, empty fold. She opened a large trunk and jerked out some blankets. Lange and Sokol bent to help. There was enough space for one of them. Lange urged Sokol into the trunk. They threw some blankets back on top of him and closed the lid. The girl hid Lange in a wardrobe. She stuffed another blanket around his feet. He tried to suppress his heavy breath—couldn't. The clothes around him trembled with each exhalation. His heart hammered. He hoped they had been wrong about the black car.

Minutes passed. The apartment was silent, except for Lange's own breath. Someone banged on the door. Voices, loud and gruff, came. A softer voice, from the man with the crutches. Again, Lange wished he knew what they said. The conversation was calm but went on a while. The girl's voice broke in once or twice. Then all the talking ceased. The door closed.

Heavy, uneven footsteps, like a man on crutches, came into the bedroom, and pattering steps, the girl. She opened the door to the wardrobe. Her eyes were bright and excited. The man balanced on his crutches, yammering at her. Sokol popped up from the trunk. Blankets spilled onto the floor. The man reached for Lange's hand, shook it. Then the man shook Sokol's hand.

Sokol patted the man on the shoulder. "The Huns told them we're traitors. *Resiste.*"

"They think we're Resistance?" Lange said, in disbelief. It was one of the few French words he had come to know.

Sokol nodded, then smiled at the man. "RAF," he said, patting his own chest. Then he tapped at Lange's shoulder. "Yank." He made a swooping motion with his hands—two planes in a dogfight. The girl flitted gleefully around them. The man seemed delighted and kept on shaking their hands.

CHAPTER 27

"*Rescue*"

Justine slept on the cot Clothilde kept in the small room beyond the upstairs kitchen. It had been a long time since four a.m., but she was sleepy all the time, now. Nina said it was a side effect of pregnancy. Clothilde said the sleepiness would improve but, so far, it had not.

It was the smell that woke her. A burning smell so strong it infiltrated her dream. She came up from the cot, certain the whole building was ablaze. In the kitchen, smoke poured from one of the ovens. She burned her hand on the door handle and choked on the black cloud that mushroomed into her face. The plum *flaugnarde* —a specialty of the bakery—were a charred ruin.

She wanted to cry. She had only meant to rest for a minute, while the *flaugnarde* browned. Clothilde would fume over this waste. She hadn't yet got over the ruined apricot *couronne* from two days ago. Twice she had mentioned the money lost, the hard-to-get ingredients. At this rate, Justine thought, Clothilde might change her mind about the arrangement and send Justine back to Garance. Clothilde hadn't wanted to agree to it in the first place and wouldn't have if not for François. He had overruled Clothilde, a thing he didn't do often. Justine had overheard an argument they had right after she arrived. If she were Nina and Joie, or Peter, Justine believed the atmosphere would have been different. Clothilde had never liked her.

When the German army came they all fled Paris together. Clothilde had belittled Justine for packing party clothes, lotions, and bathing salts. True, Justine had never used those bathing salts at Mémé's farmhouse. For one thing, there had been no proper bathtub there. But Justine had not known beforehand what to expect once they got to the country. She couldn't be blamed for packing incorrectly.

Neither François or Clothilde knew the coming baby's father was a German soldier. François knew nothing except that Nina had asked for help. Justine felt sure Clothilde had suspicions. If she knew the baby belonged to a German officer, they would most likely kick her out on the street. They were fearful people, afraid the least thing would be the ruin of their beloved shop. The shop came before everything.

Justin used a wide spatula to remove the ruined *flaugnarde* from the pan. She hated to toss it in the garbage. There were such shortages. She wrapped it in a strip of paper and slid it into the bread bin. Later, she knew, she would have to listen to Clothilde berate her, but it was possible François might know how to save the *flaugnarde* so they, at least, could eat it and not have it go to waste.

The kitchen door burst open, and François stepped in. His face was drawn and serious. He looked exhausted—sunken cheeks, dark eyes. His long apron could wrap twice around him. So different from the robust man before the war. Immediately, she began to apolgize for the burnt *flaugnarde*. She imagined the smell had made it into the shop downstairs.

"Justine, come, come," he said, stopping her mid-sentence. "Come downstairs."

"I fell asleep," she said, still trying to explain the smoke.

He waved that aside. "Two men are here," he said. "One speaks no French at all. They are asking questions. I need for you to translate."

"I don't know them," she said, quickly, automatically defensive. She wanted nothing to do with any more *Wehrmacht* soldiers. Not after the way Archie had deserted her. And anyway, her German was poor at best.

"Come here, *chérie*. Speak to them. You know English." He held out one long arm and waggled his bony fingers at her to follow.

"English?"

She hung back a second longer, but he kept insisting she come, so she finally went through the short hallway and down the stairs to the front of the shop. Clothilde was behind the bakery cases, rearranging loaves of *pain d'Epi* and *baguette*. She gave Justine a condemning look.

In the center, near the front door, stood two tattered strangers. One was blond and medium height. The other was dark and tall. They looked like pitiful tramps.

"I don't know them," she said again to François, this time with more certainty.

The blond one said, in poor French, "We search for the babies of Sunny DeLony."

Justine gaped at him in surprise. How did he know her mother's name? She shied backwards.

The tall one moved forward and in English said, "Nina?"

The use of her sister's name startled her. "Who are you?" she said in English.

"Is this the Monnier's bakery?" the tall, thin one said, then to François, "Do you have a son named Emile."

"He doesn't speak English," she said. "Tell me who you are." She eased closer to François. These strangers frightened her. "My mother was Sunny Lange. She died six years ago."

"You must be Nina." The tall man smiled. "Please, don't be afraid. I can't believe I found you. I'm Lange. I'm your uncle. Your mother, Sunny, was my sister. Lange was our mother's maiden name. You real last name is Dailey."

Justine gasped. He had to be lying. He was a German spy and had somehow found out about her background. That was the only possibility. But why? What had she done to cause them to come for her? She started to run away, back up the stairs.

"Don't be afraid," the tall man said, still smiling. "I know it's a surprise."

She glanced at the blond one, came back to the one who claimed to be her uncle. Mama had one younger brother who lived in America, in Texas. There was a photograph, long ago, that had sat on a shelf beneath the window of their apartment. It had been of a fifteen-year-old boy, black and white, standing before a two-wing aeroplane. The person in front of her seemed too tall, too old to be the boy in that photograph.

She inspected him up and down, took in his ragged clothes, the scraggly beard, unwashed hair. The sleeve of his coat was torn. She frowned. "Uncle Ding?"

"Yes!" He smiled widened. He laughed. He seemed delighted with her. "Yes! Yes! That's me! That's what your mother...that's what Sunny called me."

He stepped forward as if to embrace her, but she retreated again. She continued to study him warily and thought perhaps—perhaps—there was something familiar in his face. He was definitely American. He sounded just like Mama.

He said, "Where are Justine and Pete?"

She felt suddenly dizzy. She barely heard the last question. And anyway, he stopped asking questions when she flung herself against him. Her uncle! Mama's only brother. The aviator. That much she knew for a fact. The rest she figured out in a split second. He was here to rescue her. To take her back with him to America in his aeroplane. He was her Uncle Ding! She couldn't stop sobbing joyous tears.

~

"I DON'T KNOW any people here who can help you return to England." She sat on the small cot in the room behind the kitchen.

Her uncle sat backwards on the straight chair across from her. He understood now that she was Justine, not Nina. He held her hand and it helped to soften the blow. He had not come to take her to America at all. Instead, he was asking her for help. He had been fighting the war. His aeroplane had crashed somewhere in Belgium. She had only a vague idea of where Belgium was or how far he had come. His Czech friend stood against the wall beside the rear doorway.

"I'm sure Nina would know what to do," she said. "You can go to her. Or Peter. They both resist the occupation."

"Where are they right now?" the Czech pilot asked.

She didn't like the tone of voice he used, so she didn't answer but only gave him a glance. She wished he would stop trying to speak French. Didn't he see she could speak English perfectly well?

"Do you have papers?" she said to her uncle. "Identity papers? You will need those to go anywhere in France."

Her uncle let go of her hand to reach into his coat pocket. The Czech stopped him with a firm hand on his shoulder, shook his head in warning.

She snapped at the Czech, "Do you think I would turn you over to the Gestapo?"

"What about the man and woman?" he said, nodding towards the front of the store. "Maybe they would."

"Sokol," Uncle Ding said. "Sit down. She's my niece. She wants to help us."

"I guess he has a right to wonder." Justine stood up from the cot and confronted the Czech. He backed up one step, looked down at her. "I shall tell you about me," she said, "and then you will tell me about you."

"Not necessary," he said in French.

"You speak French worse than you do English," she said to him in French, then proceeded in English, for the uncle's sake. "I came to Paris now only because my sister wanted me to leave Garance. People hate me there. Some people. She said it was for my own safety to come here to live with the Monniers as we did before the Germans came."

"Why do people hate you there?" her uncle said.

"Because I have a baby." She rubbed her hands in a circle on her belly. "I'm sure you can see for yourself." She cast a look at the Czech. "The father is an officer of the *Wehrmacht*."

"He raped you?" the Czech said, in French again. His bluntness startled her.

"No!"

The Czech threw up his hands in disgust and acted like he wanted to stomp from the room. She watched him march in a circle. He was a peculiar one, a hot head. She looked at her uncle. He had kind eyes, the same eyes in that long-ago photograph, not light in color like mama's, but warm and kind.

"I loved him," she said to her uncle. Tears welled. "I thought he was good."

Her uncle stayed sitting in the chair. "Do you know you look exactly like your mother?"

"No, not me." She sat back on the cot, wiping at her cheeks. "That's Nina. You shall see."

"Tell me about her. She was a baby the last time I saw her."

Justine raised her chin. "She's bossy. She thinks she's always right about everything."

"Bossy, yes," the uncle laughed. "That sounds like Sunny, too. All the women in our family are bossy."

"Our family," Justine repeated in a wistful tone. She wished Nina were here. She would know how to help their uncle. "Clothilde will not let you and your friend stay here," Justine said. "This is certain. If not for you being my uncle she would most likely turn you in to the authorities. She hates trouble, and always follows rules. Even though Emile—their son—was captured by the Germans at the beginning of the war."

"Captured where?" Uncle Ding's brow furrowed.

"Near Laon."

He nodded gravely. She glanced at the Czech. He was still angry, she could see that clearly enough.

"Your friend hates me," she whispered to her uncle.

"Sokol? No, he hates the Germans. They invaded his homeland."

"They invaded mine, too." She watched Sokol pace. "What is his given name?"

"Joe. Josef."

She kept her eyes on Josef Sokol. She was certain he could hear them, but he seemed to choose not to pay attention. He stood beside the rear door, staring out through the slit window.

"Peter ran away to live in the woods with the communists," she said. "He thinks he and his *maquis* friends can defeat the Germans by force. They cut telephone lines and create trouble for patrols. At first, it was a matter of puncturing tires, but then two soldiers were found shot in the woods. I know Peter didn't do this. He is too gentle."

"Peter?" Uncle Ding interrupted. "I thought he was…"

"Deaf?" She tilted her head. "That's what you were planning to say? He does everything hearing people do. It is not good in Garance now."

Josef Sokol glanced at her from the door where he stood. "Where is Garance?" he asked.

She avoided his gaze. "Three hundred kilometers. Near Dijon. You will have to go by train. Do you have money?"

The uncle shook his head and looked at his empty hands. So did the Czech. She grimaced. She had none either.

"François might give you enough for tickets," she said, "if Clothilde doesn't find out. However, she will want to be rid of you both. She wants to be rid of me as well. I know Nina paid her to take me. I saw a letter she wrote." She squinted her eyes at her uncle. "Can we make a bargain?"

He rested his elbows on the back of the chair. He was facing her. He seemed like he wanted to laugh. "What kind of a bargain?"

"I will go with you on the train. It will be easier for you with me along. When we get to Garance, Nina and Peter will help. There is a man who lives there, too, and works for Mémé. His name is Lothaire. He will know how to get you and—" Her eyes moved to the Czech. Clearly, he was listening now, "—your friend back to England. And you will take me with you."

He uncle's hand touched her arm, just above the wrist. "I like everything you just said except that last part. It's too dangerous."

Tears clouded her vision. It was had to stay dry-eyed with someone being kind to her. "I want to leave France," she sobbed. "I wish to get to America. *Grand-pére* wanted us to come, but Nina said no. She decided for all of us. She never asked me what I wanted."

"Let's take her," the Czech said suddenly from the corner where he stood.

Her uncle took hold of her hand again. "Justine, I would never be able to live with myself if something happened to you. If you got caught with us, you could be...."

"What do I care? I'm already dying here. Your friend thinks it's a good idea. I can help you. He speaks French like a goat. I will do all the talking, and we will have no trouble."

"Why do everybody keep saying my French is bad?" the Czech said.

"It is very bad. I'm sorry. I don't mean to be cruel. Your English is no good either. Tell him to take me. Please." She turned her pleading eyes back to her uncle. "You won't make it without me. I'm not afraid. I don't want my baby to be born in France. Not now. Not with the war."

The Czech strode forward. "Let her come with us," he said, gruffly. Justine looked at him with hope. "She can show the way."

She nodded. "I can show you the way."

Her uncle rose from the chair. He shook his head. "It's too dangerous. If we're caught she goes straight to jail. And so will these people she's staying with."

"I think we might not make it without her, DeLony." Josef Sokol let his glance fall on her for a brief instant. "With my bad French."

"That's true," Justine said.

The debate went on for several long minutes. The uncle would waver and then he would repeat his warnings of the danger. She and the Czech wore him down. She was surprised to find an ally in the Czech. She began to like him a little more.

Finally Uncle Ding said, "OK. But she only goes as far as Garance." He took her hands in his. "I'm sorry, Justine. It's too risky. You know what would happen if you're caught with us."

"Firing squad," she said and shrugged to prove she was brave.

Josef Sokol burst into laughter. She laughed with him, happy that he understood her joke. Her uncle kept a grim face.

FRANÇOIS PROVIDED them with enough money for train tickets. He also let her uncle and the Czech stay the night downstairs in the back of the shop, but he made them wait outside until Clothilde had gone upstairs. He sent Justine along with her, telling them he would follow in a few minutes. It was hard to keep quiet. She let Clothilde scold her for the ruined *flaugnarde* and even for the *couronne* from two days ago. Tomorrow she would be gone. And this time she wasn't coming back. Paris had changed. She wasn't happy here. She wasn't happy in France at all. She would make the uncle see how useful she could be. He would have to give in and take her with them when they left the country.

After a while, she went back downstairs. She took the *flaugnarde*. They ate it in big bites, and didn't seem to notice it was burned. She showed them the basin in the washroom behind the shop, so they could wash. François brought down a razor so they could shave and prepare for the journey. She broomed off their clothes, mended the rip in the sleeve of the coat her uncle wore. She gathered their shoes to clean caked mud off them, found the identity disk under the sole. She studied it. It had an "O" on it.

"Are you an officer?" she asked him, and he nodded. "If we had an aeroplane, you could fly us to America?"

"To England," he said. "I doubt we'd have enough fuel to get to America." He chuckled.

"Do you know of a plane?" Josef Sokol asked her. Everything he said sounded so urgent.

"No. I just had the idea." Perhaps Peter would be able to figure out something. From England, she thought she could easily get to America.

They left early, before daybreak. The train station wasn't far, but they took the Metro. It was quicker, safer. Justine was happy to be leaving. In fact, she felt like celebrating. She had only been back in Paris since Christmas, but it felt like two years instead of two months.

On the Metro car it was decided that she and Josef Sokol would pretend to be lovers. She loved the delicious feeling of playing a part, sneaking past German solders and collaborators. She had always dreamed of becoming an actress. Maybe once she got to America, she would go to Hollywood, California.

She used François's money and bought the train tickets to Dijon. Garance was only a half hour walk from Dijon, and no train stopped there. On the train, the three of them sat away from any other people. Uncle Ding told her about his family in England. She told him about them leaving Paris in front of the invasion. He told her stories about Mama when she still lived in Texas, and about Papa, too, whom Justine had never known.

Once daylight broke, the train began to fill up on stops outside of Paris. The more people who boarded, the quieter her uncle became. He finally leaned against the window and seemed to drift off to sleep.

"He told you lies, this *Wehrmacht* soldier," Josef Sokol whispered. "They all lie, the German bastards."

"He was Austrian."

"Worse."

She laughed, pushed her arm through his, and continued to play the part. It was the last thing Josef Sokol expected. "What is your full name? Josef, what?"

"Theodor. Josef Theodor Sokol."

"I think I will call you Teddy. It sounds more American."

He grunted and looked away, out the window. On the other side of her, Uncle Ding still slept, or pretended to.

"Don't you want to go to America?" she asked softly.

"Maybe someday, sure. I don't know what will be left of my home."

"You can visit me there. In America." She squeezed his arm. "I will teach you proper French."

"Ssh," he said, half-smiling. He kept his eyes forward.

"Are you Jewish?"

He shook his head. "Catholic. What are you?"

"An orphan."

He touched her hand on his arm. "I will look after you," he said.

She smiled and hung onto him. He was a little bit handsome. She thought it wasn't bad to pretend to be in love with him. She glanced at her uncle, sleeping. She leaned closer to Teddy, and pressed her lips to his cheek.

"What has happened to your mother and father?" she whispered. "Do you know?"

He shook his head and looked down at his lap. "No."

"They wanted you to leave?"

"Yes. My father insisted." He pressed his forehead against hers. "Kiss me again," he said.

She leaned to press a feathery kiss on his cheek, but he turned his head at the last second and caught the kiss on his lips.

"*Tombeur*," she said, scolding him with a smile.

"What does that mean?"

She shrugged. "Figure it out."

CHAPTER 28

"*Garance*"

In his memory, Lange had never traveled on so many trains as he had since he'd been trying to get back to England. Beside him, Justine and Sokol huddled together, pretending to be lovers––or maybe they weren't pretending. Their laughter and intense interest in each other seemed genuine, enough to fool Lange, so he thought it would fool any Germans that might be watching, too, despite the mismatch in the clothes they wore— Sokol in his threadbare disguise, Justine with her ermine-collared coat.

What were the odds of him finding Sunny's kids in all of France, in the middle of a war? And yet, he had already found one of them and was about to meet the other two. Wouldn't Papa and Aunt Dellie be surprised and happy about that? He just wished it were under better circumstances, when he wasn't trying to evade capture. He had no intention of taking Justine with them. If they could somehow reconnect with the escape line, he felt sure he and Sokol would have to get into neutral Spain, which meant going over the Pyrenees. No journey for a young girl, let alone a pregnant one. He wondered what had happened to the bomber boys back in Paris, and to Georges and Celeste.

A woman in a red dress sat down in the empty seat across from him, so close her knees touched his. She smelled of mothballs. He let out a couple of light snores to convince her he was asleep so she wouldn't try to start a conversation. Next to him, Sokol and Justine played their parts, kept their heads close, as if in a deep, whispering, lovers' conversation. Now and then, Lange opened one eye for a peep at them. They were sure convincing. Once she even raised her mouth to kiss Sokol on his cheek.

Justine reminded Lange so much of Sunny or, anyway, his memory of Sunny. Their coloring was identical, but it was mostly her mannerisms, the fluttery way her hands moved, the sound of her laughter, the way she tipped her chin up when she was listening. It stirred something inside him, something lonely and lost that he hadn't felt since he was a kid.

Sunny was thirteen years older than him, more like a young aunt than a sister. When their mother died, she took over. She was someone he relied on and trusted, and then she left, moved off to a foreign country, and he never saw her again. To him it felt like she had died. By the time she did die, in 1938, she was almost lost from his memory. Seeing Justine, how much she favored Sunny, brought back that loss all over again.

He leaned back with his eyes closed and let his mind wander, from his sister, to Becky, to being a kid, to Mackie coming into his life, having his own kids. No doubt about it, his priorities had changed. Wandering lost in Nazi Europe had seen to that. Nothing sounded better to him than his family, his wife, and his kids. All this time, he realized he had been on hold, misunderstanding what the important things were, and that he already had them.

When he opened his eyes again, Sokol had his arm around Justine. Her head rested on his shoulder. They were both sound asleep. They looked at peace.

~

MID-AFTERNOON, the train pulled into the little station at Garance. Lange was relieved to have made it without any trouble, and something had changed in him on that train. It was a subtle difference but it was palpable. He was eager, hopeful, looked forward to meeting his other niece and his nephew. He wished he could tell Papa—no, he wished Papa was here. He could just imagine the look that would come to Papa's face, that look he got when he was pleased about something but too stubborn to say so.

Justine walked with a light step a little out in front of him and Sokol, leading the way. She looked almost glamorous in her ermine-collared coat. If she was pregnant, she sure didn't show it. As they walked into Garance, she pointed out places to them, the store where her brother had worked when they first came here, an old medieval church with crumbling walls but still in use. There had been a recent snow. It was piled along the walks and in the gutters. A stone bridge crossed over an icy stream.

She took them to a small pastry shop, told them to wait by the door. She went inside, calling out a familiar greeting, in French, of course, so Lange didn't know exactly what she said. She even spoke English with a heavy French accent, which for some reason, he hadn't expected.

Sokol watched Justine through the window. Lange gazed through the window, too. There were some fine-looking pies on display, and crusty rolls dusted with flour. His empty stomach growled. Justine stood talking to a middle-aged woman, who kept peering towards the door, wondering, no doubt, about the two vagrants waiting for Justine to return.

"I am in love, DeLony." Sokol sounded dreamy. The sun was out, but Sokol's breath made a vapor trail.

Lange laughed. "Not again."

"This time is different. She looks so little and pretty. Yes, I am sure of it. I love her."

"She's a child."

Sokol gave Lange an impatient look. "In May she is eighteen. Not a child, DeLony."

"You're too old for her, Sokol."

"Four years only."

"Jesus!" Lange stared at Sokol, then counted quickly in his head. "You mean, you're just twenty-two?" He thought about all the times Sokol had saved his hide in dogfights. He'd never considered Sokol a kid back then.

"I am eighteen when I leave my country," Sokol said, as if he had read Lange's mind. It was the first time in a while they had a moment to talk freely.

Lange said. "What about the fact that she's pregnant?"

Sokol watched intently through the window. "I don't care. I tell you, I love her. She has no one, and she is so pretty and—"

"Little. Yeah, I heard you the first time." Lange shook his head. But Sokol sounded as sincere as he had about Margot back in Brussels. Any pretty face in a storm.

Sokol's face lit up as Justine came back out to where they stood by the door. She said, "Nina isn't working today. She must be at the farm. We can walk there."

They set off, shoulder to shoulder, Justine in the middle. In just a few minutes they were out of the village streets and on a narrow dirt road, climbing a hill. Sokol reached to hold Justine's hand. Lange caught it out of the corner of his eye, smiled.

Justine cast a look at Lange, smiled, too. "I think Teddy likes the play acting," she said.

"Teddy?"

Sokol spoke up, "She calls me Teddy."

Lange chuckled. "Maybe he's not play-acting, Justine."

"Of course he is." She smiled in Sokol's direction. "He thinks I'm a *callabo*, remember?"

"I do not," Sokol jumped in.

"You thought so in Paris," she said.

"I did not say you were *collabo*," Sokol protested.

Lange wasn't even sure what they were talking about, but it struck him as funny. And Sokol was right about Justine, she was pretty and appealing. And small. Maybe five foot, if that. He could see the attraction, especially if they were nearly the same damned age. How many sorties had they flown together? He didn't think he could even count them all.

They topped the hill, rounded a bend and there, a hundred yards ahead, in the middle of nowhere, a roadblock bristled with German soldiers. They had a poor fellow waylaid and were searching him, had his pockets turned inside out, his hands spread out to his sides. While one soldier frisked him, another one spoke loudly into his face. Lange, Sokol, and Justine all froze at the same time.

"What's this," Lange said, under his breath.

Suddenly, Justine bolted off to the left and into the woods that lined the road. Sokol went right after her, and Lange followed. But it was too late; they had been spotted. More commotion began at the roadblock.

"I think they're coming after us," Lange said.

Justine and Sokol ran, darted among the trees. Lange ran, too. There was little undergrowth in the woods, which made running easier, but also made it harder to hide. With no path to follow, Lange dodged through the trees, tripped over vines, but stayed right behind Sokol. Justine seemed to know the way. She darted up hills and down through draws. She stayed well ahead. Lange's feet slipped on the leaf cover on the hill. Sokol held up for him, but Justine ran on.

The smooth soles on the street shoes Lange wore wouldn't hold purchase in the deep drifts of leaves and slippery moss. Just as he regained his balance from yet another slip, he heard a dog. His eyes snapped to Sokol's. They sprinted onward, followed the way Justine led, down into a ravine, tearing through a thicket. Lange's coat snagged on something thorny. Breath wheezed in and out of his lungs. He could still hear the dog, closer, making quick gains.

The woods seemed to go on forever. Justine ran like a deer, and Sokol went headlong after her. But the sound of the dog came, too, and the voices of soldiers pounded behind. And all at once, Lange knew they would be caught. After all this time, after making it this far, after keeping the possibility of capture out of their conversations, out of their minds, he recognized the inevitability. He couldn't outrun the dog. None of them could.

Desperation struck him, and fear—not so much for himself or Sokol as for Justine. They would know she had helped them. What would they do to her? Would they care that she was pregnant? He doubted it. He slowed up. It was an unconscious decision that quickly turned to conscious resolution. Sokol turned back.

"Go on," Lange said. "Get out of here."

"No, no, DeLony. Come! You can make it!"

Lange waved Sokol away. "Hurry. Get the hell out of here. Take care of her."

He saw reluctance flash over Sokol's face and then resignation. Sokol knew there wasn't time for argument. He turned and ran flat out to catch up to Justine. They disappeared behind thick trees. In a moment, the sound of their running footsteps disappeared as well. They would get away. He felt certain of it. Fleetingly, a thought crossed his mind with grim disappointment now he wouldn't get to meet Nina and Pete.

An instant later, the dog was upon him. Before the impact of his decision could dawn on him, before the deep loneliness could set in, he was fighting off a German Sheperd, a big one with a powerful mouth. The dog gripped his arm, shook it, nearly knocked him over, before three soldiers arrived with their guns and their brown boots. One of them shouted, and the dog loosened his hold on Lange's arm.

The sleeve of his coat was shredded but he didn't think he was physically hurt. He raised his hands and said, "I'm an American pilot. A captain in the United States Army Air Force."

He could tell they didn't understand him. Or if they did they didn't believe him. A disheveled man in battered clothes, so far behind the lines of battle. Carefully and so they could see he wasn't trying to get away, he drew his foot out of his shoe. The sheperd tried to lunge again but one of the soldiers held the dog fast by the harness. Lange plucked the single dog tag out from under the inner sole and held it palm out.

"US Army Air Force," he said, again. "I am an American pilot."

Both of them stared at the embossed metal tag. The dog strained and whined. The soldier who seemed to be in charge, the one with dirty, tobacco-stained teeth, raised his eyes.

"Pilot." Lange made an airplane with his hands.

The dirty-toothed soldier squinted one eye, watched for a second, and then the butt of a rifle came at Lange's face so fast, so unexpectedly, he had no time to dodge. It smashed into his forehead. The sound of it reverberated in his skull. He collapsed into the mulch of leaves on the ground.

THEY TOOK him to a Dijon interrogation center, stripped him, and beat him with a woven whip until his back was raw. He could feel the blood running in a rivulet down his spine. They tied his ankles and manacled his hands behind his back; they forced his head into a bathtub of water. Just before he lost consciousness, they hurled him backwards. Water poured out of him. He gagged and gasped, and before he could get his breath, they shoved him back under. Twelve times they held him under water until he felt sure he would drown. A nameless terror took hold of him but also sadness at his own loss of dignity, and a sick sense of shame that people could behave this way.

They thought he was a spy or part of the *resiste*. They wanted the name of his helpers, where the false identity papers came from, where he had stolen the metal ID from his shoe. He repeated his name and rank. He sang "The Eyes of Texas." But he wondered in his deepest self if the interrogation had gone on for another day or two, if he might have broken.

Before he had to find that out, the interrogations abruptly stopped. He was taken in the back of an automobile to a hospital, treated for six cracked ribs, and a dislocated shoulder. When he was wheeled into a private room an officer in the Luftwaffe was waiting for him. Pilot's wings adorned his smart tunic. He wore a peaked cap with silver braids.

"Major DeLony," the officer said, smiling. His English was perfect. He offered his hand for a shake. "I must apologize for the treatment you have received. In some places the foxes are guarding the hens."

"It's captain," Lange said, avoiding the handshake. "Captain DeLony not major."

He distrusted the familiar way the officer addressed him by name. There was a glass on the opposite wall and he could see his own sorry reflection compared to the spit-shined German officer standing over his bed.

"Ah, so you don't know. You must have been evading for a very long time, major. You have recently received a promotion. Congratulations." The officer's smile widened. He had straight white teeth. "You can relax now. Have some American cigarettes." The officer laid a pack of Lucky Strikes on the bedside table. Lange wondered where in hell the cigarettes had come from, right here in the middle of France. The officer said just like in a movie script, "For you, the war is over."

CHAPTER 29

Letters

12 March 1944

Dear Mackie,

I don't know where to begin. I have been given this small sheet of paper, so I can write to you. As you may already know, they have got me in the bag. At first they didn't believe I was who I said I was, but now I'm waiting to be sent somewhere and am told things will be better for me there. I wish I could say more, but the main thing is I am alive and will see you again some day. Kiss the kids for me and tell them their daddy loves them. I love and miss you more than I can say.

Yours,

Lange

~

25 March 1944

Headquarters
Fourth Fighter Group
Mrs. Allison L. DeLony
24 Process Road

Colesbury, Cambridgeshire, UK

Dear Mrs. DeLony,

We have learned from the Swiss Red Cross that your husband, Major C. L. DeLony, USAAF, is a prisoner of war at Stalag Luft I in Barth, Germany. His fighter went down on 21 October 1943. He evaded capture for several weeks but was finally detained in Garance, France on 17 February 1944. He is in good health and is being held in compliance with the terms of the Geneva Convention of 1935. You may write to him and send packages to him through this office.

I trust that this news will relieve you and your family. Major DeLony is an outstanding officer and highly respected by the members of his squadron. His loss to the squadron is deeply felt. His devotion and duty to his country remains unswerving and merits the highest praise.

Sincerely yours,

Howard C. Stringer

Brigadier General, USAAF

Commanding

~

Tuesday, 22 March 44

Stalag Luft I

Dear Mackie,

I am parked you might say. It's better than the previous camp, [CENSORED]. We are pretty much left alone. When I say we, I mean the [CENSORED] camp. Don't have much room to say much, but we will sure have a lot to talk about once we're back together. Write to me as often as you can. From what I hear around here, only about a third of the letters seem to make it, so there may be gaps, but just know the main thing I do to occupy my time is think about you and the kids. If you can, send me a picture. This is not how I chose to spend the last part of the war. I miss you more than I can say. Write to me.

Many kisses,

Lange

P.S. Remember the promise you made to me about what you would do if something happened. Well, honey, it has.

~

April 14, 1944

Colesbury, England

My Darling,

It is with such joy that I received your letters. I got the second one first, but no matter, just seeing your handwriting on the outside sent me over the moon! Darling, whatever else I feel as regards your situation, words cannot express the relief in knowing you are alive. I died a thousand deaths thinking you would not be coming back and that I would never see you again. It was truly the longest four months of my life. [CENSORED] Darling, please don't do anything foolish. Write to me as often as you can.

The children are growing and miss their daddy. The twins are beginning to talk. I'm teaching them to say "daddy." Susannah is pulling up on things and trying to walk from point A to B. Given danced for joy when your letters arrived. He's as relieved as I am that you are safe. He has been a tower of strength for his mummy.

Darling, what do you need? I'm told that I can send packages. Do you have books to read? Are there any personal items I should send? I will get a picture of the children together for you very soon. This has all come as such a welcome surprise, and I feel so unprepared to respond.

Darling, in between the arrival of your two letters, came one from [CENSORED] office. Did you know that you had made major? Maybe I shouldn't say that in a letter, I don't know what the rules are yet. I take it that this news will not be entirely unex-

pected. You certainly deserve it, but I had no idea you were up for promotion. Does this mean you intend to stay in once all this is over? [CENSORED]I know we have plenty of time to talk about this later, but maybe it helps you to think about the future. I've always said it and I mean it still, what I want most of all is to make you happy. Please, stay safe. You're in my every waking thought. You are in my dreams, too. Missing you frightfully—

Mackie

~

May 3, 1944

Colesbury, UK

Darling,

There have been no letters from you since the first two, but I guess I can't expect that it will be a back and forth sort of correspondence like we have had in the past. I have some news to share with you. Your niece is in hospital in London. I was notified by the American Consulate that she was there, and then shortly after, I had a visit from your old [CENSORED] pal, Joe. I think it will mean a lot to you to know that he came to see me. He has a big story to tell you one of these days. I am supposed to be able to bring Justine home very soon. I will keep you posted on this situation.

I hope you get the snap that I have enclosed with this letter. Aren't our babies big? Given holds Susannah by her hands and walks her all over the house. She adores her big bubbie. Honour and Hope have started into the "terrible twos" already. Even sweet Honour is cranky a lot of the time, but at least she doesn't stand and squall when she doesn't get her way or hold her breath like her sister does. But of course, I am completely devoted to them and don't know how I ever lived without them, or without you, my darling. I sometimes marvel at how lucky I was to find you. And how easily I could have missed. If they'd had a return ferry chit for me at Hawarden that day, I would have never been on that train.

I am not avoiding mention of the promise you reminded me of in your last letter. I do most certainly remember it but everything has been complicated by the situation with Justine. She lost her child, and was very sick for a long time afterwards. She has been through an awful lot and needs TLC.

We miss you so much, darling. Please, write when you can.

All my love,

Mackie

∼

May 17, 1944

Colesbury, England

Dear Dad,

I know Mum writes letters to you, so I wanted to write to you, too. Did you know you have another DFC? It came in a black box with gold writing on it. Mum opened the box. She said you wouldn't mind if I took it to school to show to my class. They had never seen one from the USAAF. It's quite heavy and has a red, white, and blue ribbon. I think you will like it lots.

It has been raining an awful lot lately. I haven't been able to get outside much. Mr. Bailey and I have been going to the stable in Auntie's car to feed Blin. Auntie says she needs to ask for a Land Girl now that we have chickens to feed.

Yesterday was Susie's first birthday. We had cake. She burned her hand on the candle, but she didn't cry one bit. She has a blister in the middle of her right palm.

How are you doing? Are you cold? Mum worries that you are cold where you are. We do so miss you around this place.

Yours truly,

Given

∼

June 8, 1944

> *Colesbury England*
>
> *Dear Lange,*
>
> *I still have not heard from you and it makes it so hard not knowing if you are all right. Justine has come to Colesbury with me. She is still very weak. I believe she had a terrible ordeal. She doesn't talk much about it, or about anything at all really. Except when Joe Sokol comes to visit her. I hear them in the other room speaking French. My own French is rusty after all my schoolgirl years, but I have retained enough to be able to tell you that they are definitely more than just friends. The other night they were discussing marriage. I don't want to discourage her if they are in love, but she is so young. I know she feels out of place here. She seems to like the children but is not well enough to have a lot to do with them. She doesn't speak at all about the child she lost, other than to say she thought she might die, and I believe that was a real possibility. However, the whole thing is a mystery, and it wouldn't be wise for me to go into much detail, but I will tell you that you are quite the hero to both of them. I hope they will both always be grateful for the second chance you gave to them. Honestly, I am trying not to be resentful. Your sacrifice was also mine.*
>
> *Everything else is all right except that I miss you terribly. Your friend, Jim, brought your barracks bag over a few days ago. You have another DFC, all shiny and in its case, and gold major's leaves, too. I put them on your dress uniform. You are getting quite a fruit salad on there, Major.*
>
> *Darling, I wish for the war to be over by autumn. I pray for it. This family needs you with us. I will close this letter for now. Send me one, darling. I need so much to hear from you.*
>
> *All my love,*
> *Mackie*

1 July 1944

    Stalag Luft I

    Dear Mackie,

    I have been writing to you but I guess my letters aren't reaching you. I'm sorry, honey. Please, don't worry over me. I am getting by all right. We have a sort of library here and some of the fellows who have knowledge in certain fields are teaching classes. The Red Cross has been providing the books, and I am taking some classes in engineering. Maybe I'll learn something that will help me after I get out of here.

    I was surprised and happy to hear the news about Justine. I know there's no way for you to know, but she is so much like my sister. Being around her brought back a lot of memories. I think she must be just as fearless as Sunny. She should go to Aunt Dellie's, and you, honey, should go with her. Take the children. I want all of you there when I get home. I don't want to have to travel all over the world gathering up my family.

    Remember I love you. Keep writing to me. Kiss the babies. Tell Given Daddy loves hearing from him, too, and to write to me some more.

    Your darling,

    Lange

～

July 17, 1944

    Colesbury, UK

    My Darling,

    Yippee!! I finally got a letter from you. Such joy to see your handwriting. Keep writing. I have to know you're all right. Yes, you are my "darling." You always have been, right from the beginning.

    Engineering sounds like a perfect fit for you. Learn all you can and keep busy. I should think time would go by faster if you stay busy. Next time I'm in London I'll pop over to Charing Cross and see if I can locate some books on engineering that might be of interest to you.

Lange, I have tried to set the wheels in motion to take Justine and the kids to Aunt Dellie's, but I was told that all transportation is occupied at the moment. I suppose we both know by now why that is. Do you get any war news? Things have got a bit dicey around here lately. I would explain in detail but I'm afraid it will be censored. Suffice it to say, I want to get the children away as soon as possible. Who knew those little "doodle bugs" could be so dangerous? [CENSORED]

Seems we may have a situation in reverse to the usual one for war brides. Your pal, Joe, will soon be your nephew. How will that feel? He asked Justine to marry him and she said yes. He has been VERY busy but as soon as he gets a forty-eight, they are going to go through with it. The ceremony will be here at Colesbury. They seem to think they have all the details worked out for when the war is over. Which will be soon. I think that is clear enough now.

Stay safe, my darling. Keep writing. I will do my part on this end.

Remember I love you,
Mackie

~

July 29, 1944
Colesbury, UK
Darling,
This will be a hurried letter and short, and don't fret if some time elapses before you get another from me. I am keeping my promise to you. We are to be ready at a moment's notice. I am so glad to have Justine along. She will be immense help with the children. Aunt Dellie has written several times to let me know they are ready and waiting. She says they are fixing up the house where Gabe and Lettie lived. That must be the bunkhouse you

told me about. Anyway, you can rest easy about your family, darling.

Speaking of Justine, she and Josef were married last week in Aunt Kath's garden. It was lovely. Some of his squadron mates attended, and several of them asked about you. Your extended family is taking on a distinctively international flare. Justine says after the war ends, Joe (she calls him Teddy, for some reason) plans to live with her in America. I hope you take this as good news—the rest of us certainly do. I believe Justine would be lost right now without him in her life. Just as I would be without you, darling. But I really feel as if time will go fast, now, for everyone. All the signs for a quick end are in the air. Maybe it will be done by Christmas. I hope this letter hasn't been completely blacked out by the censors.

All my love,
Mackie

CHAPTER 30

"Trophies"

In the photograph, Ding was all decked out in his military get-up, looking official, grown up. Dane couldn't wrap his brain around it. Seemed like just yesterday Ding was a barefoot kid, running around the old home place, chasing chickens or catching toad frogs. He had an old busted-wheel tricycle he hauled around everywhere. One day, he painted it blue and got paint all over himself, before Tessa saw him through the kitchen window. Fixing things. Always fixing things, and tinkering.

After Tessa was gone, he turned into a quieter boy, smart but stubborn. Dane figured Ding could do just about anything he turned his mind to, fly an airplane, become an officer in the Army Air Corps. Now, he had all them damned kids, and a British wife. What with all of them waiting for him, it was hard to imagine that Ding wouldn't get his bounce back again pretty quick.

Dane stared at the picture on his lap and with sheer force of will, inched his finger over onto Ding's face. His boy. Holed up in some goddamn filthy Nazi prison camp. Ever since the wire cable came five months ago Dane had been having dreams, and he never was given to dreams before. Mostly these new dreams were about Ding when he was little, but sometimes Tessa showed up in one, too. He hadn't dreamed about Tessa in more than twenty years. Dreams didn't do much for restful sleep. He had gotten so's he would just as soon avoid sleep altogether. Explained him falling off to sleep all day long.

An hour ago, right before Dellie left the house, she had rolled Dane's chair closer to the window in the front room, opened the curtains the way she always did, so he could look up the road and see when the Buick was coming. They had gone down to the station to meet the ten-forty. Those babies had been cooped up on a train for two days, probably had stored-up energy to last them for a week. He wasn't much in the mood for a bunch of wild hellions. He was used to a quiet house. He preferred quiet.

The Mexican woman Dellie had hired—Rosalee--had already started cooking dinner. Smells from the kitchen made his mouth water. At least since Rosalee came they had good meals to eat. He still enjoyed eating his meals, hoped his teeth would hold out. Hell to outlive your teeth, and his had been feeling loose since last winter.

Way off down the road, a dust cloud rose. Dellie's Buick, with Gabe driving. He always drove too fast, slung dust and gravel every-where. Dane looked again at the photo on his lap and counted: One, two, three, four children. Little fellow had been busy over there in England. Was a wonder he had any time at all for fighting a war. Dane guessed they could fit all them kids in the Buick, but it was probably a tight squeeze. He pictured the squirming and fretting.

What he tried hard not to picture was Ding behind barbed wire, but sometimes the thought crossed his mind anyway. He hoped Ding wasn't suffering. In fact, Dane prayed about it, and it had been a hell of a long time since he'd prayed about anything. He didn't want Ding to come home scarred and beat down by the goddamned Germans the way so many soldiers were after the last war. A kind of lingering darkness that had settled over the house since that cable arrived. That was months ago now.

The Buick came closer. Sure enough, Gabe was behind the

wheel. Dane watched the Buick swerve into the driveway. Dust billowed out from under the tires. It came in through the front windows and settled on everything. Dane coughed.

"Mister Dane!" Rosalee came prancing in from the kitchen. He felt her hands grab his chair handles and whirl him around. "You want to go meet your grandbabies, don't you?" She wheeled him towards the back hallway.

He heard them before he saw them, just as he knew he would—noisy, thundering up the back steps, chattering. Dellie called out, "Yoohoo! We're home!" He could tell by her voice she was over-excited. She had always been a high-strung woman.

She came up the hallway towards him, a whole passel of folks behind her. She held one of the young'uns in her arms—a fat baby with blond hair. "Oh Dane, we have got the biggest surprise for you."

And he could see that rightly enough—babies, babies, and more babies, and a boy that gave Dane a start when he first laid eyes on him. Looked just like Ding for a second.

"Say hello to Papa Dane," a slender blond woman said to the boy, pushing him forward. She knelt in front of Dane's chair with the boy beside her. She smelled sweet and clean.

"We've come a long way to meet you," she said in her British voice. "This is Given. That's Susannah there with Aunt Dellie, and Honour and Hope are..." She twisted to look around behind her. "Well, they're somewhere." She laughed. It was a nice cheerful laugh. She was pretty enough, blond and blue-eyed. Ding had always gone for a pretty face. "And this..."

She reached for a pale woman-child with honey blonde hair, drew her in front of Dane. He felt his spine stiffen, his head got woozy. He tried to reach for her—a ghost. His mouth moved. A string of slobber was all that came out. The British woman wiped it away from his chin. She pulled the pale girl closer.

"This is Justine," she said. "I know what you're thinking, Papa Dane. Lange says he felt the same way."

Dellie leaned into Dane's line of vision. "It's Sunny's daughter, Dane. The youngest one. They brought her with them. Doesn't she favor her mama?" Dellie patted the girl on her shoulder. "Say something, dear. Let him hear you so he'll know you're real. You look so much like your mother, I believe you've got him dazzled."

The girl smiled—Sunny's smile. She took his hand in her soft one. "Papa," she said, kind of sing-songing the word, and he didn't understand a single thing she said after that. She was talking in French or what sounded like French to him.

He heard a rumble rise from somewhere inside him. There was so much he wanted to ask her. Where were her brother and sister? He glanced for them but saw nothing but babies. Why was she here without the other two? All he could do was rumble and drool and watch her pretty little sweetheart mouth move.

THE BRITISH WOMAN called herself Mackie, but he could have sworn Ding's wife was named Allison. He stayed confused about that for the first few days after they were all there. Dellie kept reminding him of who was who, but it didn't start to straighten out until he got past his shock over Justine. Sunny's youngest—the baby. He had only seen pictures of her. She was a woman, now, and that idea had not crossed his mind—that she would be all grown up.

Even though all the babies were cute as bugs, they rattled Dane's nerves. Too many new faces. Too much to try to swallow. Dellie was overwrought with the newcomers herself, tried to hide it, stayed busy readying the old bunkhouse, flitted around doing this and that for Ding's family.

Most days, Justine sat a while with him on the back porch. She talked to him, but she was just too hard for him to understand so he gave that up and just listened to the music of her voice. It pleased him enough to have her to look at—brought Sunny a little closer to him. He wished the other two were there, but he was happy with this one.

After a while, little by little, with help from Dellie, he came to understand some of Justine's story. Her brother and sister had been living in another town a long way from Paris. Ding had gone to the bakery where she worked in Paris, and they set out together to the town where the others lived. And somehow, Ding had rescued Justine. Dane wasn't sure exactly how that part happened or how Ding ended up in a POW camp while Justine ended up here in McDade, but knowing the boy played a role in it was enough to satisfy Dane's curiosity. Ding had gone over there to get those kids out of France, and he had, sure enough, got one of them.

Over the next few days, the whole extended family came by to visit and to meet Ding's family. They wanted to see the babies. They wanted to see Sunny's daughter. There was talk of a husband, somebody named Teddy. Dane couldn't keep it all straight. It took a while for him to realize that little Justine had married an RAF pilot. So he guess that meant there would be another Limey showing up around here before long.

He sat in the hallway and watched the activity around him: Julianne came and went, Dellie, too, one or two other relatives he didn't see often enough to remember. Nieces, nephews, a sister-in-law. Back and forth, in and out of the kitchen, the front room, all around him, chattering, bustling. Kids everywhere slamming in and out, hollering through the back screened door. Now and then, one of them would stop and peer at him, say a few nonsense words at him. Talking at him. That's all anybody seemed to do anymore: talk *at* him.

The boy—that older, dark-haired one—passed by Dane several times, eyeing him. He was quieter than the others. A watcher. He had the same color hair as Ding, same build for that age. Nice flat ears. The women were in the kitchen, feeding babies, fussing around like women do. Their voices came trilling down the hallway like a flock of birds.

The boy leaned down in front of Dane's chair, looked into

Dane's eyes. "My mum says it's all right if I speak to you, but that you can't speak back to me at the moment."

Dane watched the boy's mouth move. If it weren't for that British accent, it would be easy to get confused, believe he was hallucinating again. This boy had blue eyes and the other, long-ago boy's eyes had been dark brown. But other than that, he was the spitting image.

The boy pulled two small boxes out from his pockets. He sat one box on the hall table and the other he pried open with his slender fingers. "This is my dad's," he said. "Your son."

He held out the box like he wanted Dane to take it from him, then realized. Dane's hand spread on his lap, willing but unable. The boy fingered out the object and held it up. The metal part dangled.

"This is a DFC. Distinguished Flying Cross. Dad got this one from the RAF. You have to shoot down five German aircraft to earn this." He laid the medal on Dane's knee. "Now, this one..." He lifted the other box from the table. "This DFC is from the United States Army Air Force. Dad hasn't actually got to see this one yet. Would you like to hold it?" The boy pulled the medal out of the box and tucked it inside the clutches of Dane's hand.

Dane stared down at the thing in his hand, the red, white and blue ribbon, the metal cross. The boy's finger pointed. "See the propeller on top of the cross?"

The boy lifted the box off the table, turned it over. "It says right here, 'Major C.L. DeLony.'" He held the box up so Dane could read the typewriting on the label.

"Given?" The boy's mother peered around the kitchen doorway. The boy snatched the first medal off Dane's knee. She came towards Dane's wheelchair. "What are you up to in here? Are you bothering Papa Dane?"

Dane wished he could answer. He would tell her that the boy was just having a little conversation, not bothering anybody at all.

"I was showing him Dad's medals. See, he's holding it. I put it in his hand, and he's holding it."

She stood still in front of Dane for a moment, then knelt down to his level. "I hope Given wasn't being a nuisance. He thinks his dad hung the moon." She reached for Dane's hand, and he thought she was about to take away the medal. Instead, she closed his grip tighter around it. "I'm certain Lange would want you to have that," she said.

Then she leaned to kiss him on the forehead. For a second, he imagined she was Tessa, Ding's mother instead of Ding's wife. They smelled the same, womanly, like flowers.

Later that evening, Gabe came to wheel Dane out on the back porch, away from the commotion and fuss. It was cool out in the air. Gabe positioned Dane's chair, so he was facing west and could watch the sun go down.

"What you got there?" Gabe pried the medal out of Dane's hands, held it up for an inspection. "This belong to Ding?" He held the cigarette he was smoking between his lips and unfastened the bar on the back of the medal. He leaned to pin it on Dane's shirt. Smoke got in Dane's eyes. He blinked. Gabe stood back to admire his handiwork, whistled. "Don't you look sharp?" He chuckled. Dane felt ignorant.

With his pocketknife and his thumb, Gabe opened a bottle of beer and sat down on the porch steps. He let out a groan. He'd been working his cows all day, separating out calves for market. Inside the house, piano music played. Laughter and kids shrieking. They were having a big time inside.

Gabe took a swig of his beer, wiped his mouth, said, "That piano has sat in there since I was a boy and not a note has ever been played on it. Not till Ding's woman got here. Mama's beside herself having somebody who can play the damned thing. Sounds out of tune to me. But you know women. They like things like music and babies."

Dane sat there staring at the sunset, rolling those words in his mind...*Ding's woman. Ding's babies.* Hard to get used to the sound of that.

"I saw her over there by the bunkhouse this morning, already digging out a flower bed. That's the kind of stuff they do, too, women. Plant flowers and then fret when bugs eat it all up. Or the deer. She won't be able to keep out the deer. Had her boy helping her." Gabe took another swig of the beer. "He come out to the barn the other day. Seemed like he wanted to talk. Cute little British feller. Asked me did I know Tom Mix."

Gabe laughed. Took a deep draw on his coffin nail. The smoke swirled out into the twilight. The piano music was softer now. Made a person kind of drowsy. Kids had got quieter, too. Night frogs were beginning to sing.

Gabe took out his handkerchief, blew his nose. His voice got more serious. "Heard on the radio while ago, they liberated Paris today. Be moving over the Rhine pretty soon. Shove those bastards back where they belong." Gabe turned, glanced over at Dane. "Ol' Ding'll be home before you know it." He leaned back against the second step and took another swig from the can, wiped his mouth with his sleeve. "Maybe this time those goddammed bastards will stay beat."

Dane nodded his head or thought he did. Instead of a grin, a glob of slobber ran out onto his chin. He thought he must have something in his eye, too, because it sure felt salty. He blinked at the first star of the night and wondered if Ding could see that same star, wherever he was at in Germany.

CHAPTER 31

"Operation Revival"

O n April 30, 1945, the German guards scurried out in the middle of the night like the rats they were. The boom of the advancing Russian army was close at their backs. It was not a big surprise. Lately, Allied bomber armadas had been filling the sky, coming over high, above the flak, with fighters escorting them this far into Germany. Lange hated he had missed out on the P-51, but quite a few Mustang pilots had been bagged and thrown into this camp, so he knew all about it, how it had that beautiful Rolls-Royce engine he had loved in the Spitfire, coupled with the sturdiness of old Gunslinger, and twice the fuel range.

The day after the German guards disappeared, the Russians rode in like Cossacks on horseback. The commanding officer of the Americans in the camp, struck up a conversation with them about the lack of food, and later that evening, another group of Russians came herding cattle and pigs into camp, on the hoof. Lange and some of the other fellows who had been raised around livestock, took care of wrangling the cows and slaughtering them. For the next few days, they barbecued meat and ate like gluttons. Some of the POWs got sick, their stomachs having been empty for so long.

Lange still wore the trousers Tatiana had given to him, but they were now held up with a length of rope tied around his waist. The German-issued sweater and thin coat hung on him. He reckoned he had lost about forty or fifty pounds. Some of the men still had their military uniforms, and some of the lucky, recent arrivals had even managed to keep their A-2 leather jackets. Lange often thought with regret about surrendering his uniform to the beet farmer's nephews.

Since winter, food shortage had been bad. Red Cross boxes were slow to get through. When they did come, they were parceled out eight men to a box. Soup had been served in horse toughs. They lined up and held their bowls out for a ladle full. There might be a leaf of cabbage floating on top, or a chunk of fat, but it was mostly water and caused terrible bouts of diarrhea. Bread was mealy, tasted like sawdust, probably was mostly sawdust. The winter had been brutally cold, with little coal for the camp heaters. It was harder to keep warm when you were hungry.

On the eighth of May, word came from the BBC over the crystal set in Compound Three that the German Army had surrendered. The war was over. It was a clear, beautiful, blue-sky day. There was a lightness in camp, but no church bells rang. The CO ordered all the compounds to be opened.

Four days later, the first reconnaissance B-17 arrived. There was an abandoned German airfield south of the camp. The American CO organized work parties to go clean up as much as possible, to make the landing strip usable. Others stayed behind to cut up sheets for armbands. The Russians had occupied the town. They were rowdy and would shoot anybody they thought might be a German. The armbands helped to prevent tragedies. After all the months of being locked up, nobody wanted to have it end in disaster amid the confusion.

The first group of B-17s arrived early on May 13. They came in a steady stream, one after the other. Wounded and sick went first, then in order of how long a man had been in the camp. The airlift was more orderly than Lange would have imagined: a plane landed, taxied in a line, stopped, thirty men boarded, and off they went, without ever shutting down their engines. As a senior officer, and one who had been interred for less than two years, Lange was part of the "evacuation crew." He helped gather the men into groups of thirty. He checked off names on the rosters and watched thousands of men head off—into the wild blue yonder. Back to sanity.

That night, the camp was restless. Some of the men didn't believe any more B-17s would be coming. Lange tried to quell rumors. A few men left the camp but came back soon. The Russians were pillaging the countryside. They all agreed to take turns on watch outside the barracks. Lookouts were posted in the abandoned guard towers.

During Lange's turn on watch, he was approached by a stranger he didn't know, a small fellow with dark piercing eyes and a face so narrow and gaunt his cheekbones were etched. It was not a face Lange recognized. He waved the man over, asked him to identify himself. The man answered in French. After Lange's four months on the run, he recognized French when he heard it, even if he still couldn't understand much of it.

"Do you speak English?" he asked.

The man held up his thumb and one finger, pinched together with a half-inch between them. "I cook," he said, patting his chest. "Bake...uh, *pardon*. Bread. I cook."

Lange straightened. He hadn't realized they had French cooks in camp. He thought maybe he recognized the pants the fellow wore as having once been part of a military uniform. The man was so clearly beaten down; he had most certainly been a prisoner for a long time.

"You." The man pointed at Lange. He said something Lange couldn't understand for a second, then realized the fellow was trying to say, "Texas?" Asking it as a question.

Lange nodded, figuring the fellow had seen him among the cow wranglers a few days before. Lange held up his hand for the man to wait a second, and went to the barracks door. Lange leaned in and hollered out, "Anybody in here speak French?"

Zach Prejean, a navigator on a B-24, a first lieutenant from Thibodaux, Louisiana, came outside. He said he could speak Cajun French.

"Find out this fella's story," Lange said. "I think he's saying he was one of our cooks. Did you know we had French cooks?"

"Sure didn't taste like it." Prejean went over and spoke some words to the scraggily Frenchman. They had a little back and forth. The cook kept pointing at Lange, and finally Prejean gave Lange a doubtful look.

"He believes he's related to you," Prejean said. "At least that's what I think he said."

"*Oui*," the cook said. "Yes. Texas."

"What the hell's his name?" Lange said, a premonition creeping over him. He stepped up closer to the fellow. "Where were you taken prisoner?"

Prejean translated the question, got an answer. "He says Laon. He says his name is—"

"Emile Monnier," the Frenchman said. "*Nous sommes une famille. Nina est ma femme.*"

LANGE'S PLACE in line to leave came on the second day, one of the last planes to land, a big C-47. He added Emile's name to the bottom of the roster and took him along without asking permission. He sat Emile down on one of the row benches along the wall and took the next seat. Lange had kept Prejean back for this transport, too, to ease the language problem. Emile could speak a little English, but damned little. Lange needed Prejean to find out how Emile had ended up at the camp. It had been the fourth one he had been at in as many years. Once the Germans learned he was the son of a baker, he had been put in camp kitchens all over Germany. He sat quietly on the plane beside Lange, his expression unreadable.

The big C-47 took off, roaring up over Barth, Germany. Outside the window, every building in the town flew a white bed sheet or flag. The POWs onboard let out a big cheer and clapped, almost drowning out the engine noise. It was the first genuine emotion Lange had seen on Emile's narrow face.

Flying at 10,000 feet, all the bombed-out buildings, the cratered roads, and the destruction, were plainly visible. Lange felt a pang of remorse that he had missed that part of the war, invading the continent, knocking out bridges and factories. The opportunity to do all those things would have brought him such satisfaction.

"What're you going to do when you get back, Major?" Prejean said, raising his voice above the din.

The question startled Lange. It was almost as if Prejean had been reading his mind, but Lange didn't have to think long for his answer. "Kiss my wife and kids. How about you?"

Prejean paused, then said, "Well, I sure as hell won't be doing much world traveling."

THEY LANDED at Camp Lucky Strike in France and were herded to a check-in tent. Immediately, Lange spotted the hospital tent—big white cross over the open flap—and veered out of the line with Emile in tow. After being a prisoner since 1940, Emile needed a physical. He looked like a waif, a dirty one. Lange left him with a sweet-faced Red Cross nurse. He could tell Emile didn't want him to go.

"I'll be back," Lange assured him.

Lange got a shower, a meal, a fresh uniform, and was issued sleeping quarters in a big circus tent among the thousand of other circus tents, housing 60,000 POWs from all the camps in Eastern Europe—except they weren't to be called POWs anymore. Their new designation was RAMPs—Recovered Allied Military Personnel.

He made his way to the headquarters to find out how he could get Emile de-mobbed or whatever needed to happen. He knew he had spotted some Free French racing around in Jeeps. Maybe they could take him back to Paris. Now, that Lange was back in uniform again, wherever he went, salutes kept cracking at him. They had been more informal about that in the POW camp. It felt odd and otherworldly. That morning he had been filthy and still wearing POW clothes.

When he checked in at the commander's office, he learned he would have to be debriefed, put on the list for transport back to the States. Nobody could tell him how long it would take before he got a ship bound for New York. They weren't interested in helping him with Emile's situation either. He left there aggravated at the usual military red tape and prepared to take matters into his own hands.

He had spent too many months confined in a POW camp to spend much more time in this one. Enough was enough. He decided he would pull rank and managed to finagle a ride on a cargo plane back to England. He figured if he could get to England he could get back to the States a lot quicker than waiting at this relocation camp for a ship. The cargo pilot told him where to be. "We leave at nineteen hundred hours," the pilot said, and Lange agreed to be there. But first he had to take care of Emile.

He made his way back across the enormous camp to the hospital tent. By then most of the day had passed. The sweet, little nurse was still there. She looked harried and exhausted, red in the face from the close confines of the stuffy tent. She didn't remember Lange. He guessed he looked different clean and in uniform. He began to explain to her again.

"Oh, you're the one who brought in the French POW." She shook her head. "He was in bad shape. We really needed to keep him for a while, but he left. Said he wanted to go home. We couldn't force him to stay since he isn't one of ours."

Lange thanked her and stepped out of the hospital tent. People were everywhere, scurrying like ants. Military vehicles charged through the camp streets. Groups of men lined up or walked from here to there. Construction crews were stringing electrical wires.

Aircraft came in low for the landing strip. All around him was a whirlwind of activity.

Standing there, in the midst of it, he was struck by what he had just survived, what the world had survived—the magnitude of it. He was ready, more than ready, to get on with his life, get home to Mackie and the kids, and decide from there what would come next. He thought about the cargo pilot and the promise of a quick ride to England. Lange had flown over this part of France enough to know how close he was—twenty minutes by air and he would be there. But could he leave without knowing what happened to Emile?

He started to walk. The camp had everything, a PX, commissary, movie theater, bowling alley. He flagged down one of the Jeeps, asked how a person could get a vehicle. The driver, a sergeant, told him to get in. Lange had an idea of commandeering one of the Jeeps, a can of gasoline, and driving to Paris if he had to. He thought he might be able to navigate back to the Monnier's bakery on Rue d'Odessa. Maybe now that the war had ended, the reception he would get there would be friendlier than the last time. He could wait there for Emile, or maybe Emile would have already made it by then. He knew it was an outlandish plan, but it was all he had.

The sergeant driver was reckless and kept beeping his horn at people in the middle of the road. At one point, he almost rear-ended a deuce-and-a-half filled with soldiers, POWs or rather RAMPs. The traffic snarled up so badly, that Lange decided to go it on foot. The sergeant gave Lange some vague directions to the transportation depot. He hopped out of the Jeep and started up the line of traffic.

Supply trucks loaded with bedding passed him, another with uniforms. Food trucks. Personnel carriers. After all those months in a POW camp, all the movement, the racket, the chaos, rattled him. He felt lost in a maze. He kept on walking in the direction the sergeant had pointed.

From behind him, he thought he heard his name. He turned. Sure enough, nothing. No one knew him here. A second later, it came again.

"Major! DeLony!"

He turned inagain just as Emile Monnier bounded out of one of the stopped trucks. He had come by a powder blue uniform cap, some regiment of the French army. Somehow, he looked healthier, smiling, happy. He sprinted over to Lange. The cap was too big, covered most of his brow.

He pulled a half-assed, unnecessary salute, said, "Thank you," only it sounded like *tank you*. He gestured at the wild-looking men in the back of the truck he had just exited. "Home. For me."

"They're from your regiment?" Lange said, doing the old mime hand-dance.

Emile nodded exuberantly. "*Oui*. Yes. Thank you." He clutched Lange's arm. "I call..." He made his hand into a telephone pressed to his ear.

"You'll call?"

"*Oui*. Yes. I call Nina."

"Nina? You talked to Nina?" Lange said, surprised.

"Yes. *Oui*, Nina." Emile rattled off a lot of French then, and the only word Lange caught was Par-ee.

"Paris? Nina's in Paris?" he said.

"*Oui*. Yes." Emile bobbed up and down a little, grasped Lange in a sort of embrace. The truck with his buddies was grinding gears, beginning to move. "Thank you. Yes. *Merci*. Et Peter...eeh..." He paused, searching for words.

"Peter? What?" Lange nodded, encouraged Emile to go on. "Wait a minute. Pete's in Paree?"

"*Oui*. Yes, yes. Pete, yes."

Almost overcome with relief and joy at this sudden news, Lange grabbed Emile in a bear hug. They were safe. They had made it through the war, too. Emile held on for a moment. Indecision clouded Lange then. It was a chance to see his niece and his nephew, a chance he might never get again. But if he did that, he would miss the chance to get back to Mackie, to his kids. He hadn't seen them in nineteen long months. He didn't want to make it twenty.

When they broke apart, Lange held onto Emile's narrow shoulders. "Tell them Justine is in Texas. Tell them she's in Texas."

Emile nodded, but Lange wasn't sure he'd understood until he said, "Justine?"

"Yes. Justine. She's OK. Understand?"

"OK." Emile was grinning ear to ear. "*Oui*. Thanks. Yes. *Sil vous plait.*"

Lange made the pencil on paper gesture. "Tell Nina to write to us. Letters. Tell her to write."

Emile gave Lange's shoulder a last, parting squeeze, then sprinted back to the already rolling truck. He held onto his big blue cap as his fellow soldiers grabbed his hand and hauled him up into the cargo bed with them, all of them jabbering, laughing. The truck began to move away. Emile raised his hand in goodbye. Lange did the same.

What were the odds he would meet up with Emile in all of goddamned Europe? What were the chances of that? He felt overwhelmed for a moment, as he watched the truck full of Frenchmen drive away.

He got to the airstrip ahead of the cargo pilot. He waited, breathing in the old familiar smells: oil, high-octane gas, airplane dust. He watched engineers loading war materiel—equipment, apparatus, the supplies of a military force—onto palleted crates. This side of the camp seemed to be dismantling, already packing away the war.

The cargo pilot arrived, spoke briefly to Lange, before he started his walk-around. The crew came in a Jeep. The co-pilot told Lange to climb on board. He was given the jump seat and tossed a headset as the pilots started their cockpit drill: Run up of both engines. Co-pilot waved away the chocks. It seemed an eternity before the big heavy C-46 attained lift. As the big bastard lumbered into the air, Lange felt the pull of "G." He closed his eyes. So many times he thought he would never get this far. Freedom. Home. One door shuts, another one opens. In a few minutes—such a few—the white cliffs came into view, gleaming like golden beacons across the Channel.

IT TOOK three days to get out of England, on a C-53 to New York. Then a train ride from Union Station to Washington for a de-brief and to collect his back pay. They offered him a peacetime commission. He didn't know what Mackie would think of it but he didn't have any other hot offers and he really wanted a crack at the P-51, even if there would be no Germans to fight. And jets—jets were on the way. Hell, he was a flyer. What else was he going to do?

He had a wad of cash in the bag he'd bought in England, along with a change of clothes and re-enlistment papers, when he caught the Gooney Bird to Kelly Field in San Antonio. Julianne plucked him out of the mayhem there and drove him to Stinson's Field where Sterling kept his planes parked. He and Troy Lee were both flying for the Navy now, down in Corpus Christi.

"He said for me to give you the Taylorcraft to get home. He said we would get it back here some way or another." She gave him a big hug, held him by the shoulders at arm's length for just a moment. "You are sight for sore eyes, honey."

HE COULDN'T GET over how much everything had changed. He had flown over this country a hundred times, learned to fly in these skies. The high wings of the Taylorcraft gave him a good line of sight. He passed over Camp Swift, enormous in size, now, the cemetery, more overgrown than it used to be, his shabby old schoolhouse, the train tracks that cut the town in half. Twenty more seconds and there was Aunt Dellie's house, trees lined up along the back pasture, two cars, the bunkhouse, clothes flapping on the clothesline.

Gabe's cattle ran as he buzzed the place. He grinned ear to ear. He pulled up to go around again. He would use the same approach Troy Lee had used for joy rides that Thanksgiving a million years ago. Back to front, so he would be facing the house.

He came down low, slow. He thought he would be rusty but it was like riding a horse, or like cropdusting. At 50 MPH, the stall alarm screamed and he reigned in. The little plane bounced down twice. When he looked up, they were all running towards him, pouring out the back door and down the steps like cream. It was 11:30, a Sunday morning, 27 May 1945. Sunshine beat down and flooded his eyes. The smell of dirt and cows and home found him as he alighted from the cockpit. He hit the ground just before Mackie leaped into his arms.

"Darling," she said, and covered him with kisses. He swung her around, kissed tears off her cheeks.

They swarmed him—Aunt Dellie, the babies, Given, Gabe, slapping at him, hugging him, chattering all at once. His arms weren't big enough to hold them all the way he wanted to. He felt like Lucky Lindy when he landed the Spirit of St. Louis. It was one of those perfect, epic moments they would talk about for years: "Remember when Dad flew home from the war and landed in Gabe's cow pasture. Remember how he buzzed the house and we all came running." Nobody would remember it better than he did. He spotted Papa on the back porch, in his wheelchair, waiting.

THE END

About the Author

Cindy Bonner's first novel, LILY, was a runner-up for the Western Writers of America's Medicine Pipe Bearer Award. Her fourth. novel, RIGHT FROM WRONG, won the PEN/Texas Award and was first runner-up for the Willa Award. Her novels have been translated into Spanish and German and have been named Best Books by the American Library Association. Her manuscripts are collected in the Southwestern Writers Collection, a distinguished and steadily growing archive at Texas State University. Bonner lives in Texas where she writes full-time.